Praise for The Untouchable

'This great novel can be approached from many angles: as an impeccable art of ventriloquism, as a treatise on art history, as a socio-political novel with fine sections on wartime London and Ulster childhood, as a thesis on camp and stoicism'

Chris Petit, *Guardian*, Books of the Year

'In many ways a comic masterpiece, the novel culls the best from the modernist tradition of retrospective, ironic narrative, and with breathtaking, cutting humour renders Victor Maskell's private and public worlds – his marriage and his homosexuality, his professionalism, his royalism and Marxism, the Second World War and the Cold War, Cambridge and Ireland – with rare intensity. Banville is a physical pleasure to read'

Edward W. Said, *Times Literary Supplement*, Books of the Year

'Banville's evocation of pre-war debauchery is deft and sensational, tricked out in the fastidious prose of his deeply unreliable narrator'   **David Profumo, *Daily Telegraph***

'In *The Untouchable*, his novel of espionage, sacrifice and betrayal, he was unerring'

Ruth Rendell, *Sunday Times*, Books of the Year

'Critics who condemned *The Untouchable* as exploitative failed to see that it is no more about Anthony Blunt or Louis MacNeice than *Henry V* is about Henry V. A brilliant study of fakery, deceptions and conspiracy, with an entirely appropriate Irish twist, it was easily top of my Booker list'

Stella Tillyard, *Guardian*, Books of the Year

'From the contra~~diction of a flawed life~~, ~~Banville~~ has fashioned a work of dry p~~o~~   ~~Su~~*nday Telegraph*

'Banville's novel is inspired, intelligent, literary. *The Untouchable* is compelling. The narrative of Burgess and Maclean's defection particularly so in its pathos, humour, excitement'

Brian Martin, *Financial Times*

'His newest work represents both a broadening and an apotheosis: his habitual high aesthetics and shimmering sensuousness of language now leaving the realm of enigmatic dream for observable historical fact, earthed in the familiar and endlessly tantalising story of Anthony Blunt. *The Untouchable* has exquisite humour, aching irony, swooningly luscious sentences'

Catherine Lockerbie, *Scotsman*

'John Banville's prose is clear, fluent and possessed of authentic energy – the real thing, in fact'   Anita Brookner, *Spectator*

'His books are brilliant, glowing objects, intricate puzzles, exquisitely written'   Tom Adair, *Scotland on Sunday*

'*The Untouchable* moves with seamless ease between the recent past and the formative decades of this century which produces men like Maskell–Blunt: boozy, ideologically charged afternoons in Trinity or evenings in pre-war Soho; crackling characterisations of the main and minor players'   Steve Grant, *Time Out*

'Banville's achievement is to show the tragic consequences of Maskell's detachment while naming him an appealingly human, even noble, figure . . . His narrative voice is a marvellous invention by turns caustic, wistful, lush, self-mocking and filled with regret. In some ways *The Untouchable* is an elegy for espionage as it once was. But then you can never quite pin down this marvellous novel'   Katy Emck, *New Statesman*

'Banville has written a coolly intelligent novel in which art and other kinds of understanding are inextricably linked'

Brian Morton, *Times Educational Supplement*

'Banville spies everything. And, at best, his prose is transfixing. Like Virginia Woolf, he can unwrap an unseen world. You recognise something which you have never before seen put into words. It is a rare gift. Banville has long been a master of the most seductive prose, a writer of the most extraordinary and exquisite powers . . . frequently on each page one does have to stop and sigh with pleasure over Banville's swoon-making sentences'   **Kate Kellaway, *Punch***

'To have grasped a man of such complexity – spy and aesthete of rude Irish origin – and to demonstrate how those rivulets of personality flow into the wider currents of twentieth-century history is Banville's rare achievement'   ***Esquire***

'Banville is a faultless conjuror with aspects of authenticity, teasing, probing, and possessing what is perhaps the novelist's most precious gift: the courage to endlessly take risks'
Irish Times

'This is a book of surprises. Fluent and articulate, it also carries a remarkable narrative strength . . . This is a fable for our times that deserves to be a bestseller'   **Hayden Murphy, *Herald***

'The prose is stunning; every sentence is perfectly judged in length and weight, every simile is piercingly apposite . . . The language is formal and dense, intoxicating in its precision'
Elspeth Barker, *Independent on Sunday*

'In the grace of its style and the vividness of its parts it shows that John Banville is one of the most compelling novelists on earth'   ***Sydney Morning Herald***

'Victor Maskell is one of the most fascinating fictional characters I have encountered in years'
Australian Bookseller and Publisher

The Untouchable

JOHN BANVILLE was born in Wexford, Ireland, in 1945.
He is the author of fourteen other novels including
The Sea, which won the 2005 Man Booker Prize.
He has received a literary award from the
Lannan Foundation. He lives in Dublin.

Also by John Banville

Long Lankin

Nightspawn

Birchwood

Doctor Copernicus

Kepler

The Newton Letter

Mefisto

The Book of Evidence

Ghosts

Athena

Eclipse

Shroud

The Sea

The Infinities

JOHN BANVILLE

The Untouchable

PICADOR

First published 1997 by Picador

First published in paperback in this revised edition 1998 by Picador
an imprint of Pan Macmillan, a division of Macmillan Publishers Limited
Pan Macmillan, 20 New Wharf Road, London N1 9RR
Basingstoke and Oxford
Associated companies throughout the world
www.panmacmillan.com

ISBN 978-0-330-33932-2

9 10 8

A CIP catalogue record for this book is available from
the British Library.

Typeset by SetSystems Ltd, Saffron Walden, Essex
Printed in the UK by CPI Mackays, Chatham ME5 8TD

Visit **www.picador.com** to read more about all our books
and to buy them. You will also find features, author interviews and
news of any author events, and you can sign up for e-newsletters
so that you're always first to hear about our new releases.

to Colm and Douglas

ONE

FIRST DAY of the new life. Very strange. Feeling almost skittish all day. Exhausted now yet feverish also, like a child at the end of a party. Like a child, yes: as if I had suffered a grotesque form of rebirth. Yet this morning I realised for the first time that I am an old man. I was crossing Gower Street, my former stamping ground. I stepped off the path and something hindered me. Odd sensation, as if the air at my ankles had developed a flaw, seemed to turn – what is the word: viscid? – and resisted me and I almost stumbled. Bus thundering past with a grinning blackamoor at the wheel. What did he see? Sandals, mac, my inveterate string bag, old rheumy eye wild with fright. If I had been run over they would have said it was suicide, with relief all round. But I will not give them that satisfaction. I shall be seventy-two this year. Impossible to believe. Inside, an eternal twenty-two. I suppose that is how it is for everybody old. Brr.

Never kept a journal before. Fear of incrimination. Leave nothing in writing, Boy always said. Why have I started now? I just sat down and began to write, as if it were the most natural thing in the world, which of course it is not. My last testament. It is twilight, everything very still and poignant. The trees in the square are dripping. Tiny sound of birdsong. April. I do not like the spring, its antics and agitations; I fear that anguished seething in the heart, what it might make me do. What it might *have made* me do: one has to be scrupulous with tenses, at my age. I miss my children. Goodness, where did that come from? They are hardly what you could call children any more. Julian must be – well, he must be forty this year, which makes

Blanche thirty-eight, is it? Compared to them I seem to myself hardly grown-up at all. Auden wrote somewhere that no matter what the age of the company, he was always convinced he was the youngest in the room; me, too. All the same, I thought they might have called. *Sorry to hear about your treachery, Daddums.* Yet I am not at all sure I would want to hear Blanche sniffling and Julian tightening his lips at me down the line. His mother's son. I suppose all fathers say that.

I mustn't ramble.

Public disgrace is a strange thing. Fluttery feeling in the region of the diaphragm and a sort of racing sensation all over, as of the blood like mercury slithering along heavily just under the skin. Excitement mixed with fright makes for a heady brew. At first I could not think what this state reminded me of, then it came to me: those first nights on the prowl after I had finally admitted to myself it was my own kind that I wanted. The same hot shiver of mingled anticipation and fear, the same desperate grin trying not to break out. Wanting to be caught. To be set upon. To be manhandled. Well, past all that now. Past everything, really. There is a particular bit of blue sky in *Et in Arcadia Ego*, where the clouds are broken in the shape of a bird in swift flight, which is the true, clandestine centre-point, the pinnacle of the picture, for me. When I contemplate death, and I contemplate it with an ever-diminishing sense of implausibility in these latter days, I see myself swaddled in zinc-white cerements, more a figure out of El Greco than Poussin, ascending in a transport of erotic agony amid alleluias and lip-farts through a swirl of clouds the colour of golden tea head-first into just such a patch of pellucid bleu céleste.

Switch on the lamp. My steady, little light. How neatly it defines this narrow bourn of desk and page in which I have always found my deepest joy, this lighted tent wherein I crouch in happy hiding from the world. For even the pictures were more a matter of mind than eye. Here there is everything that—

That was a call from Querell. Well, he certainly has nerve,

I'll say that for him. The telephone ringing gave me a dreadful start. I have never got used to this machine, the way it crouches so malevolently, ready to start clamouring for attention when you least expect it, like a mad baby. My poor heart is still thudding in the most alarming way. Who did I think it would be? He was calling from Antibes. I thought I could hear the sea in the background and I felt envious and annoyed, but more likely it was just the noise of traffic passing by outside his flat, along the Corniche, is it? – or is that somewhere else? Heard the news on the World Service, so he said. 'Dreadful, old man, dreadful; what can I say?' He could not keep the eagerness out of his voice. Wanted all the dirty details. 'Was it sex they got you on?' How disingenuous – and yet how little he realises, after all. Should I have challenged him, told him I know him for his perfidy? What would have been the point. Skryne reads his books, he is a real fan. 'That Querell, now,' he says, doing that peculiar whistle with his dentures, 'he has the measure of us all.' Not of me, he hasn't, my friend; not of me. At least, I hope not.

No one else has called. Well, I hardly expected that he would . . .

I shall miss old Skryne. No question now of having to deal with him any more; that is all over, along with so much else. I should feel relieved but, oddly, I do not. We had become a kind of double act at the end, he and I, a music hall routine. *I say I say I say, Mr Skryne! Well, bless my soul, Mr Bones!* He was hardly the popular image of an interrogator. Hardy little fellow with a narrow head and miniature features and a neat thatch of very dry, stone-coloured hair. He reminds me of the fierce father of the madcap bride in those Hollywood comedies of the thirties. Blue eyes, not piercing, even a little fogged (incipient cataracts?). The buffed brogues, the pipe he plays with, the old tweed jacket with elbow patches. Ageless. Might be anything from fifty to seventy-five. Nimble mind, though, you could practically hear the cogs whirring. And an amazing memory.

'Hold on a sec,' he would say, stabbing at me with his pipe-stem, 'let's run over that bit once more,' and I would have to unpack the delicate tissue of lies I had been spinning him, searching with frantic calmness as I did so for the flaw he had detected in the fabric. By now I was only lying for fun, for recreation, you might say, like a retired tennis pro knocking up with an old opponent. I had no fear that he would discover some new enormity – I have confessed to everything by now, or almost everything – but it seemed imperative to maintain consistency, for aesthetic reasons, I suppose, and in order to be consistent it was necessary to invent. Ironic, I know. He has the tenacity of the ferret: never let go. He is straight out of Dickens; I picture a crooked little house in Stepney or Hackney or wherever it is he lives, complete with termagant wife and a brood of cheeky nippers. It is another of my besetting weaknesses, to see people always as caricatures. Including myself.

Not that I recognise myself in the public version of me that is being put about now. I was listening on the wireless when our dear PM (I really do admire her; such firmness, such fixity of purpose, and so handsome, too, in a fascinatingly mannish way) stood up in the Commons and made the announcement, and for a moment I did not register my own name. I mean I thought she was speaking of someone else, someone whom I knew, but not well, and whom I had not seen for a long time. It was a very peculiar sensation. The Department had already alerted me to what was to come – terribly rude, the people they have in there now, not at all the easygoing types of my day – but it was still a shock. Then on the television news at midday they had some extraordinary blurred photographs of me, I do not know how or where they got them, and cannot even remember them being taken – apt verb, that, applied to photography: the savages are right, it is a part of one's soul that is being taken away. I looked like one of those preserved bodies they dig up from Scandinavian bogs, all jaw and sinewy throat and hooded eyeballs. Some writer fellow, I have forgotten or suppressed his name – a 'contemporary historian', whatever that may be – was about to identify me, but the government got in first, in what I must say was a clumsy attempt to save face; I was embarrassed for the PM, really I was. Now here I am, exposed again, and after all this time. Exposed! – what a shiversome, naked-sounding word. Oh, Querell, Querell. I *know* it was you. It is the kind of thing you would do, to settle an old score. Is there no end to life's turbulences? Except the obvious one, I mean.

What is my purpose here? I may say, *I just sat down to write*, but I am not deceived. I have never done anything in my life that did not have a purpose, usually hidden, sometimes even from myself. Am I, like Querell, out to settle old scores? Or is it perhaps my intention to justify my deeds, to offer extenuations? I hope not. On the other hand, neither do I want to fashion for myself yet another burnished mask ... Having pondered for a moment, I realise that the metaphor is obvious: attribution, verification, restoration. I shall strip away layer after layer of grime – the toffee-coloured varnish and caked soot left by a lifetime of dissembling – until I come to the very thing itself and know it for what it is. My soul. My self. (When I laugh out loud like this the room seems to start back in surprise and dismay, with hand to lip. I have lived decorously here, I must not now turn into a shrieking hysteric.)

I kept my nerve in face of that pack of jackals from the newspapers today. *Did men die because of you?* Yes, dearie, swooned quite away. But no, no, I was superb, if I do say so myself. Cool, dry, balanced, every inch the Stoic: Coriolanus to the general. I am a great actor, that is the secret of my success (*Must not anyone who wants to move the crowd be an actor who impersonates himself?* – Nietzsche). I dressed the part to perfection: old but good houndstooth jacket, Jermyn Street shirt and Charvet tie – red, just to be mischievous – corduroy slacks, socks the colour and texture of porridge, that pair of scuffed brothel creepers I had not worn in thirty years. Might have just come up from a weekend at Cliveden. I toyed with the idea of a tobacco pipe *à la* Skryne, but that would have been to overdo it; and besides, it requires years of practice to be a plausible pipeman – never take on cover that you can't do naturally, that was another of Boy's dicta. I believe it was a nice piece of strategy on my part to invite the gentlepersons of the press into my lovely home. They crowded in almost sheepishly, jostling each other's notebooks and holding their cameras protectively above their heads. Rather touching, really: so eager, so awkward. I felt as if I were back at the Institute, about to deliver a lecture. Draw the shades, Miss Twinset, will you? And Stripling, you switch on the magic lantern. Plate one: *The Betrayal in the Garden*.

*

I have always had a particular fondness for gardens gone to seed. The spectacle of nature taking its slow revenge is pleasing. Not wilderness, of course, I was never one for wilderness, except in its place; but a general dishevelment bespeaks a right disdain for the humanist's fussy insistence on order. I am no Papist when it comes to husbandry, and side with Marvell's mower against gardens. I am thinking, here in this bird-haunted April twilight, of the first time I saw the Beaver, asleep in a hammock deep in the dappled orchard behind his father's house in North Oxford. Chrysalis. The grass was grown wild and the trees needed pruning. It was high summer, yet I see apple blossoms crowding on the boughs; so much for my powers of recall (I am said to have a photographic memory; very useful, in my line of work – my *lines* of work). Also I seem to remember a child, a sullen boy standing knee-deep in the grass, knocking the tops off nettles with a stick and watching me speculatively out of the corner of his eye. Who could he have been? Innocence incarnate, perhaps (yes, I am stifling another shriek of terrible mirth). Shaken already after separate encounters with the Beaver's unnerving sister and mad mother, I felt foolish, dithering there, with grass-stalks sticking up my trousers legs and a truculent bee enamoured of my hair oil zigzagging drunkenly about my head. I was clutching a manuscript under my arm – something earnest on late cubism, no doubt, or the boldness of Cézanne's draughtsmanship – and suddenly, there in that abounding glade, the idea of these pinched discriminations struck me as laughable. Sunlight, swift clouds; a breeze swooped and the boughs dipped. The Beaver slept on, holding himself in his arms with his face fallen to one side and a gleaming black wing of hair fanned across his forehead. Obviously this was not his father, whom I had come to see, and who Mrs Beaver had assured me was asleep in the garden. 'He drifts off, you know,' she had said with a queenly sniff; 'no concentration.' I had taken this as a hopeful sign: the idea of a dreamily inattentive publisher appealed to my already well-developed sense of myself as an infiltrator. But I was wrong. Max Brevoort – known as Big Beaver, to distinguish him from Nick – would turn out to be as wily and unscrupulous as any of his Dutch merchant forebears.

I close my eyes now and see the light between the apple trees and the boy standing in the long grass and that sleeping beauty folded in his hammock and the fifty years that have passed between that day and this are as nothing. It was 1929, and I was – yes – twenty-two.

Nick woke up and smiled at me, doing that trick he had of passing in an instant effortlessly from one world to another.

'Hullo,' he said. That was how chaps said it in those days: *hull*, not *hell*. He sat up, running a hand through his hair. The hammock swayed. The small boy, destroyer of nettles, was gone. 'God,' Nick said, 'I had the strangest dream.'

He accompanied me back to the house. That was how it seemed: not that we were walking together, but that he had bestowed his company on me, for a brief progress, with the ease and diffidence of royalty. He was dressed in whites, and he, like me, was carrying something under his arm, a book, or a newspaper (the news was all bad, that summer, and would get worse). As he walked he kept turning sideways towards me from the waist up and nodding rapidly at everything I said, smiling and frowning and smiling again.

'You're the Irishman,' he said. 'I've heard of you. My father thinks your stuff is very good.' He peered at me earnestly. 'He does, really.' I mumbled something meant to convey modesty and looked away. What he had seen in my face was not doubt but a momentary gloom: *the Irishman*.

The house was Queen Anne, not large, but rather grand, and maintained by Mrs B. in slovenly opulence: lots of faded silk and *objets* supposedly of great value – Big Beaver was a collector of jade figurines – and a rank smell everywhere of some sort of burnt incense. The plumbing was primitive; there was a lavatory close up under the roof which when it was flushed would make a horrible, cavernous choking noise, like a giant's death-rattle, that could be heard with embarrassing immediacy all over the house. But the rooms were full of light and there were always fresh-cut flowers, and the atmosphere had something thrillingly suppressed in it, as if at any moment the most amazing events might suddenly begin to happen. Mrs Brevoort was a large, beaked, bedizened personage, imperious and excitable, who went in for soirées and mild spiritualism. She played the piano – she had studied under someone famous – producing from the instrument great gaudy storms of sound that made the window panes buzz. Nick found her irresistibly ridiculous and was faintly ashamed of her. She took a shine to me straight off, so Nick told me later (he was lying, I'm sure); she had pronounced me sensitive, he said, and believed I would make a good medium, if only I would try. I quailed before her force and relentlessness, like a skiff borne down upon by an ocean-going liner.

'You didn't find Max?' she said, pausing in the hallway with a copper kettle in her hand. She was darkly Jewish, and wore her hair in ringlets, and displayed a startling, steep-pitched shelf of off-white bosom. 'The beast; he must have forgotten you were coming. I shall tell him you were deeply wounded by his thoughtlessness.'

I began to protest but Nick took me by the elbow – after half a century I can still feel that grip, light but firm, with the hint of a tremor in it – and propelled me into the drawing room, where he flung himself down on a sagging sofa and crossed his legs and leaned back and gazed at me with a smile at once dreamy and intent. The moment stretched. Neither of us spoke. Time can stand still, I am convinced of it; something snags and stops, turning and turning, like a leaf on a stream. A thick drop of sunlight seethed in a glass paperweight on a low table. Mrs Beaver was in the garden dosing hollyhocks with a mixture from her copper kettle. Tinny jazz-band music came hiccuping faintly down from upstairs, where Baby Beaver was in her bedroom practising dance steps to the gramophone (I know that was what she was doing; it was what she did all the time; later on I married her). Then abruptly Nick gave himself a sort of shake and leaned forward briskly and picked up a silver cigarette box from the table and proffered it to me, holding it open with a thumb hooked on the lid. Those hands.

'She's quite mad, you know,' he said. 'My mother. We all are, in this family. You'll find out.'

What did we talk about? My essay, perhaps. The relative merits of Oxford and Cambridge. *The Eighteenth Brumaire of Louis Bonaparte*. I can't remember. Presently Max Brevoort arrived. I do not know what I had expected – *The Laughing Publisher*, I suppose: apple cheeks and a big moustache and snowy ruff – but he was tall and thin and sallow, with an amazingly long, narrow head, bald and polished at its point. He was the gentile but he looked more Jewish than his wife. He wore black serge, somewhat rusty at the knees and elbows. He gazed at me, or through me, with Nick's large black eyes and the same still, dreamy smile, though his had a glint in it. I babbled, and he kept talking over me, not listening, saying *I know, I know*, and chafing his long brown hands together. What a lot we all did talk in those days. When I think back to then, from out of this sepulchral silence, I am aware of a ceaseless hubbub of voices loudly saying things no one seemed in the least inclined to listen to. It was the Age of Statements.

'Yes, yes, very interesting,' Big Beaver said. 'Poetry is very marketable, these days.'

There was a silence. Nick laughed.

'He's not a poet, Max,' he said.

I had never before heard a son address his father by his first name. Max Brevoort peered at me.

'But of course you're not!' he said, without the least embarrassment. 'You're the art critic.' He rubbed his hands harder. '*Very* interesting.'

Then we had tea, served by an impertinent maid, and Mrs Beaver came in from the garden and Big Beaver told her of his having mistaken me for a poet and they both laughed heartily as if it were a wonderful joke. Nick lifted a sympathetic eyebrow at me.

'Did you drive over?' he asked quietly.

'Train,' I said.

We smiled, exchanging what seemed a kind of signal, conspirators in the making.

And when I was leaving, it was he who took my essay, relieving me of it gently as if it were some wounded, suffering thing, and said he would make sure his father read it. Mrs Beaver was talking about cigarette ends. 'Just pop them in a jam jar,' she said, 'and keep them for me.' I must have looked baffled. She lifted the copper kettle and shook it, producing a slushy sound. 'For the greenfly,' she said. 'Nicotine, you know. They can't abide it.' I backed out and the three of them held their places, as if waiting for applause, the parents beaming and

Nick darkly amused. Baby was still upstairs, playing her jazz and rehearsing for her entrance in act two.

*

Midnight. My leg has gone to sleep. Wish the rest of me would go with it. Yet it is not unpleasant to be awake like this, awake and alert, like a nocturnal predator, or, better yet, the guardian of the tribe's resting place. I used to fear the night, its dreads and dreams, but lately I have begun to enjoy it, almost. Something soft and yielding comes over the world when darkness falls. On the threshold of my second childhood, I suppose I am remembering the nursery, with its woolly warmth and wide-eyed vigils. Even as a babe I was already a solitary. It was not so much my mother's kiss that I Proustianly craved as the having done with it, so that I could be alone with my self, this strange, soft, breathing body in which my spinning consciousness was darkly trapped, like a dynamo in a sack. I can still see her dim form retreating and the yellow fan of light from the hall folding across the nursery floor as she lingeringly closed the door and stepped backwards in silence out of my life. I was not quite five when she died. Her death was not a cause of suffering to me, as I recall. I was old enough to register the loss but too young to find it more than merely puzzling. My father in his well-meaning way took to sleeping on a camp bed in the nursery to keep my brother Freddie and me company, and for weeks I had to listen to him thrashing all night long in the toils of his grief, mumbling and muttering and calling on his God, heaving long, shuddering sighs that made the camp bed crack its knuckles in exasperation. I would lie there intently, trying to listen beyond him to the wind in the trees that ringed the house like sentinels, and, farther off, the boxy collapse of waves on Carrick strand and the drawn-out hiss of waters receding over the shingle. I would not lie on my right side because that way I could feel my heart beating and I was convinced that if I were going to die I would feel it stop before the terrifying final darkness came down.

Strange creatures, children. That wary look they have when adults are about, as if they are worrying whether they are doing a convincing enough impersonation of what we expect them to be. The nineteenth century invented childhood and now the world is full of child actors. My poor Blanche was never any good at it, could not remember her lines or where to stand or what to do with her hands. How my heart would fold into itself in sorrow at the school play or on prize-giving day when the line of little girls being good would develop a kink, a sort of panicky quaver, and I would look along the row of heads and sure enough there she would be, on the point of tripping over her own awkwardness, blushing and biting her lip, and sloping her shoulders and bending her knees in a vain attempt to take a few inches off her height. When she was an adolescent I used to show her photographs of Isadora Duncan and Ottoline Morrell and other big, bold women from whose example she might take comfort and whose extravagance she might emulate, but she would not look at them, only sit in miserable silence with bowed head, picking at her hangnails, her wiry hair standing on end, as if a strong current were passing through it, and the heartbreakingly defenceless pale back of her neck exposed. Now Julian, on the other hand . . . No; I think not. That subject is the very stuff of insomnia.

Among the newspaper pack this morning there was a girl reporter – how these terms date one! – who reminded me of Blanche, I don't quite know why. She was not big, like my daughter, but in her manner she had something of the same intent watchfulness. Clever, too: while the rest kept elbowing each other aside in order to ask the obvious questions, such as whether there are more of us still to be unmasked (!), or if Mrs W. had known all along, she sat fixed on me with what seemed a sort of hunger and hardly spoke at all, and then only to ask for names and dates and places, information which I suspect she already possessed. It was as if she were carrying out some private test on me, checking my responses, measuring my emotions. Perhaps I, in turn, reminded her of her father? Girls, in my admittedly limited experience of them, are ever on the lookout for their Dad. I considered asking her to stay to lunch – that was the kind of giddy mood I was in – for suddenly the thought of being alone after they had vacated the place was not at all attractive. This was strange; I have never suffered from loneliness in the past. Indeed, as I said already, I have always considered myself to be a perfectly reconciled solitary, especially after poor Patrick died. But there was something about this girl, and not just her indefinable resemblance to Blanche, that attracted my attention. A fellow loner? I did not get her name and do not even know which of the papers she works for. I shall read them all tomorrow and see if I can identify her style.

Tomorrow. Dear God, how can I face a tomorrow.

*

Well, I am everywhere. Pages and pages of me. This must be how it feels to be the leading man on the morning after a stupendously disastrous first night. I went to a number of newsagents, for the sake of decency, though it got increasingly awkward as the bundle of newspapers under my arm steadily thickened. Some of the people behind the counters recognised me and curled a contemptuous lip; reactionaries to a man, shopkeepers, I have noticed it before. One chap, though, gave me a sort of sad, underhand smile. He was a Pakistani. What company I shall be in from now on. Old lags. Child molesters. Outcasts. The lost ones.

It has been confirmed: the K is to be revoked. I mind. I am surprised how much I mind. Just Doctor again, if even that; maybe just plain Mister. At least they have not taken away my bus pass, or my laundry allowance (the latter an acknowledge-ment, I imagine, that over the age of sixty-five one tends to dribble a lot).

That writer chap telephoned, requesting an interview. What effrontery. Well-spoken, however, and not at all embarrassed. Brisk tone, faintly amused, with a hint almost of fondness: after all, I am his ticket to fame, or notoriety, at least. I asked him to say who it was that betrayed me. That provoked a chuckle. Said even a journalist would go to gaol rather than reveal a source. They love to trot out that particular hobby-horse. I might have said to him, *My dear fellow, I have been in gaol for the best part of thirty years*. Instead, I rang off.

The *Telegraph* sent a photographer to Carrickdrum, site of my bourgeois beginnings. The house is no longer the bishop's residence, and is owned, the paper tells me, by a man who deals in scrap metal. The sentinel trees are gone – the scrap merchant must have wanted more light – and the brickwork has been covered with a new facing, painted white. I am tempted to work up a metaphor for change and loss, but I must beware turning into a sentimental old ass, if I am not one already. St Nicholas's (St Nicholas's! – I never made the connection before) was a grim and gloomy pile, and a bit of stucco and white paint can only be an improvement. I see myself as a little boy sitting head on hand in the bay window in the parlour, looking out at the rain falling on the sloping lawn and the far-off, stone-grey waters of the Lough, hearing poor Freddie wandering about upstairs crooning like a dreamy banshee. That's Carrickdrum. When my father married again, with what struck me even at the age of six as unseemly haste, I awaited the appearance of my stepmother – they had married in London – with a mixture of curiosity, anger and apprehension, expecting a witch out of an Arthur Rackham illustration, with violet eyes and fingernails like stilettos. When the happy couple arrived, mounted, with odd appropriateness, on a jaunting car, I was surprised and obscurely disappointed to find that she was nothing like my expectations of her, but a big, jolly woman, broad in the beam and pink of cheek, with a washerwoman's thick arms and a loud, trembly laugh. Coming up the front steps she spotted me in the hallway and broke into a wallowing run, big red hands lifted, and fell upon my neck, nuzzling me wetly and uttering distressful little grunts of joy. She smelled of face powder and peppermints and female sweat. She unclasped me and stepped back, rubbing at her eyes with the heel of a hand, and threw a histrionically fervent glance back at my father, while I stood frowning, trying to cope with a welter of sensations I did not recognise, among them a faint premonition of that unexpected happiness she was to bring to St Nicholas's. My father wrung his hands and grinned sheepishly and avoided my eye. No one said anything, yet there was the sense of loud and continuous noise, as if the unexpected gaiety of the occasion were producing a din of its own. Then my brother appeared on the stairs, descending sideways with his Quasimodo lurch and drooling – no, no, I am exaggerating, he was not really that bad – and brought the moment to its senses. 'And this,' said my father, fairly bellowing in his nervousness, 'this is Freddie!'

How difficult that day must have been for my mother – I always think of her as that, my natural mother having bowed out so early – and how well she managed it all, settling herself upon the house like a great warm roosting bird. That first day, she embraced poor Freddie stoutly, and listened to the gaggings and strangled howls that with him passed for speech, nodding her head as if she were understanding him perfectly, and even produced a hanky and wiped the spittle from his chin. I'm sure my father must have told her about him, but I doubt if any mere description could have prepared her for Freddie. He gave her his broadest gap-toothed grin and put his arms tightly about her big hips and laid his face against her stomach, as if he were welcoming her home. Most likely he thought she was our real mother come back transformed from the land of the dead. Behind her my father heaved a queer, groaning sort of sigh, like that of someone setting down at long last a toilsome and unmanageable burden.

Her name was Hermione. We called her Hettie. Thank God she did not live to see me disgraced.

*

Day three. Life goes on. The anonymous telephone calls have abated. They did not start up until first thing yesterday, after the story had appeared in the morning papers (and I thought everyone got their news these days from the telly!). I had to leave the receiver off the hook; whenever I replaced it, the damned instrument would immediately start shrilling at me, seeming to dance in rage. The callers are men, for the most part, belt-and-braces types by the sound of them, but there have been a few females as well, refined old things with gentle, reedy voices and the vocabulary of a navvy. The abuse is entirely personal. It is as if I had embezzled their pensions. At first I was polite, and even got into conversations of a sort with the less mad among them (one chap wanted to know if I had met Beria – I think he was interested in the Georgian's love life). I should have recorded them, it would have made a revealing cross-section of the English national character. One call, however, I welcomed. She announced herself diffidently while giving the impression that she expected me to know her. And she was right: I did not recognise her name, but I remembered the voice. Which paper was it again? I asked. There was a pause. 'I'm freelance,' she said. That explained why I could not find her trace in yesterday's accounts of my press conference (my press conference! – gosh, how grand it sounds). She is called Vandeleur. I wondered if there was an Irish connection – lots of Vandeleurs in Ireland – but she says not, and even seemed a bit put out by the suggestion. The Irish are not popular these days, with IRA bombs going off in the city every other week. I have forgotten her first name. Sophie? Sibyl? Something quaintly archaic, anyway. I told her to come round in the afternoon. I don't know what I was thinking of. Then I had an attack of the fidgets while I waited for her, and burned my hand cooking lunch (grilled lamb chop, sliced tomato, a leaf of lettuce; no booze – felt I should keep a clear head). She arrived on the dot, muffled in a big old coat that looked as if it had belonged to her father (there's Dad again). Dark short hair like fine fur and a little heart-shaped face and tiny, cold-looking hands. She made me think of a delicate, rare, very self-possessed small animal. Josefina the Songstress. What age is she? Late twenties, early thirties. She stood in the middle of the living room, one of those little claws braced in a peculiar, old-womany way on the lacquered edge of the Japanese table, and looked about carefully, as if to memorise what she saw.

'What a nice flat,' she said flatly. 'I didn't notice, last time.'

'Not as nice as the flat at the Institute, where I used to live.'

'Did you have to give it up?'

'Yes, but not for the reasons you think. Someone died there.'

Serena, that is her name, it has just come back to me. Serena Vandeleur. Has a ring to it, certainly.

I took her coat, which she surrendered reluctantly, I thought. 'Are you cold?' I said, playing the solicitous old gent. She shook her head. Perhaps she feels less secure without that protective paternal embrace. Though I must say she strikes me as remarkably at ease with herself. It is a little unnerving, this sense of calm that she communicates. No, communicates is the wrong word; she seems wholly self-contained. She wore a nice plain blouse and a cardigan and flat shoes, though a tight, short leather skirt lent a certain slinky raciness to the ensemble. I offered her tea but she said she would prefer a drink. That's my girl. I said we should have some gin, which gave me an excuse to escape to the kitchen, where the sting of ice cubes and the sharp tang of limes (I *always* use limes in gin; so much more *assertive* than the dull old workaday lemon) helped me to regain something of my composure. I do not know why I was so agitated. But then, how would I not be in a state? In the past three days the tranquil pool that was my life has been churned up and all sorts of disturbing things have risen from the depths. I am beset constantly by a feeling the only name for which I can think of is nostalgia. Great hot waves of remembrance wash through me, bringing images and sensations I would have thought I had entirely forgotten or successfully extirpated, yet so sharp and vivid are they that I falter in my tracks with an inward gasp, assailed by a sort of rapturous sorrow. I tried to describe this phenomenon to Miss Vandeleur when I returned to the living room with our drinks on a tray (so much for keeping a clear head). I found her standing as before, her face inclined a little and one hand with steepled fingers pressing on the table, so still and seemingly posed that the suspicion crossed my mind that she had been searching the room and had darted back to this position only when she had heard the approaching tinkle of ice and glass. But I am sure it is just my bad mind that makes me think she had been snooping: it is the kind of thing that I used to do automatically, in the days when I had a professional interest in discovering other people's secrets.

'Yes,' I said, 'I can't tell you how strange it is, to be suddenly thrust into the public gaze like this.'

She nodded distractedly; she was thinking of something else. It struck me that she was behaving oddly, for a journalist.

We sat opposite each other by the fireplace, with our drinks, in a polite, unexpectedly easy, almost companionable silence, like two voyagers sharing a cocktail before joining the captain's table, knowing we had a whole ocean of time before us in which to get acquainted. Miss Vandeleur studied with frank though unemphatic interest the framed photographs on the mantelpiece: my father in his gaiters, Hettie in a hat, Blanche and Julian as children, my ill-remembered natural mother wearing silks and a lost look. 'My family,' I said. 'The gener-ations.' She nodded again. It was one of those volatile April days, with enormous icebergs of silver-and-white cloud hurtling slowly across the sky above the city, bringing rapid alternations of glare and gloom, and now suddenly the sunlight in the window was switched off almost with a click and I thought for a moment I was going to cry, I could not say why, precisely, though obviously the photographs were part of it. Very alarming, it was, and a great surprise; I was never the tearful type, up to now. When was the last time that I wept? There was Patrick's death, of course, but that does not count – death does not count, when it comes to weeping. No, I think the last time I really cried was when I went round to Vivienne's that morning after Boy and the Dour Scot had fled. Driving like a madman through Mayfair with the wipers going full belt and then realising it wasn't rain that was splintering my vision but salt tears. Of course, I was tight, and in an awful funk (it looked as if the whole game was up and that we would all be hauled in), but I was not accustomed to losing control of myself like that, and it was a shock. I learned some remarkable things that day, and not only about my propensity to tears.

Miss Vandeleur had taken on a grey look and was huddling rather in her chair. 'But you *are* cold,' I said, and despite her protests that she was perfectly comfortable I got down on one knee, which startled her and made her shrink back – she must have thought I was going to kneel before her and blurt out some ghastly, final confession and swear her to secrecy – but it was only to light the gas fire. It uttered its gratifying *whumpf* and did that little trick of sucking the flame from the match, then the delicate filigree of wires glowed and the ashy waffle behind them began slowly to turn blush-pink. I have a great fondness for such humble gadgets: scissors, tin-openers, adjustable reading lamps, even the flush toilet. They are the unacknowledged props of civilisation.

'Why did you do it?' Miss Vandeleur said.

I was in the process of rising creakily from that genuflexion, one hand on a quivering knee, the other pressed to the small of my back, and I almost fell over. But it was a not unreasonable question, in the circumstances, and one which, curiously enough, none of her colleagues had thought to ask. I slumped into my armchair with a laughing sigh and shook my head.

'Why?' I said. 'Oh, cowboys and indians, my dear; cowboys and indians.' It was true, in a way. The need for amusement, the fear of boredom: was the whole thing much more than that, really, despite all the grand theorising? 'And hatred of America, of course,' I added, a trifle jadedly, I fear; the poor old Yanks are by now a rather moth-eaten bugbear. 'You must understand, the American occupation of Europe was to many of us not much less of a calamity than a German victory would have been. The Nazis at least were a clear and visible enemy. Men enough to be damned, to paraphrase Eliot.' At that I gave her a twinkly smile: wise age acknowledges educated youth. I stood up with my drink and walked to the window: sun-polished slates, a skittle-stand of blackened chimney pots, television aerials like a jumbled alphabet consisting mainly of aitches. 'The defence of European culture—'

'But you were,' she said evenly, interrupting me, 'a spy *before* the war. Weren't you?'

Now, such words – spy, agent, espionage, etc. – have always given me trouble. They conjure in my mind images of low taverns and cobbled laneways at night with skulking figures in doublet and hose and the flash of poniards. I could never think of myself as a part of that dashing, subfusc world. Boy, now, Boy had a touch of the Kit Marlowes about him, all right, but I was a dry old stick, even when I was young. I was what was needed, someone safe to chivvy the rest of them along, to look after them and wipe their noses and make sure they didn't run out into the traffic, but now I cannot help wondering if I sacrificed too much of myself to the . . . I suppose I must call it the cause. Did I squander my life on the gathering and collating of trivial information? The thought leaves me breathless.

'I was a connoisseur, you know, before I was anything else,' I said. I had turned from the window. She was sitting with shoulders hunched, gazing into the pallid flame of the gas fire.

In my glass an ice cube cracked with an agonised plink. 'Art was all that ever mattered to me,' I said. 'I even tried to be a painter, in my student days. Oh yes. Modest little still-lifes, blue jugs and violent tulips, that kind of thing. I dared to hang one in my rooms at Cambridge. A friend looked at it and pronounced me the finest lady painter since Raoul Dufy.' That was Boy, of course. That wide, cruel, voracious smile. 'So you have before you, my dear,' I said, 'a failed artist, like so many other egregious scoundrels: Nero, half the Medicis, Stalin, the unspeakable Herr Schicklgruber.' I could see that last one passing her by.

I returned and sat down again in the armchair. She was still gazing into the undulating pale flame of the fire. She had hardly touched her drink. I wondered what it could be that she was pondering with such concentration. Time passed. The gas flame hissed. Sunlight came and went in the window. Idly I admired the little Bonington watercolour behind her, one of my few genuine treasures: oyster-shell mud and a fried-rasher sky, fisher-lads in the foreground, a distant, lofty barquentine with sails furled. At last she raised her eyes and met mine. That inner struggle she had been engaged upon had given her the drawn look of a Carracci madonna. She must have taken my Bonington ogle – Nick always said I looked positively coital when contemplating a picture – for a benison directed upon her, for suddenly she decided to come clean.

'I'm not really a journalist,' she said.

'I know.' I smiled at her surprise. 'Takes one deceiver to recognise another. Did Skryne send you?'

She frowned. 'Who?'

'Just one of my keepers.'

'No,' she said, shaking her head violently and twisting the gin glass in her fingers, 'no, I'm . . . I'm a writer. I want to write a book on you.'

Oh dear. Another contemporary historian. I suppose my face must have fallen, for she launched at once defensively into a stumbling account of herself and her plans. I hardly listened. What did I care for her theories on the connection between espionage and the bogus concept of the English gentleman ('I'm not English,' I reminded her, but she took no notice) or the malign influence on my generation of the nihilistic aesthetics of Modernism? I wanted to tell her about the blade of sunlight cleaving the velvet shadows of the public urinal that post-war spring afternoon in Regensburg, of the incongruous gaiety of the rain shower that fell the day of my father's funeral, of that last night with Boy when I saw the red ship under Blackfriars Bridge and conceived of the tragic significance of my life: in other words, the real things; the true things.

'Do you know philosophy?' I asked. 'I mean ancient philosophy. The Stoics: Zeno, Seneca, Marcus Aurelius?' Cautiously she shook her head. She was plainly baffled by this turn in the conversation. 'I used to consider myself a Stoic,' I said. 'In fact, I was quite proud to think of myself thus.' I put down my glass and joined my fingers at their tips and gazed off in the direction of the window, where light and shade were still jostling for position. I was born to be a lecturer. 'The Stoics denied the concept of progress. There might be a little advance here, some improvement there – cosmology in their time, dentistry in ours – but in the long run the balance of things, such as good and evil, beauty and ugliness, joy and misery, remains constant. Periodically, at the end of aeons, the world is destroyed in a holocaust of fire and then everything starts up again, just as before. This pre-Nietzschean notion of eternal recurrence I have always found greatly comforting, not because I look forward to returning again and again to live my life over, but because it drains events of all consequence while at the same time conferring on them the numinous significance that derives from fixity, from completedness. Do you see?' I smiled my kindliest smile. Her mouth had fallen open a tiny way and I had an urge to reach out a finger and tip it shut again. 'And then one day I read, I can't remember where, an account of a little exchange between Josef Mengele and a Jewish doctor whom he had salvaged from the execution line to assist him in his experiments at Auschwitz. They were in the operating theatre. Mengele was working on a pregnant woman, whose legs he had bound together at the knees prior to inducing the onset of the birth of her child, without the benefit of anaesthetics, of course, which were much too valuable to waste on Jews. In the lulls between the mother's shrieks, Mengele discoursed of the vast project of the Final Solution: the numbers involved, the technology, the logistical problems, and so on. How long, the Jewish doctor ventured to ask – he must have been a courageous man – how long would the exterminations go on? Mengele, apparently not at all surprised or put out by the question, smiled gently and without looking up from his work said, *Oh, they will go on, and on, and on* . . . And it struck me that Dr Mengele was also a Stoic, just like me. I had not realised until then how broad a church it was that I belonged to.'

I liked the quality of the silence that fell, or rather rose – for silence *rises*, surely? – when I ceased speaking. At the end of a well-made period I always have a sense of ease, a sort of blissful settling back, my mind folding its arms, as it were, and smiling to itself in quiet satisfaction. It is a sensation known to all mental athletes, I am sure, and for me was one of the chief pleasures of the lecture hall, not to mention debriefings (a term that never failed to elicit a chuckle from Boy). It rather took the shine off my bliss, however, when Miss Vandeleur, of whose mousy yet persistent presence I was beginning to tire slightly, mumbled something about not having known the Stoics were a church. Young people are so literal-minded.

I stood up. 'Come,' I said to her, 'I want you to see something.'

We went through to the study. I could hear her leather skirt creaking as she walked behind me. When she first arrived she had told me her father was an admiral, and I had misheard her to say that her father was admirable. Although this piece of filial piety had struck me as disconcertingly supererogatory, I had hastened to assure her that I had no doubt that he was. There followed an inadvertently comic exchange which at the end subsided into one of those awful, sweaty silences that such glimpses of the world's essential absurdity always provoke. I remember at one of Mrs W.'s stiflingly grand occasions conversing with the lady herself as we made our way slowly up an interminable, red-carpeted staircase behind the ample back parts of the Dowager Duchess of Somewhere, and both of us noticing at the same instant, what the Duchess herself was magnificently unaware of, that on her way into the Palace she had trod in corgi-shit. At moments like that I always felt grateful for the difficulties of leading a multiple life, which lent a little weight to matters, or at least provided something for the mind to turn to in a time of need. As a child at school, when I had to keep myself from laughing in the face of a bully or a particularly mad master, I would concentrate on the thought of death; it always worked, and would still, I'm sure, if there were need.

'Here,' I said, 'is my treasure, the touchstone and true source of my life's work.'

It is a curious phenomenon, that paintings are always larger in my mind than in reality – I mean literally larger, in their physical dimensions. This is true even of works with which I am thoroughly intimate, including my *Death of Seneca*, which I have lived with for nigh on fifty years. I know its size, I know, empirically, that the canvas is seventeen and a quarter inches by twenty-four, yet when I encounter it again even after a brief interval I have the uncanny sense that it has shrunk, as if I were viewing it through the wrong side of a lens, or standing a few paces farther back from it than I really am. The effect is disconcerting, as when you go to the Bible and discover that the entire story of the expulsion from the Garden of Eden, say, is dispatched in a handful of verses. Now as always the picture did its trick and for a moment as I stood before it with Miss

Vandeleur intermittently creaking at my side it seemed diminished not only in scale but in – how shall I say? – in substance, and I experienced a strange little flicker of distress, which, however, I do not think was detectable in my tone; anyway, persons of her age are impervious to the tics and twitches by which the old betray the pain of their predicament.

'The subject,' I said, in what I think of as my Expounding Voice, 'is the suicide of Seneca the Younger in the year AD 65. See his grieving friends and family about him as his life's blood drips into the golden bowl. There is the officer of the Guard – Gavius Silvanus, according to Tacitus – who has unwillingly conveyed the imperial death sentence. Here is Pompeia Paulina, the philosopher's young wife, ready to follow her husband into death, baring her breast to the knife. And notice, here in the background, in this farther room, the servant girl filling the bath in which presently the philosopher will breathe his last. Is it not all admirably executed? Seneca was a Spaniard and was brought up in Rome. Among his works are the *Consolationes*, the *Epistolae morales*, and *The Apocolocyntosis, or 'Pumpkinification', of the Divine Claudius* – this last, as you may guess, is a satire. Although he professed to despise the things of this world, he still managed to amass an enormous fortune, much of it derived from moneylending in Britain; the historian Dio Cassius says that the excessive interest rates charged by Seneca was one of the causes of the revolt of the Britons against the occupier – which means, as Lord Russell has wittily pointed out, that Queen Boadicea's rebellion was directed against capitalism as represented by the Roman Empire's leading philosophical proponent of austerity. Such are the ironies of history.' I stole a sideways glance at Miss Vandeleur; her eyes were beginning to glaze; I was wearing her down nicely. 'Seneca fell foul of Claudius's successor, the aforementioned Nero, whose tutor he had been. He was accused of conspiracy, and was ordered to commit suicide, which he did, with great fortitude and dignity.' I gestured at the picture before us. For the first time it occurred to me to wonder if the painter was justified in portraying the scene with such tranquillity, such studied calm. Again the shiver of disquiet. In this new life I am condemned to, is there nothing that is not open to doubt? 'Baudelaire,' I said, and this time I did seem to detect the tiniest quaver in my voice, 'Baudelaire described Stoicism as a religion with only one sacrament: suicide.'

At this, Miss Vandeleur suddenly gave a sort of shudder, like a pony balking at a jump.

'Why are you doing this?' she said thickly.

I looked at her with a mildly enquiring frown. She stood with her fists clenched in front of her hip bones and her little face thrust forward, sulky-sullen, glaring at an ivory paperknife on my desk. Not so serene after all.

'Why am I doing what, my dear?'

'I know how well read you are,' she said, almost spitting, 'I know how *cultured* you are.'

She made the word sound like an ailment. I thought: she can't be from Skryne, he would never send someone with so little self-control. After a beat of flushed silence I said softly:

'In my world, there are no simple questions, and precious few answers of any kind. If you are going to write about me, you must resign yourself to that.'

Still fixed on that paperknife, she set her lips so tightly they turned white, and gave her head a quick, stubborn little shake, and I thought, almost with fondness, of Vivienne, my sometime wife, who was the only supposedly grown-up person I ever knew who used actually to stamp her foot when she was angry.

'There *are*,' she said, in a surprisingly restrained tone, 'there *are* simple questions; there *are* answers. Why did you spy for the Russians? How did you get away with it? What did you think you would achieve by betraying your country and your country's interests? Or was it because you never thought of this as your country? Was it because you were Irish and hated us?'

And at last she turned her head and looked at me. What fire!

I would never have expected it. Her father, the admirable Admiral, would be proud of her. I looked away from her, smiling my weary smile, and considered *The Death of Seneca*. How superbly executed are the folds of the dying man's robe, polished, smooth and dense as fluted sandstone, yet wonderfully delicate, too, like one of the philosopher's own carven paragraphs. (I must have the picture valued. Not that I would dream of selling it, of course, but just now I find myself in need of financial reassurance.)

'Not the Russians,' I murmured.

I could feel her blink. 'What?'

'I did not spy for the Russians,' I said. 'I spied for Europe. A *much* broader church.'

*

This really is the most unsettling weather. Just now out of nowhere a violent shower started up, pelting big fat splatters against the windows in which the watercolour sunlight shines unabated. I should not like just yet to leave this world, so tender and accommodating even in the midst of its storms. The doctors tell me they got all of it and that there is no sign of any new malignancy. I am in remission. I feel I have been in remission all my life.

MY FATHER was a great bird's-nester. I could never learn the trick of it. On Sunday mornings in springtime he would take Freddie and me walking with him in the fields above Carrickdrum. I imagine he was escaping those of his parishioners – he was still rector then – who made it a practice to call to the house after service, the boisterously unhappy country wives in their pony-and-traps, the working people from the back streets of the town, the glittery-eyed mad spinsters who spent their weekdays doing sentry-go behind lace-curtained windows in the villas on the seafront. I wish I could describe these outings as occasions of familial conviviality, with my father discoursing to his wide-eyed sons on the ways and wiles of Mother Nature, but in fact he rarely spoke, and I suspect he was for the most part forgetful of the two little boys scrambling desperately over rock and thorn to keep up with him. It was rough country up there, skimpy bits of field isolated between outcrops of bare grey stone, with whin bushes and the odd stand of mountain ash deformed by the sea gales. I do not know why my father insisted on bringing Freddie with us, for he always grew agitated in those uplands, especially on windy days, and went along uttering little moos of distress and tearing at the skin around his fingernails and gnawing at his lips until they bled. At the farthest limit of our trek, however, we would come down into a little hollow ringed by rocks, a miniature valley, with meadow-grass and gorse bushes and banks of hawthorn, where all was still and hummingly silent, and where even Freddie grew calm, or as near to calm as he ever got. Here my father, in plus-fours and gaiters and an old fawn pullover and

30

still wearing his dog collar, would stop suddenly, with a hand lifted, hearkening to I do not know what secret signal or vibration of the air, and then strike off from the path and approach this or that bush, with surprising lightness of tread for such a large-made man, and carefully part the leaves and peer in and smile. I remember it, that smile. There was simple delight in it, of course – it made him look as I imagined Freddie would have looked if he had not been a half-wit – but also a sort of grim, sad triumph, as if he had caught out the Creator in some impressive yet essentially shoddy piece of fakery. Then with a finger to his lips he would beckon us forward and lift us up one after the other to see what he had discovered: a finch's or a blackbird's nest, sometimes with the bird herself still on it, throbbing tinily and looking up at us in dull fright, as at the side-by-side big faces of God and his son. Not the birds, though, but the eggs, were what fascinated me. Pale blue or speckled white, they lay there in the scooped hollow of the nest, closed, inexplicable, packed with their own fullness. I felt that if I took one in my hand, which my father would never have permitted me to do, it would be too heavy for me to hold, like a piece of matter from a planet far more dense than this one. What was most striking about them was their *difference*. They were like themselves and nothing else. And in this extreme of selfness they rebuked all that stood round about, the dissolute world of bush and briar and riotous green leaf. They were the ultimate artefact. When I first spotted *The Death of Seneca*, shining amidst the dross in the back room at Alighieri's, I thought at once of those Sunday mornings of my childhood, and of my father with infinite delicacy parting the foliage and showing me these fragile and yet somehow indestructible treasures nestling at the heart of the world.

*

To take possession of a city of which you are not a native you must first of all fall in love there. I had always known London;

my family, although they hardly ever went there, considered it our capital, not dour Belfast, with its rain-coloured buildings and bellowing shipyard sirens. It was only in that summer I spent in London with Nick, however, that the place came fully alive for me. I say I spent the summer with him but that is wishful exaggeration. He was working – another exaggeration – for his father at Brevoort & Klein, and had moved down from Oxford to a flat above a newsagent's shop off the Fulham Road. I remember that flat with remarkable clarity. There was a small living room at the front with two peaked mansard windows that made an incongruously ecclesiastical effect; the first time Boy came there he clapped his hands and cried: 'Fetch me my surplice, we must have a black mass!' The flat was known as the Eyrie, a word neither Nick nor I was sure how to pronounce, but it suited, for certainly it was eerie – Nick favoured tall candles and Piranesi prints – and airy, too, especially in spring, when the windows were filled with flying sky and the timbers creaked like the spars of a sailing ship. Nick, who was by nature a unique mix of the aesthete and the hearty, let the place run to appalling squalor: I still shudder when I think of the lavatory. At the back was a poky bedroom with a sharply canted ceiling, in which there was wedged skew-ways an enormous brass bed Nick claimed to have won in a poker game in a gambling den behind Paddington Station. It was one of Nick's stories.

He did not often sleep at the flat. His girls refused to stay there, because of the filth, and anyway in those times girls rarely stayed overnight, at least not the kind of girl that Nick consorted with. Mostly it was a place to throw parties in, and to recover in from the resulting hangovers. On these occasions he would take to his bed for two or three days, surrounded by an accumulating clutter of books and boxes of sweets and bottles of champagne, supplied by a succession of friends whom he would summon to him by telephone. I can still hear his voice on the line, an exaggeratedly anguished whisper: 'I say, old man, do you think you could come round? I do believe I'm dying.' Usually when I arrived a small crowd would already have assembled, another party in embryo, sitting about on that vast raft of a bed eating Nick's chocolates and drinking champagne from tooth-glasses and kitchen cups, with Nick in his nightshirt propped against a bank of pillows, pale as ivory, his black hair standing on end, all eyes and angles, a figure out of Schiele. Boy would be there, of course, and Rothenstein, and girls called Daphne and Brenda and Daisy, in silks and cloche hats. Sometimes Querell would come round, tall, thin, sardonic, standing with his back against the wall and smoking a cigarette, somehow crooked, like the villain in a cautionary tale, one eyebrow arched and the corners of his mouth turned down, and a hand in the pocket of his tightly buttoned jacket that I always thought could be holding a gun. He had the look of a man who knew something damaging about everyone in the room. (I realise that I am seeing him not as he was then, young, and gauche, surely, like the rest of us, but as he was in his late thirties, when the Blitz was on, and he seemed the very personification of the times: embittered, tense, offhand, amusedly despairing, older than his, and our, years.)

Those parties: did anyone really enjoy them? What I chiefly recall is the air of suppressed desperation that pervaded them. We drank a lot, but drink seemed only to make us frightened, or despairing, so that we must shriek all the louder, as if to scare off demons. What was it that we feared? Another war, yes, the worldwide economic crisis, all that, the threat of Fascism; there was no end of things to be afraid of. We felt such deep resentments! We blamed all our ills on the Great War and the old men who had forced the young to fight in it, and perhaps Flanders really did destroy us as a nation, but— But there I go, falling into the role of amateur sociologist that I despise. I never thought in terms of *us*, or *the nation*; none of us did, I am convinced of it. We *talked* in those terms, of course – we never *stopped* talking thus – but it was all no more than a striking of attitudes to make ourselves feel more serious, more weighty, more authentic. Deep down – if we did, indeed, have deeps – we cared about ourselves and, intermittently, one or two others; isn't that how it always is? *Why did you do it?* that girl asked me yesterday, and I replied with parables of philosophy and art, and she went away dissatisfied. But what other reply could I have given? *I* am the answer to her question, the totality of what I am; nothing less will suffice. In the public mind, for the brief period it will entertain, and be entertained by, the thought of me, I am a figure with a single salient feature. Even for those who thought they knew me intimately, everything else I have done or not done has faded to insignificance before the fact of my so-called treachery. While in reality all that I am is all of a piece: all of a piece, and yet broken up into a myriad selves. Does that make sense?

So what we were frightened of, then, was ourselves, each one his own demon.

Querell when he phoned the other day had the grace not to pretend to be shocked. He knows all about betrayal, the large variety and the small; he is a connoisseur in that department. When he was at the height of his fame (he has slipped somewhat from the headlines, since he is old and no longer the hellion he once was) I used to chuckle over newspaper photographs of him hobnobbing with the Pope, since I knew that the lips with which he kissed the papal ring had most likely been between some woman's thighs a half-hour previously. But Querell too is in danger of being shown up for what he really is, whatever that might be. That fishy look he always had is becoming more pronounced with age. In yet another interview recently – where did he ever get the reputation for shunning publicity? – he made one of those seemingly deep but in fact banal observations that have become his trademark. 'I don't know about God,' he told the interviewer, 'but certainly I believe in the Devil.' Oh yes, one always needed a long spoon to sup with Querell.

He was genuinely curious about people – the sure mark of

the second-rate novelist. At those parties in the Eyrie he would stand for a long time leaning with his back against the wall, diabolical trickles of smoke issuing from the corners of his mouth, watching and listening as the party took on an air of monkey-house hysteria. He drank as much as the rest of us, but it seemed to have no effect on him except to make those unnervingly pale-blue eyes of his shine with a kind of malicious merriment. Usually he would slip away early, with a girl in tow; you would glance at the spot where he had been standing and find him gone, and seem to see a shadowy after-image of him, like the paler shadow left on a wall when a picture is removed. So I was surprised when during a party one August afternoon he accosted me in the corridor.

'Listen, Maskell,' he said, in that insinuatingly truculent way of his, 'I can't take any more of this filthy wine – let's go and have a real drink.'

My head felt as if it were stuffed with cotton wool and the sunlight in the mansard windows had taken on the colour of urine, and for once I was content to leave. A girl was standing weeping in the bedroom doorway, her face in her hands; Nick was not to be seen. Querell and I walked in silence down the clattery stairs. The air in the street was blued with exhaust fumes; strange to think of a time when one still noticed the smell of petrol. We went to a pub – was it Finch's then, or had it another name? – and Querell ordered gin and water, 'the tart's tipple', as he said with a snicker. It was just after opening time and there were few customers. Querell sat with one foot hooked on the rung of his stool and the other delicately braced *en pointe* on the floor; he did not undo the buttons of his jacket. I noticed the frayed shirt cuffs, the shine on the knees of his trousers. We were of an age, but I felt a generation younger than him. He had a job on the *Express*, or perhaps it was the *Telegraph*, writing juicy tidbits for the gossip column, and as we drank he recounted office anecdotes, drolly describing the eccentricities of his fellow journalists and the public-school asininity of the editor of the day in what were obviously pre-prepared paragraphs of admirable fluency and precision. Tight though I was I saw clearly that this was a performance, from behind which he was studying me with the detached intentness that was to become his trademark as a novelist. He was already an expert at putting up smokescreens (literally as well as figuratively: he smoked without cease, apparently the same, everlasting cigarette, for I never seemed able to catch him in the act of lighting up).

He came to the end of his stories and we were silent for a while. He ordered more drinks, and when I tried to pay for them he waved my money away with that matter-of-fact assumption of superiority that was another of his characteristics. I don't know why he should have assumed I was broke; on the contrary, I was comparatively well off at the time, thanks to my column for the *Spectator* and occasional lectures at the Institute.

'You're pretty fond of the Beaver, aren't you,' he said.

It was said with such studied casualness that I grew wary, despite the gin.

'I haven't known him for very long,' I said.

He nodded. 'Of course, you were a Cambridge man. Not that I saw a great deal of him at Oxford.' Nick had said to me of Querell that in their college days he had been too busy whoring to bother much with friendships. Despite recent rumours to the contrary, Querell was an incorrigible hetero, whose fascination with women ran almost to the level of the gynaecological. I thought he always *smelled* faintly of sex. I hear he is still chasing girls, in his seventies, down there on the Côte d'Azur. 'Quite a boy, the Beaver,' he said, and paused, and then gave me a peculiar, sidelong look and asked: 'Do you trust him?' I did not know what to answer, and mumbled something about not being sure that I thought that anyone was really to be trusted. He nodded again, seemingly satisfied, and dropped the subject and began to talk instead about a fellow he had bumped into recently, whom he had known at Oxford.

'He'd interest you,' he said. 'He's a red-hot Sinn Feiner.'

I laughed.

'I'm from the other side of the fence, you know,' I said. 'My people are black Protestants.'

'Oh, Protestants in Ireland are all Catholics, really.'

'Rather the opposite, I should have thought. Or we're all just plain pagans, perhaps.'

'Well, anyway, the place is interesting, isn't it? I mean the politics.'

I wonder – good lord, I wonder if he was putting out feelers with a view to recruiting me, even then? That was the summer of 'thirty-one; was he already with the Department, that early? Or maybe it was just the question of religion that interested him. Although none of us knew it, he was already taking instruction at Farm Street. (Querell's Catholicism, by the way, has always seemed to me far more of an anachronism than my Marxism.) And in fact now he dropped the subject of politics and went on to talk about religion, in his usual oblique way, telling me a story about Gerard Manley Hopkins preaching at some sort of women's gathering in Dublin and scandalising the congregation by comparing the Church to a sow with seven teats representing the seven sacraments. I laughed, and said what a sad poor fool Hopkins was, trying for the common touch like that and failing ridiculously, but Querell gave me another long, measuring look and said: 'Yes, he made the mistake of thinking that the way to be convincing is to put on a false front,' and I felt obscurely confounded.

We finished our drinks and left the pub, I very bleary indeed by now, and Querell hailed a taxi and we went to Curzon Street, where there was an opening at Alighieri's. The work, by an émigré White Russian whose name I have forgotten, was hopeless trash, a combination of supremacist sterility and Russian-icon kitsch that turned my already drink-insulted stomach. He was all the rage, though, this Supremavitch, and the crowd was so large it had overflowed from the gallery, and people were standing about the pavement in the evening sunshine, drinking white wine and sneering at passers-by, and producing that self-congratulatory low roar that is the natural collective voice of imbibers at the fount of art. Ah, what heights of contempt I was capable of in those days! Now, in old age, I have largely lost that faculty, and I miss it, for it was passion of a sort.

Nick's party seemed to have transferred itself here intact. There was Nick himself, still tousled, still barefoot, with a pair of trousers pulled on over his nightshirt, and Leo Rothenstein in his three-piece suit, and the silken Daphnes and Daisys, and even the weeping girl, red eyed but laughing now, all of them drunk and embarrassingly loud. When they saw Querell and me approaching they turned on us, and someone shouted something at which everyone laughed, and Querell swore and turned on his heel and stalked away in the direction of the park, narrow head held aloft and elbows pressed tightly to his sides; in his high-shouldered dark-brown suit he reminded me of an HP Sauce bottle.

Remarkable how sobering it is to arrive in the midst of people more drunk than oneself; within minutes of stopping on the pavement among that sodden, billowing crowd I began to taste copper at the back of my mouth and felt a headache starting up and knew that I must have more drink or face the rest of the evening in a state of ashen melancholy. Boy had buttonholed me and was shouting into my ear some outrageous tale about an encounter with a negro sailor ('. . . like a length of bloody hawser!') and breathing garlic fumes all over me. I wanted to talk to Nick but the girls had got him, and were hilariously admiring his bare and extremely dirty feet. I broke away from Boy at last and plunged into the interior of the gallery, where, though crowded, it seemed less confined than outside on the pavement. A glass of wine materialised in my hand. I was at that clear-eyed yet hallucinatory stage of inebriation in which the commonplace takes on a sort of comically transfigured aspect. The people standing about seemed the most bizarre of creatures; it struck me how amazing, and amazingly droll, it was that human beings should go about upright and not on all fours, which would surely be more natural, and that of those gathered here, practically everyone, including myself, was equipped with a glass which he or she must hold upright while at the same time talking at the highest possible speed and volume. It all seemed quite mad and laughable and at the same time acutely, achingly moving. I turned away from the Russian's daubs, which everyone else was ignoring anyway, and made my way into the back rooms, where Wally Cohen had his offices. Wally, a little roly-poly fellow with curls ('Shylock's shy locks' – Boy), made a sort of running gag of his Jewishness, rubbing his hands and smiling oilily and referring to his co-religionists as Jewboys and snipcocks. I suspect he was at heart an anti-Semite, as a lot of the Jews whom I knew were, in those pre-war days. I came upon him in a storeroom, one ham perched on the corner of a table, swinging a chubby little leg and talking animatedly to a dark-haired young woman whom I seemed vaguely to recognise.

'Victor, my boy!' he cried. 'You have a haunted, hungry look.'

Wally had been a Marxist since his teens, one of the first of us to contract the virus.

'I've been drinking with Querell,' I said.

He chuckled. 'Ah, the pontiff; yes.'

The young woman, whom he had not bothered to introduce, was regarding me with a sceptical eye, trying, so it seemed to me, not to laugh. She was short and dark and compactly made, with bruised shadows under her eyes. She wore one of those tube-shaped dresses of the time, made of layers of bronze-black silk along which the light darkly shimmered and flashed, and I thought of a scarab beetle, locked in its brittle, burnished carapace. Wally resumed his conversation with her and she turned her attention slowly away from me. He was going on about some painter whose work he had lately discovered – José Orozco, someone like that. Wally was one of those genuine enthusiasts the world at the time was still capable of producing. He was to die seven years later, with Cornford's brigade, at the siege of Madrid.

'It's the only thing that's possible any longer,' he was saying. 'People's art. The rest is bourgeois self-indulgence, masturbation for the middle classes.'

I glanced at the young woman: words like masturbation were not uttered as lightly then as now. She gave a jaded laugh and said:

'Oh, do shut up, Wally.'

He grinned and turned to me. 'What do you say, Victor? Sure and begorrah, isn't it the revolution itself that's coming to this land of the oppressor?'

I shrugged. Bumptious Jews like Wally were hard to stomach; the camps had not yet made his tribe into the chosen people once again. Besides, he had never liked me. I suspect he knew how much I hated my name – only bandleaders and petty crooks are called Victor – for he used it at every opportunity.

'If you're so much in favour of Socialist art,' I said, 'why are you exhibiting that White trash out there?'

He lifted his shoulders, grinning, and showed me his merchant's palms. 'It sells, my boy; it sells.'

Nick came wandering in then, his bare feet slapping the floorboards and his drunken smile askew. He exchanged a sardonic and, as it seemed to me, curiously complicit glance with the young woman and a second later I realised who she was.

'Look at us,' he said happily, sweeping his wineglass in an unsteady arc that encompassed himself and the party behind him, as well as Wally and his sister and me. 'What a decadent lot.'

'We were just anticipating the revolution,' Wally said.

Nick laughed at that. I turned to Baby.

'I'm sorry,' I said, 'I knew I knew you but . . .'

She lifted an eyebrow at me and answered nothing.

The room was painted greyish white and the ceiling was a shallow dome. Two filthy windows side by side looked out on a cobbled yard thick with evening sunlight shining straight from Delft. Pictures were stacked against the walls under a fur of mouse-grey dust. Unnerved by Baby's challenging, slightly bulbous gaze, I went and poked amongst them. Failed fashions of past years, tired, sad and shamefaced: orchards in April, the odd wan nude, some examples of English cubism that were all soft angles and pastel planes. And then there it was, in its chipped gilt frame, with a cracked coating of varnish that made it seem as if hundreds of shrivelled toenails had been carefully glued to the surface. It was unmistakable what it was, even at first glance, and in poor light. I laid it back quickly against the wall, and a sort of hot something began swelling outward from a point in the centre of my breast; whenever I look at a great picture for the first time I know why we still speak of the heart as the seat of the emotions. My breathing grew shallow and my palms were moist. It was as if I had stumbled on something indecent; this was how I used to feel as a schoolboy when someone would pass me a dirty picture under the desk. I am not exaggerating. I have never cared to examine the roots of my response to art; too many tendrils coiling about each other down there in the dark. I waited a moment, telling myself to be calm – the alcohol in my system had suddenly all evaporated – and then, taking a deep breath, I lifted out the picture and carried it to the window.

Definitely.

Wally was on to me at once.

'Seen something you like, Victor?' he said.

I shrugged, and peered closely at the brushwork, trying to appear sceptical.

'Looks like *The Death of Seneca*, by what's-his-name,' Nick said, surprising me. 'We saw it in the Louvre, remember?' I imagined myself kicking him, hard, on the shin.

Wally came and stood at my shoulder, breathing. 'Or another working of the same subject,' he said thoughtfully. 'When he found a subject he liked, he stuck to it until it was done to death.' He was interested now; my reviews annoyed him, but he respected my eye.

'Well, I think it's school of,' I said, and put the picture back in its place, with its face to the wall, expecting it to cling to my hand like a child about to be abandoned. Wally was eyeing me with malicious speculation. He was not fooled.

'If you want it,' he said, 'make me an offer.'

Nick and Baby were sitting side by side on Wally's table in an oddly crumpled attitude, heads hanging and legs limply dangling, graceful and lifeless as a pair of marionettes. Suddenly I was shy in their presence, and said nothing, and Wally looked at them and then at me and nodded, closing his eyes and slyly smiling, as if he understood my predicament of the moment, which I did not: something to do with art, and embarrassment, and desire, all mixed together.

'Tell you what,' he said. 'Five hundred quid and it's yours.'

I laughed; that was a fortune in those days.

'I could manage a hundred,' I said. 'It's an obvious copy.'

Wally put on one of his shtetl expressions, narrowing his eyes and setting his head to the side and hunching a shoulder. 'What are you saying to me, my man – a copy, is it, a copy?' Then he straightened up again and shrugged. 'All right: three hundred. That's as low as I'll go.'

Baby said: 'Why don't you get Leo Rothenstein to buy it for you? He has pots of money.'

We all looked at her. Nick laughed, and jumped down nimbly from the table, suddenly animated.

'That's a good idea,' he said. 'Come on, let's find him.'

My heart sank (odd formulation, that; the heart does not

seem to fall, but to *swell*, rather, I find, when one is alarmed).
Nick would turn the thing into a rag, and Wally would get
peeved, and I would lose my chance, the only one I was ever
likely to have, to take possession of a small but true masterpiece.
I followed him and Baby (I wonder, by the way, why she was
called that – her name was Vivienne, cool and sharp, like her)
out to the pavement, where the crowd had thinned. Leo
Rothenstein was there still, though, we heard his booming,
plummy tones before we saw him. He was talking to Boy and
one of the blonde, diaphanous girls. They were discussing the
gold standard, or the state of Italian politics, something like
that. Small talk on large topics, the chief characteristic of the
time. Leo had the matt sheen of the very rich. He was
handsome, in an excessively masculine way, tall, full-chested,
with a long, swarth, Levantine head.

'Hello, Beaver,' he said. I got a nod, Baby a sharp, appraising
look and the shadow of a smile. Leo was parsimonious with his
attentions.

'Leo,' Nick said, 'we want you to buy a picture for Victor.'

'Oh, yes?'

'Yes. It's a Poussin, but Wally doesn't know it. He's asking
three hundred, which is a snip. Think of it as an investment.
Better than bullion, a picture is. You tell him, Boy.'

Boy, for reasons that I could never understand, was considered to have something of a feeling for pictures, and on
occasion had advised Leo's family on its art collection. It
amused me to imagine him in the company of Leo's father, an
august and enigmatic gentleman with the look of a Bedouin
chieftain, the two of them pacing the showrooms and gravely
pausing before this or that big brown third-rate canvas, Boy all
the while struggling to suppress a laugh. Now he did his
gargoyle grin: eyes bulging, nostrils flared, the thick, fleshy
mouth turned down at the corners. '*Poussin?*' he said. 'Sounds
tasty.'

Leo was measuring me with genial distrust.

'I have a hundred,' I said, with the sense of setting a foot down firmly on a sagging tightrope. When Leo laughed his big, soft laugh you could almost see the sound coming out of his mouth spelled out in letters: *Ha, Ha, Ha.*

'Oh, go on,' Nick said and scowled in tipsy petulance from Leo to me and back again, as if it were his game and we were laggards. Leo looked at Boy and something passed between them, then he turned his measuring eye back on me.

'You say it's genuine?' he said.

'If I had a reputation I'd stake it on it.'

The tightrope thrummed. Leo laughed again and shrugged.

'Tell Wally I'll send him a cheque,' he said, and turned away.

Nick punched me softly on the shoulder. 'There,' he said; 'told you.' He seemed suddenly quite drunk. I had a sensation of helpless, happy falling. Baby squeezed my arm. The blonde girl stepped close to Boy and whispered, 'What's a Poussin?'

*

I wonder if that really was August, or earlier in the summer? I recall a white night, with an endlessly lingering glimmer in the sky over the park and shadows the colour of dirty water lying in the muffled streets. Suddenly the city was a place I had not seen before, mysterious, exotic, lit as if from within by its own dark radiance. We seemed to walk for hours, Nick and Baby and I, strolling aimlessly arm in arm, dreamily drunk. Nick had managed to find a pair of oversized carpet slippers, which he kept stepping out of by mistake, and had to be supported while he backtracked and wriggled into them again, swearing and laughing. The feel of his bony, tremulous fingers on my arm was somehow the physical counterpart of the glow at the back of my mind where the image of the picture, *my* picture, floated as in a darkened gallery. Fearing a renewed bout of sobriety, we went to a club in Greek Street where Nick got us in; someone had money – Baby, perhaps – and we drank some bottles of vile champagne, and a girl in feathers with a whinnying laugh came and sat on Nick's lap. Then Boy arrived and took us to a party in a flat in the War Office – I think it was the resident clerk's billet – where Baby was the only female present. Boy stood with his fists on his hips amidst the cigarette smoke and the drunken squeals and shook his head in disgust and said loudly: 'Look at all these bloody pansies!' Later, when we came out into Whitehall, a headachy dawn was breaking, with small rain sifting down out of clouds that were the same plumbeous colour as the shadows under Baby's eyes. A giant seagull stood on the pavement and looked at us with cold surmise. Boy said, 'Damn this climate,' while Nick sadly contemplated his slippers. I was filled with airy elation, a sort of swooning, breathy happiness that not even the acquisition of a picture, no matter how marvellous, could fully account for. We found a taxi to take us to Nick's flat for breakfast, and in the depths of the back seat – were taxis bigger then than now? – while Boy and Nick exchanged outrageous nuggets of gossip they had picked up at the party, I found myself kissing Baby. She did not resist, as girls were expected to, and I drew back in faint alarm, tasting her lipstick and still feeling in the nerves of my fingertips the brittle, glassy texture of her silk dress. She sat and looked at me, studying me, as if I were a new variety of some hitherto familiar species. We were silent; there did not seem to be any necessary words. Although nothing else was to happen between us for a long time, I think we both knew that in that moment, for better or worse, and it would mostly be for the worse, our lives had become inextricably joined. When I turned my head I found Nick watching us with an intent, small smile.

*

Miss Vandeleur has not telephoned now for two days. I wonder if she has lost interest in me already? Perhaps she has found a better subject for her attentions. I would not be surprised; I suspect my personality is not one to quicken the pulse of an ambitious biographer. Reading over these pages, I am struck by how little I impinge on them. The personal pronoun is every-where, of course, propping up the edifice I am erecting, but what is there to be seen behind this slender capital? Yet I must have made a stronger impression than I remember; there were people who hated me, and a few even who claimed to have loved me. My dry jokes were appreciated – I know I was considered quite a wag in some quarters, and I once overheard myself described as an Irish wit (at least, I *think* that was the word). Why then am I not more vividly present to myself in these recollections I am setting down here with such finicking attention to detail? After a long pause for thought (funny there is no mark in prose to indicate lengthy lapses of time: whole days could pass in the space of a full stop – whole years) I have come to the conclusion that my early espousal of the Stoic philosophy had the inevitable consequence of forcing me to sacrifice an essential vitality of spirit. Have I lived at all? Sometimes the chill thought strikes me that the risks I took, the dangers I exposed myself to (after all, it is not far-fetched to think that I might have been bumped off at any time), were only a substitute for some more simple, much more authentic form of living that was beyond me. Yet if I had not stepped into the spate of history, what would I have been? A dried-up scholar, fussing over nice questions of attribution and what to have for supper ('Shivershanks' was Boy's nickname for me in later years). That's all true; all the same, these kinds of rationalisation do not satisfy me.

Let me try another tack. Perhaps it was not the philosophy by which I lived, but the double life itself – which at first seemed to so many of us a source of strength – that acted upon me as a debilitating force. I know this has always been said of us, that the lying and the secrecy inevitably corrupted us, sapped our moral strength and blinded us to the actual nature of things, but I never believed it could be true. We were latter-day Gnostics, keepers of a secret knowledge, for whom the world of appearances was only a gross manifestation of an infinitely subtler, more real reality known only to the chosen few, but the iron, ineluctable laws of which were everywhere at work. This gnosis was, on the material level, the equivalent of the Freudian conception of the unconscious, that unacknowledged and irresistible legislator, that spy in the heart. Thus, for us, *everything was itself and at the same time something else*. So we could rag about the place and drink all night and laugh ourselves silly, because behind all our frivolity there operated the stern conviction that the world must be changed and that we were the ones who would do it. At our lightest we seemed to ourselves possessed of a seriousness far more deep, partly because it was hidden, than anything our parents could manage, with their vaguenesses and lack of any certainty, any rigour, above all, their contemptibly feeble efforts at being good. Let the whole sham fortress fall, we said, and if we can give it a good hard shove, we will. *Destruam et aedificabo*, as Proudhon was wont to cry.

It was all selfishness, of course; we did not care a damn about the world, much as we might shout about freedom and justice and the plight of the masses. All selfishness.

And then, for me, there were other forces at work, ambiguous, ecstatic, anguished: the obsession with art, for instance; the tricky question of nationality, that constant drone-note in the bagpipe music of my life; and, deeper again than any of these, the murk and slither of sex. *The Queer Irish Spy*; it sounds like the title of one of those tunes the Catholics used to play on melodeons in their pubs when I was a child. Did I call it a *double* life? Quadruple – quintuple – more like.

The newspapers all this week have portrayed me, rather flatteringly, I confess, as an ice-cold theoretician, a sort of philosopher-spy, the one real intellectual in our circle and the guardian of ideological purity. The fact is, the majority of us had no more than the sketchiest grasp of theory. We did not bother to read the texts; we had others to do that for us. The working-class Comrades were the great readers – Communism could not have survived without autodidacts. I knew one or two of the shorter pieces – the *Manifesto*, of course, that great ringing shout of wishful thinking – and had made a determined start on *Kapital* – the dropping of the definite article was de rigueur for us smart young men, so long as the pronunciation was *echt deutsch* – but soon got bored. Besides, I had scholarly reading to do, and that was quite enough. Politics was not books, anyway; politics was action. Beyond the thickets of dry theory milled the ranks of the People, the final, authentic touchstone, waiting for us to liberate them into collectivity. We saw no contradiction between liberation and the collective. Holistic social engineering, as that old reactionary Popper calls it, was the logical and necessary means to achieve freedom – an orderly freedom, that is. Why should there not be order in human affairs? Throughout history the tyranny of the individual had brought nothing but chaos and butchery. The People must be united, must be melded into a single, vast, breathing being! We were like those Jacobin mobs in the early days of the French Revolution, who would go surging through the streets of Paris in a rage for fraternity, clasping the Common Man to their breasts so fiercely they knocked the stuffing out of him. 'Oh, Vic,' Danny Perkins used to say to me, shaking his head and laughing his soft laugh, 'what sport my old dad would have had out of you and your pals!' Danny's dad had been a Welsh miner. Died of emphysema. An uncommon man, I have no doubt.

Anyway, of all our ideological exemplars, I always secretly preferred Bakunin, so impetuous, disreputable, fierce and irresponsible compared to stolid, hairy-handed Marx. I once went so far as to copy out by hand Bakunin's elegantly vitriolic description of his rival: 'M. Marx is by origin a Jew. He unites in himself all the qualities and defects of that gifted race. Nervous, some say, to the point of cowardice, he is immensely malicious, vain, quarrelsome, as intolerant and autocratic as Jehovah, the God of his fathers, and like Him, insanely vindictive.' (Now, who else does that bring to mind?) Not that Marx was any less ferocious than Bakunin, in his way; I admired in particular his intellectual annihilation of Proudhon, whose *petit-bourgeois* post-Hegelianism and country-bumpkin faith in the essential goodness of the little man Marx held up to cruel and exhaustive ridicule. The spectacle of Marx mercilessly destroying his unfortunate predecessor is horribly exciting, like watching a great beast of the jungle plunging its jaws into the ripped-open belly of some still-thrashing, delicate-limbed herbivore. Violence by proxy, that is the thing: stimulating, satisfying, safe.

How they do bring one back to the days of youth, these ancient battles for the soul of man. I feel quite excited, here at my desk, in these last, unbearably expectant days of spring. Time for a gin, I think.

It will seem strange – it seems strange to me – but Boy was the most ideologically driven of the lot of us. God, how he would talk! On and on, superstructure and substructure and the division of labour and all the rest of it, endlessly. I remember coming home to sleep in my room in the house in Poland Street in the early hours one morning during the Blitz – the sky redly lit and the streets loud with fire engines and drunks – and finding Boy and Leo Rothenstein, both in full evening dress, sitting in the first-floor parlour in armchairs on either side of a cold fire, bolt upright, whiskey glasses in hand, the two of them dead asleep, and it was obvious from their slack-jawed expressions that Boy had knocked them both into unconsciousness by an evening of sustained wielding of that ideological bludgeon of his.

Mind you, there was more to Boy than talk. He was quite the activist. At Cambridge he had set about organising the gyps and bedders into a union, and joined in strike protests by bus drivers and sewerage workers in the town. Oh yes, he put us all to shame. I can see him still, marching down King's Parade on the way to a strike meeting, shirt collar open, dirty old trousers held up with a workman's broad belt, a figure straight out of a

Moscow mural. I was jealous of his energy, his boldness, his freedom from that self-consciousness which froze me solid when it came to practical activism, I mean the activism of the streets. But in my heart I despised him, too, for what I could not but think of as his crassness in seeking to turn theory into action, in the same way that I despised the Cambridge physicists of my day for translating pure mathematics into applied science. This is what I marvel at still, that I could have given myself over to such an essentially *vulgar* ideology.

Boy. I miss him, despite everything. Oh, I know, he was a clown, cruel, dishonest, slovenly, careless of himself and others, but for all that he maintained a curious kind of – what shall I call it? – a kind of grace. Yes, a kind of splendourous grace, it is not too much to say. When I was a child and heard about angels, I was both frightened and fascinated by the thought of these enormous, invisible presences moving in our midst. I conceived of them not as white-robed androgynes with yellow locks and thick gold wings, which was how my friend Matty Wilson had described them to me – Matty was the possessor of all sorts of arcane knowledge – but as big, dark, blundering men, massive in their weightlessness, given to pranks and ponderous play, who might knock you over, or break you in half, without meaning to. When a child from Miss Molyneaux's infant school in Carrickdrum fell under the hoofs of a dray-horse one day and was trampled to death, I, a watchful six-year-old, knew who was to blame; I pictured his guardian angel standing over the child's crushed form with his big hands helplessly extended, not sure whether to be contrite or to laugh. That was Boy. 'What did I *do*?' he would cry, after another of his enormities had come to light, 'what did I *say* . . . ?' And of course, everyone would have to laugh.

Odd, but I cannot remember when I first met him. It must have been at Cambridge, yet he seems to have been always present in my life, a constant force, even in childhood. Singular though he may have seemed, I suppose he was of a type: the toddler who pinches the little girls and makes them cry, the boy at the back of the class showing off his erection under the desk, the unabashed queer who can spot instantly the queer streak in others. Despite what people may think, he and I did not have an affair. There was a drunken scuffle one night in my rooms at Trinity in the early thirties, long before I had 'come out', as they say now, that left me shaking with embarrassment and fright, though Boy shrugged it off with his usual insouciance; I recall him going down the ill-lit stairs with half his shirt-tail hanging out and smiling back at me knowingly and wagging a playful, minatory finger. While revelling in its privileges, he held the world of his parents and their circle in jocular contempt (his stepfather, I've just remembered, was an admiral; I must ask Miss Vandeleur if she knew that). At home he subsisted mainly on a horrible gruel-like stuff – I can smell it still – that he boiled up from oatmeal and crushed garlic, but when he went out it was always the Ritz or the Savoy, after which he would lumber into a taxi and make his raucous way down to the docks or the East End to trawl through the pubs for what with a smacking of those big lips he referred to as 'likely meat'.

He could be subtle, if subtlety was what was needed. When we joined with Alastair Sykes in the putsch on the Apostles in the summer term of 1932, Boy turned out to be not only the most energetic activist of the three of us but also the smoothest plotter. He was skilled too at curbing Alastair's more hair-raising flights of enthusiasm. 'Look here, Psyche,' he would say with cheerful firmness, 'you just belt up now, like a good chap, and let Victor and me do the talking.' And Alastair, after a moment's hesitation during which the tips of his ears would turn bright pink while his pipe belched smoke and sparks like a steam train, would meekly do as he was told, although he was the senior man. He got the credit for packing the society with our people, but I am sure it was really Boy's doing. Boy's charm, at once sunny and sinister, was hard to resist. (Miss

Vandeleur would be agog; not much is known publicly, even still, about the Apostles, that absurd boys' club, to which only the most gilded of Cambridge's golden youth were admitted; being Irish and not yet queer, I had to work hard and scheme long before I managed to worm my way in.)

The Apostles' meetings that term were held in Alastair's rooms; as a senior Fellow he had ampler quarters than any of the rest of us. I had met him my first year up. Those were the days when I still thought I had it in me to be a mathematician. The discipline held a deep appeal for me. Its procedures had the mark of an arcane ritual, another secret doctrine like that which I was soon to discover in Marxism. I relished the thought of being privy to a specialised language which even in its most rarefied form is an exact – well, *plausible* – expression of empirical reality. *Mathematics speaks the world*, as Alastair put it, with an uncharacteristic rhetorical flourish. Seeing the work that Alastair could do was what convinced me, more than my poor showing in the exams, that my future must lie in scholarship and not science. Alastair had the purest, most elegant intellect I have ever encountered. His father had been a docker in Liverpool, and Alastair had come up to Cambridge on a scholarship. In appearance he was a fierce, choleric little fellow with big teeth and a spiky bush of black hair standing straight up from his forehead like the bristles of a yard-brush. He favoured hob-nailed boots and shapeless jackets made from a peculiar kind of stiff, hairy tweed that might have been run up specially for him. That first year we were inseparable. It was a strange liaison, I suppose; what we shared most deeply, though we would never dream of speaking of it openly, was that we both felt keenly the insecurity of being outsiders. One of the wits dubbed us Jekyll and Hyde, and no doubt we did look an ill-assorted pair, I the gangling youth with pointed nose and already pronounced stoop loping across Great Court pursued by the little man in the boots, his stumpy legs going like a pair of blunt scissors and tobacco pipe fuming. It was the theoretical side of mathematics that interested me, but Alastair had a genius for application. He adored gadgets. At Bletchley Park during the war he found his true and perfect place. 'It was like coming home,' he told me afterwards, his eyes shiny with misery. That was in the fifties, the last time I saw him. He had fallen into an enticement trap in the gents in Piccadilly Circus and was due in court the following week. The heavies from the Department had been tormenting him, he knew he could expect no mercy. He would not go to prison: on the eve of his court appearance he injected cyanide into an apple (a Cox's pippin, the report said; very scrupulous, the heavies) and ate it. Another uncharacteristic flourish. I wonder where he got the poison, not to mention the needle? I had not even known that he was queer. Perhaps he had not known it himself, before that jug-eared copper with his trousers round his ankles beckoned to him from his stall. Poor Psyche. I imagine him in the weeks before he died, lying between army-surplus blankets in that dreary bedsit he had off the Cromwell Road, miserably turning over the ruins of his life. He had broken some of the most difficult of the German army's codes, thus saving God knows how many Allied lives, yet they hounded him to death. And they call me a traitor. Could I have done something for him, pulled a few strings, put a word in with the internal security people? The thought gnaws at me.

Alastair, now, Alastair had read the sacred texts. Whatever scraps of theory I knew, I learned from him. The cause of Ireland was his great enthusiasm. His Irish mother had made him into a Sinn Feiner. Like me, he regretted that it was in Russia the Revolution had occurred, but I could not agree with him that Ireland would have been a more congenial battle-ground; the notion seemed to me utterly risible. He had even taught himself the Irish language, and could swear in it – though to my ears, I confess, the language in general sounds like a string of softly vehement oaths strung haphazardly together. He berated me for my lack of patriotism, and called me a dirty Unionist, not wholly in jest. However, when I asked him one day for specific details of his knowledge of my country he grew evasive, and when I pressed him he blushed – those reddening ears – and admitted that in fact he had never set foot in Ireland.

He did not much care for the company of the majority of the Apostles, with their plush accents and aesthete manners. 'You could be speaking in bloody code, you lot, when you get started,' he complained, digging a blackened thumb into the burning dottle of his pipe. 'Bloody public schoolboys.' I used to laugh at him, with not much malice, but Boy gave him an awful time, mimicking perfectly his Scouse accent and bullying him into drinking too much beer. Alastair thought Boy was not sufficiently serious about the cause, and considered him – with remarkable prescience, as it turned out – to be a security risk. 'That Bannister,' he would mutter angrily, 'he'll get us all shopped.'

Here is a snapshot from the bulging album I keep in my head. It is sometime in the thirties. Tea, thick sandwiches and thin beer, the sun of April on Trinity court. A dozen Apostles – some Fellows, such as Alastair and myself, a couple of nondescript dons, one or two earnest postgraduate scholars, every one of us a devout Marxist – are sitting about in Alastair's big gloomy living room. We favoured dark jackets and fawn bags and open-necked white shirts, except for Leo Rothenstein, always suavely magnificent in his Savile Row blazers. Boy was more flamboyant: I recall crimson ties and purple waistcoats and, on this occasion, plus-fours in a bright-green check. He is pacing up and down the room, dropping cigarette ash on the threadbare carpet, telling us, as I have heard him tell many times before, of the event that, so he insisted, had made him a homosexual.

'God, it was frightful! There she was, poor Mother, flat on her back with her legs in the air, shrieking, and my huge father lying naked on top of her, dead as a doornail. I had the hell of a job getting him off her. The smells! Twelve years old, I was. Haven't been able to look at a woman since without seeing Mater's big white breasts, colour of a fish's belly. The paps that gave me suck. In dreams those nipples still stare up at me cock-eyed. No Oedipus I, or Hamlet, either, that's certain. When she threw off her widow's weeds and remarried I felt only relief.'

I used to divide people into two sorts, those who were shocked by Boy's stories and those who were not, though I could never decide which was the more reprehensible half. Alastair had begun to huff and puff. 'Look here, we've got a motion before us which we should consider. Spain is going to be the next theatre of operations' – Alastair, who had never heard a shot fired in anger, had a great fondness for military jargon – 'and we've got to decide where we stand.'

Leo Rothenstein laughed. 'That's obvious, surely? We're hardly in favour of the Fascists.' At the age of twenty-one Leo had come into an inheritance of two million, along with Maule Park and a mansion in Portman Square.

Alastair fussed with his pipe; he disliked Leo and was at pains to hide the fact, afraid of being thought an anti-Semite.

'But the point is,' he said, 'will we fight?'

It strikes me how much talk of fighting there was throughout the thirties, among our set, at least. Did the appeasers talk about appeasement with the same passion, I wonder?

'Don't be a fathead,' Boy said. 'Uncle Joe won't let it come to that.'

A chap called Wilkins, I've forgotten his first name, weedy type with glasses and a bad case of psoriasis, who was to die at El Alamein in command of a tank, turned from the window with a glass of beer in his fist and said:

'According to a man I spoke to the other day who's been over there, Uncle Joe has too much of a job on his hands trying to feed the masses at home to think of sending aid abroad.'

A silence followed. Bad form on Wilkins's part: we did not

speak of the Comrades' difficulties. Doubt was a bourgeois self-indulgence. Then Boy gave a nasty little laugh. 'Surprising,' he said, 'how some of us can't recognise propaganda when we hear it,' and Wilkins threw him a baleful look and turned back to the window.

Spain, the kulaks, the machinations of the Trotskyites, racial violence in the East End – how antique it all seems now, almost quaint, and yet how seriously we took ourselves and our place on the world stage. I often have the idea that what drove those of us who went on to become active agents was the burden of deep – of intolerable – embarrassment that the talk-drunk thirties left us with. The beer, the sandwiches, the sunlight on the cobbles, the aimless walks in shadowed lanes, the sudden, always amazing fact of sex – a whole world of privilege and assurance, all going on, while elsewhere millions were preparing to die. How could we have borne the thought of all that and not—

But no. It will not do. These fine sentiments will not do. I have told myself already, I must not attempt to impose retrospective significance on what we were and did. Is it that I believed in something then and now believe in nothing? Or that even then I only believed in the belief, out of longing, out of necessity? The latter, surely. The wave of history rolled over us, as it rolled over so many others of our kind, leaving us quite dry.

'Oh, Uncle Joe is sound,' Boy was saying. 'Quite sound.'

They are all dead: Boy the outrageous, Leo and his millions, Wilkins the sceptic, burnt to a cinder in his sardine tin in the desert. I ask again: Have I lived at all?

I DO NOT think I can continue to call this a journal, for it is certainly more than a record of my days, which, anyway, now that the furore has died down, are hardly distinguishable one from another. Call it a memoir, then; a scrapbook of memories. Or go the whole hog and call it an autobiography, notes toward. Miss Vandeleur would be upset if she knew I was pre-empting her. She came round this morning to ask me about my visit to Spain with Nick at Easter in 1936. (How portentous and stirring a mere date can be: *Easter, 1936!*) The things she wants to know about surprise me. I could understand if she were eager for details of my adventures in Germany in 1945, say, or of the exact nature of my relations with Mrs W. and her ma (which fascinates *everyone*), but no, it is the ancient history that she is after.

Spain. Now there's ancient, all right. A hateful country. I recall rain, and a dispiriting smell everywhere, that seemed a mixture of semen and mildew. There were wall-posters, the hammer and sickle on every street corner, and violent-looking young men in red shirts whose flat, weathered features and evasive glances reminded me of the tinkers who in my child-hood used to go about Carrickdrum selling tin cans and leaky saucepans. The Prado of course was a revelation, the Goyas hair-raisingly prophetic in their blood and muck, El Greco frightened out of his wits. I preferred the Zurbaráns, haunting in their stillness, their transcendent mundanity. In Seville in Holy Week we stood glumly in the rain watching a procession of penitents, a spectacle from which my Protestant soul recoiled. A deposition scene was borne aloft on a litter, shaded from the rain by a tasseled baldachin of gold brocade; the plaster Christ, laid out naked at his mother's plaster feet, was a faintly obscene, orgasmic figure (after The Greek – a long way after), with creamy skin and agonised mouth and copiously spouting wounds. When this thing appeared, swaying and lurching, two or three elderly men near us fell to their knees, making a noise like that of collapsing deckchairs, crossing themselves rapidly, in a kind of holy terror, and one of them with surprising nimbleness ducked under the litter to lend it a supporting shoulder. I remember too a young woman stepping out of the crowd and handing to one of the black-mantillaed penitents – her mother or her aunt – a gaudy red-and-white striped umbrella. At Algeciras we watched the gratifying and thrilling spectacle of a mob desecrating a church and stoning the town's mayor, a portly man with a shiny, brown bald head, who fled from his tormentors at a rapid walk, trying to hold on to his dignity. Rain rattled in the palm trees and a quicksilver bolt of lightning rent the glans-brown sky above the railway station. Peeling wall-posters flapped in a sudden wind. Later we tried to cross the border but found Gibraltar shut for the night. The inn at La Linea was filthy. I lay awake for a long time listening to the dogs yapping and a wireless set somewhere muttering of war, and watched the rain-light's faint phosphorescence playing over Nick's uncovered back where he lay prone and snoring softly on the narrow bed a mile away from me at the other side of the room. His skin had a thick, faintly slimed look to it; I thought of the Saviour's statue. Next day we took ship for England. There were dolphins in the Strait, and in the Bay of Biscay I was sick.

Will that do, Miss V.?

I have been finding out a little more about her. It is difficult, for she is almost more secretive than I am. I feel like a restorer chipping away the varnish from a damaged portrait. Damaged? Why did I say damaged? There is something about her reticence, her profound, stalled silences, that bespeaks a deep-seated constraint. She is too old for her years. I have the sense of an ineradicable disaffection for things in general. She keeps reminding me of Baby – those silences, the bruised eyes, that surly stare she directs at inanimate objects – and certainly Baby was damaged. When I asked Miss Vandeleur this morning if she lived alone she did not answer, and pretended that she had not heard me, then later on suddenly began to tell me about her young man, with whom she shares a flat in Golders Green (another of my old haunts, by the way). He is a mechanic, in a garage. Sounds like rough trade to me; now I understand the leather skirt. I wonder what the Admiral thinks of this ménage? Or does anyone care about such matters any more? She complained of the rigours of the Northern Line. I told her I had not been on an Underground train in thirty years and she ducked her head and glared resentfully at my hands.

The morning was warm enough for us to have tea on the back balcony. That is, she had tea while I had a small glass of something, despite the early hour. She makes me jittery, I have to take a little fortification when dealing with her. (Balconies make me jittery too, but that is another matter. Patrick! My Patsy, poor Pat.) Besides, at my age I can drink at any hour of the day without the need of an excuse; I foresee a time when I shall be breakfasting on cocktails of gin and Complan. From the balcony we could just see the tops of the trees in the park. They are at their loveliest stage just now, the black boughs lightly dusted with the most delicate puffs of green. I remarked how the city's pollution imparts to the sky a wonderful depth of colour, like that dense, gulp-inducing blue you see when the aeroplane banks and you peer up into nothingness. Miss Vandeleur was not listening. She sat on the other side of the little metal table, slumped in her greatcoat and frowning into her cup.

'Was he a Marxist?' she asked. 'Sir Nicholas?'

I had to think for a second who it was she meant.

'Nick?' I said. 'Lord, no! In fact . . .'

In fact it was on that voyage home from Spain that we had our one and only serious conversation about politics. I can't remember how it started. I suppose I had attempted a bit of proselytising; I had all the zeal of the convert in those early, heady days, and Nick never did care to be preached at.

'Do shut up, for God's sake,' he said, not quite managing to laugh. 'I'm sick of listening to you and your historical dialectic and all the rest of that tommyrot.'

We were leaning at the rail in the bows, contemplatively smoking, under the dome of the great soft calm marine night. The further north we sailed the warmer the weather was becoming, as if the climate like everything else in the world had been turned topsyturvy. A huge, bone-white moon hung above the prostrate sea, and the ship's wake flashed and writhed like a great silver rope unravelling behind us. I was giddy and slightly feverish after my recent bout of seasickness.

'There must be action,' I said, with the doggedness of the dogmatist. 'We must act, or perish.'

That is, I'm afraid, the way we talked.

'Oh, action!' Nick said, and this time he did laugh. 'Words, for you, are action. That's all you do – jaw jaw jaw.'

That stung; it amused Nick, when he was being the bruiser, to mock me for my sedentary ways.

'We can't all be soldiers,' I said huffily. 'There is a need for theorists, too.'

He flicked his cigarette end over the rail and gazed off at the glimmering horizon. A breeze lifted the hanging lock of hair at his forehead. What did I think it was I felt for him? How did I account for the hopeless, silent sob that welled up in my breast when I looked at him at moments such as this? I suppose school had accustomed us to crushes and all that – though how I could think *this* was only a crush, I don't know.

'If I were a Communist,' he said, 'I shouldn't bother with theory at all. I should think only of strategy: how to get things done. I'd use whatever means come to hand – lies, blackmail, murder and mayhem, whatever it takes. You're all idealists pretending to be pragmatists. You think you care only for the cause while really the cause is only something to lose yourselves in, a way to cancel the ego. It's half religion and half Romanticism. Marx is your St Paul, and your Rousseau.'

I was taken aback, and not a little bemused; I had never heard him talk like this before, with his intellect's lip curled, so to speak. He turned to me, smiling, leaning sideways on an elbow on the rail.

'It's rather sweet,' he said, 'the way you deceive yourselves, but a little contemptible, too, don't you think?'

'Some of us are ready to fight,' I said. 'Some of us are already signing up to go to Spain.'

His smile turned pitying.

'Yes,' he said, 'and here you are, sailing home from Spain.' I felt a flash of anger, and had a strong desire to give him a slap – a slap, or something like it. 'The trouble with you, Vic,' he said, 'is that you think of the world as a sort of huge museum with too many visitors allowed in.'

Miss Vandeleur was saying something, and I came back with a jolt.

'My dear, I'm sorry,' I said, 'my attention strayed. I was thinking about the Beaver – Sir Nicholas. Sometimes I wonder if I knew him at all. Certainly I never spotted whatever it was in him – just will-power, I suppose – that would drive him to such giddy heights of power and influence later on.' Miss V. had gone into that state of suspended animation, her head lowered and features fallen slack in a faintly idiotic looking way, that I have come to recognise as her mode of deepest listening. She would not make a good interrogator, she shows her interest too plainly. I told myself to proceed with caution. 'But then,' I said, slipping into my bland old-boy routine, 'which of us ever really recognises the true nature of others?'

She is very interested in Nick. I would not want to see him harmed. No, I would not want that, at all.

*

Another ship, another trip, to Ireland, this time. It was just after Munich, and I was glad to get away from London, with its blimps and rumours, and fear pervasive and palpable as fog. While the world was collapsing, however, my personal fortunes were soaring. Yes, that year I was very full of myself, as Nanny Hargreaves would have said. I had a modest but rapidly growing international reputation as a connoisseur and scholar, I had moved up from the *Spectator* to the altogether more austere and rarefied pages of the *Burlington* and the Warburg *Journal*, and in the autumn I was to take up the Deputy Directorship of the Institute. Not bad for a man of thirty-one, and an Irish man, at that. Perhaps more impressive than any of these successes was the fact that I had spent the summer at Windsor, where I had embarked on the task of cataloguing the great and, until I took it in hand, chaotic collection of drawings that had been accumulating there since the days of Henry Tudor. It was hard labour, but I was sustained in it by an acute awareness of its value, not only to art history, but also to the furtherance of my own multiple interests (God, you can't beat a spy for smugness!). I got on well with HM – he had been up at Trinity not many years before me. Despite his enthusiasm for boys' clubs and tennis, he was, like his mother, a shrewd and jealous guardian of the royal possessions. Often in those last months before the war, while we all waited in a state of dreamy tension for hostilities to break out, he would come up to the print room and sit on a corner of my desk, swinging one leg, the fingers of his slender, somewhat fidgety hands laced together and resting on his thigh, and talk about the great collectors among his predecessors on the throne, all of whom he spoke of with amused, rueful familiarity, as if they were so many generous but faintly disreputable uncles, which you might say they were,

I suppose. Though he was not very much older than me, he reminded me of my father, with his diffidence, and air of vague foreboding, and sudden fits of somewhat unnerving playfulness. Certainly, I preferred him greatly to his bloody wife, with her hats and her drinkies and her after-dinner games of charades, into which I was repeatedly dragooned, to my distress and intense embarrassment. Her name for me was Boots, the origin of which I never could discover. She was a cousin of my dead mother. Moscow, of course, was entranced by these connections. Great snobs, the Comrades.

At the end of that summer I was in a state of profound nervous exhaustion. When, ten years previously, I had failed mathematics, or it had failed me, I had understood clearly what the consequences would be: an entire remaking of the self, with all the dedication and unremitting labour that such an exercise would entail. Now I had managed the transformation, but at great cost in physical and intellectual energy. Metamorphosis is a painful process. I imagine the exquisite agony of the caterpillar turning itself into a butterfly, pushing out eye-stalks, pounding its fat-cells into iridescent wing-dust, at last cracking the mother-of-pearl sheath and staggering upright on sticky, hair's-breadth legs, drunken, gasping, dazed by the light. When Nick suggested a recuperative jaunt ('You're looking even more cadaverous than usual, old chap') I agreed with a suddenness that surprised even myself. It was Nick's idea that we should go to Ireland. Did he mean, I wondered nervously, to get the goods on me, nose out my family secrets (I had not told him about Freddie), place me in my class? He was full of enthusiasm for the trip. We would go to Carrickdrum to rest up, as he said, then travel on out to the far west, where, I had told him, my father's people came from. It seemed a wonderful notion. The thought of having Nick to myself for weeks on end was intoxicating, and stilled whatever qualms I might have had.

I bought the tickets. Nick was broke. He had long ago drifted out of his editorial job at Brevoort & Klein and was existing on an allowance from a grudging and ceaselessly complaining Big Beaver, supplemented by numerous small loans from his friends. We took the Friday night steamer, and travelled down from Larne on a rackety train through the glaucous light of a late-September dawn. I sat and watched the landscape making its huge, slow rotation around us. Antrim that morning wore a particularly tight-lipped aspect. Nick was subdued, and sat huddled in a corner of the unheated compartment with his overcoat pulled close around him, pretending to sleep. When the hills of Carrickdrum came into view a kind of panic seized me and I wanted to wrench open the carriage door and leap out and be swallowed in the engine's steam and flying smoke. 'Home,' Nick said in a sepulchral voice, startling me. 'You must be cursing me for making you come.' He had an unnerving ability sometimes to guess what one was thinking. The train passed along a raised embankment from which the garden and, presently, the house were to be seen, but I did not point out the view to Nick. Doubt and foreboding had set in.

My father had sent Andy Wilson with the pony-and-trap to meet us. Andy was the gardener and general handyman at St Nicholas's, a wiry little man, like a wood-sprite, with bowed arms and legs and a baby's washed-blue eyes. He was ageless, and seemed not to have changed at all since I was an infant, when he used to terrify me by putting frogs into the pram with me. He was a ferocious and unregenerate Orangeman and played the Lambeg drum in the town's Twelfth parade every year. He took to Nick straight away and formed a jeering alliance with him against me. 'Thon's the lad won't lift a finger,' he said as he heaved our bags into the trap, nodding towards me and nudging Nick and winking. 'Never would, aye, and never will.' He cackled, shaking his head, and took the reins and clicked his tongue at the pony, and Nick smiled at me lopsidedly, and with a wallowing, backward lurch we were off.

We skirted the town, the little pony going along at a fastidious trot, and began the ascent of the West Road. A weak sun was struggling to shine. With a pang I caught the buttery smell of gorse. Presently the Lough came into view, a great flat flaky sheet of steel, and something in me quailed; I have always disliked the sea, its surliness, its menace, its vast reaches and unknowable, shudder-inducing depths. Nick was asleep again, or pretending to be, with his feet on his bags. I thought how much I envied him his ability to escape the tedium of life's interludes. Andy, wielding the reins, cast a fond glance back at him and softly exclaimed:

'Och, the gentleman!'

The trees surrounding the house looked darker than ever, more blue than green, pointing heavenward in urgent, mute admonishment. Freddie was the first to appear, lumbering diagonally across the lawn to meet us with his arms spread, grinning and gibbering. 'Here's the boss,' said Andy. 'Will you look at him, the gawnie!' Nick opened his eyes. Freddie drew level, and putting a hand on the wing of the trap turned and trotted along beside us, moaning in excitement. He gave me one of his sliding glances and did not look at Nick at all. Strange, that one so severely afflicted should be prey to something so subtle as shyness. He was a big fellow, with big feet and big hands and a big head topped by a thatch of straw-coloured hair. To look at him in repose, if he could ever be said to be in repose, you would hardly have known his condition, if it were not for those helplessly flickering eyes, and the scabs around his fingernails and his mouth where he picked and chewed at himself ceaselessly. He was nearly thirty by now, but despite his bulk he still had the rumpled, shirt-tails-and-catapults air of an obstreperous twelve-year-old. Nick raised his eyebrows and nodded in Andy's direction. 'His son?' he murmured. In my agitation and shame all I did was shake my head and look away.

When we drew up at the house my father popped out at once, as if he had been waiting behind the door, which probably he had. He was wearing his dog collar and bishop's starched front and a moth-eaten pullover, and was clutching a handful of papers – I think I never saw my father at home without a sheaf of scribbled notes in his hand. He greeted us with his usual mixture of warmth and wariness. He looked smaller than I remembered, like a slightly out-of-scale model of himself. Recently he had suffered a second heart attack, and there was a sort of lightness about him, a wispy, tentative something, that I supposed must be the effect of the subdued but ever-present fear of sudden death. Freddie ran up and hugged him and laid his big head on his shoulder and looked back at us with a sly, proprietorial leer. I could tell by the alarmed way my father took in the Beaver that he had forgotten I had said I would be bringing a guest. We got down from the trap, and I tackled the introductions. Andy was making a racket with our bags, and the pony put its snout into the small of my back and tried to push me over, and Freddie, moved by the agitation and awkwardness of the moment, began to howl softly, and just when I thought everything would turn irretrievably into ruinous farce, Nick stepped forward briskly, like a doctor taking over at the scene of an accident, and shook my father's hand with just the right proportions of deference and familiarity, murmuring something about the weather.

'Yes, well,' my father said, vaguely smiling, and patting Freddie soothingly on the back. 'You're very welcome. Both of you, very welcome. Did you have a good crossing? Usually it's calm this time of year. Do stop that, Freddie, there's a good boy.'

Then Hettie appeared. She also seemed to have been lurking in the hallway, waiting for her moment. If my father had shrunk over the years, Hettie had swelled to the dimensions of one of Rowlandson's royal doxies. She was in her sixties but still retained the bloom of youth, a big pink person with teary eyes and dainty feet and an uncontrollable, wobbly smile.

'Oh, Victor!' she cried, clasping her hands. 'How thin you've grown!'

Hettie came of a wealthy Quaker family and had spent her

youth in a vast grey stone mansion on the south shore of the Lough doing good works and needlepoint. I think that she is the only human being I have ever encountered, apart from poor Freddie, of whom I can say with complete conviction that she had not a trace of wickedness in her (how can there be such people as these, in such a world as this?). If she had not been my stepmother and therefore more or less a part of the furniture, I surely would have found her an object of amazement and awe. When she arrived in our lives I had tried hard to resent and thwart her, but her jollity had been too much for me. She had won me over at once by getting rid of Nanny Hargreaves, a fearsome Presbyterian frump who since my mother's death had ruled over my life with malevolent efficiency, dosing me weekly with castor oil and subjecting Freddie and me to sulphurous homilies on sin and damnation. Nanny Hargreaves would not have known how to play; Hettie, though, loved children's games, the rowdier the better – perhaps her Quaker parents had disapproved of such godless frivolities when she was little, and she was making up for lost opportunities. She would get down on hands and knees and chase Freddie and me about the drawing-room floor, growling like a grizzly bear, her face bright red and her great bosom swinging. In the evenings before our bedtime she read us stories of the foreign missions, featuring brave, pure girls and stout-hearted men with beards, and the odd martyr, staked out in the desert to die or boiled in a pot by capering Hottentots.

'Come in, come in,' she said, flustered, I could see, by Nick's exotic good looks. 'Mary will make you an Ulster fry.'

My father disengaged himself from Freddie's embrace and we all bustled into the hall, Andy Wilson coming behind us with the bags and swearing mildly under his breath. Andy's son, Matty, had been what I suppose I may call my first, precocious love. Matty was my age: black curls, blue eyes, and hardy, like his father. Is there any figure in childhood more invitingly vulnerable, any presence more sinisterly suggestive, than the son of a servant? Matty had died, drowned while swimming in Colton Weir. I had not known what to do with my sorrow, it had sat in me for weeks like a great brooding bird. And then one day it just flew off. Thus does one learn about the limits of love, the limits of grief.

Nick was smiling at me reprovingly. 'You didn't tell me you had a brother,' he said.

By now I had realised the full magnitude of the mistake I had made in bringing him here. The home returned to is a concatenation of sadnesses that makes one want to weep and at the same time sets the teeth on edge. How dingy the place looked. And that smell! – tired, brownish, intimate, awful. I was ashamed of everything, and ashamed of myself for being ashamed. I could hardly bear to look at my shabby father and his fat wife, I flinched at Andy's mutterings behind me and cringed at the thought of red-haired Mary, our Catholic cook, slapping a plate of rashers and black pudding down in front of Nick (did he eat pork? – Oh God, I had forgotten to ask). My greatest shame, however, was Freddie. When we were children I had not minded him, deeming it right, I suppose, that anyone born into the family after me should be defective. He had been someone for me to order about, a makeweight in the intricate games that I devised, an uncritical witness to my cautiously daring escapades. I used to perform experiments on him just to see how he would react. I gave him methylated spirits to drink – he gagged and retched – and put a dead lizard in his porridge. One day I pushed him into a bed of nettles and made him scream. I thought I would be punished, but my father only looked at me with deep, droop-eyed sadness, shaking his head, while Hettie sat down on the lawn like a squaw and rocked Freddie in her arms and pressed dock leaves to his livid arms and his swollen knock-knees. In adolescence, when I developed a passion for the Romantics, I conceived of him as a noble savage, and even wrote a sonnet about him, composed of Wordsworthian apostrophes (*O! thou princely child of Nature, list!*), and made him tramp the hills with me in all weathers, to his distress, for he was as much afraid of the outdoors as he had been as a child. Now, suddenly, I saw him through Nick's eyes, a poor, shambling, damaged thing with my high forehead and prominent upper jaw, and I walked down the hall in a hot sweat of embarrassment and would not meet Nick's amused, quizzical eye, and was relieved when Freddie sloped off to the garden to take up again whatever obscure doings he had been engaged in when we arrived.

In the dining room, while Nick and I ate breakfast, Hettie and my father sat and watched us in a sort of hazy wonderment, as if we were a pair of immortals who had stopped off at their humble table on the way to some important piece of Olympian business elsewhere. Mary the cook kept bringing us more things to eat, fried bread and grilled kidneys and racks of toast, walking around the table with her apron lifted to protect her fingers from the heat of the plates, glancing at Nick – his hands, that hanging lock of hair – from under her almost invisible, pale eyelashes and blushing. My father talked about the threat of war. He always had an acute sense of the weight and menace of the world, conceiving it as something like a gigantic spinning-top at whose pointed end the individual cowered, hands clasped in supplication to a capricious and worryingly taciturn God.

'Say what you like about Chamberlain,' he said, 'but he remembers the Great War, the cost of it.'

I glared at a sausage, thinking what a hopeless booby my father was.

'Peace in our time,' Hettie murmured, sighing.

'Oh, but there *will* be war,' Nick said equably, 'despite the appeasers. What is this, by the way?'

'Fadge,' Mary blurted, and blushed the harder, making for the door.

'Potato cake,' I said between clenched teeth. 'Local delicacy.' Two days ago I had been chatting with the King.

'Mm,' Nick said, 'delicious.'

My father sat blinking in distress. Light from the leaded window glinted on his balding pate. Trollope, I thought; he's a character out of Trollope – one of the minor ones.

'Is that what people feel in London,' he said, 'that there will be war?'

Nick pondered, head to one side, looking at his plate. I can see the moment: the thin October sunlight on the parquet, a curl of steam from the teapot's spout, the somehow evil glitter of the marmalade in its cut-glass dish, and my father and Hettie waiting like frightened children to hear what London thought.

'Of course there'll be a war,' I said impatiently. 'The old men have let it happen all over again.'

My father nodded sadly.

'Yes,' he said, 'you must consider our generation has rather let you down.'

'Oh, but we want peace!' Hettie exclaimed, as close to indignation as it was possible for her to get. 'We don't want young men to go out again and be killed for . . . for nothing.'

I glanced at Nick. He was working away unconcernedly at his plate; he always did have a remarkable appetite.

'The fight against Fascism is hardly what you could call *nothing*,' I said, and Hettie looked so abashed it seemed she might burst into tears.

'Ah, you young people,' my father said softly, batting a hand at the air before him in a gesture which must have been a secular modification of the episcopal blessing, 'you have such certainty.'

At this Nick looked up with an expression of real interest.

'Do you think so?' he said. 'I feel we're all rather . . . well, *unfocused*.' Pensively he buttered a piece of cold toast, lathering on the butter like a painter applying cadmium yellow with a palette knife. 'Seems to me that chaps of my age lack any sense of purpose or direction. In fact, I think we could do with a jolly good dose of military discipline.'

'Shove 'em in the army, eh?' I said bitterly. Nick went on

calmly buttering his toast and, preparing to take a bite, glanced at me sideways and said:

'Why not? Those louts one sees standing on street corners complaining that they can't get work – wouldn't they be better off in uniform?'

'They'd be better off in *work*!' I said. 'Marx makes the point that—'

'Oh, Marx!' Nick said through a crackling mouthful of toast, and chuckled.

I felt my forehead turning red.

'You should try reading Marx,' I said. 'Then you might know what you're talking about.'

Nick only laughed again.

'You mean, then I might know what *you* are talking about.'

An uneasy silence fell and Hettie looked at me apprehensively but I avoided her eye. My father, troubled, cleared his throat and with anxious fingers traced an invisible pattern on the tablecloth.

'Marxism, now,' he began, but I cut him off at once, with that particular form of corrosive savagery that grown sons reserve for their bumbling fathers.

'Nick and I are thinking of going to the west,' I said loudly. 'He wants to see Mayo.'

Guilt is the only affect I know of that does not diminish with time. Nor does the guilty conscience have any sense of priority or right proportion. In my time I have, knowingly or otherwise, sent men and women to terrible deaths, yet I do not feel as sharp a pang when I think of them as I do when I recall the gleam of light on my father's bowed pate at the table just then, or Hettie's big sad soft eyes looking at me in silent beseeching, without anger or resentment, asking me to be kind to an ageing, anxious man, to be tolerant of the littleness of their lives; asking me to have a heart.

After breakfast I had to get out of the house, and made Nick walk with me down to the harbour. The day had turned blustery, and the shadows of clouds scudded over the white-flecked sea. The Norman castle on the shore looked particularly dour today, in the pale, autumn light; as a child I had believed it was made of wet sea-sand.

'Good people,' Nick said. 'Your father is a fighter.'

I stared at him.

'You think so? Just another bourgeois liberal, I would have said. Although he was a great Home Ruler, in his day.'

Nick laughed.

'Not a popular position for a Protestant clergyman, surely?'

'Carson hated him. Tried to stop him being made bishop.'

'There you are: a fighter.'

We strolled along the front. Despite the lateness of the season there were bathers down at the water, their cries came to us, tiny and clear, skimming the ribbed sand. Something in me always responds, shamefacedly, to the pastel gaieties of the seaside. I saw, with unnerving clarity, another version of myself, a little boy playing here with Freddie (Wittgenstein accosted me one day by the Cam and clutched me by the wrist and stuck his face close to mine and hissed: *'Is the dotard the same being that he was when he was an infant?'*), making castles and trying surreptitiously to get him to eat sand, while Hettie sat placidly in the middle of a vast checked blanket doing her knitting, sighing contentedly and talking to herself in a murmur, her big, mottled legs stuck out before her like a pair of windlasses and her yellow toes twitching (a parishioner once complained to my father that his wife was down on the strand 'with her pegs on show for all the town to see').

Nick halted suddenly and gazed about him histrionically at sea and beach and sky, his overcoat billowing in the breeze like a cloak.

'God,' he muttered, 'how I loathe nature!'

'I'm sorry,' I said, 'perhaps we shouldn't have come.'

He looked at me and put on a glum grin, pulling down his mouth at the sides. 'You mustn't take everything personally, you know,' he said. We walked on and he patted his stomach. 'What was that stuff called? Fudge?'

'Fadge.'

'Amazing.'

I had watched him throughout breakfast, while my father talked platitudes and Hettie stoutly nodded her support. One smile from him at their quaintness, I had told myself, and I shall hate him for life. But he was impeccable. Even when Freddie came and pressed his nose and his scabbed lips against the dining room window, smearing the glass with snot and spittle, Nick only chuckled, as at the endearing antics of a toddler. *I* was the one who had sat with lip curled in contemptuous impatience. Now he said:

'*Young people*, your father called us. I don't feel young, do you? The Ancient of Days, rather. It's we who are the old men now. I shall be thirty next month. Thirty!'

'I know,' I said. 'On the twenty-fifth.'

He looked at me in surprise. 'How did you remember?'

'I have a head for dates. And that's a momentous one, after all.'

'What? Oh, yes, I see. Your glorious Revolution. Didn't it in fact take place in November?'

'Yes. Their November, Old Style. The Julian calendar.'

'Ah, the Julian calendar, yes. What-ho for jolly old Julian.'

I winced; he never sounded more Jewish than when he came out with these Woosterisms.

'Anyway,' I said, 'the symbol is all. As Querell likes to remark, the Catholic Church is founded on a pun. *Tu es Petrus.*'

'Eh? Oh, I see. That's good; that's very good.'

'Pinched it from someone else, though.'

We walked into the shadow of the castle wall and Nick's mood darkened with the air.

'What will you do in this war, Victor?' he asked, his voice going gruff and Sydney Cartonish. He stopped and leaned against the harbour rail. The sea wind was chill, and sharp with salt. Far out to sea a flock of gulls was wheeling above a patch of brightness on the water, wheeling and clumsily diving, like blown sheets of newsprint. I fancied I could hear their harsh, hungry cries.

'You really think there will be a war?' I said.

'Yes. No question but.' He walked on and I followed a pace behind him. 'Three months, six months – a year at the most. The factories have been given the word, though the War Office hasn't told Chamberlain about it. You know he and Daladier worked together in secret for months to strike a deal with Hitler over the Sudetenland? And now Hitler can do whatever he pleases. Have you heard what he said about Chamberlain? *I feel sorry for him, let him have his piece of paper.*'

I was staring at him.

'How do you know all this?' I asked, laughing in surprise. 'Chamberlain, the factories, all that stuff?'

He shrugged.

'I've been talking to some people,' he said. 'You might like to meet them. They're our sort.'

My sort, I thought, *or yours?* I let it pass.

'You mean, people in the government?'

He shrugged again.

'Something like that,' he said. We turned from the harbour and set off back up the hill road. While he had talked, a sort of slow, burning blush had come over me from breast to brow. It was as if we were a pair of schoolboys and Nick thought he had discovered the secrets of sex but had got the details all wrong. 'Everything's gone rotten, don't you think?' he said. 'Spain finished the whole thing for me. Spain, and now this beastly Munich business. Peace in our time – ha!' He stopped and turned to me with an earnest frown, brushing the lock of hair back from his forehead. Eyes very black in the pale light of morning, lip trembling with emotion as he struggled to maintain a manful mien. I had to look away to hide my grin. 'Something has to be done, Victor. It's up to us.'

'Our sort, you mean?'

It was said before I knew it. I was terrified of offending him – I had a vision of him sitting grim-faced in the trap, with eyes averted, demanding to be taken back to the station at once, while my father and Hettie, and Andy Wilson, and even the pony, looked at me accusingly. I need not have worried; Nick was not one to spot an irony; egotists never are, I find. We turned to the hill again. He walked with his hands jammed in his overcoat pockets and eyes on the road, his jaw set, a muscle in it working.

'I've felt so useless up to now,' he said, 'playing the exquisite and guzzling champagne. You've at least done something with your life.'

'I hardly think a catalogue of the drawings in the Windsor Castle collection will stop Herr Hitler in his tracks.'

He nodded; he was not listening.

'The thing is to get involved,' he said; 'to *act*.'

'Is this the new Nick Brevoort?' I said, in as light a tone as I could manage. Embarrassment was giving way in me now to a not quite explicable and certainly unjustified annoyance – after all, everyone that autumn was talking like this. 'I seem to remember having this conversation with you some years ago, but in reverse. Then I was the one playing at being the man of action.'

He smiled to himself, biting his lip; my annoyance shot up a couple of hot degrees.

'You think I'm playing?' he said, with just the hint of a contemptuous drawl. I did not let myself reply. We went on for a while in silence. The sun had retreated into a milky haze. 'By the way,' he said, 'I have a job, did you know? Leo Rothenstein has hired me as an adviser.'

I thought this must be one of Leo's practical jokes.

'An adviser? What kind of an adviser?'

'Well, politics, mostly. And finance.'

'*Finance?* What on earth do you know about finance?'

He did not reply for a moment. A rabbit came out of the hedge and sat up on its hind legs at the side of the road and looked at us in amazement.

'His family is worried about Hitler. They have money in Germany, and a lot of relations there. He asked me to look in on them. He knew I was going over, you see.'

'Are you? To Germany?'

'Yes – didn't I say? Sorry. The people I've been talking to have asked me to go.'

'And do what?'

'Just . . . look around. Get the feel of things. Report back.'

I let out a loud laugh.

'Good God, Beaver,' I cried, 'you're going to be a spy!'

'Yes,' he said, with a rueful smirk, proud as a boy scout. 'Yes, I suppose I am.'

I did not know why I should have been surprised: after all, I had been in the secret ranks myself for years, though on the other side from him, and his sort. What would have happened, I ask myself, if I had said to him then, *Nick, my love, I'm working for Moscow, what do you think of that?* Instead I stopped and turned and looked back down the hill to the harbour and the roughening sea.

'I wonder what those gulls were after,' I said.

Nick turned too and vaguely peered.

'What gulls?' he said.

WE DID NOT go to Mayo. I cannot remember what excuse I made to my father and Hettie, or if I even bothered to offer one. We were both anxious to get back to London, Nick to his spying and I to mine. Father was hurt. The west for him was the land of youth, not only the scene of his childhood holidays – his grandfather had kept a farm on a rocky islet in Clew Bay – but the place where his people had originated, mysterious autochthons stepping out of the mists of the western seaboard, the mighty O Measceoils, warriors, pirates, fierce clansmen all, who just in time to avoid the ravages of the Famine had changed their religion and Anglicised the family name and turned themselves into Yeats's hard-riding country gentlemen. I had no wish to introduce Nick to these legends, and much less to walk with him through the sites where had stood the stone cottages of my forebears and the base beds from which they had sprung. In these matters he and I observed a decorous silence: he did not speak of his Jewishness nor I of my Catholic blood. We were both, in our own ways, self-made men. Three days at Carrickdrum was enough for us; we packed up our books and our unworn hiking boots and took ship for what I realised now was home. Leaving Ireland and my father's house, I had the sense of having committed a small but particularly brutish crime. Throughout the journey I could feel my father's wounded, forgiving gaze fixed like a spot of heat on the already burning back of my neck.

London that autumn had an abstracted, provisional air; the atmosphere was hectic and hollow, like that of the last day of school term, or the closing half-hour of a drunken party. People would drift off into silence in the middle of a sentence and look up at the tawny sunlight in the windows and sigh. The streets were like stage-sets, scaled down, two-dimensional, their bustle and busyness tinged with the pathos of something set in motion only so that it might be violently halted. The squawks of the news-vendors had an infernal ring – cockney chirpiness has always grated on my nerves. At evening the sunset glare in the sky above the roofs seemed the afterglow of a vast conflagration. It was all so banal, these hackneyed signs and wonders. Fear was banal.

For some, the times were grimly congenial. Querell, for instance, was in his element. I remember meeting him in the Strand one drizzly afternoon late in that November. We went to a Lyons Corner House and drank tea that was the same colour as the rain falling on the pavement outside the steamy window where we sat. Querell looked even more the spiv than usual, in his narrow suit and brown trilby. Within minutes, it seemed, he had filled to overflowing the tin ashtray on the table between us. I was well established at the Department by then, but I rarely saw him there – he was on the Balkans desk, I was in Languages – and when we chanced upon each other in the outside world like this we felt embarrassed and constrained, like two clergymen meeting the morning after an accidental encounter in a brothel. At least, *I* felt embarrassment, *I* felt constraint; I do not think Querell would ever allow himself to succumb to sensations so weak-kneed and obvious. I could not take seriously the self-deluding, school-brigade, boys-with-men's-moustaches world of military intelligence; the atmosphere of mingled jollity and earnestness in which the Department went about its work was amusing at first, then obscurely shaming, then merely tedious. Such asses one had to deal with! Querell was different, though; I suspected he despised the place as much as I did. It had taken me a long time, and much vigorous yanking on the lattices of the old-boy network, to get in; in the end Leo Rothenstein managed it for me. He was – and had been for years, I was surprised to discover – something very high up in the Middle East section. 'It's in the blood,' Querell said, with a pursed smile. 'His family has been running spies for centuries. They got early news of Waterloo and made their fortune out of it on the Stock Exchange, did you know that? Crafty; very crafty.' Querell did not care for Jews. He was watching me out of those unblinking, protuberant pale eyes of his, two lazy streams of cigarette smoke flaring out of his nostrils. I busied myself eating a sticky bun. His mention of spies had startled me; it was not a word Department people used, even amongst ourselves. Sometimes it crossed my mind that he too, like me, might be more than he was admitting – he had just published a thriller called *The Double Agent*. The idea of having Querell as a secret sharer was not appealing. When I looked up from my bun he shifted his gaze to the legs of a passing waitress. I had never succeeded in pinning down his politics. He would talk of the Cliveden crowd or Mosley and his thugs with a sort of wistful admiration, then in the next breath he would be the worker's champion. In my innocence I thought it was his Catholicism that afforded him this breadth of casuistry. At Maules one weekend when the Moscow show trials were going on he overheard me castigating Stalin. 'Thing is, Maskell,' he said, 'a bad pope doesn't make a bad church.' Leo Rothenstein, draped on a sofa, his long legs crossed before him, shifted himself and laughed lazily. 'My God,' he said, 'a Bolshie in the house! My poor papa would turn in his grave.'

'Have you seen Bannister recently?' Querell asked now, still with his eye on the waitress's crooked seams. 'I hear he's taken up with the Fascists.'

Boy was working at the BBC, in charge of what he portentously referred to as Talks. He was endearingly proud of this job, and regaled us with stories about Lord Reith and his boyfriends, which at the time we refused to believe. By then he too was with the Department; after Munich, pretty well everyone in our set had joined the Secret Service, or been press-ganged into it. I imagine we were not unaware that intelligence work was likely to be far preferable to soldiering – or am I being unfair to us? Boy took to his undercover role with childish enthusiasm. He would always love the secret life, and missed it painfully after he defected. He enjoyed especially the role-playing; for cover, he had lately joined a Tory ginger group of Nazi sympathisers calling itself the Chain ('I'm pulling the Chain for Uncle Joe,' was Boy's catchphrase), and had attached himself to a notorious pro-Hitler MP called Richard Someone, I have forgotten the name, an ex-Guards officer and a lunatic, for whom he was acting (the right word) as unofficial private secretary. His chief duty, he told us, was to be a pander for the Captain, who had an insatiable appetite for working-class young men. Recently Boy and his mad Captain had undertaken a jaunt to the Rhineland, escorting a band of schoolboys from the East End on a visit to a Hitler Youth camp. It was the kind of preposterous thing that went on in the run-up to war. The pair had returned in ecstasies ('Oh, those blond beasts!'), though Captain Dick had contracted a painful dose of anal thrush; not so clean-limbed after all, *die Hitlerjugend.*

'The best part of the joke,' I said, 'is that the trip was sponsored by the Foreign Relations Council of the Church of England!'

Querell did not laugh, only gave me one of his swift, bug-eyed glances, which always made me feel as if a bottle had been rolled across my face, the way at country house parties they used to roll empty champagne bottles over the ballroom floors to impart a final polishing (ah, the days of our youth – the youth of the world!).

'Maybe you should have gone with them,' he said.

That gave me pause. I could feel myself beginning to redden.

'Not my kind of thing, old boy,' I said, meaning it to come out lazy and insolent, though it sounded, to my own ears, incriminatingly prim. I passed on quickly. 'Boy says the Krauts have finished rearming and are just waiting for the word.'

Querell shrugged. 'Well, we hardly needed to send a pansy over to find out that for us, did we.'

'He and the Captain were shown around an aerodrome. Line upon line of Messerschmitts, all pointing at us.'

We were silent. In the traffic noise from the street outside I seemed to hear the whirr of propellers, and I shivered with eager anticipation: *let it come, let it all come!* Querell looked idly about the room. At the table next to us a fat man in a greasy suit was speaking vehemently in a low voice to a wan young woman with hennaed hair – his daughter, it seemed – telling her in a level undertone that she was nothing but a tart; they were to turn up again a couple of years later, disguised as a Jewish refugee and his doomed young wife, on board *The Orient Express*, the first of Querell's overrated Balkan thrillers.

'I wonder if we shall survive,' Querell said. 'All this, I mean.' He waved a hand, taking in the other tables, and the waitress, and the woman at the cash register, and the fat man and his miserable daughter, and, beyond them, England.

'What if we don't?' I said, cautiously. 'Something better might take our place.'

'You want Hitler to win?'

'Not Hitler, no.'

It is hard now to recapture the peculiar thrill of moments such as that, when one risked everything on a throwaway remark. It was akin to the rush of vertiginous glee I felt when I made my first parachute jump. There was the same sensation of being light as air and yet far weightier, of far more significance, somehow, than a mere mortal should ever expect to be. Thus a minor god might feel, flying down from the clouds to try out a disguise on one of Arcady's more experienced nymphs. We sat, Querell and I, unspeaking, looking at each other. That was another thing about those moments of absolute risk: the powerful, charged neutrality that took over one's facial expressions and one's tone of voice. When I met T. S. Eliot at a Palace function after the war, I recognised at once in that shadowed, camel-eyed gaze and timbreless voice the marks of the lifelong, obsessive dissembler.

Querell was the first to look away; the moment passed.

'Well,' he said, 'it hardly matters who wins, since it will be left to the Yanks as usual to come in and mop up after us.'

We went off then and got drunk together at the Gryphon. When I look back, I am surprised at how much time I have spent in Querell's company over the years. There was no warmth between us, and we had few interests in common. His Catholicism was as incomprehensible to me as he claimed my Marxism was to him; though each was a believer, neither could credit the other's faith. Yet there was a bond of some sort between us. Ours was like one of those odd attachments at school, when two unlovely misfits sidle up to each other out of mutual need and form a sort of humid, hapless friendship. The Gryphon and the George were our version of the trees behind the playing fields, where we could sit through long hours of shared melancholy in a haze of cigarette smoke and alcohol fumes, indulging in occasional rancorous exchanges, and glaring and grinning at our fellow drinkers. Being with Querell was, for me, a kind of slumming. I did not subscribe – in those days, anyway – to his Manichean version of the world, yet I found myself drawn to the idea of it, this dark, befouled yet curiously dauntless place through which he slouched, always alone, with a fag in his mouth and his hat raked to the side and one hand ever ready in his jacket pocket, cradling that imaginary gun.

It was a tumultuous evening. After the Gryphon, when we were good and soused, we collected his Riley from the RAC garage and drove to an awful dive somewhere off the Edgware Road. Querell had said the place specialised in child prostitutes. There was a low basement room that smelled of carbolic, with a balding, red-velvet sofa and spindle-backed cane chairs and brown lino on the floor scarred from trodden-on cigarette butts. A feebly burning table lamp wore a crooked shade the stuff of which had the uncanny look of dried human skin. The girls sitting about vacantly in their slips had ceased being children a long time ago. The couple who ran the place were out of a seaside postcard, she a big blancmange with a wig of brass curls, he a lean little whippet of a fellow with a Hitler tash and a tic in one eye. Mrs Gill kept sweeping in and out of the room like a watchful duenna, while Adolf plied us with brown ale, scurrying about at a crouch with a tin tray expertly balanced on the bunched fingers of his left hand while with his right he deftly distributed bottles and grimed glasses. It all seemed to me very jolly, in a bleary, sin-soaked, Stanley Spencerish sort of way (*Belshazzar's Feast at Cookham*). I found myself sitting with a freckled, red-haired girl perched on my lap in the attitude of an overgrown infant, her head resting awkwardly on my shoulder and her knees braced sideways against my chest, while under us the cane chair cackled scornfully to itself. She told me with great pride that her mam and dad had once been Pearly King and Queen (do they still have that custom?), and offered to suck me off for ten bob. I fell asleep, or passed out briefly, and when I came to, the girl was gone, and so were her companions, and Querell, too, though presently he reappeared, with a strand of his thin, oiled hair hanging down his forehead; I found it very worrying, that bit of discomposure in one usually so fanatically shined and smoothed.

We left, and climbed the basement steps to the street, not without difficulty, and found that it was raining heavily – what a surprise the weather always is when one is drunk – and Querell said he knew another place where there were definitely children for sale, and when I said I had no wish to sleep with a child he went into a sulk and refused to drive the car, so I took the keys from him, although I had never driven before, and we jerked and juddered off through the rain in the direction of Soho, I leaning forward anxiously with my nose almost touching the streaming windscreen, and Querell slumped beside me in wordless anger, his arms furiously folded. I was so drunk by now I could not focus properly and had to keep one eye shut in order to stop the white line in the middle of the road from splitting in two. Before I knew where I was going we had pulled up outside Leo Rothenstein's house in Poland Street, where Nick was already living – most of us would lodge there, on and off, in the coming years; it was what would nowadays be called a commune, I suppose. There was a light in Nick's window. Querell leaned on the bell – by now he had forgotten whatever it was he had been sulking about – while I stood with my face uplifted to the rain, declaiming Blake:

Awake! awake O sleeper of the land of shadows, wake! expand!

Nick opened a window and stuck out his head and swore at us. 'For Christ's sake, go home, Victor, there's a good chap.' He came down, however, and let us in. He was in evening dress, looking very pale and satanic. We followed him up the narrow stairs, bumping from banisters to wall and back again, and Querell took up the refrain of *Jerusalem*:

I am in you and you in me, mutual in love divine:
Fibres of love from man to man thro' Albion's pleasant land.

In the flat a small after-party party was in progress. Boy was there, and Abercrombie the poet, and Lady Mary Somebody, and the Lydon sisters. They had been to a party at the Rothenstein mansion in Portman Square (*Why wasn't I invited?*) and were finishing a magnum of champagne. Querell and I stopped in the doorway and goggled at them.

'I say,' I said, 'you all do look splendid.'

And they did: like a flock of languorous penguins.

Nick did his nasty laugh.

'How English you're coming to sound, Vic,' he said. 'Quite the native.'

He knew very well how much I hated to be called Vic.

Querell drew a bead on him and in a slurred voice said, 'At least he didn't come here via Palestine.'

The Lydon sisters giggled.

Nick fetched a couple of beer glasses from the kitchen and poured a gulp of champagne into each. Now I noticed for the first time, sitting in an armchair in a corner, ankle crossed on knee, an unknown yet disturbingly familiar, delicate youth in a silk evening suit, with brilliantined hair brushed tightly back, smoking a cigarette and watching me with cool amusement out of shadowed eyes.

'Hello, Victor,' this person said. 'You look somewhat the worse for wear.'

It was Baby. The others laughed at my astonishment.

'Dodo here bet her a gallon of bubbly she couldn't get away with it,' Nick said. Lady Mary – Dodo – clasped her hands in her lap and drew her thin shoulders together and put on an expression of comic ruefulness. Nick made a face at her. 'She lost,' he said. 'It was the damnedest thing. Even Leo didn't recognise her.'

'And I made a pass at her,' Boy said. 'So that will tell you.'

More laughter. Nick crossed the room with the champagne bottle.

'Come on, old girl,' he said, 'we've got to finish up your winnings.'

Baby, still with her eyes on me, lifted her glass to be filled. Dark-blue velvet curtains were drawn over the tall window behind her chair, and on a low table a clutch of washed-pink roses was expiring in a copper bowl, the packed petals heavy and limp as wetted cloth. The room shrank, became a long, low box, like the inside of something, a camera, or a magic lantern. I stood and swayed, with champagne bubbles detonating in my nostrils, and, as I watched them, in my poor fuddled vision brother and sister seemed to merge and separate and merge again, dark on dark and pale on glimmering pale, Pierrot and Pierrette. Nick glanced at me and smiled and said:

'Better sit down, Victor, you have a distinct look of Ben Turpin.'

A blank then, and then I am sitting on the floor, beside Baby's chair, my legs crossed under me tailor-fashion and my chin practically leaning on the armrest beside her suddenly significant hand with its short, fatly tapering fingers and blood-red nails; I want to take each one of those fingers between my lips and suck and suck until the painted nails turn transparent as fish-scales. I am telling her earnestly about Diderot's theory of statues. There is a stage of drunkenness when all at once one seems to step with startling, with laughable, ease through a door that all night one had been struggling in vain to open. On the other side all is light and definition and the calm of certitude.

'Diderot said,' I said, 'Diderot said that what we do is, we erect a statue in our own image inside ourselves – idealised, you know, but still recognisable – and then spend our lives engaged in the effort to make ourselves into its likeness. This is the moral imperative. I think it's awfully clever, don't you? I know that's how *I* feel. Only there are times when I can't tell which is the statue and which is me.' This last struck me as profoundly sad and I thought I might cry. Behind me Boy was loudly reciting 'The Ball of Inverness' and the Lydon sisters were delightedly shrieking. I covered Baby's hand with mine. How cool it was; cool, and excitingly unresponsive. 'What do you think,' I said in a voice thick with emotion. 'Tell me what you think.'

She sat in her chair as motionless as – yes, as motionless as a statue, one silk-trousered leg still crossed on the other and her arms stretched out along the armrests, androgynous, hieratic and faintly, calmly crazed-looking, with her hair drawn back so tight her eyes were slanted at the corners; her head was turned toward me, and she looked at me, saying nothing. Or looked not at me, but around me, rather. It was a way she had. Her gaze would stray no farther than one's face yet one would seem to be taken in all of a piece, defined, somehow, and set apart, as if by her scrutiny she were generating around one a kind of invisible corona, a forcefield inside of which one stood isolated, inspected, alone. Do I give her too much weight, do I make her seem a sort of sphinx, a sort of she-monster, cruel and cold and impossibly, untouchably distant? She was just a human, like me, groping her way through the world, yet when she looked at me like that I felt my sins shine out of me, illumined forth for all to see. It was an intoxicating sensation, especially for one already so intoxicated.

At four in the morning Querell drove me home. In Leicester Square he ran the car gently into a lamp-post, and we sat for a while listening to the radiator ticking and watching an illuminated advertisement for Bovril blinking on and off. The square was deserted. Squalls of wind pushed dead leaves back and forth over the pavements from which the recently ceased rain was drying in big map-shaped patches. It was all very desolate and beautiful and sad, and I thought again that I might weep.

'Bloody people,' Querell muttered, starting up the stalled engine. 'Bloody war will fix 'em.'

At dawn I sprang awake suddenly, completely, in a transport of certitude. I knew exactly what I must do. I did not so much get out of bed as levitate from it; I felt like one of Blake's shining figures, transformed and aflame. The telephone rattled in my hands. Baby answered on the first ring. She did not sound as if she had been asleep. Behind her voice there lay a vast, waiting silence.

'Look here,' I said, 'I have to marry you.' She did not reply. I imagined her floating in that sea of silence, fronds of black silk undulating about her. 'Vivienne? Are you there?'

How strange her name sounded.

'Yes,' she said, 'I'm here.' She seemed as always to be suppressing laughter, but I did not mind.

'*Will* you marry me?'

She paused again. A seagull alighted on the sill outside my

window and looked at me with a bright, blank eye. The sky was the colour of pale mud. I had the sense that all this had happened before.

'All right,' she said.

And hung up.

*

We met later that day for lunch at the Savoy. It was a curious occasion, strained and somewhat stagey, as if we were taking part in one of those self-consciously smart drawing-room comedies of the time. The restaurant was littered with people we knew, which intensified our sense of being on display. Baby wore her habitual black, a suit with padded shoulders and a narrow skirt, which in daylight had to my eye the look of widow's weeds. She was as always both watchful and remote, though I thought I could detect a hint of agitation in the way she kept reaching out and fiddling with my cigarette case, turning it this way and that on the tablecloth. I did not help matters by saying, first thing, how awful I was feeling. And I was: my eyes felt as if they had been torn out and held over hot coals and then thrust back into the throbbing sockets. I showed her my shaking hands, told her how my heart was wobbling. She made a grimace of disdain.

'Why do men always boast about their hangovers?'

'There's so little else for us to be boastful about, I suppose, these days,' I said sulkily.

We looked away from each other. The silence stretched, thinner and thinner. We were like hesitant swimmers who have come to the water's grey and uninviting edge. Baby was the first to plunge in.

'Well,' she said, 'I've never been proposed to over the telephone before.'

Her laughter had a nervous sparkle. She had recently ended a messy affair with some sort of an American. *My Yank*, was how she would refer to him, with a bitter, resigned little smile.

No one seemed to have met him. It came to me with a kind of slow amazement how little I knew about her.

'Yes,' I said, 'I'm sorry, but it seemed the thing to do, at the time.'

'And does it still?'

'What?'

'Seem the thing to do.'

'Well, yes, of course. Don't you think?'

She paused. That gaze of hers, it seemed to originate somehow at the back of her eyes.

'Nick is right,' she said, 'you *are* turning into an Englishman.'

The waiter appeared then and we bent with relief over our menus. During lunch we talked in a studiedly desultory fashion about my new post at the Institute, Nick's bizarre hiring of himself as an adviser to the Rothensteins, Boy Bannister's latest scrape, the coming war. I had assumed she would have no politics and was obscurely irritated to discover that she was fiercely anti-appeasement – quite bellicose, in fact. While our plates were being cleared away she opened my cigarette case and took a cigarette – from the brusqueness of her movements, she too seemed irritated – and paused with the match burning and said:

'You do love me, I take it?'

The waiter glanced at her quickly and away. I took her wrist and drew her hand toward me and blew out the match. We had started on our second bottle of wine.

'Yes,' I said, 'I love you.'

I had never said it to anyone before, except Hettie, when I was little. Baby nodded once, briskly, as if I had cleared up some small, niggling matter that had been on her mind for a long time.

'You'll have to see Mummy, you know,' she said. I stared blankly. She permitted herself an ironic smile. 'To ask for my hand.'

We both looked at where my fingers were still lightly holding her wrist. Had there really been an audience, the moment would have raised a scatter of laughter.

'Shouldn't it be your father that I talk to?' I said. Big Beaver was about to publish a monograph of mine on German baroque architecture.

'Oh, he won't care.'

In the taxi we kissed, turning sideways suddenly toward each other and grappling awkwardly, like a pair of shop-window mannequins come jerkily alive. I remembered the same thing happening, what, six, seven years before? and thought how strange life was. Her nose was chill and faintly damp. I touched a breast. A strong cold wind was blowing along Oxford Street. Baby leaned her forehead against my neck. Her fat-fingered little hand rested in mine.

'What shall I call you?' she said. 'Victor is hardly a name, is it. More a title. Like someone in ancient Rome.' She lifted her head and looked at me. The lights of the shut shops as we passed them by flashed in miniature across her eyes, like so many slides flickering past the lenses of a faulty projector. In the darkness her smile seemed bright and brave, as if she were holding back tears. '*I* don't love *you*, you know,' she said softly.

I closed my fingers on hers.

'I know that,' I said. 'But it doesn't matter, does it.'

*

I went up to Oxford by train on one of those deceptively soft, glowing days of late October. Everything was melodramatically aflame, so that the world seemed poised not on the edge of winter but of some grand, blazoned beginning. I was wearing a new and rather smart suit, and as we sped along I admired the line of the trouser-leg and the chestnut gleam on the toecaps of my well-polished shoes. I had a clear and definite image of myself: smooth, well-groomed, primped and pomaded, a man with a mission. I was quite calm about the impending confrontation with Mrs Beaver, was even looking forward to it, in a mood of amused condescension. What could I have to fear from such a scatter-brain? Yet as we went along, I began to be affected by something in the inexorability of the way the lumbering, seemingly unstoppable train ticked off the station halts, and the smoke rolling past the window took on an infernal aspect, and by the time we drew into Oxford, blank terror had fixed its claw upon my heart.

The maid who opened the door to me was new, a heavy-haunched, flat-faced girl who gave me a sceptical look and took my hat as if it were something dead I had handed her. The Brevoorts were proud of their reputation for keeping impossible servants; it fed Mrs Beaver's bohemian notions of herself. 'Madam is in the pantry,' the girl said, and I found the nursery-rhyme echo of it oddly disconcerting. There was a warm, sickly-sweet odour. I followed the girl's joggling haunches through to the drawing room, where she left me, stepping backwards and closing the door on me with a definite smirk. I stood in the middle of the floor listening to my heart and looking through the bottle-glass window panes at the iridescent and somehow derisively gaudy garden. Time passed. I thought of the first time I had been in this room, nearly a decade ago, with Nick lounging on the sofa and Baby upstairs playing her jazz records. I felt suddenly, immensely old, and saw myself now not as the polished man of the world I had seemed at the outset of my journey, but a sort of freak, desiccated and obscenely preserved, like one of those fairground midgets, a man in a boy's wrinkled body.

Without warning the door flew open and Mrs Brevoort stood there in her Sarah Bernhardt pose, a hand on the knob and her head thrown back, her bared embonpoint pallidly aheave.

'Plums!' she said. 'Such impossible fecundity.'

She was wearing a tasselled shawl affair and a voluminous velvet dress the colour of old blood, and both arms were busy almost to the elbows with fine gold bangles, like a set of springs, which suggested the circus ring more than the seraglio. I realised what it was she always reminded me of in her looks: one of Henry James's worldly schemers, a Mme Merle, or a Mrs Assingham, but without their wit, or their acuity. She advanced, moving as always as if mounted on a hidden trolley, and grasped me by the shoulders and kissed me dramatically on both cheeks, then thrust me from her and held me at arm's length and gazed at me for a long moment with an expression of tragic weight, slowly nodding her great head.

'Baby spoke to you?' I said tentatively.

She nodded more deeply still, so that her chin almost dropped to her breast.

'Vivienne,' she said, 'telephoned. Her father and I have had a long chat. We are so . . .' It was impossible to tell what might have followed. She went on contemplating me, seemingly lost in thought, then suddenly she roused herself and grew brisk. 'Come along,' she said, 'I need a man's help.'

The pantry was a stylised model of a witch's cave. Through a low little window giving on to the vegetable garden there entered a dense, sinister green glow which seemed something at once more and less than daylight. An enormous vat of plum jam was turbidly boiling on a squat black gas stove that stood with delicate feet braced, like a weightlifter about to bend to his task, while on the draining board beside the chipped sink there was ranged a waiting squadron of jam jars of varying sizes. Mrs B. bent over the bubbling cauldron, her eyes slitted and the wings of her great beaked nose flaring, and lifted a ladleful of the jam and examined it doubtfully.

'Max expects one to do this sort of thing,' she said, turning off the gas, 'I can't think why.' She glanced at me sideways with a Grimalkin grin. 'He's a great tyrant, you know. Would you like an apron? And do take off your jacket.'

I was to hold the jars while she ladled the jam into them. 'You've got to do it while the jam is hot, you see, or the seals won't work.' The first jar cracked from the heat of the boiling fruit, in the second the jam overflowed and burned my fingers, at which I uttered an oath, which Mrs B. pretended not to hear.

'Well,' she said, 'perhaps we should allow it to cool a little. Let's go into the garden. Such a perfect day. Should I offer you a drink, or is it too early? Maude shall bring us something. Maude! Dear me, where is the girl. Oh, there you are; how you do lurk. What will you take, Mr Maskell? People tell me my dandelion wine is really quite good. Gin? Well, yes, I'm sure we must have, somewhere. Maude, bring Mr Maskell some gin. And . . . tonic, and so on.' Maude looked at me and let another sardonic smile cross her large face briefly, and slouched off. Mrs Brevoort sighed. 'I suspect her of insolence, but I can never quite catch her in the act. They are so sly, you know, and so clever, too, in their way.'

The garden was at its last, glorious gasp, all gold and green and umber and rose madder. A strong autumnal sun was shining. We walked over the crisp grass, smelling eucalyptus and the thin, hot stink of verbena, and sat down on a weather-beaten wooden bench that knelt at a tipsy angle against a rough stone wall under a tangled arch of old roses. A very bower of unbliss.

'Is your hand terribly painful?' Mrs B. said. 'Perhaps we should have put something on it.'

'Dock leaves,' I said.

'What?'

'It was a cure my mother had. My stepmother.'

'I see.' She cast about the garden with an air of vague helplessness. 'I don't know that there are any *dock* leaves . . .'

Maude approached then with my gin, and a green goblet of urine-coloured liquid for Mrs Beaver which I took to be the celebrated dandelion wine. I knocked back half my drink in one go. Mrs B. once more pretended not to notice.

'You were telling me about your stepmother,' she said, and took a sip of wine, eyeing me keenly over the rim of the glass.

'Was I? Her name is Hermione,' I said, floundering.

'Very . . . pretty. And is she Irish, too?'

'Yes. Her people were Quakers.'

'Quakers!' she said, uttering the word as a high-pitched squawk, and opened her eyes very wide and clapped a hand with fingers splayed to her sloped chest with an audible little smack. I had the impression she was not at all sure what a Quaker was. 'Well, of course, one can't be held accountable for one's people,' she said. '*I* should know that!' And she threw back her head and produced a great full raucous trill of laughter, humourless and mad, like the heroine's laugh in a tragic opera. I thought of mentioning my maternal connection with the Queen; one isn't a snob, of course, but it is a thing that does impress.

I had finished my gin, and kept twirling the empty glass ostentatiously in my fingers, but she refused to take the hint.

'And you have a brother, yes?'

She had suddenly become very interested in the nap of the velvet stuff of her dress where it was stretched over her large, round knees.

'Yes,' I said. My voice sounded extraordinarily thin and strained, like that of a meek murderer replying to the prosecution's first, frightening question.

'Yes,' she said, softly. 'Because you did not say.'

'It did not arise.'

'We rather thought you were an only child.'

'I'm sorry.' I was not sure what I was apologising for. A wave of anguished anger broke over me. Nick: Nick had told them. Mrs Brevoort placed her wineglass on the bench beside her and rose and paced a little way on to the lawn, and stopped and turned, gazing pensively down upon the grass at her feet.

'Of course,' she said, 'we should require a certificate.'

'A certificate . . . ?'

'Yes. From a doctor, you know; Max will find a dependable man. So often these things run in the family, and we could not dream of exposing Vivienne to anything of that nature. You do see that, don't you?' She was standing now canted forward at a slight angle, her hands clasped under her bosom, gazing at me with an earnest, kindly, melancholy little smile. 'We have no doubt that *you*, Mr Maskell—'

'Call me Victor, please,' I murmured. A bubble of manic, miserable laughter was now pushing its hot way upward in my chest and threatening to choke me.

'We have no doubt,' she pressed on, irresistible as a battle-ship, 'that you, of course, are not personally . . . infected, if I may put it that way. But it's the *blood*, you see.' She brought up her clasped hands and tucked them under her chin in a winsomely histrionic gesture and turned and paced a few steps to the left and back again. 'We are, Mr Maskell, despite extremes of sophistication, a primitive people. I mean, of course, *my* people. The Hebrew race has suffered much, and no doubt will again in the future' – she was right: her brother and his wife and their three children were to perish in Treblinka – 'but throughout the thousands of years of our history we have held fast to essentials. The family. Our children. And blood, Mr Maskell: blood.' She dropped her hands from under her chin and turned and paced again, this time to the right, and again returned to centre stage. I felt like a theatre-goer trapped in the middle of a long second act who hears, outside, a fire engine howling past in the direction of his own house.

'Mrs Brevoort—' I began, but she held up a hand as broad as a traffic policeman's.

'Please,' she said, with a large, icy smile. 'Two words more, and then silence, I promise.' I could see the maid moving about behind the drawing room window and toyed desperately with the possibility of shouting for her to bring me another drink – to bring the bloody bottle. Is there anything more dispiriting than an empty, hand-warmed, sticky gin glass? I thought of sucking on the slice of lemon but knew that even that would not have been sufficient sign of desperation for Mrs B., in full flight as she was. 'When Vivienne telephoned,' she was saying, 'to tell us of your engagement, which came, you understand, as a great . . . surprise' – *shock* was the word she had suppressed – 'to her father and to me, I shut myself away in the music room for an entire afternoon. I had much to think about. Music is always a help. I played Brahms. Those great, dark chords. So filled with sadness and yet so . . . so sustaining.' She bowed her head and let her eyelids gently close and stood for a moment as if in silent prayer, and then looked at me again suddenly, piercingly. 'She is our only daughter, Mr Maskell; our only, precious girl.'

I stood up. The musky smell of roses, along with everything else, was giving me a headache.

'Mrs Brevoort,' I said, 'Vivienne is twenty-nine. She is not a child. We love each other' – at that she shot up her thick, shiny eyebrows and gave her head a dismissive little toss, Mrs Touchett to the life – 'and we think it is time that we should marry.' I faltered; somehow that was not what I had meant to say, or at least not how I had meant to say it. 'My brother suffers from a syndrome the name of which would mean nothing to you and which, besides, I have temporarily forgotten.' This was going from bad to worse. 'His condition is not hereditary. It is the result of a depletion of oxygen to the brain while he was in the womb.' At that word she gave a definite start; I pressed on. 'We would have hoped for your blessing, and that of Mr Brevoort, but if you withhold it we shall go ahead regardless. I feel you should understand that.' Matters suddenly were improving, as the rhetoric heated. I could feel an invisible starched stock sprouting up about my throat, and would not have been surprised to look down and find myself in frock coat and riding boots: Lord Warburton himself could not have struck a haughtier aspect. I would have felt thoroughly in command were it not for the troubling persistence of that word *womb*, still wallowing between us like a half-inflated football that neither of us would dare either to pick up or kick away.

We were silent. I could hear myself breathe, a soft, stertorous roaring down the nostrils. Mrs B. made a peculiar little move-ment of her upper body, half shrug half bridle, and said:

'Of course you shall have our blessing. Vivienne shall have our blessing. That is not the matter at all.'

'Then what is the matter?'

She made to speak but instead stood silent, her mouth working and her eyes going glossily out of focus. I was afraid she might be having a seizure – the word *apoplexy* popped up in my mind, and I thought, I don't know why, of the Punch and Judy show that used to be set up on Carrickdrum strand in summer when I was a child, and which filled me with unease even while I shrieked with laughter – but then, to my astonish-ment and dismay, she began to weep. I had never seen her lose control like this before, and would not see it again. I suspect she was as surprised as I was. She was angry at herself too, which added tears of rage to whatever the other kind were. 'Ridiculous, ridiculous,' she muttered, scrubbing at her eyes, her bangles jingling, and shaking her head sideways as if to dislodge something from her ear, and I caught a glimpse of what she would look like as an old, old woman. I felt sorry for her, but there was another feeling also, which I was ashamed of but could not deny: it was exultation; nasty, secret and small-scale, but exultation for all that. These are the moments, rare, and seldom as clear-cut as this one, when power passes from one opponent to another, silently, instantaneously, like an electric charge jumping between electrodes. I began to offer her some futile and probably spurious words of comfort but she brushed them aside with an angry sweep of her hand, as if pushing away a wasp. She was quickly regaining control of herself. Her tears ceased. She gave a great sniff and lifted her head and pointed her chin at me.

'I do not wish us to be enemies, Mr Maskell.'

'No,' I said, 'that would not be wise.'

Max Brevoort arrived a little after that, when I was standing in the drawing room again and Mrs B. had gone off somewhere to repair her face. I thought the tip of his thin nose quivered as he sniffed carefully at the atmosphere. He had a marvellously fine sense for the danger of an occasion. He did have something of the beaver about him, with his sleekness and his hand-rubbing and that delicately probing snout.

'I'm told we are to gain a son,' he said, and gave me one of his fierce, humourless grins. 'Congratulations.'

There seemed nothing more to say after that and we stood awkwardly, looking at our feet. Then we both began to speak at once and lapsed again into painful silence. Mrs B. came back, and was her accustomed imperial self again, but I caught Max giving her a sharp, searching glance and deciding, on the evidence, to proceed with caution.

'Perhaps we should have a drink?' he said, and added, gingerly: 'To mark the occasion.'

'Yes, indeed,' his wife said, flashing at him a brilliant, brittle smile. 'Some champagne. We've been having a chat.' She turned to me. 'Haven't we, Mr Maskell.'

'Victor,' I said.

*

The wedding was a quiet affair, as the saying was in those days. The ceremony took place at Marylebone register office. The Beavers were there, Nick and his parents and an ancient aunt I had never met before – she had money – and Boy Bannister, of course, and Leo Rothenstein, and a couple of Baby's girlfriends, mature flappers in ridiculous hats. My father and Hettie had come over the night before on the ferry, and looked frightened and country-mousey, and I was embarrassed for them, and by them. Nick was best man. Afterwards we went to Claridges for lunch, and Boy got drunk and made a disgraceful speech, throughout which Mrs Beaver sat with a terrible, fixed smile, twisting and twisting a napkin in her hands as if she were wringing the neck of some small, white, boneless animal. The honeymoon was spent in Taormina. It was hot, and Mount Etna wore a stationary, menacing plume of smoke. We read a lot, and explored the ruins, and in the evenings, over dinner, Baby told me about her former lovers, of whom there had been an impressive number. I do not know why she felt the need to recount these adventures, which sounded uniformly melancholy, to me; perhaps it was a form of exorcism. I did not mind. It was even pleasant, in a peculiar way, to sit sipping my wine while this ghostly line of bankers and polo players and hapless Americans threaded its way through the hotel's lugubriously ornate dining room and disappeared into the steamy, starstruck night.

Sex turned out to be easier than I had expected, or feared. I was pleased to encounter a version of Baby – warm, yielding, languorous, even – very different from the alarmingly hard-edged one I had married, while she was amused, and touched, to discover that she had married a thirty-one-year-old virgin. I had some difficulty getting going, and she laughed, and pushed back her hair, and said, 'Poor darling, let me help you, I'm a sucker for this sort of thing.' On our last night we made a solemn, if tipsy, vow that we would not have children. And by Christmas she was pregnant.

TWO

DEAR MISS VANDELEUR. I have been neglecting you, I know. More, I have been avoiding you: I was here this morning when you called, but did not answer the bell. I knew it was you because I had seen you from the window, crossing the square, in the rain (what is it young women have against the employment of umbrellas?). I felt like an elderly spinster (but then, when do I not feel like an elderly spinster?), peeping out from behind lace curtains at a world of which she is growing increasingly afraid. I have not been well. Heartsick, is the word. Too much brooding, here, under the lamp, just me and the scratching of my pen, and the distracting noise of the birds in the trees outside, where spring has come to a frantic head and toppled over into full-throated Keatsian summer. Such rude good weather strikes me as heartless; I have always been prone to the pathetic fallacy. I took things too quickly, I think; I should have allowed myself time to recuperate after that public exposure and the resulting humiliation. It is like having had an operation, or what it must be like to have been shot; you come round and you think, Well, this is not so bad, I'm still here, and there is hardly any pain – why are all these people about me behaving in such an exaggerated way? And you feel almost euphoric. It is because the system has not absorbed the shock, or because the shock is acting as an anaesthetic. But this little interval of exhilaration ends, the excited attendants rush off to the scene of some new emergency, and then comes night and darkness and the dawning astonishment of pain.

I was genuinely surprised when they stripped me of the knighthood, and Cambridge revoked the honorary doctorate, and the Institute delicately indicated that my continued presence there, even for the purposes of research, would not be welcomed. (I have heard nothing from the Palace; Mrs W. does hate a scandal.) What have I done, to be so reviled, in a nation of traitors, who daily betray friends, wives, children, tax inspectors? I am being disingenuous, I know. I think what they find so shocking is that someone – one of their own, that is – should actually have held to an ideal. And I did hold to it, even in the face of my own innate, all-corroding scepticism. I did not deceive myself as to the nature of the choice I had made. I was not like Boy, with his puerile conviction of the perfectibility of man, and not like Querell, either, wandering the world and dropping in to argue fine points of dogma over the Bishop of Bongoland's best port. Oh, no doubt for me Marxism was a recrudescence, in a not greatly altered form, of the faith of my fathers; any back-street Freudian could tease that one out. But what comfort does belief offer, when it contains within it its own antithesis, the glistening drop of poison at the heart? Is the Pascalian wager sufficient to sustain a life, a real life, in the real world? The fact that you place your bet on red does not mean that the black is not still there.

I often think how differently things might have gone for me if I had not encountered Felix Hartmann when I did. Naturally, I fell a little in love with him. You will not have heard of this person. He was one of Moscow's most impressive people, both an ideologue and a dedicated activist (dear me, how easily one falls into the jargon of the Sunday papers!). His front was a fur trading business in the vicinity of Brick Lane, or some such insalubrious place, which gave him frequent opportunities for travel, both within the country and abroad. (I trust, Miss V., you are taking notes.) He was a Hungarian national of German and Slav extraction: father a soldier, mother a Serb, or a Slovenian, something like that. It was said, though I do not know where the story originated (it may even be true), that he had been ordained a Catholic priest and had served in the Great

War as a chaplain in the Austro-Hungarian army; when I asked him once about this period of his life he would say nothing and only gave me one of his studiedly enigmatic smiles. He had suffered a shrapnel wound – 'in a skirmish in the Carpathians' – which had left him with an attractive Byronic limp. He was tall, straight-backed, with glossy blue-black hair, soft eyes, an engaging, if somewhat laboured, ironical smile. He could have been one of those Prussian princes out of the last century, all gold braid and duelling scars, so beloved of operetta composers. He claimed he had been captured in battle by the Russian army, and when the Revolution came had joined the Reds and fought in the civil war. All this gave him the faintly preposterous air of fortitude and self-importance of the Man Who Has Seen Action. In his own eyes, I suspect, he was not the Student Prince, but one of those tormented warrior priests of the Counter-Reformation, trailing his bloodied sword through the smoking ruins of sacked towns.

It was Alastair Sykes who introduced me to him. Summer of 1936. I had travelled up to Cambridge in the middle of August – I still had rooms at Trinity – to finish work on a long essay on the drawings of Poussin. The weather was hot, and London impossible, and I had a deadline from Brevoort & Klein. War had broken out in Spain, and people were excitedly preparing to go off and fight. I must say it never occurred to me to join them. Not that I was afraid – as I was later to discover, I was physically not uncourageous, except on one unfortunately memorable occasion – or that I did not appreciate the significance of what was happening in Spain. It is just that I have never been one for the grand gesture. The John Cornford type of manufactured hero struck me as self-regarding and, if I may be allowed the oxymoron, profoundly frivolous. For an Englishman to rush out and get his head shot off in some arroyo in Seville or wherever seemed to me merely an extreme form of rhetoric, excessive, wasteful, futile. The man of action would despise me for such sentiments – I would not have dreamed of expressing them to Felix Hartmann, for example – but I have a different definition of what constitutes effective action. The worm in the bud is more thorough than the wind that shakes the bough. This is what the spy knows. It is what I know.

Alastair, of course, was in a high state of excitement over the events in Spain. The remarkable thing about the Spanish war – about all ideological wars, I suppose – was the fiery single-mindedness, not to say simple-mindedness, that it produced in otherwise quite sophisticated people. All doubts were banished, all questions answered, all quibbling done with. Franco was Moloch and the Popular Front were the children in white whom the West was offering to the fiend in heartless and craven sacrifice. The fact that Stalin, while flying to the aid of the Spanish Loyalists, was at the same time systematically extermi-nating all opposition to his rule at home, was conveniently ignored. I was a Marxist, yes, but I never had anything other than contempt for the Iron Man; such an *unappetising* person.

'Come on, Victor!' Alastair said, wrenching the stem of his pipe from its socket and shaking dribbles of black goo out of it. 'These are dangerous times. The Revolution has to be protected.'

I sighed and smiled.

'The city must be destroyed in order to save it, is that what you mean?'

We were sitting in deckchairs in the sun in the little back garden below the windows of his rooms in Trinity. Alastair tended the garden himself and was touchingly proud of it. There were roses and snapdragons, and the lawn was as smooth as a billiard table. He poured out tea from a blue pot, daintily holding the lid in place with a fingertip, and slowly, gloomily, shook his head.

'Sometimes I wonder about your commitment to the cause, Victor.'

'Yes,' I said, 'and if we were in Moscow you could denounce me to the secret police.' He gave me a wounded look. 'Oh,

Alastair,' I said wearily, 'for goodness' sake, you know as well as I what's going on over there. We're not blind, we're not fools.'

He poured tea into his saucer and slurped it up through exaggeratedly pouted lips; it was one of his ways of demonstrating class solidarity; it struck me as ostentatious and, I'm afraid, slightly repulsive.

'Yes, but what we *are* is believers,' he said, and smacked his lips and smiled, and leaned back on the faded striped canvas of the deckchair, balancing the cup and saucer on the shelf of his little pot belly. He looked so smug, in his sleeveless Fair Isle pullover and brown boots, that I wanted to hit him.

'You sound like a priest,' I said.

He grinned at me, showing the gap between his rabbity front teeth.

'Funny you should say that,' he said. 'There's a chap coming round shortly who used to be a priest. You'll like him.'

'You forget,' I said sourly, 'I come from a family of clergymen.'

'Well, you'll have a lot to talk about then, won't you.'

Presently Alastair's gyp appeared, a cringing, forelock-pulling semi-dwarf – God, how I despised those people! – to announce that there was a visitor. Felix Hartmann wore black: black suit, black shirt, and, remarkably in the surroundings, a pair of narrow, patent-leather black shoes as delicate as dancing pumps. As he crossed the lawn to meet us I noticed how he tried to hide his limp. Alastair introduced us and we shook hands. I should like to be able to say that a spark of excited recognition of each other's potential passed between us, but I suspect that significant first encounters only take on their aura of significance in retrospect. His handshake, a brief pressure quickly released, communicated nothing other than a mild and not wholly impolite indifference. (Yet what a strange ceremony it is, shaking hands; I always see it in heraldic terms: solemn, antiquated, a little ridiculous, slightly indecent, and yet, for all that, peculiarly affecting.) Felix's soft, Slavic eyes, the colour of toffee – that toffee which, when I would come home from Miss Molyneaux's school on winter evenings, Hettie used to help me make from burnt sugar poured out in a pan – rested on my face a moment, and then he turned them vaguely aside. It was one of his tactics to seem always just a bit distracted; he would pause for a second in the middle of a sentence and frown, then give himself a sort of infinitesimal shake, and go on again. He had a habit also, when being spoken to, no matter how earnestly, of turning very slowly on his heel and limping a little way away, head bowed, and then stopping to stand with his back turned and hands clasped behind him, so that one could not be sure that he was still listening to what one was saying, or had sunk into altogether more profound communings with himself. I could never finally decide whether these mannerisms were genuine, or if he was merely trying things out, rehearsing in mid-play, as it were, like an actor walking into the wings to have a quick practice of a particularly tricky move while the rest of the cast went on with the drama. (I hope you do not wonder, Miss V., at my use of the word *genuine* in this context; if you do, you understand nothing about us and our little world.)

'Felix is in furs,' Alastair said, and giggled.

Hartmann smiled wanly.

'You are such a wit, Alastair,' he said.

We stood about awkwardly on the grass, the three of us, there being only two deckchairs, and Felix Hartmann studied the glossy toes of his shoes. Presently Alastair, squinting in the sunlight, put down his cup and muttered something about fetching another chair, and scuttled off. Hartmann shifted his gaze to the roses and sighed. We listened to the buzz of summer about us.

'You are the art critic?' he said.

'More an historian.'

'But of art?'

'Yes.'

He nodded, looking now in the vicinity of my knees.

'I know something of art,' he said.

'Oh, yes?' I waited, but he offered nothing more. 'I have a great fondness for the German baroque,' I said, speaking over-loudly. 'Do you know that style at all?'

He shook his head.

'I am not German,' he said, with a lugubrious intonation, frowning to one side.

And we were silent again. I wondered if I had offended him somehow, or if I were being a bore, and I felt faintly annoyed; we cannot all be winged in skirmishes in the Carpathians. Alastair came back with a third deckchair and set it up with much struggling and cursing, pinching his thumb badly in the process. He offered to make a fresh pot of tea but Hartmann silently declined, with a throwaway motion of his left hand. We sat down. Alastair heaved a happy sigh; gardeners have a particularly irritating way of sighing when they contemplate their handiwork.

'Hard to think of Spain and a war starting,' he said, 'while we sit here in the sun.' He touched the sleeve of Felix's black suit. 'Aren't you hot, old chap?'

'Yes,' Hartmann said, nodding again with that peculiar mixture of indifference and frowning solemnity.

Pause. The bells of King's began to chime, the bronzen strokes beating thickly high up through the dense blue air.

'Alastair thinks we should all go to Spain and fight Franco,' I said lightly, and was startled and even a little unnerved when Hartmann lifted his gaze and fixed it on me briefly, with a positively theatrical intensity.

'And perhaps he is right?' he said.

If not a Hun, I thought, then Austrian, surely – somewhere German-speaking, at any rate; all that gloom and soulfulness could only be the result of an upbringing among compound words.

Alastair sat forward earnestly and clasped his hands between his knees, putting on that look, like that of a constipated bulldog, that always heralded an attack of polemics. Before he could get started, however, Hartmann said to me:

'Your theory of art: what is it?'

Strange now to think how natural a question like that seemed then. In those days we were constantly asking each other such things, demanding explanations, justifications; challenging; defending; attacking. Everything was gloriously open to question. Even the most dogmatic Marxists among us knew the giddy and intoxicating excitement of exposing to doubt all that we were supposed to believe in, of taking our essential faith, like a delicate and fantastically intricate piece of spun glass, and letting it drop into the slippery and possibly malevolent hands of a fellow ideologue. It fed the illusion that words are actions. We were young.

'Oh, don't get him started,' said Alastair. 'We'll have significant form and the autonomy of the object until the cows come home. His only belief is in the uselessness of art.'

'I prefer the word inutility,' I said. 'And anyway, my position has shifted on that, as on much else.'

There was a beat of silence and the atmosphere thickened briefly. I glanced from one of them to the other, seeming to detect an invisible something passing between them, not so much a signal as a sort of silent token, like one of those almost impalpable acknowledgements that adulterers exchange when they are in company. The phenomenon was strange to me still but would become increasingly familiar the deeper I penetrated into the secret world. It marks that moment when a group of initiates, in the midst of the usual prattle, begin to go to work on a potential recruit. It was always the same: the pause, the brief tumescence in the air, then the smooth resumption of whatever the subject was, though all, even the target, were aware that in fact the subject had been irretrievably changed. Later, when I was an initiate myself, this little secret flurry of speculative activity always stirred me deeply. Nothing so tentative, nothing so thrilling, excepting, of course, certain manoeuvres in the sexual chase.

I knew what was going on; I knew I was being recruited. It was exciting and alarming and slightly ludicrous, like being summoned from the sideline to play in the senior-school game. It was *amusing*. This word no longer carries the weight that it did for us. Amusement was not amusement, but a test of the authenticity of a thing, a verification of its worth. The most serious matters amused us. This was something the Felix Hartmanns never understood.

'Yes,' I said, 'it is the case that I did once argue for the primacy of pure form. So much in art is merely anecdotal, which is what attracts the bourgeois sentimentalist. I wanted something harsh and studied, the truly lifelike: Poussin, Cézanne, Picasso. But these new movements – this surrealism, these arid abstractions – what do they have to do with the actual world, in which men live and work and die?'

Alastair did a soundless slow handclap. Hartmann, frowning thoughtfully at my ankle, ignored him.

'Bonnard?' he said. Bonnard was all the rage just then.

'Domestic bliss. Saturday night sex.'

'Matisse?'

'Hand-tinted postcards.'

'Diego Rivera?'

'A true painter of the people, of course. A great painter.'

He ignored the lip-biting little smile I could not suppress; I remember catching Bernard Berenson smiling like that once, when he was making a blatantly false attribution of a tawdry piece of fakery some unfortunate American was about to purchase at a fabulous price.

'As great as . . . Poussin?' he said.

I shrugged. So he knew my interests. Someone had been talking to him. I looked at Alastair, but he was engrossed in examining his sore thumb.

'The question does not arise,' I said. 'Comparative criticism is essentially Fascist. Our task' – how gently I applied the pressure on that *our* – 'is to emphasise the progressive elements in art. In times such as this, surely that is the critic's first and most important duty.'

There followed another significant silence, while Alastair sucked his thumb and Hartmann sat and nodded to himself and I gazed off, showing him my profile, all proletarian modesty and firmness of resolve, looking, I felt sure, like one of those figures in fanned-out relief on the pedestal of a socialist-realist monument. It is odd, how the small dishonesties are the ones that snag in the silk of the mind. Diego Rivera – God! Alastair was watching me now with a sly grin.

'More to the point,' he said to Hartmann, 'Victor's looking forward to being made Minister of Culture when the Revolution comes, so he can ransack the stately homes of England.'

'Indeed,' I said, prim as a postmistress, 'I see no reason why masterpieces pillaged by our hunting fathers in successive European wars should not be taken back for the people and housed in a central gallery.'

Alastair heaved himself forward again, his deckchair groaning, and tapped Hartmann on the knee. 'You see?' he said happily. It was obvious he was referring to something more than my curatorial ambitions; Alastair prided himself on his talent-spotting abilities. Hartmann frowned, a pained little frown like that of a great singer when his accompanist hits a wrong note, and this time made a point of paying him no heed.

'So, then,' he said to me slowly, with a judicious tilt of the head, 'you are opposed to the bourgeois interpretation of art as luxury—'

'Bitterly opposed.'

'—and consider the artist to have a clear political duty.'

'Like the rest of us,' I said, 'the artist must contribute to the great forward movement of history.'

Oh, I was shameless, like a hoyden set on losing her virginity.

'Or . . . ?' he said.

'Or he becomes redundant, and his art descends to the level of mere decoration and self-indulgent revery . . .'

Everything went still then, subsided softly to a stop, and I was left hanging in vague consternation; I had thought we were in the middle and not at the end of this interesting discussion. Hartmann was looking at me directly for what seemed the first time, and I realised two things: first, that he had not for a moment been taken in by my stout declarations of political rectitude, and, second, that instead of being disappointed or offended, he was on the contrary gratified that I had lied to him, or at least that I had offered a carefully tinted version of what might be the truth. Now, this is difficult; this is the nub of the matter, in a way. It is hard for anyone who has not given himself wholeheartedly to a belief (and I say again, Miss V., that is how it is: you *give* yourself to it, it does not fall upon you like sanctifying grace from Heaven) to appreciate how the believer's conscious mind can separate itself into many compartments containing many, conflicting, dogmas. These are not sealed compartments; they are like the cells of a battery (I think this is how a battery works), over which the electrical charge plays, leaping from one cell to another, gathering force and direction as it goes. You put in the acid of world-historical necessity and the distilled water of pure theory and connect up your points and with a flash and a shudder the patched-together monster of commitment, sutures straining and ape brow clenched, rises in jerky slow motion from Dr Diabolo's operating table. That is how it is, for the likes of us – I mean the likes of Felix Hartmann, and myself, though not, perhaps, Alastair, who was essentially an innocent, with an innocent's faith in the justice and inevitability of the cause. So when Hartmann looked at me that day, in the lemon-and-blue light of Psyche's sun-dazzled garden in Cambridge, as the Falangist guns were firing five hundred miles to the south of us, he saw that I was exactly what was required: harder than Alastair, more biddable than

Boy, a casuist who would split an ideological hair to an infinitesimal extreme of thinness – in other words, a man in need of a faith (*No one more devout than a sceptic on his knees –* Querell *dixit*), and so there was nothing left to say. Hartmann distrusted words, and made it a point of pride never to use more of them than the occasion required.

Alastair suddenly stood up and began fussily gathering the teacups, making a great show of not treading on our toes, and walked off, muttering, with a sort of resentful flounce, bearing the tea tray aloft before him like a grievance: I suppose he too was a little in love with Felix – more than a little, probably – and was jealous, now that his matchmaking exercise had proved so successful so quickly. Hartmann, however, seemed hardly to notice his going. He was leaning forward intently, head bowed, with his elbows on his knees and his hands clasped (it must be a mark of true grace to be able to sit in a deckchair without looking like a discommoded frog). After a moment he glanced up at me sideways with a crooked, oddly feral smile.

'You know Boy Bannister, of course,' he said.

'Of course; everyone knows Boy.'

He nodded, still with that fierce leer, an eyetooth glinting.

'He is going to make a journey to Russia,' he said. 'It's time for him to become disenchanted with the Soviet system.' By now his look was positively wolfish. 'Perhaps you would care to accompany him? I could arrange it. We – they – have many art treasures. In public galleries, of course.'

We both laughed at once, which left me feeling uneasy. It will sound strange, coming from me, but the complicity suggested by that kind of thing – the soft laugh exchanged, the quick pressure of the hand, the covert wink – always strikes me as faintly improper, and shaming, a small conspiracy got up against a world altogether more open and decent than I or my accomplice in intimacy could ever hope to be. Despite all Felix Hartmann's dark charm and elegant intensity, I really preferred the goons and the thugs with whom I had to deal later on, such as poor Oleg Kropotsky, with his awful suits and his pasty face like that of a debauched baby; at least they made no bones about the ugliness of the struggle in which we were unlikely partners. But that was much later; as yet the eager virgin was only at the kissing stage, and still intact. I smiled back into Felix Hartmann's face and with an insouciance I did not fully feel said that yes, a couple of weeks in the arms of great Mother Rus might be just the thing to harden up my ideological position and strengthen my ties of solidarity with the proletariat. At this his look turned wary – the Comrades never were very strong in the irony department – and he frowned again at his shiny toecaps and began to speak earnestly of his experiences in the war against the Whites: the burned villages, the raped children, the old man he had come upon one rainy evening somewhere in the Crimea, crucified on his own barn door, and still alive.

'I shot him through the heart,' he said, making a pistol of finger and thumb and silently firing it. 'There was nothing else to do for him. I see his eyes still in my dreams.'

I nodded, and I too looked grimly at my shoes, to show how thoroughly ashamed I was of that facetious reference to Holy Mother Russia; but just below the lid of my sobriety there was squeezed a cackle of disgraceful laughter, as if there were an evil, merry little elf curled up inside me, hand clapped to mouth and cheeks bulging and weasel eyes malignantly aglitter. It was not that I thought the horrors of war were funny, or Hartmann completely ridiculous; that was not the sort of laughter that was threatening to break out. Perhaps laughter is the wrong word. What I felt at moments such as this – and there would be many such: solemn, silent, fraught with portent – was a kind of hysteria, made up of equal parts of disgust and shame and appalling mirth. I cannot explain it – or could, perhaps, but do not want to. (One can know too much about oneself, that is a thing I have learned.) Someone has written somewhere, I wish I could remember who, of the sensation of gleeful anticipatory horror he experiences in the concert hall when in the middle of a movement the orchestra grinds to a halt and the virtuoso draws back his arm preparatory to plunging his bow into the quivering heart of the cadenza. Although the writer is a cynic, and as a Marxist (am I a Marxist, still?) I should disapprove of him, I know exactly what he means and secretly applaud his baleful honesty. Belief is hard, and the abyss is always there, under one's feet.

Alastair came back. Seeing Hartmann and me sunk in what must have looked like silent communion, and perhaps was, he grew more cross than ever.

'Well,' he said, 'have you decided the future of art?'

When neither of us responded – Hartmann looked up at him with a vacant frown as if trying to remember who he was – he threw himself down on the deckchair, which gave a loud, pained grunt of protest, and clamped his stubby arms across his chest and glared at a bush of shell-pink roses.

'What do you think, Alastair?' I said. 'Mr Hartmann—'

'Felix,' Hartmann said smoothly, 'please.'

'—has offered me a trip to Russia.'

There was something about Alastair – the combination of that not quite convincing bulldog ferocity and an almost girlish tentativeness, not to mention the hobnailed boots and hairy tweeds – that made it impossible to resist being cruel to him.

'Oh?' he said. He would not look at me, but folded his arms more tightly still, while under his glare the roses seemed to blush a deeper shade of pink. 'How interesting for you.'

'Yes,' I said blithely, 'Boy and I are going to go.'

'And one or two others,' Hartmann murmured, looking at his fingernails.

'Boy, eh?' Alastair said, and essayed a nasty little laugh. 'He'll probably get you both arrested on your first night in Moscow.'

'Yes,' I said, faltering a little (*Others? – what others?*), 'I'm sure we'll have some amusing times.'

Hartmann was still examining his nails.

'Of course, we shall arrange guides for you, and so on,' he said.

Yes, Comrade Hartmann, I'm sure you will.

Did I mention that we were all smoking away like railway engines? Everyone smoked then, we stumbled about everywhere in clouds of tobacco fumes. I recall with a pang, in this Puritan age, the Watteauesque delicacy of those grey-blue, gauzy billows we breathed out everywhere on the air, suggestive of twilight and misted grass and thickening shadows under great trees – although Alastair's belching pipe was more the Potteries than Versailles.

'I'd like to see Russia,' Alastair said, his irritation giving way to wistfulness. 'Moscow, the Nevsky Prospect . . .'

Hartmann coughed.

'Perhaps,' he said, 'another time . . .'

Alastair did a sort of flip and wriggle, as if the canvas of his chair had turned into a trampoline.

'Oh, I say, old chap,' he said, 'I didn't mean . . . I mean I . . .'

Where exactly had it occurred, I wondered, the moment when Hartmann and I had joined in tacit alliance against poor Alastair? Or was it only me? – I am not sure that Hartmann was capable of keeping in mind anyone or anything that was not the immediate object of his attention. Yes, probably it was just me, pirouetting alone there, a Nijinsky of vanity and petty spitefulness. I do not want to exaggerate the matter, but I cannot help wondering if the disappointment he suffered that day – no gallops across the steppes, no earnest talks with horny-handed sons of the soil, no stroll down Moscowburg's Nevsky Prospect with a handsome spoiled priest by his side – was not a biggish pebble lobbed on to the steadily accumulating mountain of woe that Psyche would disappear under twenty years later, crouched on his bunk in his dank room and gnawing on a poisoned apple. I have said it before, I shall say it again: it is the minor treacheries that weigh most heavily on the heart.

'Tell me,' I said to Hartmann, when Alastair had stopped bouncing on the springs of his embarrassment, 'how many will be travelling?'

I had a terrible vision of myself being shown around a tractor factory in the company of psoriatic City clerks and dumpy, fur-hatted spinsters from the Midlands, and cloth-capped Welsh miners who after borscht and bear-paw dinners in our hotel would entertain us with evenings of glee-singing. Do not imagine, Miss Vandeleur, that Marxists, at least the ones of my variety, are gregarious. Man is only lovable in the multitude, and at a good distance.

Hartmann smiled, and showed me his upturned innocent hands.

'Don't worry,' he said. 'Just some people. You will find them interesting.'

I would not.

'Party people?' I said.

(By the way, Miss V., you do know, don't you, that I was never a Party member? None of us was. Even at Cambridge in my – picture an ironic smile here – firebrand days, the question of joining never arose. The Apostles was Party enough for us. We were undercover agents before we had heard of the Comintern or had a Soviet recruiter whispering blandishments in our ears.)

Hartmann shook his head, still smiling, and lightly let drop his dark-shadowed, long-lashed eyelids.

'Just . . . people,' he said. 'Trust me.'

Ah, trust: now *there* is a word to which I could devote a page or two, its shades and gradations, the nuances it took on or shed according to circumstance. In my time I have put my trust in some of the most egregious scoundrels one could ever hope not to meet, while there were things in my life, and I am not speaking only of sins, that I would not have revealed to my own father. In this I was not so different from other people, burdened with far fewer secrets than I was, as a moment's reflection will show. Would you, dear Miss Vandeleur, tell the Admiral of what you and your young man get up to below decks in Golders Green of a night? If my life has taught me anything it is that in these matters there are no absolutes, of trust, or belief, or anything else. And a good thing, too. (No, I suppose I am not a Marxist, still.)

Above us in the dream-blue zenith a tiny silver plane was laboriously buzzing. I thought of bombs falling on the white towns of Spain and was struck, as earlier Alastair had been, by the hardly comprehensible incongruity of time and circumstance; how could I be here, while all that was happening there? Yet I could feel nothing for the victims; distant deaths are weightless.

Alastair attempted to introduce the topic of Ireland and Sinn Fein, but was ignored, and went back to sulking again, and refolded his arms and glared off, trying, it seemed, to wither those poor roses on their stems.

'Tell me,' I said to Hartmann, 'what did you mean when you said it was time for Boy to become disenchanted with Marxism?'

Hartmann had a peculiar way of holding a cigarette, in his left hand, between the third and middle fingers and cocked against his thumb, so that when he lifted it to his lips he seemed to be not smoking, but taking a tiny sip of something from a slim, white phial. A standing shape of smoke, the same shade of silver-grey as the aeroplane, that was gone now, drifted sideways away from us on the pulsing light of noon.

'Mr Bannister is a . . . a person of consequence, shall we say,' Hartmann said carefully, squinting into the middle distance. 'His connections are excellent. His family, his friends—'

'Not forgetting his boyfriends,' Alastair said sourly, and, I could see, immediately regretted it. Hartmann did his smiling nod again, with eyelids lowered, dismissing him.

'The advantage of him for us – you understand by now, I am sure, who it is I mean when I say *us*? – the advantage is that he can move easily at any level of society, from the Admiralty to the pubs of the East End. That is important, in a country such as this, in which the class divisions are so strong.' Abruptly he sat up straight and clapped his hands on his knees. 'So we have plans for him. It will be, of course, a long-term campaign. And the first thing, the truly important thing, is for him to be seen to abandon his past beliefs. You understand?' I understood. I said nothing. He glanced at me. 'You have doubts?'

'I imagine,' Alastair said, trying to sound arch, 'that Victor, like me, finds it hard to believe that Boy will be capable of the kind of discipline necessary for the campaign of dissimulation you have in mind.'

Hartmann pursed his lips and examined the ashy tip of his cigarette.

'Perhaps,' he said mildly, 'you do not know him as well as you think you do. He is a man of many sides.'

'As we all are,' I said.

He nodded with excessive courtesy.

'But yes. That is why we are here' – by which he meant, that is why *I* am here – 'having this important conversation, which to the ears of the uninitiated would seem no more than an aimless chat between three civilised gentlemen in this charming garden on a beautiful summer day.'

Suddenly I found his Mitteleuropan unctuousness intensely irritating.

'Am *I* one of the initiated?' I said.

He turned his head slowly and let his glance slide over me from toe to brow.

'I am trusting that you are,' he said. 'Or that you *will* be . . .'

There it was again, that word: trust. Yet I could not resist that hooded, meaning gaze. Slender, black suited, with his pale, priestly hands clasped before him, he sat in the sunlight not so much watching as attending me, waiting for . . . for what? For me to surrender to him. Fleetingly, unnervingly, I understood what it would be like to be a woman whom he desired. My own gaze faltered and slipped as the ratchets of my self-possession disengaged for a second with a soft jolt, and I brushed busily at a non-existent patch of dust on the sleeve of my jacket and in a voice that sounded to my ears like a querulous squeak I said:

'I hope your trust is not misplaced.'

Hartmann smiled and relaxed and sat back on his chair with a look of satisfaction, and I turned my face aside, feeling gulpy and shy all of a sudden. Yes, how deceptively light they are, the truly decisive steps we take in life.

'Your ship will sail in three weeks' time from London port,' he said. 'Amsterdam, Helsinki, Leningrad. She is called the *Liberation*. A good name, don't you think?'

*

A good name, but a poor thing. The *Liberation* was a blunt-ended, low-slung merchant vessel carrying a cargo of pig iron, whatever that is, destined for the People's smelters. The North Sea was rough, a jostling waste of clay-coloured waves, each one half the size of a house, through which the little ship snuffled and heaved, like an iron pig, indeed, going along with its snout rising and falling in the troughs and tail invisibly twirling behind us. Our captain was a black-bearded Dutchman of vast girth who had spent the early years of his career in the East Indies engaged in activities which from his colourful but deliberately vague descriptions of them sounded to me suspiciously like the slave trade. He spoke of the Soviet Union with jovial detestation. His crew, made up of a medley of races, were a slovenly, furtive, piratical-looking bunch. Boy could hardly believe his luck; he spent most of the voyage below decks, changing bunks and partners with each watch. We would catch the noise of drunken revels rising from the bowels of the ship, with Boy's voice dominant, singing sea shanties and roaring for rum. 'What a filthy gang!' he would croak happily, emerging red-eyed and barefoot on to the passenger deck in search of cigarettes and something to eat. 'Talk about close quarters!' It always baffled me, how Boy could get away with so much. Despite his disgraceful doings on that voyage, he remained a favourite at Captain Kloos's table, and even when a complaint was lodged against him by one of the younger crewmen, a Friesian Islander pining for his girl, the matter was hushed up.

'It's that famous charm of his,' Archie Fletcher said sourly. 'Some day it will let him down, when he's old and fat and clapped-out.'

Fletcher, himself a charmless hetero, was disapproving of our party in general, considering it far too frolicsome for a delegation handpicked by the Comintern to be the spearhead of its English undercover drive. (Yes, Miss V., I mean Sir Archibald Fletcher, who today is one of the most poisonous spokesmen of the Tory right; how we do oscillate, we ideologues.) There was also a couple of Cambridge dons – pipes, dandruff, woollen mufflers – whom I knew slightly; Bill Darling, a sociologist from the LSE, who even then I could see was too neurotic and excitable to be a spy; and a rather pompous young aristo named Belvoir, the same Toby Belvoir who in the Sixties would renounce his title to serve in a Labour cabinet, for which piece of Socialist good faith he was rewarded with a junior ministry in charge of sport or some such. So there we were, a boatload of superannuated boys, bucketing through autumn storms along the Skagerrak and down into the Baltic, on our way to encounter the future at first-hand. Needless to say, what I see is a *Ship of Fools* by one of the anonymous medieval masters, with curly whitecaps and a stylised porpoise bustling through the waves, and our party, in robes and funny hats, crowded on the poop deck, peering eastwards, an emblem of hope and fortitude and, yes, innocence.

I know that this, my first and last visit to Russia, should have been, and perhaps was, one of the formative experiences of my life, yet my recollections of it are curiously blurred, like the features of a weather-worn statue; the form is still there, the impression of significance and stony weight: only the details are largely gone. Petersburg was an astonishment, of course. I had the sense, looking down those noble prospects (poor Psyche!), of a flare of trumpets sounding all around me, announcing the commencement of some grand imperial venture: the declaration of a war, the inauguration of a peace. Years later, when the Comrades were urging me to defect, I passed a sleepless night weighing in the scales the losing of the Louvre against the gaining of the Hermitage, and the choice, I can tell you, was not as straightforward as I might have expected.

In Moscow there were few architectural magnificences to distract one's attention from the people passing by in those impossibly wide, sleet-grey streets. The weather was unseasonably cold, with a wind in which one could feel already the glass-sharp edge of winter. We had been warned of shortages, and although the worst of the famines in the countryside were over by then, even the most enthusiastic among our party found it hard, in contemplating those hunched crowds, not to recognise the marks of deprivation and dull fear. Yes, Miss V., I can be honest: Stalin's Russia was a horrible place. But we understood that what was happening here was only a start, you see. The temporal factor is what you must always keep in mind if you wish to understand us and our politics. The present we could forgive for the sake of the future. And then, it was a matter of choosing; as we trooped past the glorious monuments of Peter's northern Venice, or tossed in our lumpy beds in the Moscova Nova, or stared in a bored stupor through the grimy windows of a rattling railway carriage at mile after mile of empty fields on the way south to Kiev, we could hear in our mind's ear, off to the west, faintly but with unignorable distinctness, the stamp and rattle of drilling armies. Hitler or Stalin: could life be simpler?

And there was art. Here, I told myself, here, for the first time since the Italian Renaissance, art had become a public medium, available to all, a lamp to illumine even the humblest of lives. By art, I need not tell you, I meant the art of the past: socialist-realism I passed over in tactful silence. (An aphorism: *Kitsch is to art as physics is to mathematics – its technology*.) But can you imagine my excitement at the possibilities that seemed to open before me in Russia? Art liberated for the populace – Poussin for the Proletariat! Here was being built a society which would apply to its own workings the rules of order and harmony by which art operates; a society in which the artist would no longer be dilettante or romantic rebel, pariah or parasite; a society whose art would be more deeply rooted in ordinary life than any since medieval times. What a prospect, for a sensibility as hungry for certainties as mine was!

I recall a discussion on the topic that I had with Boy on the last night before we docked in Leningrad. I say discussion, but really it was one of Boy's lectures, for he was drunk and in hectoring mood as he expounded what he grandly called his Theory of the Decline of Art under Bourgeois Values, which I had heard many times before, and which anyway I think was largely filched from a refugee Czech professor of aesthetics whom he had hired to give a talk on the BBC but whose accent was so impenetrable the talk could not be broadcast. It was hardly original, consisting mainly of sweeping generalisations on the glory of the Renaissance and the humanistic self-delusions of the Enlightenment, and all boiled down in the end to the thesis that in our time only the totalitarian state could legitimately assume the role of patron of the arts. I believed it, of course – I still do, surprising as it may seem – but that night, stimulated, I suppose, by Hollands gin and the needle-sharp northern air, I thought it a lot of fatuous twaddle, and said so. Really, I was not prepared to be lectured to by the likes of Boy Bannister, especially on art. He stopped, and glared at me. He had taken on that bulbous, froggy look – thick lips thicker than ever, eyes bulging and slightly crossed – that the combination of drink and polemics always produced in him. He was sitting cross-legged on the end of my bunk in shirt-sleeves, his braces loosed and his flies half unbuttoned; his big feet were bare and crusted with dirt.

'Trespassing on your territory, am I?' he said, all scowl and slur. 'Touchy old Vic.'

'You don't know what you're talking about, that's the trouble,' I said.

As so often when he was stood up to, he chose not to fight. The bloodshot scowl slackened and slid.

'America,' he said after a while, nodding ponderously to himself. 'America is the real bloody enemy. Art, culture, all that: nothing. America will sweep it all away, into the trash-can. You'll see.'

An enormous whey-faced moon – which, I noticed, bore a striking resemblance to his own large pale head and swollen visage – was swinging gently in the porthole at his shoulder. The wind had abated and the night was calm, with the mildest of breezes. The sky at midnight was still light at the edges. I have always been susceptible to the romance of shipboard.

'What about the Germans?' I said. 'You don't think they are a threat?'

'Oh, the Germans,' he growled, with a drunkenly mountain-ous shrug. 'We'll have to fight them, of course. First they'll beat us, then the Americans will beat them, and that'll be that. We'll be just another Yank state.'

'That's what Querell thinks, too.'

He batted the air with a big soiled hand.

'Querell – pah.'

The ship's hooter blared; we were approaching landfall.

'And there's Russia, of course,' I said.

He nodded, slowly, solemnly.

'Well, it's the only hope, old chap, isn't it?' I should remark that from the start of the voyage Boy and I had found ourselves somewhat estranged. I believe Boy had been annoyed to discover that I was to accompany him on this momentous visit.

He had thought he had been the only one of our circle to be chosen. He glanced at me now, sullen and suspicious, from under his brows. 'Don't you think it's the only hope?'

'Of course.'

We were silent for a time, nursing our tooth-glasses of gin, then Boy in a tone that was too casual said:

'Have you a contact in Moscow?'

'No,' I answered, immediately on the alert. 'What do you mean?'

He shrugged again.

'Oh, I just wondered if Hartmann had given you a name, or something. You know: a contact. Nothing like that?'

'No.'

'Hmm.'

He brooded glumly. Boy adored the trappings of the secret world, the code names and letter-drops and the rest. Brought up on Buchan and Henty, he saw his life in the lurid terms of an old-fashioned thriller and himself dashing through the preposterous plot heedless of all perils. In this fantasy he was always the hero, of course, never the villain in the pay of a foreign power.

He need not have felt cast down. No sooner had we arrived in the capital – tank-grey sky, great sloping spaces spectrally peopled with ugly, disproportionate statuary, and always that constant, icy wind cutting into one's face like a flung handful of ground glass – than he disappeared for an afternoon, and turned up at dinnertime looking insufferably pleased with himself. When I asked where he had been he only grinned and tapped a finger along the side of his nose, and peered in happy horror at his plate and said loudly:

'Good Christ, is this to eat, or has it been eaten already?'

My turn came to be singled out. It was on our last night in Moscow. I was walking back to the hotel, having been at the Kremlin Palace for most of the day. As always after a long time spent among pictures (or an hour in bed with a boy), I felt light-headed and tottery, and at first did not register the motor car chugging along beside me at walking speed. (Really, that is the kind of thing they did; I suspect they got it from Hollywood movies, of which they were depressingly fond.) Then, with the car still moving, the door opened and a tall, thin young man in a tightly belted, ankle-length black leather overcoat stepped nimbly on to the pavement and approached me rapidly at a sort of stiff-armed march, his heels coming down so violently on the pavement it seemed they must strike sparks from the stone. He wore a soft hat and black leather gloves. He had a narrow, hard face, but his eyes were large and soft and amber-coloured, and made me think, incongruously, of my stepmother's warm, wistful gaze. A hot qualm of fear was spreading slowly upwards from the base of my spine. He addressed me in a harsh growl – all Russians sounded like drunks to me – and I began flusteredly to protest that I did not understand the language, but then realised that he was speaking in English, or an approximation of it. Would I please to come with him. He had car. He indicated car, which had come to a stop and, the engine still going, stood shuddering like a hot horse.

'This is my hotel,' I said, in a loud, foolish voice. 'I am staying here.' I pointed to the marble entryway, where the doorman, a blue-chinned heavy in a dirty brown uniform, stood looking on with knowing amusement. I do not know what sort of sanctuary I thought I was claiming. 'My passport is in my room,' I said; it sounded as if I were reading from a phrase-book. 'I can fetch it if you wish.'

The man in the leather coat laughed. Now, I must say something about this laugh, which was peculiar to Soviet officialdom, and especially prevalent among the security establishment. It varied from Leathercoat's brief, bitten-off snicker to the melodeon wheeze of the ones at the top, but essentially it was the same wherever one heard it. It was not the mirthless snarl of the Gestapo man, nor the fat chuckle of a Chinese torturer. There was real, if bleak, amusement in it, almost, one might say, a kind of attenuated delight; Here's another one, it seemed to say, another poor dolt who thinks he has some weight in the world. The chief ingredient of this laugh, however, was a sort of bored weariness. The one who laughed had seen everything, every form of bluster and bombast, every failed attempt at cajoling and ingratiation; had seen it, and then had seen the abasements, the tears, had heard the cries for mercy and the heels clattering backwards over the flagstones and the cell doors banging shut. I exaggerate. I mean, I am exaggerating my perspicacity. It is only with hindsight that I am able to dismantle this laugh into its component parts.

The car was a big black ugly high-built thing, shaped like one of those loaves that in my childhood were called turnovers, with a domed roof and a long, dented snout. The driver, who seemed hardly more than a boy, did not turn to look at me, but loosed the brake a second before I was seated, so that I was thrown back on the upholstery, my head bobbing and heart crouched in fright in a corner of its cage, as we shot off along the wide avenue at a lumbering but reckless speed. Leathercoat took off his hat and held it primly on his lap. His short fair hair was damp with sweat, so that the pink scalp showed through, and was moulded by the crown of the hat into a pointed shape which was almost endearing. A bit of dried shaving soap, speckled with straw-coloured stubble, was lodged under his left earlobe. Buildings rose up in the windscreen, vast, blank-faced and, to my eyes, increasingly menacing, and then collapsed silently behind us.

'Where are you taking me?' I said.

I might not have spoken. Leathercoat was sitting bolt upright, watching the passing scene with lively interest, as if he, and not I, were the visitor. I leaned back on the seat – the upholstery smelled of sweat and cigarette smoke and something that seemed to be piss – and folded my arms. A curious calm had overtaken me. I seemed to be floating a foot above myself, supported somehow by the onward movement of the car, like a bird suspended on an air thermal. I wish I could believe this was a sign of moral bravery, but the most it seemed to be was indifference. Or is indifference another name for bravery? At last we pulled off the street and crossed a cobbled square, the tyres burbling and squeaking, and I saw the onion domes gleaming in the steel-grey twilight and realised with a start, and an unexpected, apprehensive thrill, that I was being brought back to the Kremlin.

Though not to the art gallery. We drew to a lurching stop in a crooked courtyard and, while the boy driver – who may well have been a little old man – continued sitting with the back of his head firmly turned to me, Leathercoat jumped out and hurried around to my side at a canted run and wrenched open the door before I could find the handle myself. I stepped out calmly, feeling a bit like an elderly and no longer grand lady arriving by taxi at Ascot. Immediately, as if the touch of my foot on the cobbles had operated a hidden spring, a great high set of double doors in front of me was thrown open and I found myself blinking in an expressionist wedge of somehow glutinous electric light. I hesitated, and turned my head, I don't know why – perhaps in a last wild search for a means of escape – and glanced upwards, past the high, dark-windowed walls of the surrounding buildings, that seemed to lean inwards at their tops, and saw the sky, delicate, pale and depthless, where a solitary crystalline star, like a star on a Christmas card, like the star of Bethlehem itself, stood with its stiletto point poised on an onion dome, and in that moment I realised with a sharp, precise shock that I was about to step out of one life and into another. Then a richly accented voice said warmly, 'Professor Maskell, please!' and I turned to find a short, dapper, balding man in an ill-fitting, tightly buttoned three-piece suit approaching me from the doorway with both stubby little hands outstretched. He was a dead ringer for the older Martin Heidegger, with a smudge of moustache and a sinisterly avuncular smile and little black eyes shiny as marbles. Never taking those eyes off mine, he fumbled for my hand and pressed it fervently between both of his. 'Welcome, comrade, welcome,' he said breathily, 'welcome to the Kremlin!' And I was ushered inside, and felt a tingling sensation in the middle of my back, as if that star had dropped out of the sky and stabbed me between the shoulder blades.

Mouldy corridors, ill lit, with someone standing in every other doorway – sag-suited officials, clerks in drooping cardigans, secretary-looking middle-aged women – all smiling the same worrying smile as Heidegger, and nodding mute greetings and encouragement, as if I had won a prize and was on my way to be presented with it (I had something of the same experience years later, when I was escorted through the Palace to kneel before Mrs W. and her sword). Heidegger walked at my side, gripping my arm above the elbow and murmuring rapidly in my ear. Although his English was faultless – another mark of the sinister – his accent was so thick I could not properly understand what he was saying, and in my agitation and apprehensiveness was hardly listening, anyway. We arrived at another pair of tall double doors – I was, I realised, nervously humming a snatch of Mussorgsky in my head – and Leathercoat, who had been loping nonchalantly behind us with his hat in his hand, stepped forward quickly and, like a harem guard, shoulders and head down and both arms thrust out stiffly, pushed the doors open on a vast, high-ceilinged, brown-painted room hung with an enormous chandelier that was a kind of monstrous, multiple parody of the star I had seen outside in the square. Dwarf people, or so they seemed, stood about the parquet floor, uneasily nursing empty glasses; at our appearance they all turned and for a moment seemed on the point of breaking into applause.

'You see?' Heidegger whispered in my ear, in delight and triumph, as if the room and its inhabitants were all his own work and I had been sceptical of his powers. 'Let me introduce you . . .'

I met in rapid succession the Commissar of Soviet Culture

and his wife, the mayor of somewhere ending in 'ovsk', a white-haired judge of noble mien whose name I seemed to remember from reports of the show trials, and a stout, stern young woman whom I spoke to for some minutes under the impression that she was something high up in the Ministry of Science and Technology, but who turned out to be the official interpreter assigned to me for the evening. I was given a glass of sticky pink champagne – 'Georgian,' the Culture Commissar's wife said, and made a sour face – which was the signal for a general refilling of glasses, and as the attendants like first-aid workers went round with their bottles, the tension eased and a relieved, happy hum swelled in the room.

Talk. Tedium. Jaw-ache from ceaseless smiling. Standing tensely beside me, my interpreter has begun to sweat as she struggles with the definite article, manfully stacking up sentences like so many big unhandy boxes. Her rapid-fire interventions are as much a hindrance as a help to understanding: I cannot rid myself of the sense of being dogged by an impossibly rude companion for whose behaviour I should be apologising to the people struggling to get a word in edgeways as she gabbles on. I am rescued from her briefly by a shambling giant of a man in horn-rimmed spectacles, who clamps a big square hairy paw on my wrist and leads me into a corner, where, glancing behind him first over one shoulder and then the other, he reaches into an inside pocket – dear God, what *is* he going to produce? – and brings out a worn, fat leather wallet from which he lifts reverently a set of dog-eared photographs of what I take to be his wife and a grown-up son and shows them to me and waits in silence, panting softly with emotion, while I admire them. The woman wears a print dress and half turns her face away from the camera in shyness; the crop-haired young man, arms folded across his chest as if he were strapped in a straitjacket, glares into the lens, stern and vigilant, a son of the Revolution.

'Very nice,' I say helplessly, nodding like a doll. 'Are they here tonight, your family?'

He shakes his head, gulping back a sob.

'Lost,' he says thickly, stabbing a meaty finger at the figure of the son. 'Gone.'

I do not think I want to know what he means.

Then Heidegger appears silently at my shoulder again – very soft-footed, is Heidegger – and the snaps are hastily put away, and I am led off to the other side of the room, where a door that I had taken for a part of the panelling opens, and here is another ill-lit corridor, and suddenly my heart is in my mouth as I realise with incontrovertible certainty that it is Him I am about to meet. But I am wrong. At the end of the corridor is an office, or study – big desk with green-shaded lamp, shelves of books no one has ever read, a ticker-tape machine, inactive but tense with potential, on a stand in the corner – the kind of room that in films the important man slips away to, leaving his sleek wife to entertain the guests while he makes a vital telephone call, standing silk-suited, sombre and cigaretted in the light from a half-open doorway (yes, I used to go to the pictures a lot, when they were still in black-and-white; my Patrick was a great enthusiast, and even subscribed to a magazine called, if I remember correctly, *Picturegoer*, which I sometimes furtively flicked through). I think the room is empty until there steps forward from the shadows another plumpish, balding little man, who might be Heidegger's older brother. He is dressed in one of those square, shiny suits that Soviet officials seem to have specially made for them, and wears spectacles, which, remembering them, he whips off quickly and slips into his jacket pocket, as if they are a shameful sign of weakness and decadence. He must be a man of some consequence, for I can feel Heidegger trembling faintly beside me in reigned-in excitement, like a steeplechaser waiting for the off. Once again there is no introduction, and Comrade Pinstripe does not offer to shake hands, but smiles the kind of rapidly nodding, excessively enthusiastic smile that tells me he does not speak English. Then he delivers himself, in a rolling, rapid voice, of a lengthy and, I guess, elaborately embellished address. I notice again how Russians, when they speak, seem not only drunk but at the same time look as if they are juggling a hot potato in their mouths. This is true also of working people in the part of Ireland where I was brought up; for a mad moment I wonder if I might mention this – to me interesting – correspondence, perhaps offering it as evidence of an essential class solidarity stretching from the glens of Antrim to the slopes of the Urals. Ending his peroration with a sort of trilled verbal flourish, Pinstripe makes a stiff little bow and steps one pace backwards, smugly, like a star pupil at a school speech-day. There follows an awful silence. My stomach pings and rumbles, Heidegger's shoes creak. Pinstripe, with eyebrows lifted, is smiling and nodding again, with some impatience. I realise with a start that he is awaiting a reply.

'Ah,' I say stumblingly, 'yes, well, ah.' Then pause. 'I am—' My voice is too high-pitched; I adjust it to a rumbling baritone. 'I am extremely proud and honoured to be here, in this historic place, seat of so many of our hopes. Of the hopes of so many of us.' I am doing quite well; I begin to relax. 'The Kremlin—'

Here Heidegger silences me by putting a hand on my arm and giving it a not unfriendly but definitely admonitory squeeze. He says something in Russian, at which Pinstripe looks a little piqued, though he goes to the desk and from a drawer takes out a vodka bottle and three tiny glasses, which he lines up on the desktop and with tremulous care fills them to the brim. I venture a cautious sip and wince as the cold, silvery fire slithers down my oesophagus. The two Russians, however, give a sort of shout and in unison knock back their shots with a quick toss of the head, their neck tendons cracking. On the third round Heidegger turns to me and with a roguish smile cries out, 'King George Six!' and I choke on my drink and have to have my back slapped. Then the audience is at an end. The vodka bottle is put away, along with the glasses, unwashed, and Pinstripe bows to me once more and retreats backwards out of the lamplight as if on castors, and Heidegger takes my arm again and steers me to the door, walking along quickly very close up against me, his yeasty breath caressing my cheek. The great hall is empty under its menacingly icy chandelier; not a trace of the party remains, save for a sweetish after-smell of champagne. Heidegger looks gratified, whether at the success of the occasion or the thoroughness with which it has been brought to a close, I do not know. We walk back along the damp-smelling corridor to the front door. He tells me, in an excited, feathery whisper, of a visit he once paid to Manchester. 'Such a beautiful, beautiful city. The Corn Exchange! The Free Trade Hall! Magnificent!' Leathercoat is waiting for us at the door, slouched in his long coat and still holding his hat. Heidegger, his thoughts already elsewhere, shakes my hand, smiles, bows, and – surely I am mistaken? – clicks his heels, and propels me out into the glimmering night, where my single star, my talisman, has paled into a myriad of its fellows.

*

The return trip was a far jollier affair than the voyage out. It did not start auspiciously: we were flown to Leningrad by military transport, and then went on by train to Helsinki. Finland smelled of fish and fir trees. I felt wretched. We joined an English cruise ship which had been visiting the Baltic ports. On board we found a few acquaintances from London, including the Lydon sisters, scatterbrained as ever and with that faint aura of debauchery that I always suspected they had not really earned. There was a jazz band on board, and in the evenings after dinner we danced in the cocktail lounge, and Sylvia Lydon put her cool hand in mine and pressed the sharp little points of her breasts against my shirt-front, and for a night or two it seemed something might come of it, but nothing did. By day the pair of Cambridge dons, who despite deep academic differences – something to do with Hegel's concept of the Absolute – had stuck exclusively to each other's company throughout the trip, paced the deck in all weathers with their pipes and mufflers, while Boy sat in the bar propositioning the waiters, and arguing politics with young Lord Belvoir, whose strongest impression of Russia had been a distinct sense of the shadow of the guillotine, with a consequent falling-off in his enthusiasm for the cause. This placed Boy in a quandary; normally he would have countered any sign of apostasy with a storm of argument and exhortation, but since on Felix Hartmann's advice he was himself supposed to be displaying signs of disenchantment with the Soviet system he had to perform an elaborate game of verbal hide-and-seek, and the strain was showing.

'What the hell is Bannister playing at?' Archie Fletcher wanted to know, his little pink face pinched with outrage.

'It's the shock,' I said. 'You know what they say: you should never wake a sleepwalker.'

'What? What the hell is that supposed to mean?' Archie had always disliked me.

'The dream has ended for him. He has seen the future and it doesn't work. Don't you feel that, too?'

'No, I damn well don't.'

'Well,' with a show of weary regret, 'I do.'

Archie gave me an apoplectic stare and strode off. Boy, sweating in desperation, winked at me miserably over young Belvoir's shoulder.

I never did discover the identity of Heidegger or his big brother. Boy was no help. I had assumed that he, too, on his missing afternoon, had been accosted by Leathercoat and taken to meet them, but he denied it ('Oh no, old man,' he said with a smirk, 'I'm sure the ones I talked to were *much* higher up'). Year after year I scanned the newspaper photographs of Politburo members on their balcony at the May Day parades, but in vain. Certain gaps along the rows of squat heads and daintily waving hands gave me pause: had Pinstripe stood there, before he was airbrushed out? I even took the opportunity, after the

135

war, of attending one or two stiflingly boring receptions, at the Foreign Office or the Palace, for visiting Soviet delegations, in the hope of spotting a familiar pate, balder now, or a grizzled toothbrush moustache. It was no good. Those two had disappeared, as if they had been conjured into existence solely to officiate at my ceremonial induction into the arcanum, and afterwards had been disposed of, silently and efficiently. I quizzed Felix Hartmann about them, but he only shrugged; Felix was already feeling the breath of the airbrush on his own face. Whenever I thought of that mysterious pair, in the years when I was active as an agent, I experienced a faint tremor of apprehension, like the flat smack caused in the air by an unheard, distant explosion.

I was secretly as glad as Lord Belvoir to be leaving Russia behind, though I grieved to think that I would never again see the Poussins at the Hermitage or the Cézannes at the Pushkin – or, indeed, that anonymous icon, at once poignant and stoical, darkly aglow in the depths of a tiny church I had hidden in for half an hour when I had managed to give our Intourist guide the slip one breezy sunlit morning at a crossroads in the midst of vast, barren cornfields somewhere south of Moscow. The little white ship that we took out of Helsinki, with its jazzy glitter and tinkling glasses and the Lydon girls' hard, bright, careless laughter, was an antechamber to a world that in my heart I knew I would never want to give up. Russia, I realised, was finished; what seemed like a beginning was really an end, as a wake can look like a party. Oh, probably, I told myself, the Revolution would succeed, would be made to succeed – I recalled Leathercoat's grim little laugh – but all the same, the country was doomed. It had suffered too much history. In the ship's lounge one evening I stopped to look idly at a framed map of Europe on the wall and thought the Soviet Union looked like nothing so much as a big old dying dog with its head hanging, peering westward, all rheum and slobber, barking its last barks. Boy would have been scandalised, but when I thought of Russia I knew that, unlike him, I did not have to feign disenchantment. You will laugh, Miss Vandeleur (if you do laugh, for I have never heard you do so), but what I discovered, as we ploughed our way through the Baltic's increasingly wintry waves, was that I was – as was Boy, indeed; as we all were – nothing less than an old-fashioned patriot.

I ARRIVED BACK from Russia into a smoky English autumn and went straight to Cambridge. The weather on the fens was gloomy and wet; fine rain fell over the town like drifts of silver webbing. My white-walled rooms wore a pursed, disapproving aspect, seeming to hunch a cold shoulder against me, as if they knew where I had been and what I had been up to. I had always liked this time of year, with its sense of quickening expectation, so much more manageable than spring's false alarms, but now the prospect of winter was suddenly dispiriting. I had finished my long essay on the Poussin drawings at Windsor and could not disguise from myself the fact that it was a poor, dry thing. I often ask myself whether my decision to pursue a life of scholarship – if decision is the word – was the result of an essential poverty of the soul, or if the desiccation which I sometimes suspect is the one truly distinguishing mark of my scholarship was an inevitable consequence of that decision. What I mean to say is, did the pursuit of accuracy and what I call *the right knowledge of things* quench the fires of passion in me? The fires of passion: there sounds the voice of a spoiled romantic.

I suppose that is what I meant when, at the outset, Miss Vandeleur asked me why I became a spy and I answered, before I had given myself time to think, that it was essentially a frivolous impulse: a flight from ennui and a search for diversion. The life of action, heedless, mind-numbing action, that is what I had always hankered after. Yet I had not succeeded in defining what, for me, might constitute action, until Felix Hartmann turned up and solved the question for me.

'Think of it,' he said smoothly, 'as another form of academic work. You are trained in research; well, research for us.'

We were in The Fox in Roundleigh. He had motored up from London in the afternoon and picked me up at my rooms. I had not invited him in, from a combination of shyness and distrust – distrust of myself, that is. The little world with which I had surrounded myself – my books, my prints, my Bonington, my *Death of Seneca* – was a delicate construct, and I feared it might not bear without injury the weight of Felix's scrutiny. His car was an unexpectedly fancy model, low and sleek with spoked wheels and worryingly eager-looking globe headlights, over the chrome cheeks of which, as we approached, our curved reflections slid, rippling amid a speckle of raindrops. The back seat was piled with mink coats, the polished fur agleam and sinister; they looked like a large dead soft brown bloodless beast thrown there, a yak, or yeti, or whatever it is called. Hartmann saw me looking at them, and sighed sepulchrally and said, 'Business.' The bucket seat clasped me in a muscular embrace. There was a warm, womanly afterbreath of perfume; Hartmann's love life was as covert as his spying. He drove through the rain-smeared streets at a sustained forty – that was terrifically fast in those days – skidding on the cobbles, and almost ran down one of my graduate students who was crossing the road outside Peterhouse. Beyond the town the fields were retreating into a sodden twilight. Suddenly, as I looked out at the rain and the crepuscular bundles of shadow falling away on either side of our steadily strengthening, burrowing headlights, a wave of homesickness rose up and drenched me in an extravagant wash of sorrow that lasted for a second and then dispersed as quickly as it had gathered. When, next morning, a telegram arrived to tell me that my father had suffered his first heart attack the previous day, I wondered with a shiver if somehow it was an intuition of his distress that I had felt, if it was at the same moment that he was being stricken that, out on the wet road, the thought of Ireland and home had come to me unbidden and my heart, too, in its own way, had suffered a minor seizure. (What an incorrigible solipsist I am!)

Hartmann that day was in a strange mood, a sort of slow-burning, troubled euphoria – lately, with so much talk of drugs, I have wondered if he may have been an addict – and was avid for details of my pilgrimage to Russia. I tried to sound enthusiastic, but I could tell I was disappointing him. As I spoke, he grew increasingly restless, fiddling with the gearstick and drumming his fingers on the steering wheel. We came to a crossroads and he pulled the car to a lurching stop and got out and stamped into the middle of the road and stood looking in all directions, as if in desperate search of an escape route, with his fists in his overcoat pockets and his lips moving, billowed about by dark-silver wraiths of rain. Because of his bad leg he leaned at a slight angle, so that he seemed to be canted sideways against a strong wind. I waited with misgiving, not knowing quite what to do. When he came back he sat for a long moment staring through the windscreen, suddenly haggard and hollow-seeming. A tracery of raindrops fine as lace was delicately draped across the shoulders of his coat. I could smell the wetted wool. He began to speak in a gabbling way about the risks he was taking, the pressures he was under, stopping abruptly every so often and sighing angrily and staring out at the rain. This was not at all like him.

'I can trust no one,' he muttered. 'No one.'

'I don't think you need fear any of us,' I said mildly, 'Boy or Alastair, Leo – me.'

He went on looking out at the deepening dark as if he had not heard me, then stirred.

'What? No, no, I don't mean you. I mean' – he gestured – 'over there.' I thought of Leathercoat and his faceless driver, and recalled, with a not quite explicable shudder, the speck of shaving soap under Leathercoat's earlobe. Hartmann gave a brief laugh that sounded like a cough. 'Perhaps I should defect,' he said, 'what do you think?' It did not seem entirely a joke.

We drove on then to Roundleigh and parked in the village square. It was fully dark by now, and the lamps under the trees stood glowing whitely in the fine rain, like big, streaming seed-heads. The Fox in those days – I wonder if it is still there? – was a tall, teetering, crooked place, with a public bar and a chophouse, and rooms upstairs where travelling salesmen and illicit couples sometimes stayed. The ceilings, stained by centuries of tobacco smoke, were a wonderfully delicate, honeysuckle shade of yellowy-brown. There were fish mounted in glass cases on the wall, and a stuffed fox cub under a bell jar. Hartmann, I could see, found it all irresistibly charming; he had a weakness for English kitsch – they all had. The publican, Noakes, was a big brute with meaty arms and broad side-whiskers and a brow furrowed like a badly ploughed field; he made me think of a pugilist from Regency times, one of those bruisers who might have gone a few rounds with Lord Byron. He had a fierce, ferrety little wife who nagged him in public, and whom, so it was said, he beat in private. We used the place for years, right up to the war, for meetings and letter drops and even once in a while for conferences with embassy people or visiting agents, but each time we gathered there Noakes behaved as if he had never laid eyes on us before. I suspect, from the sardonic way in which he surveyed us from behind his row of beer-pulls, that he thought we were what the papers would have called a homosexual ring; a case, to some extent, of misplaced prescience.

'But tell me what it is I'm expected to *do*,' I said to Hartmann, when we had settled ourselves with our halves of bitter on high-backed benches facing each other on either side of the coke fire. (Coke: that is something else that has gone; if I try, I can still smell the fumes and feel their acid prickle at the back of my palate.)

'Do?' he said, putting on an arch, amused expression; his earlier, violent mood had subsided and he was his smooth self again. 'You do not *do* anything, really.' He took a draught of beer and with relish licked the fringe of foam from his upper lip. His blue-black oiled hair was combed starkly back from his forehead, giving him the pert, suave look of a raptor. He had rubber galoshes on over his dancer's dainty shoes. It was said that he wore a hairnet in bed. 'Your value for us is that you are at the heart of the English establishment—'

'I am?'

'—and from the information you and Boy Bannister and the others supply to us we shall be able to build a picture of the power bases of this country.' He loved these expositions, the setting out of aims and objectives, the homilies on strategy; every spy is part priest, part pedant. 'It is like – what is it called . . . ?'

'A jigsaw puzzle?'

'Yes!' He frowned. 'How did you know that was what I meant?'

'Oh, just a guess.'

I sipped my beer; I only ever drank beer when I was with the Comrades – class solidarity and all that; I was as bad as Alastair, in my way. A miniature but distinctly detailed horned red devil was glowing and grinning at me from the pulsing heart of the fire.

'So,' I said, 'I am to be a sort of social diarist, am I? The Kremlin's answer to William Hickey.'

At mention of the Kremlin he flinched, and glanced over at the bar, where Noakes was polishing a glass and whistling silently, his puckered big lips swivelled to one side.

'Please,' Hartmann whispered, 'who is William Hickey?'

'A joke,' I said wearily, 'just a joke. I had rather thought I would be required to do more than pass on cocktail party gossip. Where is my code book, my cyanide pill? Sorry – another joke.'

He frowned and began to say something but thought better of it, and instead smiled his crookedest, most winning smile, and did his exaggerated European shrug.

'Everything,' he said, 'must go so slowly in this strange business of ours. In Vienna once I had the task of watching one man for a year – a whole year! Then it turned out he was the wrong man. So you see.'

I laughed, which I should not have done, and he gave me a reproachful look. Then he began to speak very earnestly of how the English aristocracy was riddled with Fascist sympathisers, and passed me a list of the names of a number of people in whom Moscow was particularly interested. I glanced down the list and stopped myself from laughing again.

'Felix,' I said, 'these people are of no consequence. They're just common-or-garden reactionaries; cranks; dinner-party speech-makers.'

He shrugged, and said nothing, and looked away. I felt a familiar depression descending upon me. Espionage has something of the quality of a dream. In the spy's world, as in dreams, the terrain is always uncertain. You put your foot on what looks like solid ground and it gives way under you and you go into a kind of free fall, turning slowly tail over tip and clutching on to things that are themselves falling. This instability, this myriadness that the world takes on, is both the attraction and the terror of being a spy. Attraction, because in the midst of such uncertainty you are never required to *be yourself*; whatever you do, there is another, alternative you standing invisibly to one side, observing, evaluating, remembering. This is the secret power of the spy, different from the power that orders armies into battle; it is purely personal; it is the power to be and not be, to detach oneself from oneself, to be oneself and at the same time another. The trouble is, if I were always at least two versions of myself, so all others must be similarly twinned with themselves in this awful, slippery way. And so, laughable as it seemed, it was not impossible that the people on Felix's list might be not only the society hostesses and double-barrelled bores whom I thought I knew, but a ruthless and efficient ring of Fascists poised to wrest power from the elected government and set an abdicated king back on a swastika-draped throne. And there lay the fascination, and the fear – not of plots and pacts and royal shenanigans (I could never take the Duke or that awful Simpson woman seriously), but of the possibility that nothing, absolutely nothing, is as it seems.

'Look here, Felix,' I said, 'are you seriously proposing that I should spend my time attending dinners and going to weekend house parties so that I can report back to you on what I overheard Fruity Metcalfe telling Nancy Astor about the German armaments industry? Do you have any idea what conversations are like on these occasions?'

He considered his beer glass. Light from the fire lay along his jaw like a polished, dark-pink scar. This evening his eyes had a distinctly Eastern cast; did mine look Irish, to him, I wonder?

'No, I do not know what these occasions are like,' he said stiffly. 'A fur trader from the East End of London is not likely to be invited for weekends to Cliveden.'

'It's Clivden,' I said absently. 'It's pronounced Clivden.'

'Thank you.'

We supped the last of our warm beer in silence, me irritated and Hartmann bridling. A few locals had come in and sat about lumpily in the reddish gloom, their ovine, steamy smell insinuating itself amid the coke fumes. The early-evening murmur in English public houses, so wan and weary, so circumspect, always depresses me. Not that I go into public houses very often, nowadays. I sometimes find myself yearning for the ramshackle hilarity of the pubs of my childhood. When I was a boy in Carrickdrum I often ventured at night into Irishtown, a half acre of higgledy-piggledy shacks behind the seafront where the Catholic poor lived in what seemed to me euphoric squalor. There was a pub in every alleyway, low, one-roomed establishments whose front windows were painted with a lacy brown effect almost to the top, where a strip of buttery, smoke-clogged light, jolly, furtive, enticing, shone out blearily into the dark. I would creep up to Murphy's Lounge or Maloney's Select

Bar and stand outside the shut door, my heart beating in my throat – it was known for a fact that if the Catholics caught a Protestant child he would be spirited away and buried alive in a shallow grave in the hills above the town – and listen to the din inside, the laughter and the shouted oaths and jagged snatches of song, while a white moon hung above me on its invisible gibbet, sliming the cobbles of the alley with a suggestive smear of tarnished pewter. These pubs made me think of weather-beaten galleons, shut fast against the sea of night, bobbing along in mutinous merriment, the crew drunk, the captain in chains, and I, the dauntless cabin boy, ready to plunge into the midst of the roisterers and seize the key to the musket chest. Ah, the romance of forbidden, brute worlds!

'Tell me, Victor,' Hartmann said, and I could tell, by the breathy, consonantal way he uttered my name (*'Vikh-torr . . .'*), that he was about to shift into the realm of the personal, 'why do you do this?'

I sighed. I had thought he would ask it, sooner or later.

'Oh, the rottenness of the system,' I said gaily. 'Miners' wages, children with rickets – you know. Here, let me buy you a whiskey; this beer is so dreary.'

He held up his glass to the weak light and contemplated it solemnly.

'Yes,' he said, with a mournful catch. 'But it reminds me of home.'

Dear me; I could almost hear the twang of a phantom zither. When I brought back the whiskey he looked at it doubtfully, sipped, and winced; no doubt he would have preferred plum brandy, or whatever it is they drink on rainy autumn nights on the shores of Lake Balaton. He drank again, more deeply this time, and huddled tightly into himself, elbows pressed to his ribs and his legs twined about each other corkscrew fashion with one slender foot tucked behind an ankle like a cocked trigger. They do love a cosy chat, these international spies.

'And you,' I said, 'why do *you* do it?'

'England is not my country—'

'Nor mine.'

He shrugged grumpily.

'But it is your *home*,' he said, with a stubborn set of the jaw. 'This is where you live, where your friends are. Cambridge, London . . .' He made a sweeping gesture with his glass, and the measure of whiskey tilted and in its depths a sulphurous gemlike fire flashed. 'Home.'

Another phantom slither of strings. I sighed.

'Do *you* get homesick?' I asked.

He shook his head.

'I have no home.'

'No,' I said, 'I suppose you haven't. I should have thought that would make you feel quite . . . free?'

He leaned back on the bench seat, his face sinking into darkness.

'Boy Bannister gives us information that he gets from his father,' he said.

'Boy's father? Boy's father is dead.'

'His stepfather, then.'

'Retired, surely?'

'He still has contacts at the Admiralty.' He paused. 'Would you,' softly, 'would you do that?'

'Betray my father? I doubt if the secrets of the bishopric of Down and Dromore would be of great interest to our masters.'

'But would you?'

The upper part of his torso was swallowed in shadow, so that all I could see were his corkscrewed legs and one hand resting on his thigh with a cigarette clipped between thumb and middle fingers. He took a sip of whiskey, and the rim of the glass clinked tinnily against his teeth.

'Of course I would,' I said, 'if it were necessary. Wouldn't you?'

When we left the pub the rain had stopped. The night was blowy and bad-tempered, and the vast, wet darkness felt hollowed out by the wind. Sodden sycamore leaves lolloped about the road like injured toads. Hartmann turned up the collar of his coat and shivered. 'Ach, this weather!' He was on his way back to London, to catch the sleeper to Paris. He liked trains. I imagined him on the Blue Train with a gun in his hand and a girl in his bunk. Our footsteps plashed on the pavement, and as we walked from the light of one lamp to another our shadows stood up hastily to meet us and then fell down on their backs behind us.

'Felix,' I said. 'I'm not at all adventurous, you know; you mustn't expect heroics.'

We reached the car. An overhanging tree gave itself a doggy shake and a random splatter of raindrops fell on me, rattling on the brim of my hat. I suddenly saw the Back Road in Carrick-drum, and remembered myself walking with my father one wet November night like this when I was a boy: the steamy light of the infrequent gas lamps, and the undersides of the dark trees thrashing in what seemed an anguish of their own, and the sudden, inexplicable swelling of ardour inside me that made me want to howl in ecstatic sorrow, yearning for something nameless, which must have been the future, I suppose.

'As a matter of fact, there *is* something we want you to do,' Hartmann said.

We were standing on either side of the car, facing each other across the glistening roof.

'Yes?'

'We want you to become an agent of Military Intelligence.'

Another gust of wind, another spatter of raindrops.

'Oh, Felix,' I said, 'tell me that's a joke.'

He got into the car and slammed the door. He drove for some miles in an angry silence, very fast, gouging about with the gearstick as if he were trying to dislodge something from the innards of the car.

'All right, tell me, then,' I said at last. 'How am I supposed to get into the Secret Service?'

'Talk to the people at your college. Professor Hope-White, for instance. The physicist Crowther.'

'Crowther?' I said. 'Crowther is a spy master? He couldn't be. And Hope-White? He's a scholar of Romance languages, for God's sake! He writes lyric verses about boys in Provençal dialect.' Hartmann shrugged, smiling now; he liked to surprise. In the glow of the dashboard lights his face had a greenish, death's-head pallor. A fox appeared on the road in front of us and stared in venomous surprise at the headlights before putting down its tail and sliding off at a low run into the dark verge. And I remember now a rabbit hopping out of a hedge and gaping at two young men walking towards it up a hill road. 'I'm sorry, Felix,' I said, looking out at the night rushing helplessly at us in the windscreen, 'but I can't see myself passing my days decoding estimates of German rolling stock in the company of former Eton prefects and retired Indian Army officers. I have better things to do. I am a scholar.'

He shrugged again.

'All right,' he said.

It was a phenomenon with which I was to become familiar, this way they had of trying out something and then dropping it when it met even the mildest resistance. I remember Oleg in a great flap rushing around to Poland Street one day during the war after he had discovered that Boy and I were sharing rooms there ('Agents cannot live together like this, it is impossible!') and then staying to get weepily, Slavicly drunk with Boy and flopping on the couch in the living room for the night. Now Hartmann said:

'A new case officer will be arriving soon.'

I turned to him, startled.

'And what about you?'

He kept his eyes fixed on the road.

'It seems they have begun to suspect me,' he said.

'Suspect you? Of what?'

He shrugged.

'Of everything,' he said. 'Of nothing. They come to suspect everyone, in the end.'

I thought for a moment.

'You know,' I said, 'I wouldn't have agreed to work for them, if they had sent a Russian.'

He nodded.

'This one will be Russian,' he said grimly.

We were silent. In the dark sky before us a low, big-bellied bank of cinder-black cloud reflected the lights of Cambridge.

'No,' I said presently, 'it won't do. You'll have to tell them it won't do. I'll deal with them through you, or not at all.'

He gave a melancholy laugh.

'Tell them?' he said. 'Ah, Victor, you don't know them. Believe me, you do not know them.'

'Nevertheless, you must tell them: I will only work with you.'

*

I have forgotten the Russian's name. Skryne always refused to believe this, but it is true. His code name was Iosif, which struck me as dangerously obvious (the first time we made contact I asked if I might call him Joe, but he did not think it funny). He is one of the many persons from my past upon whom I do not care to dwell overmuch; the thought of him ripples across my consciousness like a draught across the back of a fever patient. He was a nondescript but dogged little sharp-faced man, who reminded me eerily of a Latin master, harsh of tongue and a fine mimic, especially of the Northern Irish accent, who had made life hell for me in my first year at Marlborough. At Iosif's insistence, our meetings took place in various pubs in the more respectable of London's suburbs, a different one each time. I believe he secretly liked these ghastly establishments; I suppose he, like Felix Hartmann, saw them as typical manifestations of an idealised England, with their horse brasses and dart boards and cravatted, ruddy-hued proprietors, who all looked to me like the kind of cheery chap who would have his wife coming along nicely in an acid bath upstairs. A belief in this mythical version of John Bull was one of the few things that the Russian and the German ruling élites and their lackeys had in common in the thirties. Iosif was proud of what he imagined was his ability to pass for a native Englander. He wore tweeds and brown brogues and sleeveless grey pullovers and smoked Capstan cigarettes. The effect was of a diligently fashioned but hopelessly inaccurate imitation of a human being, something a scouting party from another world might send ahead to mingle with Earthlings and transmit back vital data – which, when I think of it, is pretty much an accurate description of what he was. His accent was laughable, though he imagined it was flawless.

For our first meeting I was summoned one cold bright afternoon early in December to a pub beside a park in Putney. I arrived late and Iosif was furious. As soon as he had identified himself – furtive nod, strained smile, no handshake – I demanded to know why Felix Hartmann was not there.

'He has other duties now.'

'What sort of duties?'

He shrugged a bony shoulder. He was standing with me at the bar, with a glass of fizzy lemonade in his hand.

'At the embassy,' he said. 'Papers. Signals.'

'He's at the embassy now?'

'He was brought in. For his protection; the police were beginning to investigate him.'

'What became of his fur business?'

He shook his head, annoyed, pretending impatience.

'Fur business? What is this fur business? I know nothing about this.'

'Oh, never mind.'

He wanted us to go to a 'quiet table in the corner' – the place was empty – but I would not budge. Although I do not care for the stuff, I ordered vodka, just to see him flinch.

'*Na zdrovye!*' I said, and knocked back the measure Russian style, remembering the brothers Heidegger. Iosif's glittery little eyes had narrowed to slits. 'I told Felix I would work only with him,' I said.

He darted a sharp glance in the direction of the barman.

'You are not in Cambridge now, John,' he said. 'You cannot choose your colleagues.'

The door opened and a ragged old boy with a dog came in, preceded by a pallid splash of winter sunlight.

'What did you call me?' I said. 'My name is not John.'

'For us you are. For our meetings.'

'Nonsense. I'm not going to have some ridiculous code name foisted on me. I won't be able to remember it. You'll telephone me and I'll say, *There's no John here*, and hang up. It's impossible. John, indeed!'

He sighed. I could see I was a disappointment to him. No doubt he had been looking forward to a pleasant hour in the company of a British gentleman, a university type, diffident and courtly, who just happened to have access to the secrets of the Cavendish Laboratory and would pass them over with charming absent-mindedness, in the manner of an impromptu tutorial. I ordered another vodka and drank it off; it seemed to go straight upwards rather than down, and my head swam and I had the sensation of levitating for a second an inch above the floor. The fat old man with the dog subsided at a table in the corner and began to cough laboriously, making a noise like that of a suction pump in action; the dog meanwhile was studying Iosif and me, head to one side and an ear-flap dangling, like that terrier on the record label. Iosif hunched his back against the animal's alert gaze and, passing a hand across the lower half of his face in what comedians call a slow burn, said something incomprehensible.

'I can't hear you if you speak like that,' I said.

In a spasm of anger, immediately checked, he clutched my arm – a surprising and, I confess, frightening, iron grip – and put his face close beside mine, looking over my shoulder and swivelling his mouth towards my ear.

'The Syndics,' he hissed, and a prickle of spittle settled on my cheek.

'The *what*?'

I laughed. I was a little tipsy already, and everything had begun to seem at once hilarious and faintly desperate. Iosif in a hot whisper explained, amid tics and twitches and whistling breaths, like a chorister telling the boy next to him a dirty joke, that Moscow desired to procure a transcript of the deliberations of the Cambridge Syndics, under the illusion that this venerable body was some sort of clandestine union of the great and powerful of our powerful and great university, a cross between the Freemasons and the Elders of Zion.

'For God's sake,' I said, 'they're just a committee of the university senate!'

He waggled a portentous eyebrow.

'Exactly.'

'They conduct the business of the university. Butchers' bills. The wine cellar. That's all they do.'

He shook his head slowly from side to side, pursing his lips and letting his eyelids slowly drop. He knew what he knew. Oxbridge was running the country, and the Syndics were running half of Oxbridge: how could an account of their doings be anything less than fascinating to our masters in Moscow? I sighed. This was not an auspicious beginning to my career as a secret agent. There is a study to be written of the effect on the history of Europe in our century of the inability of England's enemies to understand this perverse, stubborn, sly and absurd nation. Much of my time and energy over the next decade and a half would be spent trying to teach Moscow, and the likes of Iosif, to distinguish between form and content in English life (trust an Irishman to know the difference). Their misconceptions were shamingly ludicrous. When Moscow Centre heard I was a regular visitor at Windsor, that I was friendly with HM, and was often bade stay on in the evenings to play at after-dinner games with his wife – who was also related to me, however distantly – they were beside themselves, believing that one of their men had penetrated to the very seat of power in the country. Accustomed to tsardom, old style and new, they could not understand that our sceptred ruler does not rule, but is only a sort of surrogate parent of the nation, and not for a moment to be taken seriously. At the end of the war, when Labour got in, I suspect Moscow believed it would be only a matter of time before the royal family, little princesses and all, would be taken to the Palace basement and put up against the wall. Attlee, of course, they could not fathom, and their bafflement only increased when I pointed out to them that he took his politics less from Marx than from Morris and Mill (Oleg wanted to know if these were people in the government). When the Conservatives got back they assumed the election had been rigged, unable to believe that the working class, after all they had learned in the war, would freely vote for the return of a right-wing government ('My dear Oleg, there is no stouter Tory than the English working man'). Boy was infuriated and depressed by these failures of comprehension; I, however, had sympathy for the Comrades. Like them, I too came of an extreme and instinctual race. No doubt this is why Leo Rothenstein and I got on better with them than genuine Englishmen like Boy and Alastair: we shared the innate, bleak romanticism of our two very different races, the legacy of dispossession, and, especially, the lively anticipation of eventual revenge, which, when it came to politics, could be made to pass for optimism.

Meanwhile Iosif is still standing before me, like a ventrilo-quist's dummy, with his too-long cuffs and his facial muscles that seem worked by wires, attentive and hopeful as that old man's dog, and since I am tired of him, and depressed, and sorry I ever allowed Hartmann to persuade me to throw in my lot with the likes of this absurd, this impossible person, I tell him that, yes, I will get hold of a copy of the minutes of the next Syndics meeting, if that is what he really wants, and he gives a serious, swift little nod, the kind of nod I would become familiar with later on, from self-important chumps in war rooms and secret briefing centres when I came over from the Department to deliver some perfectly useless piece of classified information. All the commentators nowadays, all the wiseacres in books and in the newspapers, underestimate the adventure-story element in the world of espionage. Because real secrets are betrayed, because torturers exist, because men die – Iosif was to end up, like so many other minor servants of the system, with an NKVD bullet in the back of his head – they imagine that spies are somehow both irresponsible and inhumanly malign, like the lesser devils who carry out great Satan's commands, when really what we most resembled were those brave but playful, always resourceful chaps in school stories, the Bobs and Dicks and Jims who are good at cricket and get up to harmless but ingenious pranks and in the end unmask the Headmaster as an international criminal, while at the same time managing to get enough clandestine swotting done to come first in their exams and win the scholarships and so save their nice, penurious parents the burden of paying to send them to one of Our Great Universities. That, anyway, is how we saw ourselves, though of course we would not have put it in those terms. We considered ourselves to be *good*, that is the point. It is hard to recapture now the heady flavour of those pre-war days when the world was going to hell with bells banging and whistles madly shrilling and we alone among our fellows knew exactly what our task was. Oh, I am well aware that young men were going off to Spain to fight, and forming trades unions, and getting up petitions, and so on, but that kind of thing, though necessary, was stop-gap action; secretly, we regarded these poor eager fellows as little more than cannon-fodder, or interfering do-gooders. What we had, and they lacked, was the necessary historical perspective; while the Spanish Brigaders shouted about the need to stop Franco, we were already planning for the transition period after the defeat of Hitler, when with a gentle shove from Moscow, and from us, the war-damaged regimes of Western Europe would fall down domino-fashion – yes, we were early proponents of that now discredited theory – and the Revolution would spread like a bloodstain from the Balkans to the coast of Connemara. And yet, at the same time, how detached we were. Somehow, despite all our talk and even some action, the great events of the time trundled past us, vivid, gaudily coloured, too real to be real, like the props of a travelling theatre being carted away on the back of a lorry, off to some other town. I was working in my rooms at Trinity when I heard the announcement of the fall of Barcelona on the wireless that was playing loudly in the room of my next-door neighbour – Welshman, some sort of physicist, liked dance-band music, told me all about the latest wizardry being worked at the Cavendish – and I continued calmly studying through my magnifying glass a reproduction of the curious pair of severed heads lying on a cloth in the foreground of Poussin's *The Capture of Jerusalem by Titus*, as if the two events, the real and the depicted, were equally far off from me in antiquity, the one as fixed and finished as the other, all frozen cry and rampant steed and stylised, gorgeous cruelty. You see . . . ?

There is one final image of Iosif I want to sketch before I pack him away for good in his tissue paper alongside so many other of the best-forgotten characters with whom my life is littered. As he was leaving the pub – he had insisted we go out separately – the old man's little dog trotted forward, coiling and uncoiling itself in that enthusiastic doggy way, as if its body, taut as a sausage, were somehow spring-loaded, and tried to rub itself against his ankle, only to be rebuffed by a deft, sideways kick from a polished toecap. The animal gave a squeal, more in sorrow than pain, and skittered away, its claws clicking on the floor tiles, and sat down again between its master's spread feet, blinking and rapidly licking its lips in puzzlement and consternation. Iosif went out, briefly letting in sunlight that played, unspurnably, at his ankles, and the old man glanced at me from under his brows with a sort of grinning scowl, and for a moment I saw what he thought he was seeing in me: another of the petty, impatient, harsh-eyed ones, the dog-kickers, the elbowers-through, the pushers-out-of-the-way, and I wanted to say to him, *No, no, I am not like that, I am not like him!* and then I thought, *But perhaps I am?* I catch that same look now-adays when some Cold War veteran or self-appointed patriotic guardian of Western Values recognises me in the street and metaphorically spits upon me.

Anyway. Thus began my career as a working spy. I recalled Felix Hartmann's hope that we scions of the loftier classes would provide Moscow with a completed jigsaw-puzzle picture of the English establishment (I had not had the heart to enquire if he had ever considered the subjects the manufacturers of such puzzles choose for illustration, but I had an image of a bunkerful of crop-headed commissars gravely poring over a caramel and sugarstick-pink scene complete with cottage and roses and rippling rill and ringleted little girl with a basket of buttercups on her dimpled arm: England, our England!). Diligently I began to accept the dinner invitations that previously I would have declined with a shudder, and found myself discussing watercolours and the price of poultry with the moustached, slightly mad-eyed wife of a Cabinet minister, or listening, befuddled with brandy and cigar smoke, while a peer of the realm with brick-red jowls and a monocle, gesturing expansively, expounded to the table on the devilishly clever methods the Jews and Freemasons had employed to infiltrate every level of government, to the point where they were now ready to seize power and murder the King. I wrote up exhaustive accounts of these occasions – discovering, by the way, an unexpected flair for narrative; some of these early reports were positively racy, if somewhat over-coloured – and passed them on to Iosif, who would scan them rapidly, frowning, and breathing loudly through his nostrils, and then stow them in an inner pocket and cast a masked glance about the bar and begin to talk with laboured blandness about the weather. Once in a while I gleaned a bit of information or gossip that elicited one of Iosif's rare, lip-biting, nervous little smiles. What Moscow considered to be my greatest, early triumph was the long and, to me, extremely tedious conversation I had at a Trinity Feast with a Private Secretary at the War Office, a portly, sleek-headed man with a small moustache, who as he prattled on reminded me of those blithe gaffe-makers in the Bateman cartoons; as the night ground along he became increasingly, solemnly, comically drunk – his dicky kept flying up, as in a music-hall farce – and told me, in indiscreet detail, how unprepared for war our armed forces were, that the armaments industry was a joke and that the government had not the will or the means to do anything to rectify the situation. I could see that Iosif, sitting at a low table in a corner of The Hare and Hounds in Highbury, crouched intently over my report, could not decide whether he should be appalled or jubilant at the implications for Europe in general, and Russia in particular, of what he was reading. What he seemed unaware of was that every newsboy in the country already knew how scandalously ill-equipped we were for war, and how spineless the government was.

This naivety on the part of Moscow and its emissaries was a cause of deep misgiving to all of us on our side; much of what passed with them for intelligence was freely available to the public. Didn't they ever, I asked Felix Hartmann in exasperation, read the papers or listen to the ten o'clock news on the wireless? 'What do your people do at the embassy all day, apart from issuing laughable communiqués about Russia's industrial output and refusing entry visas to defence correspondents of the *Daily Express*?' He smiled, and shrugged, and looked at the sky and began to whistle through his teeth. We were walking by the frozen Serpentine. It was January, the air was dense with mauve-white frost-smoke, and the ducks were waddling unsteadily about on the ice, baffled and disgruntled by this inexplicable solidification of their liquid world. After two years of duty Iosif had been abruptly recalled; I can still see the sickly sheen of sweat on his already cadaverous brow the day when he told me that this was to be our final meeting. We shook hands and in the doorway – The King's Head, Highgate – he turned back and shot me a furtive, imploring glance, silently asking me I do not know what awful, impossible question.

'Life at the embassy is somewhat . . . subdued, just now,' Hartmann said.

Since Iosif's abrupt departure I had been telephoning the embassy repeatedly, but had heard nothing until today, when Hartmann had just turned up, dressed in black as usual, wearing a black hat with the brim turned low at the front. When I asked what was going on, he had only smiled and put a finger to his lips and led me into the street and towards the park. Now he stopped and looked across the iron-coloured ice, rocking back and forth on his heels, his hands thrust deep in the pockets of his long overcoat.

'Moscow has gone silent,' he said. 'I send my messages along the usual channels, but nothing comes back. I am like a person who has survived an accident. Or like a person waiting for an accident to happen. It is a very strange sensation.'

On the bank near us a small boy attended by a black-stockinged nurse was throwing crusts of bread to the ducks; the child laughed throatily in delight to see the birds ignominiously slipping and slithering, their wings thrashing, as they chased the wildly skidding morsels. We turned and walked on. At the other side of the lake, on Rotten Row, a group of riders was jostling along untidily amid white bursts of horse-breath. In silence we reached the bridge, and there we stopped. Distant behind the tops of the black trees around us the shrouded forms of London loomed. Hartmann, dreamily smiling, stood with his head tilted to one side, as if listening for some small, expected sound.

'I am going back,' he said. 'They have told me I must come back.'

High up in the frozen mist, above the spires and the chimney pots, I seemed to see something hover for a second, a giant figure, all silver and gold and dully ashine. I heard myself swallow.

'I say, old man,' I said, 'is that wise, do you think? They tell me the climate over there is not at all congenial, these days. Quite the coldest it's been for a long time.'

He turned away from me and glanced skyward, as if he too had sensed some hovering portent.

'Oh, it will be all right,' he said absently. 'They say they want me to make a personal report, that's all.'

I nodded. Strange, how like incipient laughter dismay can feel. We set off across the bridge.

'You could always stay here,' I said. 'I mean, they can't *make* you go, can they?'

He laughed, and linked his arm through mine.

'This is what I like about you,' he said, 'all of you. Matters are so simple.' Our footsteps rang on the bridge like axe-blows. He pressed my arm against his ribs. 'I *must* go,' he said. 'Otherwise there is . . . nothing. Do you see?'

We left the bridge still arm in arm and stood on the brow of the park's gentle rise and surveyed the city crouched before us motionless in the mist.

'I shall miss London,' Hartmann said. 'Kensington Gore, the Brompton Road, Tooting Bec – is there really a place called Tooting Bec? And Beauchamp Place, which only yesterday I at last learned how to pronounce in the correct way. Such a waste, all this valuable knowledge.'

He squeezed my arm again, and glanced quickly at me sidewise, and I felt something in him falter, as if a part of an inner mechanism had suddenly, finally run down.

'Listen,' I said, 'the thing is, you mustn't go; we won't let you, you know.'

He only smiled, and turned and limped away, back in the direction we had come, over the bridge, under the massy black mist-draped trees, and I never saw him again.

I TRIED FOR YEARS to find out what had become of him. The Comrades were tight-lipped; when they drop you, you disappear between the floorboards. Tatters of rumour did drift back. Someone had seen him in the Lubyanka, in bad shape, missing an eye; another claimed he was at Moscow Centre, under surveillance but running the Lisbon desk; he was in Siberia; in Tokyo; in the Caucasus; his corpse had been spotted in the back of a car on Dzerzhinski Street. These whispers might have been coming to me from the dark side of the moon. Russia was that far away; it was always that far away. The couple of weeks I had spent there had only served to make the place more distant for me. This is a curious fact about us – I think it is curious – that the country to which we had committed ourselves was a blur in our minds, the Promised Land we would never reach, and never wanted to reach. None of us would have dreamed of going to live there voluntarily; later on, Boy, though he tried to hide it, was aghast when he came to realise that he had no choice but to defect. The opposition seemed far more familiar with the place than we were. There were people in the Department, desk men who had never been east of the Elbe, who talked as if they were in and out of the Lubyanka every day, strolling up Dzerzhinski Street – which I hardly knew how to pronounce – for a copy of *Pravda* and a packet of whatever was the most popular brand of cigarettes in Moscow in those days.

Why did he go back? He knew as well as I did what awaited him – I had read the accounts of the show trials, hunched over newspapers in solitary horror behind locked doors, my hands damp and face on fire, like an appalled adolescent devouring a manual of obstetrics. He could have made a run for it, he had the contacts, the escape routes, he could have got to Switzerland, or South America. But no; he went back. Why? I brooded on the question; I still do. I have the uneasy conviction that if I could answer it, I could answer a great many other things, too, not only about Felix Hartmann, but about myself. The blank bafflement that comes over me like a fog when I contemplate that final, fateful decision that he made is an awful indictment of a lack of something in me, something perfectly ordinary, the common fellow-feeling that others seem to come by naturally. I would try out the kind of thought experiment old Charkin, my philosophy tutor at Trinity, used to urge us to conduct, imagining myself as best I could into Felix Hartmann's mind and then plotting a plausible course of action for myself in the same circumstances. But it was no good, I could never get farther than the moment when the choice became unavoidable, whether to face one's fate, or cut and run. How would it feel to have come to that pass, to be required to sacrifice one's life for the sake of a cause – and not even for the cause itself, but only to save its face, as it were, to save the phenomena, as the old cosmologists used to say? To know that one would most likely end up in a pit in a forest with a thousand other riddled corpses, and yet to go back, regardless: was that courage, or just pride, foolhardiness, quixotic stubbornness? I felt guilty now for having laughed behind my hand at his poses and pretensions. Like a suicide – which, essentially, he was – he had both earned and verified his own legend. I would lie awake at night thinking of him, a formless heap of pain and despair in the corner of a lightless cell, shivering under a filthy blanket, listening to the skitter of rats' claws and the water pipes clanking and a young man somewhere crying for his mother. But even that I could not make real, and always it turned into melodrama, an image out of a cheap adventure yarn.

Boy laughed at me.

'You're going soft, Victor,' he said. 'Bloody man could be anywhere. They come and go like gypsies, you know that.' We were in Perpignan, in a brasserie by the river. It was August, the last weeks before the war. Purple shadows under the plane trees, and shimmying lozenges of water-light on the grey-green undersides of their big, torpid leaves. We had motored down from Calais in Boy's white roadster, and were already chafing under the burden of each other's company. I found exhausting his appetite for boys and drink, and he thought me an old maid. I had decided to go on the trip because Nick was supposed to be with us, but 'something had come up', and instead he had flown to Germany again on some secret mission or other. Now Boy gave me one of his surly, smear-eyed looks. 'Obviously you're smitten, Vic. Hartmann the heart-throb. It must have been the priestly touch, the laying on of hands. In love with your father when you were a lad, were you? Gives a new meaning to the word bishopric.'

He poured himself the last of the wine and called for another bottle.

'I suppose you don't mind at all who they shoot,' I said, 'or how many.'

'Christ, Vic, you're such a moaner.'

But he would not meet my eye. It was a bad time for the true believers such as Boy. The London embassy was practically unmanned. One case officer after another – Iosif, Felix Hartmann, half a dozen others – had been recalled and not replaced, leaving us to shift for ourselves as best we might. Lately the stuff I had been pilfering from the Department files, the kind of thing which used to send Felix Hartmann into transports – probably he was exaggerating its worth, out of old-world politeness – I now delivered through a dead-letter drop in an Irish pub in Kilburn, and could not be sure that it was getting through, or, if it was, that anyone was reading it. I do not know why I kept at it, really. If it had not been for the war I might have given up. We had to spur ourselves on, like lost explorers reminding each other of the joys of home. It was hard work. Alastair Sykes had recently published a hopeless piece of self-deluding twaddle in the *Spectator* arguing the necessity for the Moscow purges in the face of the Fascist threat; I laughed as I read it, imagining him up there in his rooms in Trinity, crouched over that antique typewriter of his, tapping away like mad with two fingers, brow furrowed and the bristles standing up on his head and his pipe firing off showers of sparks.

Boy forked up a melting wedge of cheese. 'Ah, what a stink!' he exclaimed. '*Saveur de matelot . . .*' He stopped, and frowned, staring past my shoulder. 'I say,' he said, 'look at that.' I looked. Shadows and smoke, curved shine on the fat flank of a coffee machine, the silhouette of the head and slender neck of a girl laughing into her hand, and, behind her young man's head, the window, framing a big, impressionist view of tree and sunstruck stone and dazzled water. This is what we remember, the inconsequential clutter of things. '*There*, you fool!' Boy hissed, pointing with his fork. At the table next to us a very fat bald man in pince-nez sat with chubby thighs splayed and his snout lifted, short-sightedly reading a copy of *Le Figaro* and moving his lips silently as he read. The front-page headline, in frightened black type, stood a good three inches high. Boy got up blunderingly, shedding napkin and breadcrumbs from his lap, and made a sort of lunge.

'*Votre journal, monsieur, vous permettez . . . ?*'

The fat man removed his pince-nez and stared at Boy, and frowned, the skin above his delicately whorled ears crinkling into three crescent-shaped, parallel wrinkles.

'*Mais non,*' he said, wagging a doughy finger, '*ce n'est pas le journal d'aujourd'hui, mais d'hier.*' With a fingernail he tapped the front page. '*C'est d'hier.* You understand? Is the journal of yesterday.'

Boy, purple-lipped, his eyes bulging – no one as violent as a clown in a rage – tried to snatch the paper out of his hands. The fat man resisted, and the front page tore down the middle, splitting the headline in two, thus sundering briefly the Hitler–Stalin pact, which had been signed in Moscow two days before. For ever after, that momentous alliance, the seeming betrayal of all we believed in, was to be associated in my mind with the look of that fat old fellow's pince-nez and oedemic thighs, with the sunlight on the river, with the soiled-socks smell of Camembert.

*

We went straight to our hotel and collected our bags and set off northwards. We hardly spoke. What we were most keenly conscious of was a sense of deep embarrassment; we were like a pair of siblings whose revered father had just been caught in an act of gross indecency in a public place. By nightfall we had reached Lyon, where we found rooms in a spectral hotel on a wooded road outside the town, and ate dinner in a vast, deserted, ill-lit dining room where leather-covered armchairs lurked in the shadowy corners like the ghosts of former guests, and *madame la propriétaire* herself, a stately grande dame in black bombazine and fingerless lace gloves, came and sat with us and informed us that Lyon was *le centre de la magie* of France, and that there was a Jewish cabal in the town that celebrated black masses every Saturday evening in a certain notorious house by the river (*'Avec des femmes nues, messieurs!'*). I spent a restless night in a lumpy, canopied bed, dozing and dreaming (naked harpies, Hitler in a wizard's spangled hat, that kind of thing), and rose at dawn and sat by the window huddled in a quilt and watched an enormous white sun coming up stealthily through greeny-black trees on a hill behind the hotel. I could hear Boy moving about in his room next to mine, and although I am sure he knew that I too was awake, he did not knock on the wall and summon me to come and have a drink with him, as he would have on any other morning, for he always hated to be alone and sleepless.

At Calais we passed a fretful Sunday walking about the

makeshift town and drinking too much wine at a bar where Boy had taken a fancy to the owner's teenage son. Next day we could not get a place on the ferry for Boy's roadster, and he left it behind on the dock, to be dispatched on the next sailing; it stood there looking oddly self-conscious as we pulled away, as if it were aware that it was prefiguring another, more celebrated occasion when Boy would abandon his motor car on a quayside. On the crossing to Dover the talk was all of war, and everywhere there was that grim little laugh, chin up and eyebrows ironically twitching, that is one of the things I best remember from that eerily jaunty, desperate time. Nick was there to meet us at Charing Cross. He had joined up the previous month – the Department had arranged a commission for him – and he was in his captain's uniform, looking very smart and satisfied with himself. He stepped forward out of an angry billow of steam on the platform, like a memory of Flanders. He sported a thin moustache I had not seen before, which looked like a pair of soft black feathers turned up at the tips, and which I thought a mistake. He was in one of his hearty moods.

'Hullo, you two! I say, Victor, you look distinctly peaky; is it the old *mal de mer* or are you sick at what your Uncle Joe has gorn and done?'

'Oh, give over, Nick.'

He laughed, and took my bag from me and slung it on his shoulder. The station was loud and hot, and smelled of steam and coal-gas and men. There were uniforms everywhere. Those last days before war was declared have stayed with me vividly, the crowds, the sun and smoke, the endless arrivals and departures, the shouts of the newsboys – they had never done such brisk business – the bars full to the doors, and everyone bright-eyed with a sort of hectic, happy fear. We came out of the station into the cacophonous glare of the August afternoon. Taxis in the Strand swarmed and hooted like a herd in rut, their roofs blackly shining in the sun. Nick had his car, and would not hear of it when Boy said he would make his own way home.

'I'm off duty – let's go to the Gryphon and get drunk.'

Boy shrugged. His attitude to Nick – sullen, circumspect, even a touch deferential – used always to be a puzzlement to me. Nick put our bags into the boot and did that trick he had of seeming to skip off both feet at once to land in a sort of languid slouch behind the steering wheel. I said I should see Baby.

'Ah, yes,' he said, 'of course: the little wife. Or not so little, actually. She says she feels like a barrage balloon. I tell her barrage balloons are *light*, and she must weigh at least a hundredweight. You are a hound, you know, Victor, going off like that just when she's ready to pop. Anyway, she's at my place, unravelling the day's woof and weft and eagerly awaiting the return of her footloose hero.'

We drove up Charing Cross Road and at Cambridge Circus almost ran under the back of an army lorry packed with jeering Tommies.

'General mobilisation,' I said.

'It's going to be bloody, without an eastern front, you know,' Nick said, trying to look stern, an effect which that moustache did nothing to help.

Boy, in the back seat, gave a sarcastic snort. Nick looked at him in the driving mirror and turned to me.

'What's the Party line, Vic?'

I shrugged.

'We find our friends where we can,' I said. 'Winston has Roosevelt, after all.'

Nick gave a comic groan.

'Oh, Lor'!' he said. 'Urizen speaks.'

Poland Street was uncharacteristically quiet under the torpor of the summer afternoon. When we were getting out of the car we heard the sound of jazz above us. We climbed to Nick's rooms and found Baby, in a smock, big-bellied, sitting in a wicker armchair by the window with her knees splayed, a dozen records strewn at her feet and Nick's gramophone going full blast. I leaned down and kissed her cheek. She smelled, not unpleasantly, of milk, and something like stale flower-water. She was a week overdue; I had hoped to miss the birth.

'Nice trip?' she said. 'So glad for you. Boy, darling: kiss-kiss.'

Boy lumbered to his knees before her and pressed his face against the great taut mound of her belly, mewling in mock adoration, while she gripped him by the ears and laughed. Boy was good with women. I wondered idly, as I often did, if he and Baby might have had an affair, in one of his hetero phases. She pushed his face away, and he rolled over and sat at her feet with an elbow propped on her knee.

'Your husband missed you horribly,' he said. 'I heard him every night, weeping something awful.'

She pulled his hair.

'I'm sure,' she said. 'It's obvious you've both had a terrible time. How tanned you are. Quite lust-making, really; I wish I didn't look such a frump.'

Nick was pacing restlessly. He glared at the gramophone.

'Mind if I turn off this nigger racket?' he said. 'I can't hear myself think.'

He lifted the playing arm and let the needle shriek across the grooves.

'Pig!' Baby said, indolently.

'Sow.' He dropped the record into its brown-paper sleeve and tossed it aside. 'Let's have some gin.'

'Oh, yeth pleath,' Baby said. 'Nice dwink for mummy. Or should I? Isn't it gin that shop-girls take to bring it off? Suppose it's too late for me to abort, though.'

Boy clasped her knees. 'Never say die, ducky!'

And so the evening had begun. Nick and Baby danced together for a bit, and we finished the bottle of gin, and Nick changed out of his uniform and we all went down to The Coach and Horses and had some more drinks. Later we went for dinner to the Savoy, where Boy behaved badly, and Baby egged him on, clapping her hands like a seal and laughing, and the people at the next table called the head waiter and complained about us. I tried to join in this ugly fun – we were children of the twenties, after all – but my heart was not in it. I was thirty-two, and on the verge of fatherhood; I was a scholar of no little reputation (how delicately the language allows one to express these things), but that was not sufficient recompense for the fact that I would never be a mathematician, or an artist, which were the only employments I considered worthy of my intellect (it's true, I did). It is hard, when one has to live a life always at an angle, as it were, to the life one thinks one might be living. I could not wait for the war to start.

Nick was subdued also, slumped sideways on his chair with an elbow on the table and his forehead propped on an index finger, watching the antics of Boy and his sister with dull-eyed distaste.

'Are you still playing at spies?' I said.

He turned his sullen gaze on me.

'Aren't you?'

'Oh, but I'm in Languages, that hardly counts. I picture you exchanging briefcases on a station platform in Istanbul, that kind of thing. Lots of derring-do.'

He scowled.

'Don't you think the time for smart-aleckry is past?'

How lovably ridiculous he sounded when he said such things. And he knew it. What a calculator he was.

'I'm just envious,' I said, 'dull dog that I am.'

He shrugged. His oiled black hair had the same dark lustre as his evening jacket.

'You could do something,' he said, 'get into something else. It will be all change any day now. All sorts of opportunities opening up.'

'Such as?'

Boy was balancing a wineglass on his chin. When he spoke, his clenched, disembodied voice seemed to come down from the ceiling.

'Why don't you fix him up as an MP?' he said.

Baby with an evil smile was tickling Boy's stretched throat to make him let the glass fall.

'I don't think Victor would be much good at politics,' she said. 'I can't picture him at the hustings, or making his maiden speech in the House.'

'He means the Military Police,' Nick said. 'New outfit. Billy Mytchett is in charge. Do give it up, Baby, will you? We'll have broken glass all over the table.'

'Spoilsport.'

Boy flipped the wineglass off his chin and caught it deftly. He called for a bottle of champagne. Already I could feel tomorrow morning's headache starting up. I touched Baby's arm; how silky and taut her skin was in this late stage of her pregnancy.

'I think it's time we went home,' I said.

'Gosh,' she said to the table, 'doesn't he sound like a father already?'

I realised that I was drunk, in a dull, unwilling sort of way; my lips were numb, and my cheeks felt as if they were coated with some brittle, shiny stuff, a dried-out spume. I was always interested in the effects of drunkenness, wondering, I suppose, if one day I would drink a glass too many and blurt out all my secrets. And then, when I am drunk I think this must be what it is like for other people all the time: impetuous, clumsy, sentimental, dim. Baby and Boy were playing a game with matches and coffee spoons, leaning with their heads together and giggling. Nick had lit up a grotesquely fat cigar. The champagne had a tacky texture.

'Listen,' I said to him, 'tell me about this Military Police business. Would it be amusing?'

He considered, squinting through a blear of smoke.

'I should think so,' he said doubtfully.

'How can I get in?'

'Oh, don't worry about that. I can fix that. I'll have a word with Billy Mytchett. I often run into him about the place.'

'What about my' – I shrugged – 'my past?'

'You mean the left-wing stuff? But you've given up all that, haven't you? Especially now.'

'Why don't you just join the army, like everyone else?' Baby said, giving me an unsteady, out-of-focus stare. 'That brigadier that Daddy knows could get you in. If they took Nick they'll take anyone.'

'He hankers after the cloak and the dagger,' Boy said. 'Don't you, Vic?'

Nick glanced about at the nearby tables.

'Pipe down, will you, Boy?' he said. 'We don't want half of London knowing our business.'

Baby shook her head in disgust.

'What a lot of boy scouts you all are.'

'Boysh scoush?' Boy said. 'What are boysh scoush?'

Baby struck him on the arm.

'Look here,' Nick said to me, 'come round in the morning to our side of the house and we'll find Mytchett and I'll introduce you. He's pretty straight, is old Billy. He'll see you right.'

Another bottle of champagne arrived.

'Blimey,' Baby said presently, 'I don't arf feel bad.' She was sitting with her elbows on the table, twisting a handkerchief in her fingers. She was pale, and her eyes were dull and somehow straying, as if they were trying to find a way to turn and look at something inside her head. 'Blimey,' she said again, and drew a breath in sharply. Then she hauled herself to her feet and stood swaying, one hand on the back of her chair and the other pressed tight under the slope of her belly. 'Powder my nose,' she muttered, and started toward the ladies. I stood up to help her, but she pushed me aside and made her way off by herself between the tables, tottering on her incongruously shapely ankles – the bones there always made me think of butterflies – and slender high heels.

'Do sit down, Victor,' Nick muttered irritably. 'People are staring.'

I sat. We drank some more champagne. After what seemed a long time Baby came back, stepping gingerly and holding in place a fixed, ashen smile. When she reached the table she put down a hand to steady herself and stood surveying us with an air of bright surprise.

'Who'd have believed it?' she said. 'There *is* water. It *does* break.'

*

Our son was born in the small hours of the following morning. I did not register the exact time of his birth – I was still half tight – and afterwards it did not seem tactful to ask. I suppose that might be considered the first instance of that general neglect of my son which he has always tacitly accused me of. When I heard his first cry I was pacing and smoking, as expectant fathers are supposed to do, outside the delivery room – no nonsense in those days of dragging the father in to witness the birth – and I experienced a jolt, a kind of leap, in the region of my diaphragm, as if all along there had been new life growing in me, too, unnoticed until now. I wish I could say that I felt joy, excitement, the giddy realisation of being all of a sudden spiritually increased – and I must have, surely I must have – but what I recall most clearly is a sensation of dullness, of heaviness, as if this birth had somehow really added to me, I mean to my physical self, as if Vivienne had passed over to me an unhandy extra weight that from now on I would have to carry about with me everywhere. The real infant, on the other hand, weighed almost nothing. I held him in my arms with awkward tenderness, trying to think of something to say. It was only when I tasted warm salt water dribbling in at the corners of my mouth that I realised I was weeping. Vivienne, groggy on her still bloodied bed, her eyes red-rimmed and her hair lank with sweat, tactfully ignored my tears.

'Well,' she said thickly, working her tongue, grey-hued and interestingly fat, over her cracked lips, 'at least people will have to call me by my proper name from now on. Who could speak of Baby's baby and keep a straight face?'

*

The sun was well up when I got home – home then was a flat in Bayswater that we were to keep until well into the war, though neither of us spent much time there – but the park with its newly dug, zigzag trenches was still greyed with dew and there were wisps of mist under the boughs of the already faltering trees. I lay on a sofa and tried to sleep, but the night's drink was still working in me and my mind was racing. I got up and drank coffee laced with brandy, and sat in the kitchen watching the pigeons on the fire escape preening and pushing at each other. The morning silence coming in from the streets brought with it a curious sense of lightness, as if the world were dreamily afloat, waiting for the day's noise to get going and give everything its proper weight. When I had finished eating I could not think what else to do. I drifted about the flat like an uneasy ghost. Vivienne's absence was more like a presence. The gaps on the walls added to the melancholy sense of things being somehow there and not there – anticipating air raids, I had got the Institute to let me store my pictures, including *The Death of Seneca*, in the basement vault. It was morning, and I was a father, but I seemed to be at an ending rather than a beginning. I listened to the seven o'clock news on the wireless. It was all bad. I sat down on the sofa again, just to rest for a moment and nurse my throbbing brow, and three hours later found myself struggling out of sleep, with burning eyelids and a stiff neck and a horrible coating of dried gum on my tongue. I remember it as mysteriously significant, that little sleep; it seemed a stepping out of the world, and out of myself, like the sleep the hero in a magical tale might be granted before setting off on his perilous adventures. I shaved, trying not to meet my eyes in the mirror, and went down to Whitehall to talk to Billy Mytchett.

He was a young man of thirty-five, one of those eternal

public-school types who were to come into their own in the early years of the war. He was a short, sturdy little fellow, with a touchingly open, pink face, and a shock of coarse blond hair that hung low on his forehead and rose into a complicated whorl on the crown of his head, giving him the aspect of an untidy stook of wheat. He wore tweeds, and an Eton tie with a knot that looked as if it had been tied for him by his mother on his first day at school and had not been undone since. He affected a tobacco pipe, which did not suit him and which he clearly could not manage, and kept poking at it and tamping it and plying it ineffectually with sputtering matches. His cramped office looked out on a startlingly noble prospect of arches and buttressed roofs and imperial-blue sky. He was Deputy Controller of Military Intelligence; it was hard to believe.

''Lo, Billy,' Nick said, and perched himself on a corner of Mytchett's desk, swinging one leg. I had called him from the flat, and he had been waiting for me at the security desk when I arrived, and had grinned at my drawn countenance and puffy eyes; Nick no longer suffered from hangovers: that kind of thing was for Other Ranks. 'Billy, this is Maskell,' he said now, 'chap I was telling you about. I'll expect you to treat him as you would any brother-in-law of mine.'

Mytchett hopped up, knocking a sheaf of papers off the desk, and shook hands with me vigorously.

'Splendid!' he said, grinning with mouth and eyes and ears. 'Absolutely!'

Nick deftly scooped up the papers Billy had spilled and put them back on the desk. He was always doing that, tidying things, setting things to right, as if it were his special task to smooth away without fuss the little catastrophes that others less graceful than he could not help causing as they stumbled their way through the world.

'If you're thinking he looks green around the gills,' he said, 'it's because he has been up all night – my sis, who is married to him, God help her, produced their first nipper a few hours ago.'

Mytchett's grin grew even wider and he pumped my hand again, with renewed forcefulness, though an uneasy, furtive something had come into his look; babies, now, babies were not a subject a chap should be asked to consider at the kind of moment in history at which we now found ourselves.

'Splendid!' he said again, fairly barking the word. 'Boy, was it? Jolly good. Boys are best, all round. Do sit. Have a fag?' He retreated behind the desk and sat down again. 'Now – Nick tells me you're fed up being a pen-pusher? Understandable. I hope to get out in the field myself, ASAP.'

'You think there will be war?' I said. It was a question I liked to ask these days, for it never failed to produce an amusing response. Billy Mytchett's reaction was particularly gratifying, as he mugged at me in pop-eyed, pitying surprise, and smacked a hand down on the desk and looked about him at an imaginary audience, calling its attention to my naivety.

'No question, old man. Matter of days. We may have let Johnny Czecko down – disgracefully, if you want to know moy 'umble opinion – but we're not going to desert the Poles. Friend Adolf is in for a nasty surprise this time.'

Nick, still swinging his leg, was beaming down on Mytchett proudly, as if he had invented him.

'And Billy's boys,' he said, 'are going to be at the forefront of the surprise party. Right, Bill?'

Mytchett, sucking at his pipe, nodded happily, and folded his arms tight about his chest as if to keep himself from jumping up and capering a few steps of a jig.

'We've got a place down near Aldershot,' he said. 'Big old house and grounds. That's where you'll do your basic training.'

There was a silence, through which they both sat and smiled at me.

'Basic training?' I said, faintly.

''Fraid so,' Mytchett said. 'You're in the army now, and all that. Well, not the army, exactly, but as near as dammit. See, what we are is Field Security, which is a branch of the Corps of Military Police. Lot of nonsense, these fancy monikers, but there you are.' He got up again and began pacing the patch of floor in front of his desk, pipe clamped in his teeth and one hand behind him pressed to the small of his back, a bearing he must have borrowed from some hero of his youth, an admired military uncle or an old headmaster; everything about Billy Mytchett had come from somewhere else. Nick winked at me. 'You're in Languages, yes?' Mytchett said. 'That's good, that's good. How are you with the old parley-voo?'

'French? I can get by.'

'He's being modest,' Nick said. 'He speaks it like a native.'

'Excellent. Because we're going to need French speakers. This is classified, you understand, but since you're already in the Department, I can tell you: as soon as the balloon goes up, a sizeable expedition of our troops will be dispatched over there to stiffen the morale of the Froggies – you know what they're like. Our chaps will need keeping an eye on – possible infiltration, vetting of letters, that kind of thing – which is where we come in. Know Normandy at all, that area? Good. I haven't said so' – he closed one eye and pointed a finger at me as if it were the barrel of a gun – 'but I think it's not impossible that you might be stationed not a million miles from that neck of the woods. So: get your kit together, kiss the wife and sprog day-day, and get yourself down to Bingley Manor by the first available train.'

Startled, I looked from Mytchett to Nick and back again.

'Today?' I said.

Mytchett nodded.

'Certainly. If not before.'

'But,' I said, 'what about . . . what about my present posting?'

'I told you I'd fix that,' Nick said. 'I spoke this morning to your head of section. You're released as of . . .' he consulted his watch '. . . as of now, actually.'

Mytchett threw himself down at his desk again and rubbed his hands and chuckled.

'Nick's a doer,' he said. 'We'll all need to be doers, soon.' He frowned suddenly. 'But hang on: what about a conflict of loyalties?'

I stared.

'A conflict of . . . ?'

'Yes. You're Irish, aren't you?'

'Well, I . . . Of course I . . .'

Nick leaned forward and patted me gently on the shoulder.

'He's pulling your leg, Victor.'

Mytchett spluttered delightedly.

'Sorry, old chap,' he said. 'Terrible tease, I am. You should have known me at school, I was a terror.' He stood up, and offered me his hand across the desk. 'Welcome aboard. You won't regret it. And France, they tell me, is really not at all a bad place to be, in the autumn.'

When we got outside, Nick took me to Rainer's in Jermyn Street to buy me a celebratory cup of tea '—Or char,' he said, 'as I suppose we shall have to call it from now on. The fighting man's nectar.'

A beam of thick yellow sunlight beat on the table between us, vibrating in time with the throbbing in my temples. Despite the dreamy, late-summer softness of the day, the cars passing by in the street seemed to me to have a hunched, anxious aspect.

'Jesus Christ, Nick,' I said, 'are they all going to be like that?'

'Billy, you mean? Oh, Billy's all right.'

'He's a bloody child!'

He laughed, and nodded, rolling the tip of his cigarette on the rim of the ashtray to shape it into a cone.

'Yes, he is a bit hard to take. But he's useful.' He glanced at me and away, smiling and biting his lip. 'The war will make him grow up.' The waitress brought our tea. Absent-mindedly he gave her a dazzling smile; he was always practising, was Nick. 'So,' he said when the woman had gone, 'what are you going to call this boy of yours?'

*

Vivienne, when I arrived to see her at the hospital at noon, had undergone a transformation. She was sitting up in bed wearing a pearl-white satin bed-jacket and buffing her nails. Her hair was waved ('Sacha himself came in to do me') and she had put on lipstick, and there were florin-sized dabs of rouge on her cheekbones.

'You look like a harlequin,' I said.

She made a mouth at me.

'Better than a harlot, I suppose. Or is that what you meant to say?'

There were flowers everywhere, on the window sill, on the bedside table, even on the floor, some bunches still in their tissue paper; their musky perfume cloyed the air of the room. I walked to the window and stood with my hands in my pockets looking out at a blackened brick wall webbed over with a complicated geometry of drainpipes. Diagonals of sunlight and shadow on the brick bespoke the hot summer noon going on elsewhere.

'How is the . . . how is the baby?' I said.

'The what? Dear me, for a moment I didn't know what you meant. He's here, if you must see him.' She pushed aside a hanging frond of fern to reveal a cot with a blue blanket, above the fold of which there was visible a vague small patch of angry pink. I did not move from the window. She smiled at me, an eyebrow twitching. 'Yes, irresistible, isn't he. And yet when you saw him first you wept. Or was that just from all the champagne you drank last night?'

I came and sat on the side of the bed and leaned down and gingerly drew back the blanket and contemplated the infant's hot cheek and miniature, rosebud mouth. He was asleep, and breathing very fast, a tiny, soft engine. I felt . . . shy, is the only word. Vivienne sighed.

'Have we made a mistake,' she said, 'bringing another poor mite into this awful world?' I told her about my interview with Billy Mytchett, and that I would be going away. She hardly listened, and went on gazing pensively at the child. 'I've decided on a name,' she said, 'did I tell you? Daddy will be disappointed, and I suppose your father will be too. But I do think it's wrong to burden a child with the name of a grandparent. So much to live up to – or so little. Bad either way.'

An ambulance siren started up close by, very loud, and somehow comic, and stopped as abruptly as it had started.

'Practising, perhaps,' I said.

'Mm. We had blackout drill last night. It was all very exciting and cosy. Like school. I'm sure they had a lovely time in the public wards, being cheery and so on. The nurses thought it was all a great lark.'

I took her hand. It was a little swollen, and feverishly hot. I could feel the blood swarming under the skin.

'I shan't be far away,' I said. 'Hampshire. Just down the road, really.'

She nodded, nibbling distractedly at her lip. Still she kept her gaze fixed on the child.

'Perhaps I shall go home,' she said.

'I'll get someone in to look after you.'

Delicately, and as if she were unaware of doing it, she withdrew her hand from mine.

'No, I mean Oxford. I spoke to Mummy on the telephone. They'll come down to collect me. You needn't worry.'

'I *do* worry,' I said, and sounded to myself at once hangdog and truculent.

'Yes, darling,' she said absently. 'Of course you do.'

I had not thought all this would be so difficult.

'Nick sends his love,' I said, this time sounding annoyed, though she seemed not to notice.

'Oh yes?' she said. 'I had rather thought he might come round to view his nephew. Strange, these new terms we're going to have to get used to. Nephew, I mean. Uncle. Son. Mother . . . Father.' She gave me a sort of tentative half smile, as if to apologise for something. 'Boy sent a telegram,' she said, 'look: *We knew you had it in you*. I wonder if that's original?'

'Nick will probably get in to see you before too long,' I said.

'Yes. I suppose he's terribly busy, with the army and so on. It suits him, doesn't it – being a soldier? I expect it will suit you, too.'

'I won't be a soldier, exactly; more a sort of policeman.'

She found that amusing.

'I'm sure you'll look very dashing, in your uniform.' How eerie they are, those silences that fall between intimates, making them strangers to each other, and themselves. At such moments anything might happen. I might have stood up, slowly, without a word, as the sleepwalker stands up, and gone out of that room, out of that life, never to return, and it seemed as if it would have been all right, that no one would have noticed, or cared. But I did not get up, I did not leave, and we sat for a long while, curiously at rest with ourselves and each other, cocooned inside that membrane of silence, which Vivienne when she spoke seemed not to break but somehow slip into, as she would have slipped into some dense, enveloping medium, the glair parting and then closing stickily behind her. 'Do you remember,' she said softly, 'that night at Nick's flat, when I was dressed as a boy, and you and Querell turned up drunk, and Querell tried to start a row about something or other?' I nodded; I remembered. 'You sat on the floor beside my chair and told me about that theory of Blake's, that we build imaginary statues of ourselves and try to behave according to their example.'

'Diderot,' I said.

'Hmm?'

'The idea of the statues. It was Diderot's, not Blake's.'

'Yes. But that was the gist of it, wasn't it? Erecting statues of ourselves in our heads? I thought you were so clever, so . . . passionate. My wild Irishman. And then later – just at dawn, it must have been – when you telephoned and asked me to marry you, it was the most surprising thing and yet I wasn't in the least surprised.'

She shook her head in hazy amazement, gazing into the past.

'Why do you think of that now?' I said.

She drew up her legs under the sheet, with a grimace of pain which she instantly repressed, and put her arms around her knees and hugged herself pensively.

'Oh, it was just . . .' She glanced at me wryly. 'I was just thinking, I never seem to see *you* any more, just your statue.'

I might have told her then, about Felix Hartmann, and Boy and Alastair and Leo Rothenstein, about that whole other life I had been leading for years without her knowing anything of it. But I could not bring myself to step over that brink. I never did tell her, not any of it, in all the years. Perhaps I should have? Perhaps things would have been different between us. But I did not trust her; I was afraid that she would tell Nick, and I could not have borne it if Nick were to know. And in the end, it was she who told me, all there was to know.

'I'm sorry,' I mumbled, and lowered my eyes.

She gave a glittering laugh.

'Sorry, yes,' she said. 'Everyone is sorry. It must be the times.'

I was suddenly impatient to be away. The smell of the flowers, and behind that the hospital smell – ether, boiled food, faeces – and the flocculent warmth of the room were making me nauseous. I thought of Ireland, the wind-harrowed fields above Carrickdrum and the dull-blue surface of the sea stretched tight all the way to Belfast with its gantries and spires and flat, black hills. Hettie had written me one of her rare letters recently, worrying over the prospect of war and fretting about Baby's pregnancy. It was like a document out of the last

century, the heavy, gum-smelling paper embossed with a stylised representation of St Nicholas's, and Hettie's genteel and
faintly mad handwriting, all hatted t's and startled o's and spiky,
outflung ascenders. *I hope Vivienne is not uncomfortable. I hope
you will take care of yourself and that you are eating well at this
worrying time for Diet is most Important. Your Father continues
poorly. We have had some Rain at last but not enough everything
is so dry and the garden in a Bad Way* . . . I had a fantasy, a sort
of daydream I indulged in now and then, that if things got bad –
if someone betrayed me, or if I got caught through some piece
of carelessness of my own – I would somehow make my way to
Ireland and hide out up there in the hills, in a shelter under the
rocks, among the whin bushes, and Hettie would come up
every day in the pony-and-trap with a basket of food for me
covered with a white napkin, and would sit with me while I
ate, and listen to my story, my confession, the litany of my sins.

'I must go,' I said. 'When will your parents come down?'

Vivienne blinked, and roused herself; what was *her* dream of
escape, I wonder?

'What?' she said. 'Oh, before the weekend.' In his cot the
child made a sound in his sleep like a rusty hinge being opened.
'We must think about the christening; you never know, these
days.' Vivienne still held on, with a tenacity that irritated me,
to a few tattered remnants of Christianity; it was a constant
source of friction between her and her mother. 'It should be in
Oxford, I think, don't you?'

I shrugged.

'What *are* you going to call him, by the way?' I said.

I must have sounded peeved, for she reached forward quickly
and laid a hand over mine and in a mortified tone in which she
could not quite suppress a tinkle of amusement said:

'My dear, you didn't want him to be called Victor, did you?'

'No; he would be picked on dreadfully in school by his
German prefects if we lose the war.'

I kissed her cool pale brow. As she leaned toward me to

receive the kiss, the neck of her bed-jacket opened a little way and I glimpsed her swollen, silvery breasts, and a surge of something, a sort of anguished pity, rose in me hotly like gorge.

'Darling,' I said, 'I . . . I want . . .'

I was half kneeling on the edge of the bed and in danger of toppling over; she held on to my elbow to steady me, and reached up a hand and touched my cheek.

'I know,' she murmured, 'I know.' I stepped back, buttoning my jacket and brushing at the pockets. She held her head to one side and regarded me quizzically. 'Won't it be odd,' she said, 'in the coming weeks, all that emotion, those tearful partings? Quite medieval, really. Do you feel like a knight about to go forth and do battle?'

'I'll telephone you when I get down there,' I said. 'If I can, that is. They may not allow us to call out.'

'Gosh, it does sound thrilling. Will you have a pistol and invisible ink and things? I always wanted to be a spy, you know. To have secrets.'

She kissed her fingertips at me in farewell. As I was closing the door behind me I heard the child beginning to cry. I should have told her; yes, I should have told her what I was. Who I was. But then, she should have told me, too, sooner than she did.

*

Old age, as someone whom I love once said, is not a venture to be embarked on lightly. Today I went to see my doctor, the first such visit since my disgrace. He was a little cool, I thought, but not hostile. I wonder what his politics are, or if he has any. He's a bit of a dry old article, to be honest, tall and gaunt, like me, but with a very good line in suits: I feel quite shabby beside his dark, measured, faintly weary elegance. In the midst of the usual poking and prodding he startled me by saying suddenly, but in a tone of complete detachment, 'Sorry to hear about that business over your spying for the Russians; must have been an annoyance.' Well, yes, an annoyance: not a word anyone else would have thought of employing in the circumstances. While I was putting on my trousers he sat down at his desk and began writing in my file.

'You're in pretty good shape,' he said absently, 'considering.'

His pen made a scratching sound.

'Am I going to die?' I said.

He continued writing for a minute, and I thought he might not have heard, but then he paused and lifted his head and looked upward as if searching for just the right formula of words.

'Well, we shall all die, you know,' he said. 'I realise that's not a satisfactory answer, but it's the only one I can give. It's the only one I ever give.'

'Considering,' I said.

He glanced at me with a wintry smile. And then, returning to his writing, he said the oddest thing:

'I should have thought you had died already, in a way.'

I knew what he meant, of course – public humiliation on the scale that I have experienced it is indeed a version of death, a practice run at extinction, as it were – but it's not the kind of thing you expect to hear from a Harley Street consultant, is it.

THERE WAS STILL the best part of a week to go before that Sunday morning when Chamberlain came on the wireless to tell us we were at war, but it is that endless, oneiric Tuesday, the day my son was born and I was issued with my first military uniform, that I think of as the real opening of hostilities, for me. Still hungover, and using up who knows what unreplenishable reserves of energy, I left the hospital and took a taxi straight to Waterloo, and was in Aldershot by four in the afternoon. Why does that town always smell of horses? I trudged through the hot streets to the bus station, sweating pure alcohol, and fell asleep on the bus and had to be shaken awake by the conductor ('Bloody hell, squire, I thought you was dead!'). Bingley Manor was an unlovely red-brick nineteenth-century Gothic pile, standing in a large flat park, with isolated stands of yew and weeping willow, like an extensive, ill-kept cemetery. It had been requisitioned from the relicts of some grand family, Catholics, I believe, who had been rehoused somewhere in darkest Somerset. I grew depressed at once when I saw the place. The thick gold light of evening only served to deepen the funereal atmosphere. There was an insolent corporal sitting in the great entrance hall – flagstones, antlers, crossed spears and a fur-covered shield – with his feet on a metal desk, smoking a cigarette. I filled out a form and was handed an already grubby identity card. Then I was walking up flights of stairs and along bare corridors, each one narrower and shabbier than the last, in the company of an ill-tempered, red-faced sergeant major who, despite my attempts to make conversation, maintained a kind of fuming silence, as if he were under some form of private interdiction. I told him I had just become a father. I don't know why I said it – a fatuous notion of the lower classes having a weakness for children, I suppose. Anyway, it didn't work. He gave a snort of angry laughter, his moustache twitching. 'Congratulations, sir, I'm sure,' he said, without looking at me. At least, I thought, he called me *sir*, despite – in fact, because of – my civilian suit.

I was presented with an ill-fitting uniform – I can still feel the tickle and chafe of that hairy serge – and the sergeant major showed me to my bunk in what must once have been the ballroom, a long, high, many-windowed hall with a polished oak floor and plaster flora on the ceiling. There were thirty bunks, set out in three neat rows; across those nearest the windows, delicate gold shapes of sunlight lay like broken box kites. I felt as lost and weepy as a small boy on his first day at boarding school. The sergeant major noted my distress with satisfaction.

'You're in luck, sir,' he said. 'Dinner is still being served. Come down when you're changed.' He suppressed a smirk, the angry thicket of his moustache twitching again. 'Just uniform; we don't dress here.'

A big servants' room in the basement had been converted into a mess hall. My fellow recruits were already at feed. It was a disconcertingly monastic-seeming scene, with stone floor and wooden benches, and shafts of vesperal sunlight in the mullioned windows, and monklike figures hunched over their bowls of gruel. A few heads turned when I came in, and someone sent up a derisive cheer for the newcomer. I found a place beside a man named Baxter, a brutally handsome, black-haired fellow bursting out of his uniform, who introduced himself at once and shook my hand, making my knuckles creak, and challenged me to say what I thought he did for a living in Civvy Street. I made a couple of hopeless guesses, at which he smiled and nodded happily, closing his womanly, long-lashed eyes. He was, it turned out, a contraceptives salesman. 'I travel all over –

British rubbers are greatly in demand, you'd be surprised. What am I doing here? Well, it's the lingo, see; I can speak six languages – seven, if you count Hindi, which I don't.' The soup, a thin, brown sludge with floating lozenges of fat, smelled of wet dog. Baxter lapped it up, then planted his elbows on the table and lit a cigarette. 'What about you,' he said, blowing vigorous clouds of smoke, 'what's your line? No, wait, let me guess. Civil servant? Schoolmaster?' When I told him, he grinned uneasily, as if he thought I was pulling his leg, and turned his attention to the person on his other side. After a while he turned back to me, though, looking more uneasy than ever. 'Christ,' he muttered, 'I thought you were bad, but this geezer' – indicating his neighbour with a sideways slide of eyes and mouth – 'he's an unfrocked bloody priest!'

I never saw Baxter again after that evening. Quite a number of our company were to disappear silently like that over the first few weeks. We were not told what had become of them, and we never mentioned the subject amongst ourselves; we were like the inmates of a sanatorium, waking each morning to find another bed empty, and wondering which of us the silent killer would carry off next. Many of the ones that remained seemed even less prepossessing than the rejects. They were academics, and language teachers from the grammar schools, travelling salesmen like Baxter, and a few indeterminates, shifty characters who tended to lurk, and smiled at one with vague intent, like nervous queers out for a night's cottaging. As time went on a strange web of alliances and enmities began to weave itself amongst us. Ties of class, profession, shared interests, were all undone. In fact, the wider the disparity in background between us, the better we got on. I was far more at ease with the likes of Baxter than with those who came from my own world. I wish I could say that this arbitrary mingling of the classes fostered a democratic atmosphere (not, I hasten to say, that I cared – or care – much for democracy). When I first arrived, the sergeant major had treated me with resentful deference, but once I was in uniform there was no more sirring, and on the parade ground he screamed in my face in what he thought was an Irish accent, spraying me with spit, as if I were the rawest working-class recruit hauled in from the slums. Almost immediately, however, I was promoted – by the influence of what agency I did not know – to the rank of captain, and the poor wretch had to go back to that peculiar, stolid-faced fawning which unofficial army protocol demands.

We started straight off on basic training, which to my surprise I found that I enjoyed. The bone-tiredness that felled one at the end of a day of square-bashing and kit inspection and swabbing-out of floors was almost erotic, a voluptuous, swooning lapse into oblivion. We were instructed in the art of hand-to-hand combat, which we went at with the loud enthusiasm of small boys. I particularly enjoyed bayonet practice, the licence it afforded to shriek at the top of one's lungs, as one deftly disembowelled an imaginary and yet strangely, shiveringly palpable enemy. We were taught map-reading. In the evenings, despite exhaustion, we studied rudimentary encoding techniques and the rules of surveillance. I made a parachute jump; as I leapt from the plane and the icy air caught me I was filled with a kind of exalted, almost holy terror, inexplicably pleasurable. I discovered a stamina in myself I had not known I was capable of, especially on the long treks we were forced to make over the Downs in the hay-smelling, late-summer heat. My comrades chafed under these impositions, but I saw them as the stages of a kind of purification rite. The sense of the monastic I had detected in the mess that first evening persisted; I might have been a lay brother, a worker in the fields, one of those for whom humble toil is the truest form of prayer. Like all the males of my class, I had hardly known how to tie my own shoelaces; now I was mastering all sorts of interesting and useful skills I would never have had the opportunity to learn in civilian life. It all seemed wonderful fun, really.

I was taught, for instance, how to drive a lorry. I barely knew how to drive a motor car, and this great fuming monster, with its blunt front end and shuddering rear parts, was as stubborn and unwieldy as a carthorse, yet what a thrill it was to ease out the clutch and plunge down on the quivering, two-foot-long gearstick and feel the cogs meshing and the whole huge machine surging forward as if its soul had come alive under my hands. I was captivated. There was a staff car, too, which we could borrow, on a strict rotational basis. It was an ancient grey-blue Wolseley, high and narrow, with walnut fascia and a wooden steering wheel and an ebony choke button which I always forgot to push in, so that whenever I took my foot off the accelerator the engine whined as if in pain and gouts of angry blue smoke belched out behind; the floor on the driver's side was so worn it was hardly more than a filigree of rust, and if I looked down between my knees when I was driving I could see the road rushing under me like a river in spate. The poor thing came to a sad end. One night, when it was not his turn, a chartered accountant – he spoke fluent Polish – sneaked the keys from the wall cabinet in the Base Commander's room and drove into Aldershot to see a girl he was sweet on, got drunk, and crashed into a tree on the way back, and was killed. He was our first fatality of the war. To my shame, I confess I grieved more for the car than for the accountant.

In our little settlement we had scant contact with the outside world. Once a week we were allowed to telephone our wives or girlfriends. On Saturday nights, we were told, we might venture into Aldershot, though under no circumstances were we to congregate together, or even to acknowledge that we knew each other, should we meet by chance in pub or dance hall; the result was a weekly invasion of the town by solitary drinkers and hapless wallflowers, all pining for the company of comrades whom during the rest of the week they spent their time trying to avoid.

I had of course no communication at all with Moscow, or even the London embassy. I assumed that my career as a double agent was at an end. I was not sorry. In retrospect, all that now seemed unreal, a game I used to play which I had now grown out of.

The announcement that we were at war was greeted at Bingley Manor in a curiously lackadaisical fashion, as if it had nothing particularly to do with us. When the news came we were crowded into the mess hall, which served also as a chapel – Brigadier Bradshaw, our commanding officer, had made attendance at Sunday service compulsory, in order that our morale should be kept up, as he said, though with little conviction. A young chaplain, troubled and inarticulate, was struggling with a complicated military metaphor involving St Michael and his flaming sword, when a runner arrived with a message for the Brigadier, who stood up, lifting a hand to silence the padre, and turned to the congregation and announced that the Prime Minister was about to address the nation. An enormous wireless set was wheeled forward on a tea trolley and, after a scrabbling search for a socket, was plugged in with great solemnity. The set, like a cockeyed idol, slowly opened its jade-green tuning eye as the valves warmed up, and, after clearing its throat with a series of goitrous hawks, settled down to a mantra-like hum. We waited, shifting our feet; someone whispered something, someone stifled a laugh. The Brigadier, the back of his neck reddening, went forward on tiptoe and bent to the instrument and twiddled the knobs, showing us his broad, khaki-clad backside. The wireless squeaked and babbled, blubbing its lip, and suddenly there was Chamberlain's voice, crabbed, querulous, exhausted, like the voice of God himself, helpless in the face of his ungovernable creation, to tell us that the world was coming to an end.

*

When I had first gone to work at the Department – though *work* is a strong word for what went on in the Languages section – no one had thought to enquire into my political past. I was the son of a bishop – albeit an *Irish* bishop – an Old Malburian and a Cambridge man. That I was an internationally recognised scholar might have raised doubts in some quarters – the Institute, being full of refugee foreigners, had always been viewed with suspicion in security circles. On the other hand, I was received at Windsor not only in the print room and the tower library, but in the family wing, too, and if pressed I'm sure I could have got HM to vouch for me personally. (The successful spy must be able to live authentically in each of his multiple lives. The popular image of us as smiling hypocrites boiling with secret hatred of our country and its people and institutions is misconceived. I genuinely liked and admired HM and, perhaps more impressively, made no attempt to hide from him my disdain for his feather-brained wife, who consistently failed to remember that she and I were related. The fact is, I was both a Marxist and a Royalist. This is something that Mrs W., who possesses the subtlest mind in that intellectually undistinguished family, clearly if tacitly understood. I did not have to pretend to be loyal; I *was* loyal, in my fashion.) Was I overconfident? Only Boy could get away with that gloating, schoolboy swagger into which the successful agent, smugly clutching his secrets, can so easily fall. When I was summoned to the Brigadier's office a couple of weeks after the official outbreak of war, I imagined it was to be told that I had been selected for some special assignment. The first cold tentacles of alarm uncoiled themselves in my innards when I noticed his reluctance to meet my eye.

'Ah, Maskell,' he said, delving among the documents on his desk, like a large, tawny bird hunting for worms under a drift of dead leaves. 'You're wanted up in London.' He glanced in the direction of my midriff and frowned. 'Stand easy.'

'Oh, sorry, sir.' I had forgotten to salute.

His office was in the former gun room; there were hunting prints on the walls, and I seemed to detect a faint lingering tang of fin and bloodied feather. Through the window behind him I could see a hapless squad of my colleagues in camouflage gear crawling on their knees and elbows towards the house in a simulated clandestine attack, a sight that was comic and at the same time unnerving.

'Ah, here it is,' the Brigadier said, lifting a letter out of the strew of papers before him. He held it close to his nose to read it, moving his head from side to side as he followed the lines, mumbling under his breath. '. . . *Day release . . . immediate . . . no escort required . . .* Escort? Escort? *. . . Sixteen hundred hours . . .*' He lowered the sheet and for the first time looked at me directly, his big blue jaw set and nostrils flared, showing alarmingly black, deep cavities. 'What the hell have you been up to, Maskell?'

'Nothing, sir, that I know of.'

He threw the letter back on the pile and sat casting about him furiously, his hands clasped so tightly together the knuckles whitened.

'Bloody people,' he muttered. 'What do they think we're running down here, some kind of vetting station? Tell Mytchett from me he'd better stop sending me duds or we may as well shut up shop.'

'I will, sir.'

He glanced at me sharply.

'You think this funny, Maskell?'

'No, sir.'

'Good. There's a train at noon. You won't' – with an angry snicker – 'require an escort.'

Glorious day. What a September that was. The station smelled of sun-warmed cinders and cut grass. Soldiers milled on the platforms, stooped in that characteristic, disgruntled S-shaped stance, with their kitbags hoisted on one shoulder, and nursing a fag-end in their fists. I bought a copy of the previous day's *Times* and sat blindly pretending to read it in a three-quarters empty first-class carriage. I felt hot all over, yet there was a small cold weight of foreboding inside me, as if an ice cube had been dropped into the pit of my stomach. A young woman sitting opposite me, wearing tortoiseshell spectacles and a black dress and heavy-heeled black shoes – the type that have latterly come back into fashion, I notice – kept glancing at me with an expression of baleful vacancy, as if she were not seeing me but someone I reminded her of. The train meandered along at an agonisingly slow pace, pausing irresolutely at each station, sighing and shuffling, with the air of having forgotten something and wondering whether to go back and fetch it. All the same, I arrived in London with an hour to spare. I took the opportunity to bring my uniform to Denbys to have it altered. I thought of telephoning Vivienne in Oxford, but decided against it; I could not have borne that fondly scathing tone. When I left the tailor's and was coming out of St James's into Piccadilly I almost bumped into the bespectacled young woman from the train. She looked through me and hurried past. A coincidence, I told myself, but I could not help recalling the Brigadier's snicker at the word *escort*. Another ice cube dropped inside me with a tingling little plop.

How lovely London seemed, vivid, and yet mysteriously insubstantial, like the cities in one's dreams. The air was soft and clear, with half the motor cars and buses off the roads – I had not known such vast, delicate skies since my childhood – and there was a general air of pensiveness, the opposite of that hectic atmosphere of suspense that had prevailed in the weeks leading up to the outbreak of hostilities. In Regent Street, banks of sandbags had been erected in front of the shops, sprayed with concrete and painted in carnival shades of red and blue.

When I entered his office Billy Mytchett fairly bounced up to greet me, as if propelled by a spring in the seat of his chair. This show of warmth made me more worried than ever. He pulled up a chair for me, and pressed me to take a cigarette, a cup of tea, a drink, even – 'though come to think of it, there isn't any drink in the building, except in the Controller's office, so I don't know why I offer, ha ha.' Like Brigadier Bradshaw, he too avoided looking at me directly, and instead made a great business of moving things about on his desk, producing all the while a low, unhappy whirring sound from the back of his throat.

'How are you getting on down at the Manor?' he said. 'Find it interesting?'

'Very.'

'Good, good.' A pause, in which even the frozen stones of the arches and the flying buttresses outside the window seemed to participate, hanging in suspenseful wait. He sighed, and picked up his cold pipe and gazed at it gloomily. 'The thing is, old man, one of our people has been going through your files – purely routine, you understand – and has come up with . . . well, with a trace, actually.'

'A trace?' I said; the word sounded vaguely, frighteningly medical.

'Yes. It seems—' He threw down the pipe and turned sideways in his chair, throwing out his stubby little legs before him and sinking his chin on his chest, and stared broodingly at his toecaps, his lower lip protruding. 'It seems you were something of a Bolshie.'

I laughed.

'Oh, that. Wasn't everyone?'

He gave me a startled glance.

'*I* wasn't.' He turned back to the desk again, all business suddenly, and took up a mimeographed report and thumbed through it until he found what he was looking for. 'There was this trip to Russia that you went on, you and Bannister and these Cambridge people. Yes?'

'Well, yes. But I've been to Germany, too; that doesn't make me a Nazi.'

He blinked.

'That's true,' he said, impressed despite himself. 'That is true.' He consulted the report again. 'But look here, what about this stuff you wrote, this art criticism in – what was it? – the

Spectator: "*A civilisation in decay . . . baneful influence of American values . . . unstoppable march of international socialism . . .*" What's all that got to do with art? – not, mind you, that I'm claiming to know anything about art.'

I heaved a heavy sigh, meant to denote boredom, disdain, haughty amusement, but also a determination to be patient and a willingness to try to set out complex matters in simple terms. It is an attitude – patrician, condescending, cold but not unkind – that I have found most effective, in a tight corner.

'Those pieces were written,' I said, 'when the Spanish civil war was starting. Do you recall that time, the atmosphere of desperation, of despair, almost? It seems a long time ago now, I know. But the issue was simple: Fascism or Socialism. One had to choose. And of course the choice was inevitable, for us.'

'But—'

'And as it proves, we were right. England is now at war with the Fascists, after all.'

'But Stalin—'

'—Has bought a little time, that's all. Russia will be in the fight with us before the year is out. Oh but look' – I lifted a languid hand, waving all this trivia aside – 'the point is, Billy, I know I was mistaken, but not for the reason you think. I was never a Communist – I mean, I was never a member of the Party – and that trip to Russia that has so exercised your bloodhounds only served to confirm all my doubts about the Soviet system. But at the time, three years ago, when I was about twenty years younger than I am now, and Spain was the temperature chart of Europe, I thought it was my duty, my *moral* duty, as did a great many others, to throw whatever weight I had into the battle against evil, the nature of which, for once, seemed perfectly clear and obvious. Instead of going off to Spain to fight, as I probably should have done, I made the one sacrifice it was in my power to make: I abandoned aesthetic purity in favour of an overtly political stance.'

'Aesthetic purity,' Billy said, nodding vigorously and putting on a deep frown. I had taken a calculated risk in calling him by his first name, thinking it would surely be the kind of thing he would expect a chap to do in the midst of a frank and emotional confession such as I was pretending to make.

'Yes,' I said, solemn, rueful, appealingly contrite, 'aesthetic purity, the one thing a critic must hold on to, if he is to be any good at all. So yes, you are right, and your scouts are right: I *am* guilty of treachery, but in an artistic, not a political, sense. If that makes me a security risk – if you think a man who betrays his aesthetic convictions is likely also to betray his country – then so be it. I'll collect my gear from Bingley Manor and see if I can't join the ARP or the Fire Service. For I'm determined to do some good, in however humble a capacity.'

Billy Mytchett was still gravely nodding, still frowning. Absorbed in thought, he reached out for his pipe and set it in his mouth and began slowly sucking on it. I waited, gazing out of the window; nothing like a dreamy demeanour for allaying suspicion. At last Mytchett stirred himself, and gave his shoulders a great shake, like a swimmer surfacing, and pushed the mimeographed report away from him with the side of his hand.

'Look here,' he said, 'this is all nonsense. You've no idea how much of this bumf I have to wade through in a week. I wake up in a blue funk at night, asking myself if this is how we're going to fight the war, with reports and queries and signatures required in triplicate. God! And then I'm asked to haul in perfectly decent chaps like you and put them through the wringer over something they said to their prefect when they were at school. It was bad enough before the war, but now . . . !'

'Well,' I said, magnanimously, 'it's not unreasonable, after all. There must be spies about.'

Oops. He gave me a quick, sharp look, to which I returned the blandest of bland stares, trying to control a telltale nerve under my right eye which tends to twitch when I am nervous.

'There are,' he said grimly. '—And Bingley Manor's full of 'em!' He gave a muffled shout of laughter and smacked his hands together, then immediately grew sober again. 'Listen, old chap,' he said gruffly, 'you go back down there and finish your training. I have a job for you, a very nice little number, you'll like it. Hush! Not a word for now. All in good time.' He stood up and came around the desk and hustled me to the door. 'Don't worry, I'll give old Bradshaw a tinkle and tell him we've vetted you and found you stainless as a choirboy – though when I think of some of the choirboys I've known . . .'

He shook my hand hurriedly, eager to be rid of me. I lingered, pulling on my gloves.

'You mentioned Boy Bannister,' I said. 'Is he . . . ?'

Mytchett stared.

'What – under suspicion? Lord, no. He's one of our stars. Absolute wizard. No, no, old Bannister's absolutely sound.'

*

How Boy laughed, when I phoned him from the flat later and told him he was one of Billy Mytchett's stars. 'What an ass,' he said. Behind the laughter I thought I detected a note of constraint. 'By the way,' he said, stagily loud, 'Nick is here. Hold on, he wants a word.'

When Nick came on the line he too was laughing.

'Been through the third degree, have you? Yes, Billy told me, I phoned him. Hardly the Grand Inquisitor, is he. I'm going to make sure that trace disappears from your file, by the way – I know a girl in Registry. It's the kind of thing could dog you for years. And we wouldn't want that. Especially as you and I are off on a jaunt any day now, all expenses paid.'

'A jaunt?'

'That's right, old bean. Didn't Billy tell you? No? Well, in that case I'd better keep mum too; idle talk costs whatsit. Oar revwar!'

And he hung up, laughing still and humming the 'Marseillaise'.

*

In a letter to his friend Paul Fréart de Chantelou in 1649, Poussin, referring to the execution of Charles I, makes the following observation: 'It is a true pleasure to live in a century in which such great events take place, provided that one can take shelter in some little corner and watch the play in comfort.' The remark is expressive of the quietism of the later Stoics, and of Seneca in particular. There are times when I wish I had lived more in accordance with such a principle. Yet who could have remained inactive in this ferocious century? Zeno and the earlier philosophers of his school held that the individual has a clear duty to take a hand in the events of his time and seek to mould them to the public good. This is another, more vigorous form of Stoicism. In my life I have exemplified both phases of the philosophy. When I was required to, I acted, in full knowledge of the ambiguity inherent in that verb, and now I have come to rest – or no, not rest: stillness. Yes: I have come to stillness.

Today, however, I am all agitation. *The Death of Seneca* is going for cleaning and valuation. Am I making a mistake? The valuers are very dependable, very discreet, they know me well, yet I cannot suppress the unfocused doubts that keep flying up in me darkly like a flock of restless starlings at the approach of night. What if the cleaners damage it, or in some other way deprive me of it, my last solace? The Irish say, when a child turns from its parents, that it is *making strange*; it comes from the belief that fairy folk, a jealous tribe, would steal a too-fair human babe and leave a changeling in its place. What if my picture comes back and I find that it is making strange? What if I look up from my desk some day and see a changeling before me?

It is still on the wall; I cannot summon up the courage to lift it down. It looks at me as my six-year-old son did that day when

198

I told him he was to be sent to boarding school. It is a product of the artist's last years, the period of the magnificent, late flowering of his genius, of *The Seasons*, of *Apollo and Daphne*, and the *Hagar* fragment. I have dated it tentatively to 1642. It is unusual among these final works, which taken together form a symphonic meditation on the grandeur and power of nature in her different aspects, shifting as it does from landscape to interior, from the outer to the inner world, from public life to the domestic. Here nature is present only in the placid view of distant hills and forest framed in the window above the philosopher's couch. The light in which the scene is bathed has an unearthly quality, as if it were not daylight, but some other, paradisal radiance. Although its subject is tragic, the picture communicates a sense of serenity and simple grandeur that is deeply, deeply moving. The effect is achieved through the subtle and masterful organisation of colours, these blues and golds, and not-quite-blues and not-quite-golds, that lead the eye from the dying man in his marmoreal pose – already his own effigy, as it were – through the two slaves, and the officer of the Guard, awkward as a warhorse in his buckles and helmet, to the figure of the philosopher's wife, to the servant girl preparing the bath in which the philospher will presently be immersed, and on at last to the window and the vast, calm world beyond, where death awaits.

I am afraid.

I HAVE SPENT a pleasant morning telling Miss Vandeleur about my time in the war. She wrote it all down. She is a great taker of notes. Inevitably, we have fallen into the manner of tutor and student; there is the same mixture of intimacy and indefinable unease that I remember from my teaching days; also, she betrays that thin edge of resentment that is the mark of the postgraduate chafing under the yoke of a deference which she feels by rights should no longer be required of her. I enjoy her visits, in my muted way. She is the only company I have, now. She sits before me on a low chair, with her reporter's spiral-bound notebook open on her knees and her head bent, showing me the smooth twin wings of her hair and the painfully straight parting which is the colour of slightly soiled snow. She writes at a remarkable pace, with a kind of desperate concentration; I have the impression that at any moment she might lose control of her writing hand and begin to scribble all over the page; it is quite exciting. And of course, I do love the sound of my own voice.

We speculated about the origin of the phrase, *a good war*. I said I was not sure that I had ever heard it used outside of books or the theatre. The people who wrote for the pictures were especially fond of it. In the films of the late forties and the fifties, pomaded, soft-faced chaps in cravats were always pausing by the fireplace to knock out implausible pipes and ask over their shoulders, 'Had a good war, did you?' at which the other chap, with moustache and cut-glass tumbler from which he never drank, would give one of those very English shrugs and make a little moue of distaste, in which we were supposed to see expressed the memory of hand-to-hand combat in the Ardennes, or a night landing on Crete, or a best friend's Spitfire going down in a spiral of smoke and flame over the Channel.

'And what about you?' Miss Vandeleur said, without looking up from her notes. 'Did *you* have a good war?'

I laughed, but then paused, struck.

'Well, you know,' I said, 'I do believe I did. Despite the fact that it began for me in an atmosphere of farce. French farce, at that.'

*

It was Miss Vandeleur who remarked how many of my memories of Nick Brevoort involve sea journeys. This is true, I have noticed it myself. I do not know the reason for it. I should like to be able to see something grand and heroic in it – the black ships and the bloodied foreshore and Ilium's fires on the horizon – but I am afraid the atmosphere of these recollections is not so much Homer as Hollywood. Even the crossing we made together to France early in December 1939 had a touch of ersatz, nickel-and-velvet romance to it. The night was preternaturally calm, and our troopship, a converted steamer which before the outbreak of war had ferried day trippers between Wales and the Isle of Man, glided intently as a knife through a milky, unreally moonlit sea. We passed the greater part of the voyage stretched out on wooden deckchairs in the stern, wrapped in our greatcoats and with our caps pulled low over our eyes. The pulsing tips of our cigarettes and the flying breaths of smoke we released to the night air seemed absurdly melodramatic. On board with us was a squad of raw – it is the only word – recruits on their way to join the Expeditionary Force. They had taken over the lounge, where they sprawled amid their strewn kit, staring before them in slack-jawed boredom, looking more like the stragglers from a rout than a troop on its way to join battle. All that could animate them, it seemed, was the frequent ceremony of tea and sandwiches. Did

Odysseus's men look like this as they sat down on the sand to their haunches of roast bullock and goblets of sea-dark wine? When Nick and I took a turn about the deck and glanced in through the portholes, it was like looking in at a children's party, the boy-men half happy and half worried as they watched the ship's stewards – still in their white coats – progress among them disgustedly with mighty tea-kettles and trays of corned-beef sandwiches.

'There it is,' Nick said. 'Your proletariat.'

'What a snob you are,' I said.

We were terribly excited, for all the studied world-weariness of our demeanour. From Billy Mytchett's winks and hints we imagined we were being sent to France on a secret and possibly dangerous mission; we had not actually spoken, even to ourselves, the thrilling formula, *infiltrating enemy lines*, but each knew the words were trembling on the tip of the other's tongue. In the final weeks at Bingley Manor I had conceived a great curiosity as to what it would be like actually to kill a man. While swabbing out floors or polishing my Sam Browne, I would conjure up scenes of sleek, balletic violence. It was very stirring; I was like a schoolboy entertaining dirty thoughts. Usually these imaginary, clean killings took place at night, and involved sentries. I saw myself rising up out of the darkness, deft and silent as a cat, and at the last moment saying something, making some sound, just to give poor Fritz a chance. He would whirl about, fumbling for his rifle, his eyes flashing in equine fear, and I would smile at him, briefly, coldly, before the knife went in and he collapsed on the grass in a puddle of his own black blood and expired with a soft, gargling sound, his eyes blank now and already filming over, while the reflection of an approaching searchlight steadily dilated, like another, astonished, cyclopian eye, on the brow of his helmet. I hasten to say that I never got to kill anyone, not with my bare hands, anyway. I did have a revolver, of which I was very proud. It was a six-round, .455 Webley Mark VI Service revolver, eleven and a quarter inches long, thirty-eight ounces, UK manufacture, what our shooting instructor at Bingley called a man-stopper. Never have I held anything so *serious* in my hand (with one obvious exception, of course). It came with a rather complicated holster, to which it was attached by a leather lanyard which in steamy conditions gave off a rawhide stink that seemed to me the very smell of manly daring and adventure. Although I would have been happy to fire a shot, or many shots, in anger (Wild Bill Maskell on the rampage), the opportunity did not come my way. The weapon is still somewhere about. I must see if I can find it; I'm sure Miss Vandeleur would be interested to have a look at it, if that does not sound too tiresomely Freudian.

What was I saying? This tendency to ramble is worrying. I sometimes think I am going gaga.

We spent five months in France, Nick and I, stationed in Boulogne. It was all a grave disappointment. Our job was just what Billy Mytchett had said it would be: to keep watch on the doings of the men of the Expeditionary Force in our area. 'Bloody snoops, that's all we are,' Nick said disgustedly. Officially, we had been assigned to guard against infiltration by spies, on the basis, I suppose, that it takes one to know one; in fact, we found ourselves dividing our energies between day-to-day security administration, and eavesdropping on the private lives of the battalion. I confess I derived a certain nasty enjoyment from the task of censoring the men's letters home; a prurient interest in other's people's privacy is one of the first requirements for a good spy. But this pleasure soon palled. I have a high regard for the English fighting man – I do, really – but his prose style, I am afraid, is not among his more admirable qualities. ('*Dear Mavis, What a crummy place this ~~Bolonge~~ is. ~~Frogs everywhere~~ and not a decent pint to be had. Are you wearing your lacy knickers tonight I wonder? Not a sign of ~~Jerry~~*' – the excisions, of course, are the work of my blue pencil.)

Boulogne. There are people, I have no doubt, wine-bibbers and apple-tart-fanciers, not to mention dirty-weekenders, whose blood races at the name of that untidy little port, but when I hear it, what I recall, with a shudder, is the particular mixture of boredom, misery and intermittent rage in which I passed those five months there. Because of my proficiency in the language, it was natural that I should take on the unofficial role of liaison officer with the French authorities, military and civilian. What a wretched specimen your typical Frenchman is – how could Poussin have let himself be born into such a dull-witted, reactionary race? And among the subspecies, none is more wretched than the small-town official. The military were all right – touchy, of course, and always on the lookout for slights to the nobility of their person and their calling – and I could manage even the four separate branches of the police I was compelled to deal with, but the burghers of Boulogne defeated me utterly. There is a particular attitude the French male strikes when he has decided to stand on his dignity and withdraw cooperation; it is a matter of the most minute inflections – the head tilted slightly to the left, the chin lifted a millimetre, the gaze directed carefully into the middle distance – but it is unmistakable, and the determination it silently expresses is adamantine.

Nick derived much amusement from my difficulties. It was in France that he first began to call me 'Doc', and address me in the facetious tones of a schoolboy ragging a hapless master. I suffered his jibes with forbearance; it is the price one pays for intellectual superiority. We both held the rank of captain, but by a mysterious hierarchical sleight-of-hand on his part, the trick of which still puzzles me, it was understood between us from the start that he was the superior officer. Ostensibly, of course, he was a regular soldier – our links with the Department were kept secret even from fellow officers in our area, although it quickly got about that I was one of the Bingley Boys, a breed held in contempt by the men of the Expeditionary Force, among whom we moved like – well, like spies. Nick had pulled strings and got us a billet together down a cobbled side street on the hill near the cathedral, in a crooked little house wedged between a butcher's and a baker's. The house was owned by the town mayor. The gossip was that he had used it before the war to keep a succession of mistresses in, and certainly there was something delicately lewd, something Petit Trianonish, about those narrow, high rooms with their many small-paned windows and doll's-house furniture. Nick immediately added to the bijou atmosphere by taking a mistress, a Mme Joliet, one of those bright, brittle, immaculately got-up women in their late thirties that France seems to generate fully developed, with all their sophistication and polish in place, as if they had never been young. Nick would smuggle her in at night through the little back garden that gave on to a lilac-covered lane, and she would put on an apron and cook a meal for the three of us – *omelette aux fines herbes* was her speciality – while I sat at the oilcloth-covered kitchen table uneasily fingering a glass of sweet Sauterne, and Nick stood at the sink with his tunic unbuttoned and a hand in his pocket and his ankles crossed, smoking a cigarette and winking at me as poor Anne-Marie prattled on about London fashions, and the Duchess of Windsor, and the outing she had made to Ascot one mythologised perfect English summer afternoon an indeterminate number of years before. 'This war,' she would cry, 'this terrible, terrible war!', throwing her eyes to the ceiling and making a comical square mouth, as if she were bemoaning some aberration of the weather. I felt sorry for her. Behind the fine glaze of her exterior there was detectable the lurking fear of the beautiful woman who already feels under her immaculately shod feet the first steepening incline of age. Nick's name for her was Spoils-of-War. I do not care to speculate as to the precise nature of their liaison. There were nights when I had to cover my head with a pillow so as not to hear the noises coming from Nick's room, and on more than one occasion Mme Joliet displayed in the morning the bruised mouth and blackened eye that were the testaments to a slavish devotion, and which no amount of expertly applied *maquillage* could disguise.

It was a strange little ménage, the atmosphere aquiver with unspoken intimacies and constantly fraught with the suspense of held-back tears. There was something pleasurably uncanny about this almost-life we were half leading. For me, it was a sketch, a cartoon version, of that idealised connubial domesticity I was never to experience in real life. Naturally, Mme Joliet and I formed an alliance – in Nick we even had a child, of sorts. We felt, she and I, like a pair of innocent sibling-lovers out of a fairy-tale, happy at our tasks, she with her whisk and I with my blue pencil, there in our gingerbread house in the depths of the rue du Cloître. The town had battened itself down against winter and the war. The days were short, hardly days at all, more like drawn-out, brumous twilights. Great leaden sea-clouds came shouldering in from the north, and the wind sighed and whispered in the casements, making the flames of Mme Joliet's candles stagger – she was a great one for the romantic touch, and a *bougie* burned at every repast. When I think back to then I recall the smell of beeswax and the needle-sharp sting of her perfume and, in the background, the flabby after-odour of domestic gas – so much of our time there was lived in the kitchen – and the muffled stink of drains, and the crushed-chrysanthemum staleness that rose from the tiled floors, always clammy with condensation, as if the house itself were permanently in a cold sweat.

Often Nick would leave the two of us together, going off after dinner on some supposed official errand, and coming back long after midnight, glazed and grinning, in a mood of dangerous gaiety, by which time Mme Joliet and I, leaning on our elbows in a warm dome of candlelight and Gauloise smoke, would have got cosily tipsy on that pear liqueur she liked, and which I drank only to keep her company, for it tasted to me like nail varnish. In these nocturnal tête-à-têtes she and I hardly spoke about ourselves at all. A couple of tentative questions from me on the subject of M. Joliet were met with a tightening of the lips and that almost imperceptible but wholly contemptuous shrug with which French women dismiss the failings of their menfolk. I told her a little about Vivienne, and our son, and she returned frequently to the topic, not, I think, because they were my wife and child, but because they were Nick's sister and nephew. For Nick was all that we talked about, really, even when the subject under discussion seemed to have nothing whatever to do with him. Mme Joliet, I quickly realised, was far out of her depth. What had started as a manageable little *affaire* with the handsome and careless English captain had changed into something perilously like love, and love, for her, had the destructive force of a phenomenon of nature, like lightning, or a summer storm, something to shelter from lest life and all that made it tolerable be left a blasted, smoking ruin. When she spoke of him she gave off a sort of anguished radiance which she tried in vain to subdue; there in our miniature candlelit arena she struck her desperate poses, struggling not to show her terror, like a circus performer caught in a cage with a supposedly tame animal that had suddenly turned wild. And once or twice, after yet another glass of Poire William, the sad smell of Anne-Marie's fear and longing would turn into a pure whiff of the erotic, and then it would seem that I should dash into the cage and join her, so that in each other's arms we might together face down the ravening beast. But nothing happened, the moment always passed, and we would lean away from each other, out of the candlelight, and sit gazing into our liqueur glasses, blank, motionless, at once regretful and relieved.

It would not have occurred to Nick to be jealous of us. He knew how firmly he had us in his grip; he had only to flex his claws and blood would spring from both our bosoms. I believe it amused him to leave us together at night like that, to see what we might do, what strategies of escape we might attempt.

Of the war we saw no sign. For days at a stretch I would

forget the reason for our being in France. Encountering squads of soldiers on the roads, or earnestly at their exercises in the fields and among the fruited orchards, I would find myself admiring the orderliness, the homeliness of it all, this right and proper occupation of men, as if it were not a military venture they were engaged in at all, but some vast, philanthropic work detail. Once a fortnight I drove down with Corporal Haig to the Expeditionary Force HQ at Arras, supposedly to deliver a report on activity in our sector, but since there was no activity, there was nothing to report, and the night before each trip I would spend weary hours racking my brains to put together a few plausible but meaningless pages, which would disappear without trace into the innards of the military machine. I have always been fascinated by the hunger for documentation shared by all great institutions, especially those run by supposed men of action, such as the Army, or the Secret Service. I cannot count the times I was able to foil this or that inconvenient development at the Department, not by removing or suppressing documents, but by adding new ones to an already bulging file.

Have I mentioned Corporal Haig before, I wonder? He was my batman, a music-hall version of an East Ender, all grins and winks and rollings of the eyes. At times he played the part so exaggeratedly well that I suspected he had studied it up, for behind the cheeky-chappie façade there was something uneasy about him, something lost, and fearful. Haig – his first name, unlikely though it sounds, was Roland – was short and compact, with big shoulders and tiny feet, like a boxer, and a gap in his front teeth and ears that stuck out. He seemed to have been in the army since childhood. Boy, who came down for a visit at Christmas from Dunkirk, where he was posted in some propagandist capacity, took a great shine to him. He called him The Field Marshal, and spent the holiday trying to seduce him. Perhaps he succeeded? – that might explain the evasive, guilty side of Haig's performance. I wonder what became of him, and if he survived the war. I have the feeling he did not. He was the kind of minor character that the gods test their blades on, before proceeding to deal with the Hectors and the Agamemnons.

Like the majority of the men in the Force, Haig regarded the war as a ludicrous but not entirely unenjoyable waste of time, another of those tremendous mad schemes which the Powers That Be choose to dream up, the sole purpose of which seemed to be to disrupt the otherwise placid lives of the lower ranks. The French expedition he considered particularly daft, even by Their standards. He was like a marooned day tripper, half indignant at the pointlessness of it all, and half amused by the atmosphere of unending, if dull, holiday. And of course, he was glad of the opportunity to grumble. As we sped in our little black Austin (it always reminded me of a bustling and very determined, shiny black beetle) along those narrow roads between swishing colonnades of plane trees, he would indulge in a kind of sustained aria of complaint: mucky food, stinking lavs that were no more than holes in the ground, bints who didn't speak a word of English and seemed to be laughing at him all the time, and who were probably poxed, anyway, the half of them ('I tell you, sir, I wouldn't touch the quim over here if they paid me').

On one of those jaunts to Arras we stopped at a village, I think it was Hesdin, and I took him to a restaurant on the river that Boy had recommended. The day was icy. We were the only customers. The dining room was small, low-ceilinged and somewhat dirty, and the fat old biddy who ran the place had the look of a slattern, but there was a nice wood fire, and we could hear the river clattering over stones below the rimed window, and the menu was a masterpiece. Haig was uneasy; I could see he was not at all sure that he approved of this informal mingling of the ranks. With his cap off he looked somehow shorn and vulnerable, and his ears seemed to stick out even more than usual. He kept smoothing his brilliantined hair and sniffing nervously. I had an urge to pat the back of one of his surprisingly delicate, almost girlish hands (how on earth did it take me so long to realise I was queer?). He engaged in a brief snow-fight with his napkin, then sat for a long time glaring helplessly at the menu. I suggested we start with oysters and he gulped in dismay, his adam's apple bouncing like a ball on a bat.

'What, Haig,' I said, 'never eaten an oyster? We shall have to remedy that.'

I spent a pleasant five minutes in conference with *madame la patronne*, who with much theatrical shrugging and kissing of bunched fingers persuaded me to take the sorrel soup and the *boeuf en daube*. 'All right with you, Haig?' I said, and Haig nodded, and gulped again. He wanted beer, but I would not allow it, and ordered us both a glass of the rather good local white to wash down the oysters. I pretended not to notice him waiting to see which pieces of cutlery I would pick up first. He fumbled with the oyster shells, making them clack like false teeth, and had trouble forking up the frilled, glandular morsels.

'Well?' I said. 'What do you think?'

He managed a sickly smile.

'It reminds me of . . .' He blushed, displaying an unaccustomed prudery. 'Well, I don't like to say, sir. Only it's cold.'

We ate in silence for a while, but I could feel him laboriously working himself up to something. We were finishing our soup before he finally got there.

'Mind my enquiring, sir, but were you called up or did you join?'

'Good heavens,' I said, 'what a question. Why do you ask?'

'Well, I just wondered, you being Irish and all.'

I registered the familiar faint shock, like a soot-fall in a chimney.

'Do I seem very Irish to you, Haig?'

He looked at me askance, and chuckled.

'Oh, no, sir, no,' he said, and lowered his face over his soup plate. 'Not so's you'd notice.'

There flashed into my mind then a clear and detailed picture of him, sitting in the canteen at HQ with his fellow drivers, a mug in one hand and a fag in the other, putting on a snooty face and mimicking my accent: *But my dear Haig, I'm hardly Oirish at all, at all.*

I wonder if Boy *did* manage to seduce him? Such questions are troubling, to an old man. The *boeuf en daube*, I remember, was excellent.

Having forsworn the services on offer from the local women, Haig could be of little assistance to me in my most taxing problem, which was the need for the provision of a second brothel in Boulogne for the benefit of Expeditionary Force personnel. With the arrival of the Force, the town's one such establishment – a warren of dingy rooms above a barber's shop round the corner from where Nick and I were quartered, presided over by a mole-speckled madam who, in silk kimono and drooping henna-coloured wig, bore a marked resemblance to Oscar Wilde in his later years – had risen, or reclined, energetically to the great increase in demand, but within a short time Mme Mouton's gallant *filles publiques* were overwhelmed, and amateurs stepped in to absorb the overflow of business. Soon every other bar and bakery had a room upstairs with a girl in it. There were fights, and accusations of cheating and theft, and a wide-scale spread of disease. I cannot recollect how the matter came to be my responsibility. I spent fruitless weeks traipsing between police headquarters and the *mairie*. I tried to enlist the support of the town's doctors. I even spoke to the parish priest, a foxy old boy with a game eye who proved to be suspiciously familiar with the workings of Mme Mouton's establishment. I felt like a character in a Feydeau comedy, revolving desperately through one set of misunderstandings after another, colliding everywhere with stock characters, all of them blandly knowing, openly contemptuous and wholly intransigent.

'War is hell, all right,' Nick said, and laughed. 'Why don't you get Anne-Marie to help you? I think she'd make quite a good madam.'

Mme Joliet's English was weak, and when she heard Nick speak her name in conversation with me, she had a way of smiling inquiringly, tilting her head and lifting up her fine little nose, in an unintended parody of a stage coquette.

'Nick thinks you might help me with Mme Mouton and her girls,' I said to her in French. 'I mean, he thinks you might be able to . . . that you . . .'

Her smile died, and she took off her apron, fumbling with the strings, and hurried from the kitchen.

'Oh, Doc, you are an ass,' Nick said, and smiled at me merrily.

I followed Anne-Marie. She was standing by the window in the little front parlour. Only a Frenchwoman can wring her hands convincingly. A shining tear trembled at the corner of each eye. She had swapped the soubrette role for that of Phèdre now.

'He cares nothing for me,' she said, in a voice that wobbled. 'Nothing.'

It was mid-morning, and a shaft of thin, whitish spring sunlight was piercing the brown window of the *épicerie* on the other side of the street. I could hear the gulls down at the harbour shrieking, and suddenly, with heart-shaking vividness, I saw Nick and myself standing on the seafront at Carrickdrum not much more than a year ago, in another life.

'I don't think he cares much for anyone,' I said. It was not what I had meant to say. She nodded, still with her face turned to the window. She sighed, and the sigh turned into a dry little sob.

'It is so difficult,' she murmured. 'So difficult.'

'Yes,' I said, feeling helpless and miserable; I am never any good in the presence of others' pain. After a moment of silence Mme Joliet laughed, and turned her head and looked at me, her eyes glistening with sorrow, and said:

'Well, perhaps I shall have better luck when the Germans come. Except. . . .' She faltered. 'Except that I am Jewish.'

*

Miss Vandeleur has got hold of some silly story about my bravery under fire. I have tried to explain to her that the concept of bravery is entirely spurious. We are what we are, we do what we do. At school, when I first read Homer, what struck me about Achilles was his bone-headed stupidity. I was not stupid, and I *was* afraid, but I had sufficient self-control not to show it, except once (twice, actually, but the second time there was no one to see, so it doesn't count). I performed no daring acts, did not throw myself on the grenade, or run out into no man's land to rescue Haig from the Huns. Simply, I was there, and I kept my head. It was nothing to boast about. Anyway, the shameful scramble for home that was Dunkirk had too strong an overtone of slapstick to allow one at the time seriously to consider the possibility of violent death. If bravery means the ability to laugh in the face of danger, then you may call me brave, but only because that face always seemed to me to have a clownish cast.

We knew the Germans were coming. Even before they launched their assault and the French Army collapsed, it had been obvious that nothing would stop the German armour except the Channel, and by now even that seemed not much wider than a castle moat. I was asleep on the morning when the Panzers arrived at the outskirts of the town. The noise of Haig stamping up the stairs to my room was louder than that of the German guns. He was in uniform, but a piece of his pyjamas was visible above the collar of his tunic. He hung on to the

doorframe, wild-eyed and gasping; I had not noticed before
how much like a fish he looked, with those pop-eyes and
protuberant mouth and fin-like ears.

'It's the Jerries, sir – they're bloody here!'

I sat up, primly pulling the blanket to my chin.

'You're improperly dressed, Haig,' I said, indicating the telltale edge of striped cotton at his neck. He gave a sort of
desperate grin and shook himself like a trout on a hook.

'Oh, sir, they'll be here in an hour,' he said, in an imploring
whine, like a schoolboy urging on a laggardly gamesmaster.

'Then we had better look sharp, hadn't we. Or do you feel
we should stop and make a stand against the tanks? I rather
think I have misplaced my pistol.'

It was a bracingly beautiful May morning, all glitter and flash
in the foreground, the smoke-grey distances cool and still. Haig
was waiting in the Austin with the motor running. I am always
strangely moved by the smell of exhaust fumes on the morning
air. The little car was shuddering like a calf, as if it knew what
its fate was shortly to be. Nick was lounging in the front
passenger seat with his cap rakishly tilted and his collar unbuttoned. I climbed into the back seat and we shot off down the
hill towards the harbour. When we slowed to take a corner an
old man leaning on a crutch shouted something, and spat at us.

'Grand day for a rout,' I said.

Nick laughed.

'You took your time,' he said. 'What were you doing –
praying?'

'I needed to shave.'

He looked to Haig and nodded grimly. 'The German army is
about to descend on us, and he has to have a shave.' He
swivelled toward me again, pointing. 'And what's that?'

'A swagger stick.'

'I rather thought that's what it was.'

We came upon a squad of our men marching raggedly down

the hill. They looked at us with sullen resentment as we passed by.

'Where are the others?' I asked.

'Most of the men went up to Dunkirk,' Haig said. 'They've sent a liner from Dover. The *Queen Mary*, they say. Lucky blighters.'

Nick was peering through the back window at the stragglers.

'Perhaps we should have spoken to them,' he said. 'They seemed quite demoralised.'

'One of them was carrying what looked like a ham,' I said.

'Oh dear, I do hope they haven't been looting. People tend to mind that sort of thing, especially the French.'

There was a thud nearby, we felt it through the throbbing of the engine, and a moment later a hail of fine debris tinkled on the roof of the car. Haig drew his neck down between his shoulders like a tortoise.

'Why are they firing at us?' Nick said. 'Don't they realise we've turned tail?'

'It's just exuberance,' I said. 'You know what the Germans are like.'

The harbour had a wonderfully festive look, with crowds of men milling about the quayside and craft of all kinds bobbing and jostling on the sea. The water was a stylised shade of cobalt blue and the sky was stuck all over with scraps of cottony cloud.

'You managed to say your goodbyes to Mme Joliet?' I said.

Nick shrugged, and kept the back of his head turned toward me.

'Couldn't seem to find her,' he said.

By now we were nosing our way through the crowds on the quay, Haig leaning on the horn and cursing to himself in a low mutter. I spotted a fellow I had been to school with, and made Haig stop.

'Hello, Sloper,' I said.

'Oh, hello, Maskell.'

We had not seen each other since we were seventeen. He put an elbow on the door and leaned his big pale head down at the window. I introduced Nick, and they shook hands awkwardly across the back of Nick's seat.

'I should be saluting, of course,' Nick said. It was only then that I noticed the major's insignia on Sloper's shoulder.

'Sorry, sir,' I said, and sketched a salute. He had been my senior at school, too.

With a shriek a shell landed in the harbour, sending up a tremendous waterspout and making the stones of the quayside shudder.

'Any chance of our getting off today, sir, do you think?' Nick said.

Sloper looked down, and bit his lip.

'There's only one old tub left,' he said, 'and no one's taking that because—'

A soldier with a picturesquely bandaged forehead came trotting up, clutching a signals sheet, and yelled:

'Message from Dover, sir. We're to evacuate at once.'

'Is that so, Watkins?' Sloper said, taking the signal and frowning at it. 'Well well.'

'Where can we find this boat, sir?' Nick said.

Sloper gestured vaguely and went back to his reading. I told Haig to drive on.

'Sloppy Sloper a major,' I said. 'Well I never.'

The boat was a Breton trawler with a wreath of roses painted on the bow. It wallowed languidly on its tethers; there was no one on board. The squad we had passed on the hill had arrived, and stood dejectedly on the quay, their kit at their feet, gazing mournfully in the direction of England.

'Here, you, Grimes,' I said to one of them. 'Weren't you a fisherman?' He was a squat young man, keg-shaped and bandy, with a red face and a lick of blond hair plastered across the top of his skull. 'Can you drive this thing?'

He could, and presently we were puttering our way out of the harbour toward the open sea. The boat wallowed and swayed like an old cow slopping her way across a field of mud. In the wheelhouse Grimes stood braced on his bowed legs, whistling happily. By now there were two or three shells coming every minute. Haig was crouched in the bow, cupping a cigarette and shivering.

'Cheer up, Haig,' I said. 'She had to go, you know that.' We had ditched the Austin in the harbour. He had watched in sad disbelief as the little car tipped over the harbour wall and plunged nose-first into the oily water and sank with a great gulp. 'You wouldn't have wanted Jerry to get hold of her, would you?'

He gave me a kicked-dog look and said nothing and went back to his ashen brooding. I edged my way sidewise along the crowded walkway to the front of the boat, where Nick was sitting on the deck with his back against the gunwale, his elbows on his knees and his fingers laced together, squinting thoughtfully at the sky. A shell landed thirty yards off to the left of us with a curiously understated plop.

'I've been doing a calculation,' Nick said. 'Taking into account the frequency of firing, and the distance we have to go before we're out of range, I'd put our chances at two to one against.'

I sat down by his side.

'These shells seem rather tame to me,' I said. 'Do you think one of them would sink us?'

He glanced at me sidelong and chuckled.

'Well, considering the stuff that's stored below-decks, I think it's a fair assumption.'

Why is it, I wonder, that the sea smells of tar? Or is it just that boats smell that way, and we imagine it is the sea? Life is full of mysteries.

'What,' I said, 'is down there?'

He shrugged.

'Four tons of high explosives, actually. This is a demolitions ship. Didn't you know?'

*

Lately I have developed a very faint, generalised tremor. It is a strange and, I am surprised to note, not entirely unpleasant sensation. In bed at night when I cannot sleep I am most keenly aware of it, a kind of undulant, underwater shimmer that seems to originate somewhere low down in my breast, around the area of the diaphragm, and flow outwards to the very tips of my fingers and my poor cold toes. I think of a low-voltage electric current running through a vat of some thick, warm, purplish liquid. Perhaps it is the first, shivery sign of the onset of Parkinson's disease? The bleak comedy of this possibility is not lost on me: nature being conservative, two major ailments simultaneously attacking a single organism would seem prodigal, to say the least. One would have thought cancer quite enough to be going on with. But even if it is the advance announcement of one of these newfangled maladies (does Alzheimer's disease give you the shakes?), I am convinced that somehow this quaver had its origins in that moment on the retreat from Boulogne when I realised that I was sitting on a floating bomb. That is when the tuning fork of terror was first struck, I believe, and the vibrations have only now descended to a pitch detectable to my merely human receptors. You think I am being fanciful? Profound effects are always well under way, surely, before *we* register them, with our puny powers of feeling and recognition. I am thinking of my father's amused wonderment when, in his sixties, after he had suffered his first coronary attack, the doctors told him that his condition was the result of damage caused to the ventricles of his heart by a bout of rheumatic fever he had suffered in early childhood. So it is entirely possible that this tremor that has afflicted me now, at the age of seventy-two, is the manifestation, after a forty-year lapse, of the fear that came over me but which I could not show that day in Boulogne harbour as we heaved our way homeward in gay spring sunshine with the tank shells and the seagulls shrieking around us.

I have paused for a long time between the last paragraph and this one. I was pondering the question, which I have pondered before, of whether such great revelatory moments really do occur, or if it is only that, out of need, our lives so lacking in drama, we invest past events with a significance they do not warrant. Yet I cannot shake the belief that something happened to me that day which changed me, as love, or illness, or great loss are said to change us, shifting us a vital degree or two, so that we view the world from a new perspective. I *took on* fear, as one takes on knowledge. Indeed, it did seem a form of sudden, incontrovertible knowing. My immediate sensations, when Nick gaily told me about the dynamite in the hold, were, first, an intense pressure in my chest which was, I realised, the urge to burst into laughter; if I had laughed, I should probably very soon have been screaming. Next, there flashed into my mind a fantastically clear and vivid image of *The Death of Seneca*, complete with its frame – English, late eighteenth-century, but good – and a patch of the north-lit wall in the Gloucester Terrace flat where it used to hang, and even the little lacquered table that always stood beneath it. I should have thought of wife and child, of father and brother, death, judgement and resurrection, but I did not; I thought, God forgive me, of what I truly loved. Things, for me, have always been of more import than people.

That kind of sweaty, bladder-tightening terror is not like, for instance, the dull dread that I feel nowadays when I contemplate the painful and extremely messy death that I know awaits me, sooner rather than later. What made it different was the element of chance. I have never been a gambler, but I can understand how it must feel when at the end of its counter-clockwise run the little wooden ball, making a rattle that is distractingly reminiscent of the nursery, jumps tantalisingly in and out of the slots of the roulette wheel, first the red and then the black and then the red again, with everything hanging on its whim, money, the wife's pearl necklace, the children's education, the deeds to the château in the hills, not to mention that little pied-à-terre behind the *tabac* on the sea front that no one is supposed to know about. The suspense, the anguish of it, the almost sexual expectancy – *now*? is it going to be *now*? is it *now*? – and all the time that fevered, horror-stricken sense of everything being about to change, completely, unrecognisably, for ever. That is what it is to be truly, horribly, jubilantly alive, in the magnesium glare of intensest terror.

Nick of course was not afraid. Or if he was, the effect on him was even more remarkable than it was on me. He was exultant. A kind of radiance came off him, as if he were inwardly on fire. I could smell him; above the smell of the sea and the salt reek of the deck-boards where we sat, I could smell him, and I sucked it in, the raw stink of him, sweat and leather and wet wool and the rank afterburn of the flask of coffee he had drunk in the jeep an hour ago outside the house in rue du Cloître while he and Haig waited for me and the German tanks began firing on the town. I wanted to take his hands in mine, I wanted to clasp him to me, to immolate myself in that fire. I cannot tell you how embarrassed I feel now, warbling this queasy *Liebestod*, but it is not often in life that one finds oneself so quakingly close to violent death. I hoped my terror was not visible. I smiled at him, and shrugged, trying to seem ironical and insouciant, as an officer should be, though for all the stiffness of my upper lip, I had to bite the lower one to keep it from trembling. When at last we had pulled beyond the range of the guns, and the men were cheering and dancing about the deck, Nick's eyes went dead, and he turned away from me and watched the sea, frowning, silent, spent, and I thanked God for his obliviousness to the feelings of anyone save himself.

London too was silent. Six months before, the mood of the

place had been almost festive. The bombers had not come, the storm troopers had not taken the south coast, and everything had seemed as light and distant and unreal as the elephantine barrage balloons floating above the city like an image out of Magritte. Now all that was changed, and a thoughtful, oppressive silence hung everywhere. I crossed the park, under the hazy, murmurous trees, still feeling the sway of the deck under my feet, and in my light-headed state I thought it possible that I might be dead after all, and these green acres the Elysian Fields. Black-clad nannies stark as Erinyes plied their prams. Near Clarendon Gate a big man on a little horse thudded past, a centaur in a bowler hat. In Gloucester Terrace a driverless taxi stood gasping in the sun, one of its rear doors inexplicably hanging open in suggestive invitation. I climbed the stairs to the flat and my feet seemed turned to lead and my heart to stone. Surely Odysseus himself, back from the war, must have experienced such a moment of strange dread on the threshold of home. I stopped in the hallway outside the familiar door and seemed to myself trapped at the point of intolerable pressure where two planets touched, and something swelled inside me and for a moment I could not breathe. The gristly feel of the key going into the lock made me shiver.

The flat had a different smell. Before, it had smelled of the dust of books, centuries-old pigment, bed-must, and a faint, sharp, exotic tang that I suppose must have been just gin – I used to drink a lot of it, even then. Now there was added wool and milk and watery faeces, and something like the stomach-turning pong of school dinners. Vivienne was in the living room, sitting in sunlight on the floor in front of the sofa in a puddle of strewn magazines with her stockinged feet tucked under her. She might have been posing for one of those sentimental wartime daubs – *Waiting for a Letter*, or *The Home Fires Burning* – which Brendan Bracken at the Ministry of Information used to commission from Royal Academy hacks. She was wearing a voluminous pleated skirt and a salmon-pink blouse. I noted her scarlet mouth and matching nails and experienced a silky, libidinous shiver. I set my cap down on the table and began to say something but she shot up a silencing hand and contorted her face into a look of horror.

'Ssh!' she hissed, nodding in the direction of the bedroom. 'You'll wake the slumbering fiend.'

I went to the sideboard.

'Want a drink?' I said. 'I do.'

She had everything ready: the blued gin in its high-shouldered bottle, the slices of bitter lemon, the cut-glass bowl of ice cubes. She lit a cigarette. I could feel her cool gaze, and lifted a shoulder defensively against it.

'How smart you look,' she said, 'in your uniform.'

'I don't feel smart.'

'Don't snap, dear.'

'Sorry.'

I brought her the drink. She lifted both hands to receive it, looking up at me with a pursed, quizzical smile.

'Darling, are you shaking?' she said.

'Bit of a chill. It was nippy in the Channel.'

I went and stood by the fireplace, leaning an elbow on the mantelpiece. Sunlight and leaves thronged the window. The street outside hummed to itself, dazed with the first full intimations of summer. The ice cubes congregated excitedly in my glass, tinkling and cracking. Silence. Vivienne put her drink down on the carpet beside her and looked carefully at the tip of her cigarette, nodding to herself.

'Yes,' she said, in a flat voice, 'I'm very well, thank you. The war hardly impinges. It's not as much fun, of course, with everybody amusing being away, or frightfully busy at their hush-hush jobs in the War Office. I go up to Oxford every other weekend. My parents ask after you. I tell them, no, he has not written; I'm sure he must be terribly busy, rooting out Nazi agents and so on.' She was still examining the ash of her cigarette. 'And yes, your son too is very well. His name is Julian, by the way, in case you've forgotten.'

'I'm sorry,' I said again. 'I should have written, I know. It was just . . .'

I went and sat down on the sofa and she leaned against me with an arm on my knees and looked up at me. She lifted a hand and laid the back of it against my forehead, as if to test for a sign of fever.

'Oh, don't look so grim, darling,' she said. 'It's how we are, that's all. Now, tell me about the war. How many Germans did you kill?'

I slipped a hand inside her blouse and touched her breasts; they were chill and unfamiliar, the tips coarsened from feeding the child. I rehearsed for her the escape from Boulogne. She listened distractedly, picking at a loose tuft in the carpet.

'I can't believe it was this morning,' I said. 'It seems like a lifetime ago. Nick thought it was all great fun. Sometimes I wonder if he's really human.'

'Yes,' she said absently. We were very still. I could feel the slight rise and fall of her breasts as she breathed. I took my hand from her blouse and she stood up and brought my glass to the sideboard and made me another drink. Something had ended, just like that, we had both registered it, a last, thin thread severing. 'By the way,' she said brightly, not looking at me, 'someone has been telephoning for you. A Russian, by the sound of him. Something-lotsky, or -potsky; I wrote it down. He was terribly insistent. What odd acquaintances you have.'

'Someone from the Department, I imagine,' I said. 'What did you say his name was?'

She went to the kitchen and returned with a crumpled envelope and smoothed it out and squinted at it; she was short-sighted, but too vain to wear spectacles.

'Kropotsky,' she said. 'Oleg Kropotsky.'

'Never heard of him.'

Which was true.

Julian woke up from his nap, with the hair-raising, drawn-out wail that he employed throughout his infancy, an attenuated but extraordinarily penetrating banshee cry the sound of which never failed to send a shiver rippling along my scalp and down the back of my neck; Nick said it was the poor child's Irish ancestry coming out.

'Oh, blimey,' Vivienne said, hurrying to the bedroom, 'there goes the siren.'

Julian, even at nine months, had Nick's crow-black hair and Vivienne's lustrous, unwavering gaze. The one he most resembled, though, as I saw now with a shock, was Freddie. As an adult he looks more like his poor late uncle than ever, with that big Caesarean head and those weightlifter's shoulders, so incongruous in a City gent. I wonder if he sees the resemblance? Probably not; Freddie does not figure much in the family's photograph albums. Now he squirmed inside the wrappings of his blanket, smacking his lips and blinking. He smelled like hot bread. My son.

'How big he's grown,' I said.

Vivienne nodded seriously.

'Yes, they do that, babies. Grow, I mean. Others have remarked it, down the generations.'

Presently Nick arrived, tipsy and in truculent high spirits. He was dressed in black tie and tails, his bow tie askew, like the sails of a stalled windmill.

'It's still afternoon,' Vivienne said, frowning at his dress. 'Hadn't you noticed?'

Nick threw himself on to the sofa and scowled.

'Sick of that bloody uniform,' he said. 'Thought I'd put on something entirely different. Have you got any champagne? I've been drinking champagne with Leo Rothenstein. Bloody Jewboy.' He wanted to hold the child but Vivienne would not let him. He scowled more blackly still and slumped back on the cushions. 'Did Victor tell you we were nearly blown up? I expect he's been very offhand about it, but it was a damn close thing. You'd have got him back in a gunny-sack, what they could find of him.'

The telephone rang. Vivienne took the child from my arms.

'That will be your Mr Kropotsky,' she said.

Nick sat up and peered blearily, weaving his head from side to side. He seemed drunker now than he had been when he arrived.

'Eh?' he said. 'Mr Who?'

'Some Russian that Victor is in league with,' Vivienne said. 'A spy, most likely.'

But it was Querell.

'Listen, Maskell,' he said, 'you used to be a mathematician, isn't that right?'

He was all business, yet as always I had the impression that he was laughing somehow, in that sour, muffled way that he had.

'Not really,' I said carefully. 'Not what you'd call a mathematician. Why?'

'There's a general alert out for people who are good with numbers. Can't say more on the phone. Meet me in an hour at the Gryphon.'

'I've just got back,' I said. 'Nick is here.'

There was a pause, filled with ethereal fizzes and clicks.

'Don't bring that bastard.' A pause, with breathing. 'Sorry, he's your in-law, I forgot. But don't bring him.'

Nick was at the sideboard noisily delving among the bottles.

'Who was that?' he asked over his shoulder.

'Querell,' I said. 'He sent you his regards.'

The child, swaddled in Vivienne's arms, began to cry again, but pensively this time, with a kind of wistfulness.

*

The Gryphon Club in Dean Street really was an awful dive. Much sentimental nonsense has been talked about it latterly, but the truth is it was little more than a shebeen where unemployed actors and poets with time on their hands could while away the afternoons in drinking and back-stabbing. One of that old rip Betty Bowler's many lovers, a gangland boss, so it was said, had paid her off after a botched abortion by setting her up in the club and finagling an all-day licence from someone in his pay at Scotland Yard. (Take note, Miss V.; Ancient Soho is always good for a colourful page or two.) Betty was still a handsome woman, big and blowsy, with curls and creamy skin and a fat, puckered little mouth – a sort of good-looking Dylan Thomas – and the fact that she had a wooden leg only enhanced her aura of slightly overripe magnificence. She was a little too self-consciously a character for my taste (it takes one actor to spot another). She was no fool, though; I always felt she had the measure of me, somehow. The club was a dank basement underneath a porn shop. Betty, who was a suburbanite at heart, favoured pink-shaded lamps and fringed tablecloths. Tony, the queer barman, could run up a decent sandwich, if he was in a good mood, and there was a doltish boy who for a penny tip would fetch in a plate of oysters from the fish place across the street. Goodness, how archaic and quaint and almost innocent it all seems now; Dickens's London lasted right up to the Blitz. Querell caught quite well the wartime atmosphere of the city in that thriller of his about the murderer with the club foot. What was it called? *Now and in the Hour*, something pretentiously Papist like that.

He was at the bar when I arrived, I spotted him at once despite being purblind in the gloom after the sunny street. How did he manage always to make it seem as if one had in some way compromised oneself merely by having agreed to meet him? That tilted, white-lipped smile was particularly unsettling today. He was looking more prosperous than when I had last seen him; his suit, as ever tight as a snake's skin, was expensively cut, and he was wearing a tie-pin set with what looked like a real diamond.

'Have a martini,' he said. 'One of the Yanks from the embassy told me the proper way to make them, and I've been instructing Tony here. The secret is to run the vermouth over the ice cubes and then throw the ice away. Has the taste of a reserved sin – simony, incest, one of those really interesting ones. Chin-chin.'

I smiled at him coldly. I understood, of course, that this bright talk was meant to be a parody of the trivial world of cocktails and heartless banter to which I supposedly belonged. I asked for a gin and tonic. Tony, who enjoyed watching Querell in operation, shot him a sly little grin of acknowledgement, like a magician showing the corner of a card before palming it.

'I hear you were in France,' Querell said, regarding me over the rim of his glass with a glint of amusement.

'Got back this morning. Bit of a flap, all right.'

'Our finest hour.'

'Um. What about you?'

'Oh, no chance of heroics for me. I'm just a desk man.'

Tony placed my drink before me, setting the glass down on its cork coaster with a deft little flourish of the wrist, as if he were giving a start to a spinning-top. Boy claimed that Tony – all quiff and crooked teeth and lardy pallor – was a demon in bed. One gin-numbed afternoon during the Suez crisis I made a pass at him, and was rebuffed with a scornful laugh. Sometimes I think I should have stuck to women.

Querell and I went and sat at a table in a corner under a small, rather good watercolour nude by someone whose signature I could not read – Betty Bowler had an eye for a picture, and sometimes would take work from indigent club members in return for a cleared slate; when she died in the sixties I bought a couple of things from her collection. She turned out to have a son, a plump, unhappy-looking fellow with bad breath and a wheeze; also, he had a limp, a curious echo of his mother's wooden leg, I thought. He drove a damned hard bargain, but still, on the Institute's behalf I got that early Francis Bacon out of him for a song.

'Did it ever occur to you,' Querell said, surveying the room with its scattering of shadowed, solitary drinkers, 'that this business is just an excuse for people like you and me to spend our afternoons in places like this?'

'Which business?'

He gave me a wry look. Presently he said:

'They're setting up a code-breaking centre. Place near Oxford. Very hush-hush. They're looking for people with a mathematical bent – chess players, puzzle solvers, *Times* crossword addicts, that sort of thing. Mad professors. They've asked me to ask around.'

It was a conceit of Querell's to behave as if his connection with the Department were entirely casual, a matter of his being called upon once in a way to do a favour, or carry a message.

'It doesn't sound like my kind of thing,' I said; never show eagerness, that is one of the first rules.

'Not suggesting it would be,' he said. 'You're no Albert Einstein, are you. No, I just thought you might be able to suggest some names. I don't know many Cambridge men: not the boffins, anyway.'

'Well,' I said, 'there's Alastair Sykes, he's one of the best maths people I know of.' I pointed to his empty glass. 'Want another?'

When I came back with our drinks Querell was gazing before him vacantly and picking his teeth with a matchstick. When two agents, even from the same side, begin to discuss important business, an odd effect occurs, a kind of general deceleration, as if the wave pattern of everything, the ordinary noise of self and the world, had lengthened to twice its normal frequency; through these broad highs and troughs one seems to drift, with aimless intent, buoyant and taut as a hair suspended in water. Querell said:

'As a matter of fact, Sykes is already in. He's going to be a top man in the operation.'

'Good.'

Yes, indeed.

'Another leftie, is he?' Querell said.

'He was never in the Party, if that's what you mean.'

He chuckled.

'No,' he said, 'that's *not* what I mean.' He fished the olive from his drink and nibbled on it thoughtfully. 'Not that it matters much; even the Comrades are being called on to do their bit for the realm. He needs keeping an eye on, though.' He gave me a malignant, sidelong leer. '*All* you lot do.' He finished his drink with a snap of the wrist and stood up. 'Come and see me tomorrow in the office and I'll put you in the picture. The Department is setting up a special section to monitor the decrypts. You might want to give them a hand. Not much chance of anything swashbuckling, but you've probably had enough of that, after France.'

'It really wasn't much fun, you know, France,' I said. 'Not at the end, anyway.'

He stood, on the point of going, one hand in his jacket pocket, looking down at me with the pursed remains of that evil smile.

'Oh, I know that,' he said softly, in a tone of intimate contempt. 'Everyone knows that.'

*

When Oleg Davidovich Kropotsky waddled into my life, the first thing that struck me was how remarkable an embodiment he was of his name, with its crowding syllables, its preponderance of fat *o*'s and *d*'s, that jaggedly angled capital *K* – he had something of the air of one of Kafka's clerks, did Oleg – and the *pot*, as in pot belly, sitting plump in the middle. He was not much above five feet tall. Little tubular legs, a broad, low-slung

229

torso and spreading blue-grey jowls that sat toad-fashion on his shirt collar, all made it seem as if he might once have been tall and thin but over the years had succumbed in a spectacular manner to the compressive effects of gravity. Boy used to tease him by telling him he was turning into a Chinaman – Oleg despised all Orientals – and it is true that he did bear a resemblance to one of those fat little squatting jade figures that Big Beaver used to collect. Sweat was his medium; even on the coldest days he was coated in a dully shining, putty-grey film of moisture, as if he had just been lifted out of a tank of embalming fluid. He wore a soiled mac and a squashed brown hat, and shapeless electric-blue suits with concertina trousers. When he sat down – with Oleg, the act of sitting down seemed a form of general collapse – he always kicked off his shoes, and they would stand splayed before him with their laces trailing and tongues hanging out, scuffed, cracked, turned up at the toes Turkish-slipper fashion, the very emblems of his dolefulness and physical distress.

His cover was a second-hand bookshop in a side street off Long Acre. He knew nothing about books, and was rarely at the shop, which hardly mattered, since the place attracted few customers. He detested London, because of its rigid class distinctions and the hypocrisy of its ruling élite, so he said; I suspect the real reason was that he was afraid of the place, its wealth and assurance, its cold-eyed men and svelte, terrifying women. Boy and I introduced him to the East End, where he was more at ease amid the squalor and the raucousness, and for our meetings we settled on a workman's café in the Mile End Road, with steamy windows and spit on the floor and a big brown-stained tea-urn that rumbled in its depths, like a steel stomach, all day long.

Our first encounter took place in Covent Garden. I told him of my interesting conversation with Querell at the Gryphon Club.

'Place called Bletchley Park,' I said. 'Monitoring German signals traffic.'

Oleg was inclined to be suspicious.

'And this man has offered you a job?'

'Well, hardly a job.'

I had seen right away that Oleg was not greatly impressed with me. I think the Comrades all found me a little – how shall I say? – a little uncanny. I suspect I exude a faint odour of sanctity, inherited from a long line of clerical forebears, which Oleg and his like would have mistaken for a sign of zealotry, and which would worry them, for they were practical men, and chary of ideology. They were happier with Boy's avidity and schoolboy hunger for action, and even with Leo Rothenstein's patrician disdain – though of course, being good Russians, they were all of them vigorously anti-Semitic. As we walked together round and round the market in the sunshine, smelling the pleasurably nauseating, greeny smells from the vegetable stalls, Oleg launched into an earnest apologia for the Nazi–Stalin pact. I listened politely, going along with my hands clasped at my back and an ear judiciously inclined to his tortured elucidations, all the while amusing myself by studying the antics of the sparrows hopping about nimbly under our feet. When he had done, I said:

'Look here, Mr Kropotkin—'

'Hector, please; Hector is my code name.'

'Yes, well—'

'And Kropotsky is my own name.'

'Well, Mr . . . Hector, I want to make something clear. I don't at all care for your country, I'm afraid, or for your leaders. Forgive me for saying so, but it's true. I believe in the Revolution, of course; I just wish it had happened somewhere else. Sorry.'

Oleg only nodded, smiling to himself. His head was big and round, like the globe on the pillar of a gate.

'Where do you think the Revolution should have happened?' he said. 'In America?'

I laughed.

'To anticipate Brecht,' I said, 'I think America and Russia are both whores – but my whore is pregnant.'

He stopped, and stood, a finger and thumb palping his babyish lower lip, and gave a kind of burbling snort, which it took me a moment to identify as laughter.

'John, you are right. Russia is an old whore.'

Two sparrows were fighting under a barrowload of cabbages, going at each other like a pair of amputated, feathery claws. Oleg turned aside to buy a bag of apples, counting out the pennies from a little leather purse, softly snorting still and shaking his head, his hat pushed back. I could see him as a schoolboy, fat, funny, troubled, the butt of playground jokes. We walked on again. I watched him sidelong as he ate his apple, the pink prehensile lips and yellow teeth mumbling the white mush, and was reminded of Carrickdrum and Andy Wilson's pony, which used to turn its mouth inside out at me and try to bite my face.

'A whore, yes,' he said happily. 'And if they heard me saying it . . .' He put a finger to his temple. '*Bang*.' And laughed again.

*

Another IRA bomb in Oxford Street tonight. No one killed, but a glorious amount of damage and disruption. How determined they are. All that rage, that race-hatred. We should have been like that. We should have had no mercy, no qualms. We would have brought down a whole world.

IT WAS DURING one of the first of the great daylight bombing raids on London that I received the news of my father's death. I am convinced this is the reason that I was never as frightened in the Blitz as I should have been. The shock somehow deadened my susceptibility to terror. I like to think of it as my father's final kindness to me. I had returned to Gloucester Terrace after delivering a lecture at the Institute when the telegram arrived. I was in uniform – I always wore my uniform when lecturing, being an incorrigible dresser-up – and the telegraph boy eyed my captain's pips enviously. In fact, he was not a boy but a cadaverous oldster with a smoker's cough and a Hitlerian cowlick. He also had a lazy eye, so that when I looked up from the stark news – *Father dead stop Hermione Maskell* – I thought that he was giving me a broad, conspiratorial wink. Death chooses the most unprepossessing messengers. We could hear the bombs exploding, a muffled crumpling sound like that of something vast and wooden falling slowly down a series of stone steps, and under our feet the floor quaked. He cocked an ear and grinned.

'Old Adolf's paying us a daylight visit,' he said cheerfully. I gave him a shilling. He nodded at the telegram in my hand. 'Not bad news, I hope, sir?'

'No no,' I heard myself say. 'My father has died.'

I went back into the flat. The door closed behind me with a solemn thud; how obligingly at times like this the most commonplace procedures take on an air of pomp and finality. I sat down slowly on a straight-backed chair, hands on my knees and my feet planted side by side on the carpet; what is that Egyptian god, the dog-headed one? The afternoon around me had settled into a dreamy stillness, except for the sunlight falling in the window, a pale-gold tube of teeming particles. And still the bombs were falling afar in dulled funereal cannonades. Father. A weight of guilt and dry grief descended on me, and I shouldered it wearily. How familiar it seemed! It was like putting on an old overcoat. Was I somehow remembering back to my mother's death, thirty years before?

But the person I found myself thinking of, to my surprise, was Vivienne, as if it were she and not my father I had lost. She was in Oxford, with the child. I attempted to telephone her, but the lines were down. I sat for a while listening to the bombing. I tried to imagine the people dying – now, at this moment, and close by – but could not. I recalled a phrase from my lecture that morning: *The problem for Poussin in the depiction of suffering is how to stylise it, as the rules of classical art demand, while yet making it immediately felt.*

That night I took the mail boat to Dublin. The crossing was unseasonably rough. I spent it in the bar, in the company of English travelling salesmen and Irish hod carriers mad on porter. I got vilely drunk, and tried to make maudlin conversation with the barman, who was from Tipperary, and whose mother had recently died. I leaned my forehead on the back of my wrist and wept, in that odd, detached way one does when one is drunk; it only made me feel worse. We arrived in Kingstown at three in the morning. I collapsed on a bench under a tree on the harbourfront. The wind had died, and I sat in the soft cool late-summer darkness and listened in melancholy rapture to a lone bird warbling in the leaves above me. I dozed for a while, and presently at my back the dawn came up, and I woke in anguish, not knowing for a moment where I was or what I should be doing. I found a taxi, the driver still half asleep, and travelled into the city, where I had to sit for another hour nursing my burgeoning hangover in a deserted and eerily echoing railway station while I waited for the first train to

Belfast. On the platform, ill-tempered, putteed pigeons swaggered about under my feet, and a strong, heatless sun beat upon the grimed glass roof high above me. These are the moments that lodge in the memory.

*

It was afternoon by the time I got to Carrickdrum. I was numb from travelling and the night's drinking. Andy Wilson was at the station with the pony-and-trap. He greeted me warily, avoiding my eye.

'Didn't think I would outlast him,' he said, 'I surely didn't.'

We set off up the West Road. The gorse; the pony's straw-and-sacking smell; the ash-blue sea.

'How is Mrs Maskell?' I said. For answer Andy only shrugged. 'And Freddie? Does he realise what's happened?'

'Och, he knows, right enough; how would he not?'

He talked enthusiastically about the war. Everyone was saying, he said, that Belfast and the shipyards would be bombed; he spoke of the prospect in a tone of gleeful expectation, as of a promised treat of fireworks and staying up all night.

'There was a raid on London yesterday,' I said. 'In daylight.'

'Aye, so we heard on the wireless.' He gave a wistful sigh. 'A terrible thing.'

The house as always startled me with its familiarity: all still there, all still going on, careless of my absence. As I alighted on the gravel below the front steps, Andy unprecedentedly offered me a helping hand. His palm seemed made of warm, malleable stone. I realised that in his eyes I was the master of St Nicholas's now.

I found Hettie in the big stone-flagged back kitchen, sitting on a spindle-backed chair listlessly shelling peas into a battered saucepan. Her hair, those big auburn tresses of which she had once been guiltily proud, had turned into a matted nest, with grey wisps dangling over her forehead and trailing down the back of her cardigan. She was wearing a sack-shaped brown dress and those fur-lined ankle-boots that are exclusive to decaying old women. She greeted me without surprise and cracked open another pea-pod. I leaned down awkwardly and kissed her forehead, and she shied away from me in a sort of sullen alarm, like a beast of burden more used to blows than endearments. I smelled her smell.

'Hettie,' I said, 'how are you?'

She nodded dully, giving a tremendous sniff. A tear rolled down at the side of her fat nose and plopped into the saucepan on her lap.

'You're good to have come,' she said. 'Was it dangerous, travelling?'

'No. The bombings have only been in London.'

'I read in the newspaper about these submarines.'

'Not in the Irish Sea, I think, Hettie. Not yet, anyway.'

She made a sound that was half sigh, half sob, hunching her back and letting it fall slack again, a big old bag of bones. I looked beyond her through the window to the garden, where the sunlight glistened in the leaves of the sycamore standing there in its solitude, vastly atremble, its green already tinged with autumnal grey. One day when I was small I fell out of that tree, and lay motionless in the lush grass in a kind of misty languor, with a numbed arm twisted under me, watching Hettie running in slow motion towards me across the lawn, barefoot, her arms outstretched, like one of Picasso's mighty maenads, and in that moment I experienced an inexplicable and perfect happiness, such as I had not known before, nor have since, and for which even a broken arm seemed a not unreasonable price to pay.

'How are you, Hettie?' I said again. 'How are you managing?' She seemed not to hear me. I took the saucepan from her and set it on the table. She continued to sit with shoulders hunched and head bowed, a sorrowing old buffalo, picking distractedly at her fingernails. 'Where's Freddie?' I said. 'Is he all right?'

She lifted her eyes to the sunlight and September's fading green in the window.

'He was so calm,' she said, 'so calm and good.' For a moment I thought she was speaking of my brother. She heaved another sighing sob. 'He was there in the garden, you know, putting out scraps for a fox that comes down at night from the hills. I saw him bending over, and he gave a kind of start, as if he had remembered something important. And then he just fell down.' I saw her again, billowing towards me across the lawn, bare arms outstretched, her big white legs flexing and her feet hardly seeming to touch the grass over which she ran. 'He held my hand. He told me not to worry myself. I hardly knew it when he was gone.' She put her hands on her knees and heaved herself to her feet and went to the sink and ran the cold tap and pressed wetted fingers hard into the sockets of her eyes. 'You were good to come,' she said again. 'We know how busy you must be, with the war on.'

She made tea for us, moving from sink to table to sideboard at a flat-footed, leaden pace. A friend of hers, she told me, had taken Freddie to the seaside for the afternoon – Freddie had always been fascinated by the sea, and would sit on the shingle for hours gazing out with rapt attention over this strange, unknowable, shifting element, as if he had once seen something rising out of it, a sea monster, or a tridented god, and was patiently waiting for it to appear again.

'Have you spoken to him about . . . about Father?' I said.

She peered at me in momentary puzzlement.

'Oh, but he was here,' she said. 'We were both here. He came and sat beside your father on the lawn, and held his hand as well. He knew what was happening. He cried. He wouldn't come away, I had to get Andy to help me make him go indoors while we waited for the ambulance. And when they were taking your father away he wanted to go with him.'

The teapot smoked in the pale light from the window; soon

it would be full autumn. I had a sudden vision of a world in flames.

'We shall have to think about his future, now,' I said.

She became very busy with the tea things.

'Yes, yes,' she said, 'we'll need to find a position for him.'

I thought of Freddie sitting splay-legged on the seashore, in his jersey and his stained trousers, his face lifted to the horizon, grinning happily into that vast emptiness.

'Yes, of course,' I said, faintly. 'A position.'

I went for a walk, alone, up in the hills. Even on the clearest days the sunlight here seemed hazy and somehow aswarm, falling like gauze over rocks and bushes, thickening to a milky blur the tremulous blue distances. How cunningly the grieving heart seeks comfort for itself, conjuring up the softest of sorrows, the most sweetly piercing recollections, in which it is always summer, replete with birdsong and the impossible radiance of a transfigured past. I leaned on a rock and gently wept, and saw myself, leaning, weeping, and was at once gratified and ashamed.

When I returned to the house Hettie was plying the teapot again and the kitchen seemed filled with people. Hettie's friend was there, a Mrs Blenkinsop, tall, thin, pale visaged, in a frightening hat, and Freddie, sitting with an ankle crossed on a knee and his right arm flung over the back of his chair, looking uncannily like my father in one of his rare relaxed moments. Most startling of all was the presence of Andy Wilson. He was sitting at the table with a mug of tea before him, hardly recognisable with his cap off, his bald pate pale as a blanched leek above his narrow little weather-beaten weaselly face. I had never in my life known him to come inside the house, and now that he had got in I did not like his defiantly easy, proprietorial air. I gave him a hard look, at which he refused to flinch, and he made no move to rise. The Blenkinsop woman in turn was looking hard at me, and seeming not to approve of what she saw. It is always the most unexpected people who see through one. She offered me brisk condolences and went back to talking of church matters to Hettie, who, it was evident, was not listening. Freddie was shooting me shy glances from under colourless lashes. The corner of his mouth was gnawed to pulp, always a sign in him of acute distress. I laid a hand on his shoulder, and he went into a paroxysm of affection, shivering like a gun dog, and stroking my hand convulsively with his own.

'We had a grand time at the seaside,' Mrs Blenkinsop said to me loudly in her knife-edged, Presbyterian voice. 'Isn't that right, Freddie?'

Freddie did not look at her, but another, different sort of spasm passed through him, and I knew exactly what he thought of Mrs Blenkinsop.

'Aye,' said Andy, 'he do love the strand.'

The funeral was a grim affair, even for a funeral, with urns of flesh-smelling trumpet lilies in the church, and quavery organ music, and much stylised lamentation by a succession of alternately rotund and shrivelled churchmen. Hettie stood in the front pew with Freddie clinging to her arm; they were like a pair of lost, ancient children. Now and then Freddie would send up one of his werewolf ululations to the varnished rafters, and the congregation would stir uneasily, hymnals fluttering. The weather, though fine before and after, laid on a pretty little sun-shower for the interment. Afterwards, as we walked back to the motor cars along an avenue of dripping yews, I engaged in covert consultation with a jolly old hypocrite by the name of Wetherby, who was to be my father's successor to the bishopric, and whom I knew to have special responsibility for a number of Belfast's charitable institutions. When he understood my purpose he tried to sidle away from me, but I would not let him go until I had got out of him what I needed to know, along with a reluctant promise of help. Back at the rectory I shut myself into my father's study with the telephone, and by dinnertime that evening I had the plan ready to put to Hettie. She could not take it in at first.

'You know there is no other way,' I told her. 'He'll be taken care of there; they have facilities.'

We were in the upstairs drawing room. Hettie in her widow's weeds had a monumental aspect, sitting squarely in an armchair by the window, like the figure of an ancient idol on display on a temple altar, with a rhomb of late sunlight smouldering redly on the carpet at her feet. She gazed at me unblinkingly from under hanging straggles of hair, frowning in an effort of concentration, and agitatedly twining and twining her fingers, as if she were wielding a pair of knitting needles.

'Facilities,' she said; it might have been a word in a foreign language.

'Yes,' I said. 'They'll look after him. It will be for the best. I spoke to Canon Wetherby, and I telephoned the Home. I can bring him in today.'

She opened her eyes very wide.

'Today . . . ?'

'There is no reason to delay. You have enough to cope with.'

'But—'

'And besides, I must get back to London.'

She turned her great head slowly – I could almost hear the gears working – and looked out unseeing at the hills and a distant thin brushstroke of purplish sea. Mingled gorse and heather glowed on the hillsides.

'That's what Myra Blenkinsop says too,' Hettie said, grown sullen now.

'What does Myra Blenkinsop say?'

She turned her head to look at me again, with a kind of puzzled curiosity, as if I were someone she thought she had known but now did not recognise at all.

'She says what you say, that poor Freddie should be in a Home.'

We were silent then, and sat for a long time, looking away from each other, adrift in ourselves. I wonder what it will be like to die. I imagine it as a slow, helpless stumbling into deeper and deeper confusion, a kind of mute, maundering drunkenness from which there will be no sobering up. Did my father really hold Hettie's hand and tell her not to worry herself, or did she invent the scene? How do we die? I should like to know. I should like to be prepared.

On the next day I had Andy bring out the Daimler – the Bishop's Car, as even we in the family had always called it – from the tumbledown shed behind the house, where for most of the year it bided its time in clay-smelling darkness, vast, sleek and intent, like a wild beast that had blundered into captivity and could only be let out, coughing and growling, on occasions of rare significance. Andy treated it as a sentient being, manipulating it delicately and with circumspection, sitting bolt upright and clutching the wheel and the gearstick as if they were a chair and pistol. Freddie became greatly excited, and stumped about the lawn in agitated circles, grinning and crowing. He associated the car with Christmas, and summer jaunts, and those colourful church ceremonials which he loved, and which I suspect he thought were laid on specially for his delight. Hettie brought the suitcase she had packed for him. It was an old one, stuck all over with faded travel labels, testaments of my father's *Wanderjahre*; Freddie fingered them wonderingly, as if they were the petals of rare plants from foreign lands plastered to the leather. Hettie wore a black straw hat and black gloves; she clambered into the back seat and settled herself with henlike subsidences, sweating and sighing. I had a bad moment when I got behind the wheel and Freddie leaned over from the passenger seat and put his head lovingly on my shoulder and pressed his straw-dry hair against my cheek. My nostrils filled up with his milk-and-biscuits smell – Freddie never lost the smell of childhood – and my hands faltered on the controls. But then I saw Andy Wilson standing on the grass watching me with spiteful surmise, and I put my foot down on the accelerator with merciless force, and the vast old motor surged forward on the gravel, and in the mirror I saw the house abruptly shrinking to a miniature of itself, complete with toy trees and cotton wool clouds and a toy-sized Andy Wilson with one arm lifted in hieratic and, so it seemed, scornful farewell.

The day was bright, the blue air shimmering with freshets of wind. As we progressed sedately southwards along the Lough Freddie looked out with lively interest at the scenery. Every so often a doggy shiver of excitement would make his knees knock. What can he have been anticipating? My mind kept touching the thought of the prospect before him and flinching away from it like a snail from salt. In the back seat Hettie was muttering under her breath and heaving little sighs. It struck me that soon I might well be travelling this road again, with her beside me this time, and her things in a bag in the boot, on the way to another betrayal dressed up as necessity. I saw my father's face before me, half smiling in his tentative, quizzical way, and then turning sadly aside, and fading.

The Nursing Home, as it was misleadingly referred to, was big and square, made of dark brick, standing in a dispiritingly well-tended garden in a sombre cul de sac off the Malone Road. As we turned in at the gate Freddie leaned close to the windscreen to look up at the stern frontage of the place, and I thought I detected in him the first tremor of unease. He turned to me with an enquiring smile.

'This is where you're going to live now, Freddie,' I said. He nodded vehemently, making gagging noises. It was always impossible to know how much he might understand of what was being said to him. 'But only if you like it,' I added, cravenly.

In the vestibule were cracked tiles, brown shadows, a big clay pot of dried-out geraniums; there we were greeted by a sort of nun, or lay sister, in a grey wool outfit and a complicated wimple, something like a bee-keeper's headdress, in which her small sharp beaky face, the face of a baby owl, was rigidly framed. (Where on earth did a nun come from? – was the place run by Catholics? Surely not; my memory must be up to its old tricks again.) Freddie did not like the look of her at all, and balked, and I had to take him by one quivering arm and press him forward. I was by now in a state of truculent ill-temper. This is, I have noticed, a common response in me when there is something unpleasant to be done. Freddie in particular always provoked my ire. Even when we were children, and he used to stumble along beside me in the mornings to Miss Molyneaux's infant school, I would have worked myself into such a rage by the time we got there that I would hardly notice the other children gloating at the spectacle of the rector's snooty son hustling his imbecile brother into the classroom by the scruff of his neck.

The Sister led us down a hallway, up a sombre staircase, along a green-painted corridor with a window at the far end through the frosted panes of which the sun shone whitely, the light of another world. Hettie and the Sister seemed to know each other – Hettie in her heyday had been on countless boards of visitors of institutions such as this – and they walked ahead of Freddie and me, talking about the weather, the Sister brisk and faintly contemptuous, Hettie at once vague and frantic, tottering in her unaccustomed outdoor shoes. Halfway down the corridor we stopped, and while I waited politely as the Sister searched importantly among the keys on a big metal ring attached to her belt, another self inside me yearned toward that window with its milky effulgence, that seemed the very promise of escape and freedom.

'And this,' said the Sister, hauling open a dirty-cream door, 'this will be Frankie's room.'

Metal cot with folded blanket, a rudimentary chair; on the blank white wall a framed daguerreotype of a frock-coated worthy with mutton-chop whiskers. I noted the wire mesh outside the window, the Bakelite bowl and pitcher on the washstand, the metal loops along the frame of the cot where restraining bands could be attached. Freddie stepped forward tentatively, clutching the suitcase before him in both arms and peering about him in apprehensive wonder. I looked at the back

243

of his head, the delicate, unblemished neck, the pink ears and little whorl of hair at the crown, and had to close my eyes for a moment. He was quite quiet. He looked back at me over his shoulder and smiled, his tongue lolling out briefly and then popping back in. This was his being-good mode; he knew something large was expected of him. Behind me Hettie sighed in unfocused distress.

'He'll be grand, here,' the Sister said. 'We'll take the best of care of him.' She turned to Hettie confidingly. 'The Bishop, you know, was very good to us.'

Hettie, wandering lost somewhere inside herself, stared at the woman in wild-eyed incomprehension. Freddie sat on the bed and began to bounce up and down happily, still clutching the suitcase to him as if it were a big, awkward baby. The bedsprings jangled angrily. The Sister went forward and touched him on the shoulder, not without kindness, and immediately he was still, and sat gazing up at her meekly, smiling his slow-blinking smile, his blood-pink lower lip hanging loose.

'Come along with me now,' she shouted at him cheerily, 'and we'll show you the rest of the house.'

Then it was the corridor again, with its smudged thumbprint of white light at the window end, and as we went towards the stairs the Sister came close to me and murmured, 'The poor chap, has he no words at all?'

At the foot of the stairs our little party – the Sister and me, with Hettie behind us, and Freddie, unburdened of his suitcase now, trotting at her heels and holding on to the sleeve of her coat with a finger and thumb – turned towards the interior of the house, from whence there began to come to us a noise, a muffled tumult, as of many large children at boisterous and unruly play. Freddie heard it, and set up a low, worried moaning. We stopped at a broad set of double doors, from behind which the hubbub was emanating, and the Sister, pausing for effect, looked at us over her shoulder with a tight-lipped little smile, her eyes fairly sparkling, as if she were about to give us a wonderful treat, and whispered:

'This is what we call the Common Room.'

She threw open the doors on a scene that was bizarre and at the same time eerily, though inexplicably, familiar. What struck me first was the sunlight, great pale meshes of it falling down from a long row of tall, many-paned arched windows that seemed, although we were on the ground floor, to give on to nothing but an empty expanse of white, strangely shining sky. The floor was of bare wood, which intensified the uproar, adding a deep drum-rolling effect. The people in the room were of all ages, men and women, girls, youths, but in the first moment, by some trick of expectation, I suppose, to me they all seemed to be youngish men, all of Freddie's age, with the same big hands and straw-coloured hair and agonisedly blithe, vacant smiles. They were dressed in white smocks (like doctors!) and wore no shoes, only thick woollen socks. They milled about in an oddly arbitrary, disarranged way, as if just a moment before our entrance something had fallen into their midst and scattered them like ninepins out of strictly ordered ranks. The noise was that of a menagerie. We stood in the doorway, staring, ignored by all save one or two distracted souls who peered at us suspiciously as if convinced we were no more than uncommonly solid-looking specimens of the usual daytime apparitions. Freddie was silent, his eyes wide, glazed with awe and a kind of manic delight – so many, and so mad! The Sister beamed at us, her plump, mottled little hands clasped under her breast; she might have been a mother showing off with rueful pride her numerous and happily undisciplined progeny.

But why did it all seem so familiar? What was it in the scene that made me think I had been here before – or, more accurately, what was it made me think that I, or some essential part of me, had *always* been here? The room looked like nothing so much as the inside of my own head: bone white, lit by a mad radiance, and thronged with lost and aimlessly wandering figures who might be the myriad rejected versions of my self, of my soul. A small man approached me, cherubic, pinkly bald, with baby-blue eyes and tufts of woolly grey curls above his ears, conspiratorially smiling, one eyebrow roguishly arched, and took me delicately by the lapel and said:

'I'm here for safe keeping, you know. Everyone is afraid.'

The Sister stepped forward and lowered an arm between us like a level-crossing gate.

'Now now, Mr McMurty,' she said with grim good humour, 'none of that, thank you very much.'

Mr McMurty smiled again at me, and with a regretful shrug stepped backward into the milling throng. I would not have been surprised to see sprouting from his back a pair of miniature golden wings.

'Come along now, Frankie,' the Sister was saying to Freddie, 'come along and we'll get you settled in.'

He leaned toward her docilely, but then, as if he had bethought himself, he gave a violent start and shied away from her, goggling, and shaking his head, and making a choking noise at the back of his throat. He clutched at me, sinking his shockingly strong fingers into my arm. He had realised at last what was happening, that this was no treat laid on for him, a sort of pantomime, or an anarchic version of the circus, but that here was where he was to be abandoned, the bold corner where, for misdemeanours he could not recall committing, he was to be made to stand for the rest of his life. That blustering anger boiled up inside me all the stronger, and I felt violently sorry for myself, and cruelly wronged. Hettie then, to the surprise of all, gave herself a sort of rattly shake, like one waking with an effort from a drugged sleep, and without a word took Freddie firmly by the hand and led him back along the hall and up the stairs to his room. I followed, and loitered in the corridor, watching through the half-open door as she and the Sister busied themselves unpacking Freddie's bag and putting his things away. Freddie wandered about the room for a while, crooning to himself, then stopped at the bed and sat down, holding his back very straight, and with his knees together and his hands placed flat on the mattress at his sides. And then, having settled himself, the good boy once more, he lifted his eyes and looked at me where I stood cowering in the doorway, and smiled his most ingenuous, most beatific, smile, and seemed – surely I imagined it? – seemed to nod, once, as if to say, *Yes, yes, don't worry, I understand.*

I travelled back to Dublin that evening and took the mailboat to Holyhead. Troop movements had disrupted the trains, and I did not get to London until eight o'clock in the morning. I telephoned Oleg from Euston, waking him up, and summoned him to meet me at Rainer's. The day was crisp and clear, and the fighter planes were out already, their contrails scattered in the zenith like knotted pipe-cleaners. In Tottenham Court Road the traffic was being diverted around a hole in the middle of the street from which the back end of an unexploded bomb stuck up at a drunken angle. The size of the thing was remarkable. It was also remarkably ugly. This weapon had nothing of the sleek, luciferian elegance of my revolver. It was just a big stubby iron canister with tail fins shaped like a jumbo biscuit tin. The taxi driver chuckled at the sight. Outside the blasted wreckage of John Lewis, naked plaster mannequins were strewn on the pavement like so many bloodless corpses. 'Madame Tussaud's copped it last night,' the driver said. 'You should have seen it: Hitler's head under some queen's arm!'

Oleg was at a corner table, with a cup of tea and a cigarette, looking greyly unwell; he was not a morning man. He was wearing his macintosh, and his squashed hat sat on the table beside a smeared, rolled-up copy of the *Daily Mail*. He had the look of a run-down Napoleon, with those puffy blue jowls and soft-boiled eyes and greasy widow's peak. I sat down. He considered me warily.

'Well, John?' he said. 'You have something for me?'

I asked the waitress for coffee and a bun. There was no coffee, of course.

'Listen, Oleg,' I said, 'I wish you wouldn't keep calling me by that ridiculous name. No one is paying us the slightest attention; no one ever does.'

He only smiled his fat, roguish smile.

'You are always so angry,' he said fondly.

The girl brought thin tea and a bun stuck with a glacé cherry. Oleg eyed the bun hungrily. I said:

'There is an agent of ours – I mean, of the Department's – on the Moscow Politburo staff. He has been in place for five or six years. His name is Petrov. He's one of Mikoyan's private secretaries.'

Oleg greeted this news with disconcerting equanimity. He stirred his tea slowly, gazing thoughtfully into the cup. He sighed. His sausagey fingers were deeply stained by nicotine; one does not see that kind of stain any more, even on the fingers of the heaviest smokers – I wonder why?

'Petrov,' he said, turning over the syllables. 'Petrov . . .' He glanced up at me. 'How long have you known this?'

'Why? What does it matter?' He lifted his shoulders and turned down his frog's mouth at the corners. 'I've known since I joined the Department,' I said. He nodded again, his jowls wobbling, and went back to studying the tea in his cup.

'You know what will happen, when I tell Moscow,' he said.

'They'll shoot him, I imagine?'

Another big shrug, with a glistening, mauve lower lip stuck out.

'Eventually, yes,' he said.

'Eventually.'

He turned up his eggy eyes to mine and again did that smile of a dissolute baby.

'Are you sorry now,' softly, 'that you told me?'

I shrugged impatiently.

'He's a spy,' I said. 'He knew the risks.'

Still smiling, Oleg slowly shook his head.

'So angry,' he murmured. 'So angry.' I turned away from him, and was startled by my own spectral reflection in the window beside me. Such a look in those eyes! 'Well, don't worry, John,' he said. 'We already know about this Petrov.'

I stared.

'Who told you? – Boy?'

He could resist no longer, and reached out and delicately tweaked the cherry from my untouched bun and popped it into his mouth.

'Perhaps,' he said happily. 'Perhaps.'

*

When I got to Poland Street the house reeked of cigarette smoke and bodies and stale beer. There had been a party the night before. Empty bottles everywhere, fag ends ground into the carpets, on the bathroom floor a puddle of carrot-coloured puke. I went about opening windows. In the parlour I found a large, blond young man – he turned out to be a Latvian seaman – asleep in his overcoat in an armchair. Boy too was asleep. I cleared a space in the kitchen and made tea and sat drinking it and watching a patch of sunlight move across the floor. Presently Nick arrived, with Sylvia Lydon in tow. He was in uniform.

'Where have you been?' he said.

'In Ireland.'

'Oh, yes. Sorry about your dad.'

Sylvia kept shooting sly little glances at me, biting her lip to keep from giggling. They had both been up all night.

'Doing?' Nick said. 'Oh, nothing. Just ragging about.'

Sylvia spluttered.

'Well, you both look remarkably fresh,' I said.

I had a very bad headache. Nick searched about for something to eat, while Sylvia leaned against the table and played with the string of pearls at her neck. She was wearing a green satin gown and elbow-length white gloves.

'Oh, Nicky,' she said, 'we may as well tell him.'

Nicky.

'Tell me what?'

I recalled dancing with Sylvia Lydon on shipboard as we plunged through the Baltic, her sharp, foxy scent, the feel of her meagre breasts against me.

'Go on,' she said.

Nick avoided my eye. He opened a bread bin and peered into it gloomily. Sylvia went to him and draped an arm across his shoulder and looked at me again and smiled her thin-lipped, triumphant smile. I stood up. Pounding headache now; really, very bad.

'Well, congratulations,' I said. He had not given me a word of warning, not a word. 'I'll see if I can borrow some champagne from Boy, shall I?'

*

A charming interlude: dinner last night with my children – I mean, my grown-up son and daughter. It was my birthday yesterday. They took me to one of those ghastly grand hotels off Berkeley Square. It was not my choice. I suppose it is the kind of place where Julian brings his more important clients, mostly Arabs, apparently, these days. The dead air in the darkly lit vestibule was thick with the cloying, cottony smell of over-rich food. We were met in the entrance to the dining room by a sleek-headed, fawning head waiter with a marionette's blank smile and furtive eyes, who greeted Julian with a special intimacy, spotting what he surmised was a big tipper (he was wrong). When we were seated he stood over us flourishing an outsize menu like a ringmaster cracking his whip. Julian ordered a glass of mineral water; I asked for an extra-dry martini. '. . . And for the lady?' Poor Blanche was so intimidated by now she could hardly look at the fellow. She sat hunched in a flattened Z-shape, her broad back bowed and her head drawn down between her shoulders, trying in vain to make herself small. She was wearing an unbecoming dress made from yards and yards of startling crimson stuff. Her hair stood up like clumps of wire.

'Well,' I said, 'this is nice.'

Blanche shot me one of her quick, worriedly conspiratorial smiles; Blanche always enjoys it when I am provocative, though she pretends to disapprove. Julian harrumphed, ponderously shrugging, and inserted a finger under the rim of his too-tight shirt collar and gave it a tremendous, eye-popping tug. At an adjoining table an amply fleshed woman in a strapless gown was beginning to recognise me.

'Saw Mummy today,' Julian said.

'Oh, yes? And is she well?'

He glanced at me with a mixture of reproach and distress, and that peculiar beseeching that he directs at me mutely when the subject of his mother comes up. Vivienne resides now in a nursing home in North Oxford, a victim of chronic melancholia. I prefer not to visit her; she finds my presence upsetting.

'She's not well, actually,' Julian said. 'She has been refusing her meals.'

'Well, she never was a big eater, you know.'

'This is different. The doctors are quite worried.'

'A very stubborn woman, your mother.'

His jaw was beginning to work.

'She sent you her love,' Blanche said quickly. (A likely story.) Blanche has an affecting way of making sudden, eager little feints, like a mouse dashing out of its hole to seize on a bit of cheese, and then as quickly drawing back into herself again with a gulp of fright. She works in a school for children with special needs (i.e., mad). She will never marry, now; I can see her at sixty, all brawn and Labradors, doing good works, like poor Hettie, and laughed at behind her back by Julian's bratty children. My poor girl. Sometimes I am glad that I shall soon be gone. 'I told her we were seeing you tonight,' Blanche said. 'She said she wished she could be here.'

I made no comment.

Soup was a clear, thin, tasteless broth. I pushed the plate away, deciding to wait for my sole. Blanche too was having the fish, but Julian in his manly, masterful way had ordered baron of beef. Really, his resemblance to poor Freddie is remarkable. I asked him how things were in the City and he looked at me warily; he imagines I am waiting in confident anticipation for the inevitable collapse of capitalism. I must be a grave embarrassment to him, among his stockbroking colleagues. I do appreciate his filial loyalty, really I do – no one would have blamed him, least of all myself, if he had broken with me after my public exposure – but I cannot resist teasing him, he is so entertainingly teasable.

'Your Uncle Nick,' I said, 'was at one time an adviser to the Rothenstein family, did you know that? Before the war. It was one of his more bizarre employments. They sent him to Germany to assess the Nazi threat to their holdings. Of course, we were all spies in those days.'

The word brought a silence down over the table like an awning. Blanche bit her lip, and Julian coughed and frowned and attacked a slice of beef. Heh heh. It is one of the few privileges of old age to be allowed to behave appallingly to one's children.

'Didn't Lord Rothenstein buy that picture, *The Death of Cicero*, for you?' Julian said.

'Yes,' I said shortly. 'But I paid him back the loan. One would not want to be in debt to a Rothenstein. And it's Seneca, not Cicero.'

A frightening thought occurred to me: had the Poussin been a plant, a lure, a way of putting me in their debt? Had they got Wally Cohen to leave it there among the gallery dross, where I would be bound to nose it out? The picture could have been from Rothenstein's private collection, he would have been well able to spare it. I recalled the peculiar look he and Boy had exchanged on the pavement that summer evening outside Alighieri's, and Rothenstein laughing his big soft laugh and turning away. I sat aghast, with Julian's voice buzzing incomprehensibly in my ear, as the thing opened before my appalled imagination like a chrysalis and the whole horrible nasty little plot crawled out. But then, as quickly as it had unfolded, it collapsed again, the wings were furled, the casings fell to dust, and the dust dispersed. Nonsense, nonsense; pure paranoia. I was able to breathe again. I leaned back on my chair and smiled weakly. Julian had asked me a question and was waiting for an answer. 'I'm sorry,' I said, 'what were you saying . . . ?'

'Oh, nothing.'

That woman at the table next to us had at last identified me, and was speaking eagerly into the ear of the elderly gent to her left, her bulbous eyes fixed on me excitedly and the tops of her pale plump breasts aquiver. Nice to think one can still cause a flutter. 'Funny,' I said, 'that Leo was never exposed.'

Julian stared.

'You mean he . . . ?'

'Oh yes, he was one of us. Never very active, more a sort of eminence. Our masters in Moscow were leery of him, him being a Jew and them being – well, Russians; but they valued his connections. And then there was all that money— Blanche, my dear, are you all right?'

'Yes, yes, it's just a bone . . . it's got stuck . . .'

Julian had stopped eating, and was sitting with his knife and fork upright in his fists, glowering at his blood-stained plate.

'Is this true,' he said, 'or just one of your jokes?'

'Would I lie about such a thing?'

He looked at my smirk and chose not to answer; instead he asked:

'Uncle Nick – did he know? About Rothenstein, I mean.'

Blanche, purple-faced, was still coughing and thumping herself in the chest.

'I never asked him,' I said. 'Nick was not terribly observant, you know. Vain people tend not to be. Blanche, do drink some water.'

Julian bent thoughtfully to his food again, showing me the top of Freddie's head, the same drab-yellow hair and broad crown. Strange the things the genes choose to replicate.

'*He* wasn't one of you,' he said, 'was he – Uncle Nick?'

The Sancerre Julian had ordered was really quite good, though he knows I do not like Sancerre.

'Poor Nick,' I said. 'All those years and he never noticed a thing. Vanity, you see. Whatever he looked at turned immediately into a mirror. But, ah, such charm!' Julian stopped chewing, keeping his eyes fixed on his plate. I chuckled. 'No,' I said, 'don't worry, he was always profoundly, depressingly hetero.'

Another terrible silence. Had I gone too far? Julian has never reconciled himself to my queerness – well, I would hardly have expected him to: what son would? The thought of even a heterosexual parent's sexuality is squirm-making enough. And then, he is very loyal to his mother. Blanche is more tolerant of me than Julian is; women don't really take sex seriously. She is very tender and considerate of my feelings – for I do have feelings, despite appearances to the contrary – but I'm sure she too must think I betrayed her mother. Oh, families!

'Have you talked to Uncle Nick?' she said now. 'I mean, since . . . ?'

'No, no. Nick and I have not spoken for many years. I was something of a missing rung on the ladder of his success. It was necessary for him to step over me.'

For some reason Blanche reached out and gave my hand a squeeze, her eyes going shiny; she is such a soft poor thing, much too good-hearted, really, for a daughter of mine. Julian noted the gesture, and frowned. He said:

'Did he know about . . . about you?'

'About me being a spy?' He flinched; I was feeling really

254

quite mischievous by now, thanks to my having drunk most of the bottle of wine. I told myself to go carefully. The lady of the heaving embonpoint was agog. 'Oh, no,' I said. 'Why would you think that? I'm sure he would have said. He was very straightforward, you know, very bluff and honest, at least in those days – they do say he has been involved in some murky doings on the way to his present position of power and influence. He was always a bit of a Fascist, was old Nick.'

Julian snickered, surprising me; he has never been noted for his sense of humour.

'Would that prevent him from working for the Russians?' he said.

I turned the wineglass in my fingers, admiring the brassy, fiery sunburst burning in its depths.

'Of course,' I said mildly, 'you find it hard to distinguish between opposing ideologies. Capital is colour-blind.' Stung, he was about to respond, but instead looked down at his plate again, breathing an angry sigh through his nostrils. Blanche gave me another beseeching, sorrowful look. 'Come,' I said, 'let me buy you both a drink. Julian: a brandy?' I caught the glance that they exchanged: they had agreed a time limit for the evening. I thought of the flat, with its desk and lamp, of the window holding back the glossy black night. Blanche began to say something but I interrupted her. 'And tell me, Julian, how is . . . ?' I always have trouble remembering his wife's name. 'How is Pamela?' I should have asked after the children, too, but I did not wish to have that subject opened up. The thought of grandchildren I find peculiarly dispiriting, and not for the obvious reasons. 'She's thriving, I hope?'

He nodded grimly and said nothing. He knows what I think of Pamela. She keeps horses. Abruptly, as if the mention of his wife were a signal, he brought the meal to a close, putting down his napkin with grave finality, while Blanche leaned down hurriedly and scrabbled about under her chair for her handbag; he always did bully her. He and I had a brief tussle over the bill; I let him win. In the lobby he helped me on with my overcoat. I felt suddenly old and pettish and wronged. The night was raw. As we walked along the pavement Blanche linked her arm in mine, but I held myself stiffly away from her. Julian's big black car raced purringly through the darkened streets – Julian becomes uncharacteristically impetuous when he gets behind the wheel. In Portland Place a heap of rags was thrown on the steps leading up to my door; when I stepped out of the car the rags stirred and a terrible, ruined face looked up at me blearily.

'Look,' I said to Julian, 'there's the result of your capitalism for you!'

I do not know what came over me, shouting in the street like that. It was not at all like me. Julian had not got out, and sat now staring dourly through the windscreen and tapping out an impatient rhythm with his fingers on the wheel. We said our stiff goodnights. At the corner, though, the car stopped with a squeal and the door was thrust open and Blanche came running back down the middle of the road. Where did she get those big feet from? – not my side, anyway. I already had the key in the lock. She struggled up the steps, panting. 'I just wanted to . . .' she said, 'I just wanted . . .' She stopped, and looked at the ground. Then she gave a great shrug, and a sort of exasperated, lost laugh, and kissed me quickly on the cheek and turned away. At the foot of the steps she paused, and bent over her purse, becoming Vivienne's mother for a second. A blackened hand reached up from the bundle of rags and she placed a coin in it. She glanced back at me and smiled, bravely, sadly and, I thought, with the hint of an apology – for what, I could not say – and then hurried away towards the waiting car.

What is it, I ask myself, what is it that everyone knows, that I do not know?

*

This morning early, before some busybody should come and move him on, I went down to have a look at that wretch on the steps. He was awake, reclining in his filthy cocoon, his frightful eyes fixed on horrors in the air that only he could see. Indeterminate age, cropped grey hair, scabs all over, mouth blackly agape. I spoke to him but he did not respond; I think he could not hear me. I cast about for something I might do to help him, but soon gave up, in the glum, hopeless way that one does. I was about to turn away when I saw something stir under his chin, inside the collar of his buttoned-up overcoat. It was a little dog, a pup, I think, mangy brown, with big sad eager eyes and a torn ear. It licked its lips at me and squirmed ingratiatingly. Its tongue was shocking in its stark, pink cleanness. A man and his dog. Good God. Everyone must have something to love, some little scrap of life. I went back up the steps, ashamed to have to acknowledge that I felt more sorrow for the dog than I did for the man. What a thing it is, the human heart.

MISS VANDELEUR has I think been listening to wild stories about life at the Poland Street house during the war, for whenever I make mention of the place I seem to detect in her a muffled shudder of disapproval and maidenly *pudeur*. It is true, there were some memorable debauches there when the Blitz was on, but for goodness' sake, Miss V., at that time London generally, at least at the level of our class, had the atmosphere of an Italian city state in the days of the Black Death. Although she would never admit it, liberated young woman that she is, what my biographer really reprehends is not the sexual licence of those days, but the nature of the sexuality. Like so many others, she imagines the house was inhabited exclusively by queers. I remind her that our landlord, Leo Rothenstein, was as red-blooded a hetero as his Jewish blood would allow – and there was Nick, after all; need I say more? I admit that when Boy moved in, there were always questionable young men about the place, although occasionally of a morning I would meet some dazed girl stumbling out of his room with her hair in knots and carrying her stockings over her arm.

Danny Perkins was one of Boy's discoveries.

The house was tall and narrow, and seemed to lean a little outwards over the street. Blake must have seen angels prancing in the sunlight flashing down from those high windows. The living accommodation comprised three floors above a doctor's surgery. The doctor was an elusive figure; Boy insisted that he was an abortionist. Leo, despite his grandee's manner, had a taste for louche living, and had bought the house as a refuge from the stultifying magnificence of the family mansion in Portman Square. At that time, though, he was rarely in Poland Street, having moved with his new and already pregnant wife to the safety of his place in the country. I had a bedroom on the second floor, across the corridor from the tiny dressing room where Boy lived in awesome squalor. Above us was Nick's flat. I still had the place in Bayswater, but bombs had fallen near Lancaster Gate and on the west side of Sussex Square, and Vivienne had decamped with the child to her parents' house in Oxford for the duration. I missed them, in periodic bouts of loneliness and self-pity, but I will not pretend that I was not on the whole content with the arrangement.

In the mornings I was lecturing on Borromini at the Institute – what a sense of urgency and profound pathos was lent to these occasions by the sound of bombs falling on the city – and in the afternoons I was at my desk in the Department. The cryptanalysts at Bletchley Park had broken the Luftwaffe signal codes and I was able to pass a great deal of valuable information to Oleg on the strength and tactics of the German Air Force. (No, Miss V., however you may urge me, I shall not deign to engage with criticism of my dealings with a country which at the time was supposedly in league with Hitler against us; surely by now it is clear where my loyalties would always lie, whatever worthless treaty this or that vile tyrant might put his name to.) I was, I realised, happy. Amidst the schoolroom smells of the Department – pencil shavings, cheap paper, the mouth-drying reek of ink – or pacing under the great windows of the Institute's third-floor lecture room, looking down on one of Vanbrugh's finest courtyards and paying out to an attentive handful of students the measured ribbon of my thoughts on the great themes of seventeeth-century art, I was, yes, happy. As I have already remarked, I did not fear the bombing; I confess I even exulted a little, in secret, at the spectacle of such enormous, ungovernable destruction. Are you shocked? My dear, you cannot imagine the strangeness of those times. No one now

speaks about the sense of vast comedy that the Blitz engen-
dered. I don't mean the flying chamber pots or the severed legs
thrown up on to rooftops, all that mere grotesquerie. But
sometimes in the running rumble of a stick of bombs detonating
along a nearby avenue one seemed to hear a kind of – what
shall I call it? – a kind of celestial laughter, as of a delighted
child-god looking down on the glory of these things that he had
wrought. Oh, sometimes, Miss Vandeleur – Serena – sometimes I think I am no more than a cut-price Caligula, wishing
the world had a single throat, so that I might throttle it at
one go.

The summer is ending. So too with my season. At the close
of these reddened evenings especially I feel the proximal dark.
My tremor, my tumour.

London in the Blitz. Yes. Everyone had a story, an incident.
The minesweepers on the Thames. The hundreds of barrels of
paint in a burning warehouse going up like rockets. The woman
with her skirt blown off staggering down Bond Street in her
suspenders, her husband skipping along backwards in front of
her with his jacket vainly held out to her like a bullfighter's
cape. After a stray bomb fell on the zoo, Nick, returning at
dawn from a trip to Oxford, swore he had seen a pair of zebras
trotting down the middle of Prince Albert Road; he remarked
their fine black manes, their delicate hoofs.

Und so weiter . . .

I was in the kitchen one morning shortly after my return
from Ireland when Boy came down to breakfast in his dressing
gown, barefoot and hungover. He made fried bread and drank
champagne from a tumbler. He reeked of semen and stale
garlic.

'You chose a bloody good time to skulk off,' he said. 'The
Germans haven't stopped since you left. Boom boom boom,
day and night.'

'My father died,' I said, 'did I mention it?'

'Pah! – call that an excuse?' He considered me with a merrily spiteful smile; he was half drunk already. 'You do look a toothsome old thing in that uniform, you know. Such a waste. I met a chap the other day in the bar at the Reform. Spitfire pilot, hardly more than a schoolboy. He'd been out that morning flying sorties. Got shot down over the Channel, baled out, was picked up by a lifeboat, would you believe, and there he was, three hours later, having a Pimm's. Scared eyes, big grin, very fetching bandage over one eye. We went to Ma Bailey's and took a room. Christ, it was like fucking a young horse, all nerves and teeth and flying lather. It was his first time, too – and his last, most likely. This war: it's an ill wind, I say.' He sat chewing and watched me while I prepared my breakfast. My finicking ways with these things always amused him. 'By the by,' he said, 'there's a job going that I think might be right up your street. There are these couriers for so-called friendly governments that travel up to Edinburgh on the night train every week to get their dispatches sent out by the navy. We've been told to get a look at their stuff. Frogs and Turks and so on; a tricky lot.' He poured himself another measure of champagne. The foam overflowed and he scooped it up from the greasy table top and sucked it from his fingers. 'Nick, of all people, has come up with a plan,' he said. 'Very clever, really, I was amazed. He's got this chap, some sort of bootmaker or master cobbler or whatever, who'll unpick the stitches of the dispatch bags, leaving the seals in place, you see; you take a look at the documents, committing the juicy bits to your famous photographic memory, then slip them back into the bags, and Nobbs or Dobbs the cobbler will redo the stitching and no one will be the wiser – except us, that is.'

I studied a puddle of watered sunlight on the floor at my feet. There is something about midmorning, something dulled and headachy, that I always find both depressing and obscurely affecting.

'And who is *us*?' I said.

'Well, the Department, of course. And anyone else we might

care to take into our confidence.' He winked. 'What do you think? Super wheeze, what?'

He grinned woozily, tick-tocking his head from side to side like a happy flapper; he was having trouble keeping his eyes in focus.

'How do we get the bags away from the couriers?' I said.

'Eh?' He blinked. 'Yes, well, that's where Danny comes in.'

'Danny?'

'Danny Perkins. He can get anyone to do anything. You'll see.'

Sometimes Boy displayed an impressive prophetic gift.

'Danny Perkins,' I said. 'Where on earth did you turn up a person with a name like that?'

Boy laughed, and the laugh turned into one of his horrible, twangy coughs.

'Christ, Vic,' he said, smiting himself on the chest with a flattened fist, 'you're such a prig.' He stood up. 'Come on,' he said, breathing heavily down his big, pitted nose. 'You can find out his pedigree for yourself.'

He swept ahead of me unsteadily up the stairs, and threw open the door of his bedroom. The first thing that struck me was the marked amelioration of the usual feral stink in the room. Boy's smell was still there – body grime, garlic, a rancid, cheesy something the possible sources of which the mind did not care to seek after – but underneath it there was a softer though no less pungent savour, as if a flock of pigeons, say, had been introduced into a lion house. Boy's bed was a mattress thrown on the floor, and lying there now in a nest of wadded blankets and soiled sheets was a short, compact young man with that special kind of very white skin, suety and almost translucent, that used to be the sure mark of the working class. He was wearing a vest and khaki trousers and unlaced army boots. He had one arm behind his head and an ankle crossed on a lifted knee, and he was reading a copy of *Titbits*. I found myself looking at the humid, blue-shadowed hollow of his armpit. His head was a size too small for his broad shoulders and thick trunk of neck, and the disproportion lent him a delicate, almost girlish aspect. His very fine, very black hair was cropped short at the sides, and fell across his pale and, I am sorry to say, acne-stippled forehead in a darkly gleaming scoop, and I found myself recalling that Edenic moment when I had first caught sight of the Beaver, asleep in the orchard in his father's garden in Oxford, years before.

'Ten-shun, Private Perkins!' Boy shouted. 'Don't you see there's an officer present? This is Captain Maskell. Let's have a salute there.'

Danny only smiled at him lazily, and put aside the paper and rolled himself on to his knees and squatted amidst the disordered bed things, quite at his ease, looking me up and down with frank, friendly interest.

'Pleased, I'm sure,' he said. 'Mr Bannister's told me all about you, so he has.'

His voice was a sort of soft purr, so that everything he said seemed a shared confidence. He had a Welsh accent that seemed almost a parody. Boy laughed.

'Don't believe it, Victor,' he said, 'he's a hopeless liar. I've never mentioned your name to him.'

Danny smiled again, not minding at all, and went on with his examination of me; his regard was that of a benevolent opponent in a wrestling match, searching out the hold that would bring me down with the least discomfort to us both. I realised that my palms were damp.

Lumberingly, laughing, Boy sat himself down cross-legged on the mattress and put his arm around Danny's waist. Boy's dressing gown had fallen open over his knees, and I tried not to look at his big flaccid sex lolling in its bush.

'I've been telling Captain Maskell about our plan to nobble the couriers,' he said. 'He wants to know how we're going to get the bags away from them. I said that was your department.'

263

Danny shrugged, making the bunched muscles of his shoulders ripple.

'Well, we'll just have to ask them nicely, won't we,' he said, in his cooing voice.

Boy laughed, and coughed again, and again struck himself on the breastbone.

'Look you, bach,' he said, imitating Danny's accent, 'just you hand over those papers now and I'll give you a big juicy kiss.'

He made a fumbling attempt to embrace Danny, who dealt him a good-natured push with his hip, and he went sprawling on the bed, still laughing and coughing, his gown undone and his hairy legs bicycling in the air. Danny Perkins gazed upon the spectacle and shook his head.

'Isn't he a terrible sot, Captain Maskell?'

'Victor,' I said. 'Call me Victor.'

Presently Boy fell into a tipsy slumber, his big head resting babyishly on his joined hands and his hirsute backside sticking up. Danny laid a blanket over him tenderly, and together we went down to the kitchen, where Danny, still in his vest, poured himself a mug of tepid tea and stirred four big spoonfuls of sugar into it.

'Oh, I am parched,' he said. 'He made me drink that champagne last night, and it never agrees with me.' The patch of sunlight had moved from the floor to the chair, and he was bathed in it now, a grinning, big-shouldered, dingy angel. He lifted an eye towards the ceiling. 'Have you known him for long, then?'

'We were at Cambridge together,' I said. 'We're old friends.'

'Are you another leftie, like him?'

'Is he a leftie?' For answer he only shook his head and chuckled. 'And you,' I said, 'how long have you known him?'

He picked at a pimple on his arm.

'Well, I'm a singer, see.'

'A singer!' I said. 'Good Lord . . .'

He smiled at me quizzically, without resentment, letting the

264

silence last. 'My dad used to sing in chapel,' he said. 'Lovely sweet voice he had.'

I blushed. 'I'm sorry,' I said, and he nodded, taking it as his due, which it was.

'I got a place in the chorus of *Chu Chin Chow*,' he said. 'It was lovely. That was how I met Mr Bannister. He was in his car at the stage door one night. He was waiting for someone else but then he saw me, and, well . . .' He gave a sort of roguish, melancholy grin. 'Romantic, isn't it.' He grew pensive, and sat with hunched shoulders, supping his tea and gazing wistfully into the footlit depths of his memories. 'Then this blooming war started up,' he said, 'and that was the end of me on the boards.' He gloomed for a while, then brightened. 'But we'll have some fun with this courier lark, won't we? I've always been fond of trains.'

Nick arrived then. He was got up in loud checks and a yellow waistcoat, and was carrying a rolled umbrella in one hand and a brown trilby hat in the other.

'Weekend at Maules,' he said. 'Winston was there.' He cast a sour glance in Danny's direction. 'I see you two have met. By the way, Vic, Baby was looking for you.'

'Yes?'

He looked at the teapot. 'Is that char still hot? Pour us out a cup, Perkins, like a good chap, will you? Christ, my head. We were drinking brandy until four in the morning.'

'You and Winston?'

He gave me one of his wooden stares.

'He had gone to bed,' he said.

Danny passed him the tea and he leaned against the sink with his ankles crossed, nursing the smoking mug in both hands. Soft morning, the pale sunlight of September, and, like a mirage shimmering at the very edge of vision, the limitless possibilities of the future; where do they come from, these moments of unlooked-for happiness?

'Leo Rothenstein says he had a long talk with the PM before

265

the rest of us arrived,' Nick said, in his serious voice. 'It seems we've won the air war, despite appearances to the contrary.'

'Well, good for us,' Danny said. Nick looked at him sharply, but Danny only smiled back at him blandly.

Boy reappeared from upstairs, and stood swaying in the doorway. The cord of his dressing gown was still undone, but he had put on a pair of drooping grey underpants.

'For Christ's sake, Beaver,' he said, 'have you been to a fancy-dress party? You look like a bookie. Hasn't anyone ever told you Jews are not allowed to wear tweeds? There's an ordinance against it.'

'You're drunk,' Nick said, 'and it's not half-eleven yet. And for God's sake put on some clothes, can't you?'

Boy, swaying, hesitated, regarding Nick with an unsteady, sullen stare, then muttered something and stumbled away upstairs again, and presently we heard him above us, kicking things and swearing drunkenly.

'Oh, listen to that,' Danny Perkins said, shaking his head.

'Go and smooth his brow, will you?' Nick said, and Danny shrugged amiably and went out, whistling, and thumped up the stairs in his outsize boots. Nick turned to me. 'You've talked to Perkins about the couriers and so on?'

'Yes,' I said. 'Did you really dream up the scheme?'

He looked at me suspiciously.

'Yes; why?'

'Oh, I just wondered. Ingenious, if it works.'

He snorted.

'Of course it will work. Why wouldn't it?' He came and sat in Danny's chair and put his head in his hands. 'Do you think,' he said weakly, 'you could make me some more tea? My head really is splitting.'

I went to the sink and filled the kettle. I remember the moment: the nickel glint of light on the kettle's cheek, the greyish whiff from the drain, and, through the window above the sink, the red-brick backs of houses on Berwick Street.

'What did Vivienne want with me?' I said.

Nick gave a gloomy laugh. 'I think you've put her in pod again, old boy.' The kettle clanged against the tap. He looked at me through his fingers with a death's-head grin. 'Or someone has, anyway.'

*

And so, for the second time in my life, I found myself, in autumn, on a train bound for Oxford, with a difficult encounter in view; before, it was Mrs Beaver I had been going to see, before the whole thing started, and now it was her daughter. Funny, that: I still thought of Vivienne as one of the Brevoorts. A daughter, that is; a sister; *wife* was a word to which I had never quite become reconciled. The train was slow, and extremely smelly – where did the notion of the romance of steam travel come from, I wonder? – and the first-class seats had all been taken by the time I got to the ticket window. Every compartment had its contingent of soldiers, other ranks, mostly, with the odd bored officer smoking jadedly and watching in bitter wistfulness the sunlit fields of England flowing past. I had settled down as best I could to work – I was revising the Borromini lectures, which I hoped to persuade Big Beaver to bring out in book form – when someone folded himself sinuously into the seat beside me and said:

'Ah, the admirable detachment of the scholar.'

It was Querell. I was not pleased to see him, and must have shown it, for he smiled thinly in satisfaction, and crossed his arms and his long, spidery legs and settled back happily in the seat. I told him I was going to Oxford. 'And you?'

He shrugged. 'Oh, further than that. But I'll be changing there.' Bletchley, then, I thought, with a twinge of jealousy. 'How do you find the work now, in your section?'

'Fascinating.'

He turned his head and leaned a little way forward to look at me.

'That's good,' he said, with no particular emphasis. 'I hear you're sharing a billet these days with Bannister and Nick Brevoort.'

'I have a room in Leo Rothenstein's place in Poland Street,' I said, sounding defensive even to my own ears. He nodded, tapping a long finger on the barrel of his cigarette.

'Wife left you, has she?'

'No. She's in Oxford, with our child. I'm on my way to see her.'

Why did I always feel it necessary to explain myself to him? Anyway, he was not listening.

'Bannister's a bit of a worry, don't you think?' he said.

Cows, a farmer on a tractor, the sudden, sun-dazzled windows of a factory.

'A worry?'

Querell shifted, and threw back his head and emitted a rapid thin stream of smoke towards the carriage ceiling.

'I hear him around town, at the Reform, or in the Gryphon. Always drunk, always shouting about this or that. One day it's Goebbels, who he says he hopes will take over the BBC when the Germans win, the next it's what a sound chap Stalin is. I can't make him out.' He turned his head again to look at me. 'Can you?'

'It's just talk,' I said. 'He's quite sound.'

'You think so?' he said thoughtfully. 'Well, I'm glad to hear it.' He mused for a while, working at his cigarette. 'Mind you, I do wonder what you fellows would consider *sound*.' He smiled his lizard smile, and then leaned forward again, craning towards the window. 'Here we are,' he said, 'Oxford.' He looked at the papers on my knee. 'You didn't get any work done, did you. Sorry.' He watched me while I gathered up my things. I had got down to the platform when he appeared in the door behind me. 'By the way,' he said, 'give my regards to your wife. I hear she's expecting again.'

I was leaving the station when I saw him. He had got off the train after all, and was hanging back in the ticket office, pretending to read the timetable.

*

Vivienne was reclining in a deckchair on the lawn, with a tartan rug over her knees and a sheaf of glossy magazines on the grass beside her. At her feet there was a tray with the remains of tea things, jam and buttered bread and a pot of clotted cream; apparently her condition had not affected her appetite. The bruised hollows under her eyes were a deeper shade of mauve than usual, and her black hair, Nick's hair, had shed something of its lustre. She greeted me with a smile, extending a cool, queenly hand for me to kiss. That smile: one plucked and painted eyebrow arched, the lips compressed as if to prevent an outbreak of the mocking laughter that was already there, that was always there, in her eyes. 'Do I look pale and interesting?' she said. 'Tell me I do.' I stood before her awkwardly on the grass. From the corner of my eye I could see her mother lurking among the flowerbeds at the side of the house, pretending she had not yet noticed my arrival. I wondered if Big Beaver was home; he had already written to me moaning about paper rationing and the loss of his best compositors to the army.

'How smart you look,' Vivienne said, lifting an arm to shade her eyes and scanning me up and down. 'Quite the steadfast soldier.'

'That's what Boy Bannister says, too.'

'Does he? I thought he preferred the rougher types.' She moved the magazines to make a space for me on the grass beside her chair. 'Sit; tell me all the gossip. I suppose everybody is being terribly brave despite the bombs. Even the Palace is not immune. Wasn't it gulp-inducing how the Queen made common cause with the plucky East Enders? I feel such a shirker, cowering up here; I shouldn't be surprised if one of the Oxford matrons presses a yellow feather on me in the High some morning. Or was it white feathers they used to hand out

269

to the conchies last time round? Perhaps I should hang a placard about my neck advertising my condition. Breeding for Britain, you know.'

Idly I watched my mother-in-law creeping along a bed of dahlias, plucking up snails and tossing them into a bucket of brine.

'Querell was on the train,' I said. 'Have you been seeing him?'

'*Seeing* him?' She laughed. 'What on earth do you mean?'

'I just wondered. He knew about the . . . he knew you were . . .'

'Oh, Nick will have told him.'

How cool she was! Mrs Beaver put down her bucket and straightened up with a hand pressed to the small of her back, and looked all about with a great show of absent-mindedness, still ignoring me.

'Nick?' I said. 'Why would Nick tell him?'

'He's going about telling everyone. He thinks it's a scream, for some reason. I wish I could see the funny side of it.'

'But why would he tell Querell? I thought they detested each other.'

'Oh, no; they're thick as thieves, those two, aren't they?' She turned in the chair to look at me. 'What *did* you mean, have I been seeing Querell?' I said nothing, and her face emptied and grew hard. 'You don't want this child, do you,' she said.

'Why do you say that?'

'It's true, isn't it.'

I shrugged.

'The times are hardly propitious,' I said, 'with this war, and worse to come, probably, when it's over.'

She studied me, smiling.

'What a heartless beast you are, Victor,' she said, wonderingly.

I looked away.

'I'm sorry,' I said.

She sighed, and picked with scarlet fingernails at the rug on her lap.

'So am I,' she said. Faintly we could hear the bell for evensong at Christ Church. 'It's going to be a girl.'

'How do you know?'

'I just do.' She sighed again, so lightly it was almost a laugh. 'Poor little blighter.'

Big Beaver, wearing plus-fours and a sort of shooting jacket – what a ridiculous man – came out of the conservatory, apparently intending to say something to his wife, who was on her knees now, delving in the clay with a trowel, her broad behind turned towards the lawn; seeing Vivienne and me, he stepped back smartly into the doorway and faded like a shadow behind glass and greenery.

'Have you been to the flat?' Vivienne said. 'It hasn't been blown up or anything?'

'No. I mean, it hasn't been bombed. Of course I've been there.'

'Because I rather had the impression from Nick that you were spending most of your time nowadays at Poland Street. I suppose the parties must be fun. Nick tells me you raid the doctor's surgery for rubber bones to bite on when the bombings start.' She paused. 'I hate it here, you know,' she said with quiet vehemence. 'I feel like someone in the Bible, sent unto the house of her fathers to atone for her uncleanness. I want my life. This is not my life.'

Mrs Beaver, straightening up again to ease her back, and unable decently to go on pretending I was not there, gave an exaggerated start, peering at me, and waved her trowel.

'Do you think,' I said quickly, 'you might . . . terminate it?'

Vivienne gave me that look again, stonier than before.

'*She*,' she said. 'Or he, if by some mad chance my feminine intuition is mistaken. But not *it*; don't say *it*.'

'Because,' I went on doggedly, 'something that has no past is not alive yet, is it. Life is memory; life is the past.'

'Goodness,' she said brightly, her eyes sparkling with tears, 'such a perfect statement of your philosophy! Whereas to human beings, darling, life is the present, the present and the future. Don't you see?' Mrs B. had lumbered to her feet and was bearing down on us, her great skirts billowing. Vivienne was still regarding me brightly, the tears standing in her eyes. 'I've just realised something,' she said. 'You came up here to ask for a divorce, didn't you.' She gave a little silvery laugh. 'You did; I can see it in your eyes.'

'Victor!' Mrs Beaver cried. 'What a lovely surprise!'

*

I stayed to dinner. All the talk was of Nick's engagement. The senior Beavers were quietly exultant: Sylvia Lydon, a prospective heiress, was a catch, even if she was a trifle shop-soiled. Julian, a year old now, cried piteously when I picked him up and sat him on my knee. Everyone was embarrassed, and tried to cover it with laughter and baby-talk. The child would not be mollified, and in the end I relinquished him to his mother. I remarked how much he looked like Nick – he didn't, really, but I thought the Beavers would be pleased – at which Vivienne for some reason gave me a bleak stare. Big Beaver spoke bitterly of the French collapse; he seemed to regard it as a personal affront, as if General Blanchard's First Army had shirked its main duty, which, surely, was to act as a buffer between the advancing German forces and the purlieus of North Oxford. I said I understood that Hitler had changed his mind and would not now attempt an invasion. Big Beaver scowled. 'Attempt?' he said loudly. 'Attempt? The south-east coast is being defended by retired insurance clerks armed with wooden rifles. The Germans could row over in rubber dinghies after lunch and be in London by dinner time.' He had worked himself into a high state of agitation; he sat fuming at the head of the table, convulsively rolling pellets of bread in his long brown fingers; I had been casting about for a way to introduce the topic of my

Borromini book; now, gloomily, I thought better of it. Mrs B. attempted to lay her hand comfortingly on his, but he shook her off impatiently. 'Europe is finished,' he said, glaring about at us and grimly nodding. 'Finished.' The child, nestled proprie- torially against his mother's breast, sucked his thumb and watched me with steady, unblinking resentment. I found myself inwardly giving a kind of wolf-howl – *Oh God, release me, release me!* – and glanced about guiltily, not sure that my silent cry had not been intense enough to be heard. When I was leaving, Vivienne stood with me on the front steps while Big Beaver, grumbling about his petrol ration, got out the car to drive me to the station.

'I won't do it, you know,' she said. She was smiling, but a nerve was twitching in her eyelid.

'You won't do what?'

(*Release me!*)

'I won't divorce you.' She touched my hand. 'Poor darling, I'm afraid you're stuck with me.'

*

How nice! – Miss Vandeleur has given me an Xmas (her spelling) present of a bottle of wine. I could not wait for her to leave so that I might unwrap it. Bulgarian claret. I sometimes suspect her of a sense of humour. Or am I being churlish? The gesture may have been quite sincere. Should I tell her what my wine merchant once told me, that the South Africans sell their wine clandestinely in bulk to the Bulgars, who bottle it under their own more politically acceptable labels and sell it on to all those unsuspecting left-wing liberals in the West? But of course I shan't. What a cantankerous old so-and-so I am, even to think of it.

WE MADE A splendid team, Danny Perkins, Albert Clegg and me. Albert had served his apprenticeship at Lobb's the bootmaker; he was one of those vernacular geniuses that the working class used to produce in abundance before the advent of universal literacy. He was a tiny fellow, shorter even than Danny, and much slighter. When the three of us were together, proceeding in single file down a railway platform, say, we must have looked like an illustration from a natural history textbook, showing the evolution of man from primitive but not unattractive pygmy, through sturdy villein, to the blandly upright, married and mortgaged *Homo sapiens* of the modern day. Albert did love his craft, though it tormented and maddened him, too. He was a maniacal perfectionist. When he was at work he had two states: profound, well-nigh autistic concentration, and frustrated rage. Nothing was ever right for him, or right enough; the equipment he had to work with was always shoddy, the threads too coarse or too fine, the needles blunt, the awls made from inferior steel. Nor was there ever enough time to complete the job to the standard that he imagined would have satisfied him.

He and Danny squabbled constantly, in hissing undertones; if I had not been there I believe they would have descended to scuffles. It was not my rank that inhibited them, I think, but that reserve, that genteel unwillingness to show themselves up in the presence of their betters, which used to be one of the more attractive traits of their kind. Danny would stand in the doorway of our compartment, shifting agitatedly from foot to foot and doing that tense, almost soundless whistle that he did, while Albert, perched on the swaying seat opposite me like a furious, khaki-clad elf, with the dispatch bag of the Polish government-in-exile on his knee, unpicked a line of stitching he had just painstakingly completed, preparatory to starting the job all over again. Meanwhile, in the next compartment, Jaroslav the courier, comatose on the vodka and best Baltic caviare with which Danny had been plying him all evening, would be turning over in his couchette, dreaming of duels and cavalry charges, or whatever it is the minor Polish nobility dreams about.

We supplied more than strong drink and lavish foodstuffs. There was a young woman called Kirstie who travelled with us, a delicate little person with vivid red hair and porcelain skin and a marvellously refined Edinburgh accent. I do not remember where we had found her. Boy nicknamed her the Venus Fly Trap. In her way she was as dedicated to her craft as Albert was to his. She would appear in the corridor of the train after a hard night spent entertaining an eighteen-stone Estonian dispatch carrier, and look as if she had been doing no more than enjoying a pleasant hour of mild gossip with a wee friend in a tea shop on Prince's Street. When her services were not required she would sit with me, taking sips from my whiskey flask ('What my Daddy would say if he knew I was drinking Irish!') and telling me about her plans to open a haberdashery shop when the war was over and she had earned enough to purchase a lease. She was an unofficial adjunct to our team – Billy Mytchett would have been scandalised – and I funded her, quite generously, out of what I listed as operational expenses. I had to keep her out of the way of Albert, too, for he also was something of a puritan. I do not know what he imagined was happening on those nights when Kirstie was rejected and Danny instead slipped into the next-door compartment and did not reappear until dawn was breaking over the Southern Uplands.

We had some close shaves. There was the Turk who, after only a few minutes with Kirstie, appeared in the corridor in his underwear just as Albert was getting to work on the fellow's dispatch case with his bradawl and his blade. Luckily, the Turk had prostate trouble, and by the time he came back from emptying a bladder that must have been the size of a football, looking pained and suspicious in equal measure, Albert had done up the few stitches he had unpicked, and I was able to convince Abdul that of course my man had not been tampering with his bag but, on the contrary, was merely making sure that it was all intact and sound. In some instances, however, we had to employ extreme measures. I discovered I had a talent to threaten. Even when there was little real damage we could have done, there was something in the smoothly suggestive way I delivered the menaces that proved gratifyingly persuasive. Blackmail, especially the sexual kind, was more effective in those straitlaced times than it would be now. And it was more effective still when Danny and not Kirstie was the bait. There was an unfortunate Portuguese, I remember, a middle-aged fellow of aristocratic bearing by the name of Fonseca, who came a terrible cropper. I was taking a long time over his papers, having only a rudimentary grasp of the language, when I became aware of an alteration in the atmosphere in the compartment, and Albert coughed and I looked up to find Senhor Fonseca, in a dressing gown of the most wonderful blue silk, blue as the sky in a Book of Hours, standing in the corridor, watching me. I bade him come in. I invited him to sit. He declined. He was courteous, but his otherwise sallow face was grey with anger. Danny, who had spent a strenuous couple of hours with him earlier, was sleeping in a compartment further along. I sent Albert to fetch him. He came in yawning and scratching his belly. Having told Albert to go out into the corridor for a smoke, I sat for a moment in silence, considering the toe of my shoe. Such pauses, I found, always had an unnerving effect on even the most outraged of our – victims, I was going to say, and I suppose it is the only word. Fonseca began haughtily to demand an explanation, but I interrupted him. I mentioned the laws against homosexuality. I mentioned his wife, his children – 'Two, is that right?' We knew all about him. Danny yawned. 'Would it not be best,' I said, 'if what has happened tonight, everything that has happened tonight, were to be forgotten? I guarantee you absolute discretion, of course. You have my word as an officer.'

Black rain was falling out of the darkness outside, flying raggedly against the lighted window of the speeding train. I imagined fields, crouched farms, great trees thick with darkness heaving in the wind; and I thought how this moment – night, storm, this lighted, hurtling little world in which we were sealed – would never come again, and I was pierced with strange sorrow. The imagination has no sense of the inappropriate. Fonseca was staring at me. It struck me how much he resembled Droeshout's portrait of Shakespeare, with his domed forehead and concave cheeks and watchful, wary eyes. I squared the documents on my knee and slipped them back into the dispatch case.

'I'll have Private Clegg here sew this up,' I said. 'He's very expert; no one will know.'

Fonseca gave me a queer, wild look.

'No,' he said, 'no one will know.' He turned to Danny. 'May I speak to you?'

Danny did one of his bashful, shoulder-rolling shrugs, and they stepped out into the corridor, and Fonseca looked at me again over his shoulder and slid the door shut behind them. Presently Albert Clegg returned.

'What's the matter with the dago, sir?' he said. 'He's down there by the lav with Perkins. I think he's crying.' He gave a snuffly little laugh. 'See that thing he was wearing, that blue thing? Looked like a frigging ponce in it.' He grimaced. ' 'Scuse the language, sir.'

Three hours later we arrived, pulling into Edinburgh under a soiled and angry sky. I sent Clegg to wake Fonseca. In a moment he was back, looking green, and said I had better come and see for myself. The Portuguese was on the floor of his compartment, wedged in the narrow space beside the made-up bed, a large section of his Bardic pate shot away and his magnificent blue gown spattered with blood and bits of brain. A pistol had slipped from his grasp; I noticed his long, slender hands. Later, after our people had removed the body and cleared up the mess and we were on our way back to London, I asked Danny what Fonseca had said to him in the corridor; he made a wry face and looked out at the sodden landscape through which our troop-laden train was crawling.

'Told me he loved me, that sort of thing,' he said. 'Asked me to remember him. Soppy stuff.'

I watched him carefully.

'Perkins, did you know what he was going to do?'

'Oh, no, sir,' he said, shocked. 'Anyway, we can't worry about that kind of thing, now, can we? There's a war on, after all.' Such clear, clean eyes, glossy brown, with bluish whites, and long, sable lashes. I recalled him, in his vest, dropping on one knee beside Fonseca's body and tenderly lifting the poor fellow's hands and folding them on his bloodstained breast.

*

I passed on to Oleg anything from the diplomatic pouches that I thought would be of interest to Moscow – it was not easy to tell whether this or that choice morsel would excite the Comrades or provoke one of their sulky silences. I do not wish to boast, but I think I may say that the service I provided from this source was not inconsiderable. I gave regularly updated estimates, more or less reliable, of the disposition and readiness of the various enemy forces ranged along Russia's border from Estonia to the Black Sea. I supplied the names and often the whereabouts of foreign agents at work in Russia, as well as lists of anti-Soviet activists in Hungary, Lithuania, Ukrainian Poland – I had no illusions as to the likely fate of these unfortunate people. Also, I ensured that Moscow's dispatches remained inviolate by spreading the story that the Soviets' own pouches were booby-trapped and would blow up in the face of anyone who tampered with them; a simple ruse, but surprisingly effective. Moscow's Bomb-Bags became a staple of Department mythology, and stories even began to circulate of inquisitive couriers being found sprawled under a snowfall of tattered documents with their hands and half their heads blown off.

What Moscow was most interested in, however, was the flood of signals intelligence coming out of Bletchley Park. I had access to a great deal of this material from my desk at the Department, but there were obvious gaps, where some of the more sensitive intercepts had been withheld. At Oleg's urging I sought to get myself assigned to Bletchley as a cryptanalyst, citing my linguistic skills, my gift for mathematics, my training as a decoder of the arcane language of pictorial art, my phenomenal memory. I confess I rather fancied myself as a Bletchley boffin. I urged Nick to put in a word for me with the mysterious friends in high places he claimed to have, but without result. I began to wonder if I should be worried: that trace against me from my Cambridge days, that little five-pointed red star that Billy Mytchett's researchers had spotted in the firmament of my files, was it still twinkling there, despite Nick's promise to have it extinguished?

I went to Querell and asked if he would recommend me for a transfer. He leaned back on his chair and put one long, narrow foot on the corner of his desk and looked at me for a moment in silence. Querell's silences always carried the implication of suppressed laughter.

'They don't take just anybody, you know,' he said. 'These people are the very best – really first-class brains. Besides, they're working themselves to death, eighteen-hour shifts, seven days a week; that wouldn't be your kind of thing, would it?' I was walking away when he called after me. 'Why don't you talk to your chum Sykes? He's a power in the land up there.'

Alastair when I telephoned him sounded at once vague and hysterical. He was not glad to hear from me.

'Oh, come on, Psyche,' I said, 'you can take an hour off from your crossword puzzles. I'll buy you a pint.'

I could hear him breathing, and I pictured him, peering desperately into the receiver like a trapped rabbit and running stubby fingers through his spiked hair.

'You don't know what it's like up here, Vic. It's a bloody madhouse.'

I drove up in one of the Department cars. It was early spring, but the roads were treacherous with ice. I crawled into Bletchley at twilight in a freezing fog. The pair of guards at the gate were a long time in letting me through. They were young men, pustular, the backs of their necks shaved and sore looking, their caps seeming much too big for their narrow, hollow-templed heads; as they examined my papers, frowning and scratching their downy jaws, they might have been a couple of schoolboys worrying over their homework. Behind them the huts squatted in the fog, and here and there a window was weakly aglow with sallow lamplight. Alastair met me in the canteen, a long, low shack smelling of boiled tea and chip fat. A few solitary souls were scattered among the tables, slumped like guys over mugs of tea and full ashtrays.

'Well, you chaps are really sprawling in the lap of luxury up here, aren't you,' I said.

Alastair looked wretched. He was thin and stooped, and his skin had a greyish, moist patina. When he lit his pipe the match shook in his fingers.

'It's pretty rudimentary, all right,' he said, a little huffily, as if he were head of house and I had cast aspersions on the school. 'We're promised improvements, but you know how it is. Churchill himself came up and gave us one of his pep talks – vital work, listening in on the enemy's thoughts, all that. Ugly little bloke, up close. Hadn't a clue what we actually do here. I tried to explain a bit of it but I could see it was going in one ear and out the other.' He looked about the room and sighed. 'Funny,' he said, 'the noise is the worst thing, those ruddy machines rattling and sputtering twenty-four hours a day.'

'I see some of the material you produce,' I said, 'though not all.' He gave me a sharp look. 'Listen,' I said, 'let's go to the pub, this place is awful.'

But the pub was not much better, although there was a fire. Alastair drank beer, dipping a prehensile lip into the suds and sucking up cheekfuls of the watery, warm brew, his adam's apple bobbling. He wanted to know how the war was going. 'I don't mean the propaganda they put in the papers. What's really happening? We never hear a thing, up here. Bloody ironic, isn't it.'

'It's going to be a long one,' I said. 'Years, they say; maybe a decade.'

'Christ.' He cupped his forehead in his hands and gazed gloomily at the patch of ringed and scarred counter between his elbows. 'I won't last it.' He lifted his head and looked about cautiously. 'Victor,' he whispered, 'when do you think they'll come in?'

'They?'

'You know what I mean.' He smiled anxiously. 'Are they ready, do you think? You've been there. If they break . . .'

'They won't break,' I said. I put a hand on his arm. 'Not when they have us to help them: Boy, me . . . you.'

His stuck his mouth into his beer again and took a long swallow.

'Don't know about that,' he said. 'Me, I mean.'

We stayed for an hour. He would not talk about his work, no matter how many pints I plied him with. He asked about Felix Hartmann.

'Gone,' I said. 'Back to base.'

'His choice?'

'No; he was recalled.'

That brought an awkward silence.

Alastair was due to start his shift at nine. When he climbed down from the stool he was unsteady on his feet. In the car he sat slumped beside me with his short little arms tightly folded, sighing and softly belching. At the gate, a new guard detail, who looked even younger than the first pair, peered in at us and, seeing Alastair, waved us through.

'Not supposed to do that,' Alastair said thickly. 'I'll have to report them in the morning.' He giggled. 'We might have been a couple of spies!'

I offered to drop him at his quarters – it was bitterly cold by now, and the blackout was in force – but he insisted that we stop before we got there, for he wanted to show me something. We pulled up at one of the larger huts. As we approached the door I heard, or rather felt, through the soles of my shoes, a muffled, thunderous din. Inside, the decoding machines, bronze-coloured, each one as big as a wardrobe, were churning and pounding in a kind of comic earnestness, like big dull foolish animals ranged about a circus ring performing their frantic, monotonous tricks. Alastair pulled one of them open to show me the rows of wheels spinning and clacking on their rods. 'Ugly beggars, aren't they,' Alastair shouted happily. We went outside again, into the burningly cold air. Alastair lost his footing and would have fallen over if I had not held on to him. For a moment we grappled unhandily in the dark. He smelled of beer and unwashed clothes and old pipe smoke.

'You know, Psyche,' I said in a fervent voice, 'I wish they could find a use for me up here.'

Alastair giggled again, and detached himself from me and walked away, staggering a little. 'Why don't you put in for a transfer?' he said over his shoulder. He laughed again. I failed to see what was funny.

I caught up with him, and we went along together blindly through the darkness and the motionless fog.

'When all this is over,' he said grandly, 'I shall go to America, where I'll become famous. Oops, here's my squat.'

He let himself into the hut and switched on the light; I had an impression of chaos and squalor. He remembered the blackout, and turned off the light again. I was suddenly tired of him, of his weariness and his bad breath and his air of obscure anguish. Yet we went on standing there, I on the cinder path and he in the deeper darkness of the doorway.

'Alastair,' I said, 'you've got to help me. You've got to row in.'

'No.'

He sounded like a recalcitrant child.

'Then get me in here. I won't involve you, once I'm here. Just get me in.'

He was silent for so long I wondered if he had fallen asleep on his feet. Then he sighed heavily, and dimly I could see him shaking his head.

'I can't,' he said. 'It's not . . . it's just not . . .' Another sigh, and then a tremendous sniff; was he weeping? Close by, on another pathway, someone unseen went by, whistling a snatch of the overture to *Tannhäuser*. I listened to the crunching footsteps fade. I turned away. As I walked off along the path he said behind me out of the darkness: 'Tell them I'm sorry, Victor.'

*

Nevertheless, someone did help me. Suddenly the flow of Bletchley material crossing my desk became a flood, as if someone at the source had opened a sluice-gate. Years later, when I encountered Alastair by chance one day in the Strand, I asked him if he had changed his mind after I had driven up to see him that evening. He denied it. By then he had been to America. 'And are you famous?' I asked, and he nodded judiciously and said that he supposed he was, in certain specialised circles. We were silent for a while, watching the traffic, and then he shuffled up close to me, suddenly agitated.

'You didn't tell them about Bletchley, did you?' he said. 'I

283

mean, you didn't tell them about the machines and all that, surely?'

'Good heavens, Psyche,' I said, 'what you must think of me! Besides, you refused to cooperate, remember?'

It was the Bletchley leaks which led eventually to my greatest triumph, the part I played in the great tank battle of the Kursk Salient in the summer of 1943. I shall not bore you with the details, Miss V.; probably these ancient fights seem to you as far off as the Punic wars. Suffice to say that it was a matter of a new German tank design, details of which I got via Bletchley and passed on to Oleg. I am told, and modesty will not prevent me from believing it, that it was thanks in no small part to my intervention that the Russian forces prevailed in that momentous engagement. For these and other contributions to the Soviet war effort – I am determined to keep some secrets to myself – I was presented with the Order of the Red Banner, one of the highest Soviet decorations. I was sceptical, of course, and when, at a table by the window of our caff in the Mile End Road, in the drifting, brass-coloured sunlight of a late-summer evening, Oleg produced a shoddily made wooden box and, glancing about cautiously, opened it to show me the unreal-looking medal – so shiny and unfingered, like a false coin preserved in the police museum as evidence of a foiled counterfeiter's flashy skill – I was surprised to discover that I was moved. I lifted the medal briefly from its bed of crimson velvet, and, although I had only the vaguest idea of where Kursk was, for a moment I saw the scene, as in one of those old scratchy, noisy propaganda pictures Mosfilm used to churn out: the Soviet tanks racing across the battlefield, a helmeted hero in the turret of each one, with smoke flying, and a huge, transparent flag rippling in front of everything, and an invisible choir of mighty basses bellowing out a victory hymn. Then Oleg reverently closed the lid and stowed the box away in an inner pocket of his shiny blue suit; there was of course no question of my keeping the medal. 'Perhaps,' Oleg said quietly, with wheezy wistfulness, 'perhaps, someday, in Moscow . . .' What a hope, Oleg; what a hope.

*

On the 10th of May, 1941 (those were the days of Significant Dates), I went to Oxford to see Vivienne. She had just borne our second child. The weather was warm, and we sat in the sunlit conservatory, with the baby in a Moses basket beside us shaded by a potted palm and Julian sprawled on a rug at our feet playing with his building blocks. 'How nice,' Vivienne said brightly, looking about her at the scene. 'One might almost think we were a family.' The maid brought us tea, and Mrs Beaver kept popping in and out nervously to observe us, as if she feared the familial scene must necessarily break down into some terrible altercation, perhaps with attendant violence. I wondered what account of our marriage Vivienne gave to her parents. Perhaps none; she never was one to explain herself. Big Beaver also made an appearance, shifty as always, and stood and absent-mindedly ate a biscuit, and said that he and I must have a serious talk ('On business, that is,' he added hastily, with an anxious roll of the eye), but not today, as he had to go to London. Maliciously, I offered him a lift, and looked on with enjoyment as he performed his snake dance of demurral and squirming apology; the prospect of a couple of hours on the road together was as welcome to him as it would have been to me.

'How I envy you big brave men,' Vivienne said, 'free to venture into the very heart of the inferno. I wouldn't mind watching a few buildings burn to the ground, I'm sure it must be terribly thrilling. Does one hear the cries of the dying, or are they drowned out by the fire sirens and so on?'

'They say the raids are coming to an end,' I said. 'Hitler is going to attack Russia.'

'Is that so?' Big Beaver said, brushing biscuit crumbs from the front of his waistcoat. 'That will be a relief.'

'Not for the Russians,' I said.

He gave me a glum look. Vivienne laughed.

'Didn't you know, Daddy? – Victor is a secret admirer of Stalin.'

He smiled at her with his teeth, and then grew brisk, rubbing his hands together sinuously.

'Well,' he said, 'I must be off. Vivienne, do rest. Victor, perhaps we shall meet in London' – a man-of-the-world chuckle – 'groping our way like blind men through the blackout.' Gingerly he laid a hand on Julian's head – the child, taciturn already, ignored him – and leaned over to peer into the baby's basket, his long nose quivering at the tip. 'Darling girl,' he breathed. 'Beautiful, beautiful.' Then, drolly waving a dusky hand, he gave each of us in turn a sort of glazed, smiling glance, and departed, tiptoeing past the sleeping baby with a finger to his lips in extravagant dumbshow. In the early hours of the following morning, as he was walking down a side street off Charing Cross Road, for what purpose no one knew or cared to speculate, he was struck on the forehead by a very large piece of shrapnel that was flung over the rooftops from a bomb exploding in Shaftesbury Avenue, and died on the pavement, where his body was discovered by a professional young lady as she was making her way home after a night's work in an establishment in Greek Street. I picture poor Max, sauntering along gaily, whistling a tune, hands in pockets and hat on the back of his head, an ageing *flâneur* whose very own Belle Époque was about to be brought to an abrupt close by a hurtling piece of Luftwaffe *matériel*. I wonder what time it was exactly when he died; I am interested, because in those same early hours I too underwent a profound and transformative experience.

The attack that night was the last great air raid of the Blitz. Driving down from Oxford, I was stopped at a police barrier on Hampstead Heath. I got out of the car and stood in the moonlight, the ground shuddering under my feet, and looked down, fascinated, on the city half submerged in a sea of flame. The sky was hung with the tracery of anti-aircraft fire, and searchlight

beams swung and swayed, now and then snagging on one of the
bombers, a stubby, comical-looking thing, reduced by distance
to the size of a toy and seemingly held aloft by the dense ice-
white beam fixed on it. 'Twilight of the gods, sir, eh?' an eerily
cheerful policeman beside me remarked. 'Good old St Paul's is
still standing, though.' I showed him my Department pass, and
he scrutinised it by the light of his torch with amiable scepticism. In the end, however, he let me through. 'You really
intending to drive down into that, sir?' he said.

I should have been thinking of Bosch, of Grünewald and
Altdorfer of Regensburg, those great apocalyptics, but really, I
cannot remember anything in particular going through my mind,
except what might be the best route to take to Poland Street.
When I got there, after many vicissitudes, and stopped the car,
the full weight of the noise fell on me, making my eardrums
vibrate painfully. On the pavement, I looked up and saw in the
direction of Bloomsbury a ragged trail of bombs tumbling flabbily
down the vertical chute of a searchlight beam. Blake would
have been fascinated by the Blitz. As I was letting myself into
the house, it struck me that I had never seen anything so bizarre
as this key going into this lock. The livid sky shed a tender pink
glow on the back of my hand. Inside, the entire house was
trembling, minutely, rapidly, like a dog dragged out of an icy
river. A lamp was burning in the first-floor sitting room, but the
room was empty. The chairs and sofa crouched in what seemed
an apprehensive silence, their arms braced, as if at any moment
they might get up and scuttle for safety. These raids could be
extremely tedious, and one of the abiding problems was to find
a way to pass the time. Reading was difficult, and if the bombing
was close by it was impossible to listen to music on the
gramophone, not only because of the racket, but because the
shocks kept making the needle jump out of the groove of the
record. Sometimes I would browse through a volume of Poussin
reproductions; the classical stillness of the compositions was a
calmative, but I was conscious how banal, not to say absurd, it

would be for me to be killed with such a book in my hands (Boy always had a laugh about a doctor he once knew who had been found dead of a heart attack, sitting in an armchair with a medical textbook on his lap open at a chapter dealing with the subject of angina pectoris). Drink, of course, was a possibility, but I always found that hangovers were worse than usual on the mornings after raids, I suppose because one's drunken sleep had been all din and flashing lights and shaking bedsprings. So I was pacing the sitting room, somewhat at a loss, when Danny Perkins came down, in striped calico pyjamas and slippers and Boy's ratty dressing gown, from which the cord was missing. His eyes were swollen and his hair was on end. He was annoyed.

'Asleep, I was,' he said, 'and those blooming bombs woke me up.' He might have been referring to the doings of a noisy neighbour. He stood, scratching, and peered at me. 'Been to see the wifey, have you?'

'I have a new daughter,' I said.

'Oh, that's nice.' He looked about the shadowed room vaguely, stretching sleep-gummed lips and running an explorative grey tongue-tip over his teeth. 'I wonder if the pox-doctor's office has any sleeping pills in it. I could break open a cabinet, maybe?' A tremendous explosion occurred close by, and the floor buckled and sagged alarmingly and the windows boomed and rattled. 'Listen to that,' Danny said peevishly, clicking his tongue, and briefly, although I had never met the woman, I could clearly see his mother in him.

'Aren't you at all afraid, Danny?' I said.

He considered the question.

'No,' he said, 'I don't think so. Not what you'd call properly afraid. I do get nervous, like, sometimes.'

I laughed.

'Boy should put you on the wireless,' I said, 'broadcasting to Germany. You'd be a perfect counter to Lord Haw Haw. Why don't we sit down, since it doesn't seem either of us is going to be able to sleep tonight.'

Danny sat on the sofa, and I took an armchair on the other side of the fireplace. There were charred papers in the grate, like a bunch of soot-black roses; I admired the convoluted, whorled and pleated shapes, their rich velvet texture. Boy often burned sensitive documents here. He had no sense of security.

'Is Boy in?' I asked.

Danny made a put-upon face, throwing up his eyes. The dressing gown had fallen open, and the buttonless fly of his pyjamas revealed a patch of mossy darkness.

'Oh, don't talk to me about him,' he said. 'Drunk again, and passed out up there, snoring like a hog. I say to him, I say, Mr Bannister, you'll have to leave your liver to science.' To the east of us another stick of bombs went off, crackcrack crackcrack craack. Danny grew pensive. 'When we were children,' he said, 'our dad used to tell us to count how many seconds it took for the thunder to come after a flash of lightning, and that way we'd know how many miles away the storm was. Seems silly now, doesn't it. But we believed him.'

'Is that what you always call him?' I said. He looked at me, his eyes refocusing as he came back from the valleys. 'Boy,' I said. 'Do you always call him Mr Bannister?'

He did not answer, only gave one of his sly, lewd little smiles.

'Like a cup of tea?' he said.

'No.' The silence in the room was a pool of calm in the midst of a raging storm. Danny softly hummed a snatch of song. 'I wonder what it would be like,' I said, 'if a bomb were to hit the house now. I mean, I wonder if one would know, in the second before everything collapsed?'

'Makes you think, sir, doesn't it?'

'Yes, Danny, it makes you think.'

He smiled that blameless smile of his again.

'And tell me, sir, what would you be thinking now – apart, like, from worrying about a bomb falling on our heads?'

Suddenly it felt as if there were a marble in my throat; I heard myself swallow.

'I'm thinking,' I said, 'that I would not like to die before I have lived.'

He shook his head and gave a wondering little whistle.

'Oh, that's terrible. Have you not lived, sir?'

'There are things I haven't done.'

'Well now, that's true of all of us, sir, isn't it? Why don't you come over here and sit beside me.'

'No,' I said, 'it's not true of everyone. Not of Boy, or of you, either, I suspect. Is there room for me to sit there?'

'Well, there's lots of things I haven't done,' he said. 'Lots of things.' He put out a hand and patted the space beside him. I stood up, feeling impossibly tall and teetering, as if I were on stilts. I did not so much sit beside him as tumble down on to the cushions in a heap. He had a faintly meaty, faintly rancid smell; from childhood suddenly I remembered the stink that marauding foxes used to leave behind in the garden in the early morning. I kissed him awkwardly on the mouth (*bristles!*), and he laughed, and pulled back his face and looked at me, quizzical and amused, and shook his head. 'Oh, Captain,' he said softly.

I tried to take his hand, but that did not work. I touched his shoulder and was startled by the hardness of it, the hardness, and the unaccustomed muscular responsiveness; I might have been feeling a horse's flank. He waited, tolerant, mocking, fond.

'I don't know . . . what you do,' I said.

He laughed again, and took me by the wrist and gave it a yank.

'Come here, then,' he said, 'and I'll show you.'

And he did.

*

Do not trouble yourself, Miss V., there will be no graphic descriptions of The Act, of bodies pounding in unison, of the cries and the clawings, the delighted easings, the familiar spasm in unfamiliar surroundings, and then the gentle falling into calm – no, no, none of that. I am a gentleman of the old school, awkward in such matters, a touch prudish, even. The bombs of course lent drama to the occasion, but to tell the truth, these stage effects were a bit overdone, a bit vulgarly Wagnerian, as that unlikely Hampstead policeman earlier in the night had understood. The city quaked, and I quaked, both of us under an irresistible but very different manner of assault. I had no sense of entering into a foreign or an unknown land. True, lovemaking with Danny Perkins was a wholly dissimilar experience from the cool and always faintly preoccupied ministrations of my wife, but I knew where I was; oh yes, I knew where I was. I thought it highly probable that I would not survive this night, in which the intensity of the passion I was experiencing seemed as likely to do for me as the bombs raining down on the city, but I contemplated the prospect with perfect detachment; death was a bored and slightly resentful attendant, sitting impatiently at the other side of the room, waiting for Danny and me to finish so that I might be taken up and led away to the final exit. I felt no shame in the things I was doing, and was having done to me, none of that awful sense of transgression that I might have expected. I do not think I felt any real pleasure, either, that first time. In fact, I felt like nothing so much as the volunteer in a crude and remarkably vigorous medical experiment. I hope Danny would forgive me for making this comparison, but it is, I am afraid, accurate. In subsequent encounters he inflicted such exquisite, tender torments on me that I would have wept at his feet and cried out for more – there was a particular thickening effect at the root of my tongue, an ecstatic, panicky sensation of choking, that only Danny could produce in me – but that time, as the bombs fell and thousands died around us, I was the splayed specimen and he was the vivisector.

Afterwards – what a pity, in a way, that there must always be an afterwards – Danny made us a pot of strong tea, and we sat in the kitchen drinking it, he wearing my jacket, that was much too long for him in the sleeves, and me huddled in Boy's grey dressing gown, shamefaced, and ridiculously pleased with myself, as the dawn struggled to break, and the all-clear sounded, and a sort of ringing silence descended, as if a vast chandelier had come crashing down somewhere close by and smashed into pieces.

'That was a bad one,' Danny said, 'that raid. I don't think there'll be much left standing after that.'

I was shocked. Indeed, it is not too much to say that I was outraged. This was the first time he had spoken since we had left the sofa, and all he could come out with were these wretched banalities. What did I care if the entire realm had been flattened! I watched him with sulky curiosity and a swelling sense of umbrage, waiting in vain for him to register the momentousness of the occasion. It is a reaction I in after-years was to see often in other first-timers. They look at you and think, How can he sit there, so offhand, so unmoved, so firmly back in the ordinary, when this amazing thing has happened to me? When I have had a great deal of pleasure from them, or they are very beautiful, or married and anxious (all this in the wholly inappropriate present tense, I notice), I try for their sake to pretend that I too feel that something great and transfiguring has occurred, after which neither of us will be the same ever again. And it is true, for them it has been a revelation, a transformation, a light-stricken falling down in the dust of the road; for me, however, it has been just a . . . well, I shall not use the word, which anyway I am sure Miss V. thinks only properly applies, if properly is the way to put it, to what she and her plumber, or whatever he is, I have forgotten, do together on their pull-out divan after the pub on a Saturday night.

Immediately, like a fond old roué, I sought to introduce Danny to what used to be called the finer things of life. I brought him – my God, I burn with shame to think of it – I brought him to the Institute and made him sit and listen while I lectured on Poussin's second period in Rome, on Claude Lorrain and the cult of landscape, on François Mansart and the French baroque style. While I spoke, his attention would decline in three distinct stages. For five minutes or so he would sit up very straight with his hands folded in his lap, watching me with the concentration of a retriever on point; then would come a long central period of increasing agitation, during which he would study the other students, or lean over at the window to follow the progress of someone crossing the courtyard below, or bite his nails with tiny, darting movements, like a jeweller cutting and shaping a row of precious stones; after that, until the end of the lecture, he would sink into a trance of boredom, head sunk on neck, his eyelids drooping at the corners and his lips slackly parted. I covered up my disappointment in him on these occasions as best I could. Yet he did so try to keep up, to seem interested and impressed. He would turn to me afterwards and say, 'What you said about the Greek stuff in that picture, the one with the fellow in the skirt – you know, that one by what's-his-name – that was very good, that was; I thought that was very good.' And he would frown, and nod gravely, and look at his boots.

I would not give up. I pressed books on him, including, not without shyness, *Art Theory of the Renaissance*, my favourite among my own works. I urged him to read Plutarch, Vasari, Pater, Roger Fry. I gave him reproductions of Poussin and Ingres to pin up on the wall in the little boxroom off Boy's bedroom that was his private place. I took him to hear Myra Hess playing Bach at lunchtime in the National Gallery. He endured all these trials with a sort of rueful tolerance, laughing at himself, and at me for my delusions and childish desires. One Sunday afternoon we went together to the Institute and descended through the deserted building to the vaults in the basement, where with all the solemnity of a high priest inducting an ephebe into the mysteries of the cult, I unwrapped my *Death of Seneca* from its burlap shroud and held it up for his admiration. Long silence; then: 'Why is that woman in the middle there showing off her titties?'

The price he exacted for submitting himself to so much culture was the frequent excursions that we made together into the world of popular entertainment. I had to accompany him regularly to the theatre, to musicals and farces and comedy reviews. Afterwards we would go to a pub and he would give me a detailed critique of the show. He was a harsh critic. His most scathing denunciations were reserved for the male soloists and the boys in the chorus. 'Couldn't sing for toffee, that one – hear him trying to do that high note at the end? Pathetic, I call it.' He was very fond of the music hall, too, and at least once a week I would find myself squirming on a hard seat at the Chelsea Palace of Varieties or the Metropolitan in the Edgware Road, while fat women in floppy hats sang risqué ballads, and sweating magicians fumbled with scarves and ping-pong balls, and check-suited mephistophelian comedians flung themselves about the stage on rubber legs, making double entendres, and shouting catch-phrases I could not understand but which sent the audiences into swaying transports of mirth.

Boy too had a weakness for the music hall, and often accompanied us on these jaunts Up West. He loved the noise and the laughter, the brute euphoria of the crowd. He would bob and stamp beside me in his seat, cheering the fat singers and joining in the refrains with them, hugging himself with glee at the comedians' blue jokes, making wolf whistles at the mighty-thighed, no longer young girls in the chorus. It was as well the darkness hid the rictus of contempt with which I regarded him as he swayed and shouted. Another attraction of these occasions for him was the rich opportunities there were after the show for him to pick up lonely young men. Boy knew about Danny and me, of course – Danny had told him what had occurred as soon as he had woken up that morning from his drunken stupor. I imagine they both had a good laugh. I had waited, not without trepidation, for Boy's reaction; I don't know what I had expected him to do, but Danny was supposed to be his lover, after all. I need not have worried. As soon as he heard, Boy came lumbering down the stairs and clasped me in a close and noisome embrace and gave me a fat wet kiss full on the lips. 'Welcome to the Homintern, darling,' he said. 'I always knew, you know; something in those soulful eyes.' And he cackled.

What really worried me, of course, was what Nick would think. Even the possibility that he would tell Vivienne was nothing compared with the prospect of his disapproval or, worse still, his ridicule. I should say that at that stage I did not for a moment think that I had turned overnight into a fully fledged queer. I was a married man, wasn't I, with two young children? This fling with Danny I took to be an aberration, an experiment in living, an exotic indulgence licensed by the times, the sort of thing that so many others of my acquaintance had gone through at school but which I with characteristic tardiness had only arrived at in my thirties. True, I was startled, not to say shaken, by the emotional and physical intensity of these new experiences, but that too I could take as merely another symptom of the general feverishness of the extraordinary times through which we were living. I suppose these were the kind of things I planned to say to Nick if he should challenge me. I saw myself in a Noël Coward pose, world-weary, polished, briskly turning aside his remonstrations with the flick of an invisible ebony cigarette holder. ('For goodness' sake, dear boy, don't be so conventional!') But he did not challenge me. On the contrary, he observed a total silence, which was more alarming than any expression of abhorrence would have been. It was not just that he never said anything: he did not register by the slightest sign what he was thinking. It was as if he had not noticed – in fact, sometimes I wondered if perhaps the thing was entirely beyond his comprehension, and that it was this that kept him from seeing what was happening, and from attacking me, or turning from me in disgust. As the years went on, and I acknowledged my true nature to him, if not in so many words then certainly in unignorable deeds, we developed a tacit understanding which, so I thought, embraced not only our friendship but my relations, as he saw them, with Vivienne and the children and the Brevoort family in general. I can never decide which I am more of, an innocent or a fool. Equal parts of both, perhaps.

The day after that night of revelation is lit in my memory with a garish, hallucinatory glare. At mid-morning, when Danny had gone back to his room to sleep – Danny loved to lie in bed in the daytime, wrapped in voluptuous, wool-warm communion with himself – and I was bracing myself to step out into what I was convinced would be an utterly devastated city, a telephone call came, from a person whose identity I never did manage to trace, and even whose gender was uncertain to me, but who seemed to be a Brevoort relation of some sort, to inform me of the discovery earlier that morning in Lisle Street of the body of my father-in-law, sprawled on the pavement in a tacky puddle of his own blood. I assumed a felony had been committed – that sprawl, that spilled blood – and asked if the police had been called, which provoked a puzzled, crackly silence on the line, followed by what I thought was a snort of laughter, but was probably a sob, and a long, gabbled explanation in which the words *flying shrapnel* seemed to me to strike an incongruously comic note. More phone calls followed (how had the telephone lines survived such a night?). Vivienne rang from Oxford. She sounded tight-lipped and accusatory, as if she were holding me at least partly to blame for the tragedy, which perhaps she was, since I was the only immediately available representative of the vast machine of war in which her father had been inadvertently caught and crushed. Her mother came on the line, urgent and incoherent, saying she *had known, had known all along*; I took her to mean she had foreseen Max's death and was adducing it as another confirmation of her gift of second sight. I listened to her blathering, making sympathetic noises now and then, which was all that was required of me; I was still in a state of love-drunk euphoria which nothing could fully penetrate. I thought, with callous irritation, of the lecture I had been meant to be embarking on at this very moment to my class at the Institute; Big Beaver's death, on top of the air raids, was going to mean a serious disruption of my teaching schedule in the immediate future. Then there was the question of my books: would I have to find a new publisher now, or could I count on the practically senile Immanuel Klein to continue his late partner's support of me? Really, it was all extremely inconvenient.

Vivienne had commanded me to find Nick and tell him the news. He was not in the house, and I could not reach him at the Department. It took me until lunchtime to track him down, at the Hungaria, where at one end of the dining room a noisy crowd was happily at feed, while at the other, blue-aproned waiters were sweeping up the glass and splinters from a window that had been blown in by one of last night's bombs. Nick, in uniform, was lunching with Sylvia Lydon and her sister. I hung back in the doorway for a moment, watching him talk, and smile, and turn his head sideways and up in that characteristic way of his, as if to toss back from his forehead the glossy black wing of hair that was no longer there, except in my memory (he was already balding; it rather suited him, I thought, but he was very touchy on the matter, for he had been vain of his hair). There was sunshine on the table, and the girls – Sylvia languorously feline in Nick's presence, Lydia officially a spinster by now but giddier than ever – were laughing at a joke that Nick had made, and suddenly I wanted to turn and walk away rapidly – I could see myself striding out the door and down the stairs – and leave it to someone else to extinguish that frail square of sunlight on the table, where Nick's hand rested, holding a cigarette from the tip of which there rose a thin, frost-blue plume of smoke, sinuous, hurrying, like a chain of shivery question marks. Nick turned his head then and saw me, and although his smile remained in place, something behind it faltered, and shrank. He rose, and came across the dining room, keeping his gaze on me, one hand in a pocket, the other trailing his cigarette. When he reached the doorway where I was standing he stopped short a pace and held his head to one side and looked at me, smiling, tense, apprehensive, defiantly nonchalant, all at the same time.

'Victor,' he said, in a wondering, wary sort of way, as if I were an old and not much treasured friend come back unexpectedly after a long absence.

'Bad news, old man,' I said.

That fearful something behind his gaze shrank further still into itself. He gave himself a little shake, frowning in puzzlement, and glanced beyond my shoulder, as if expecting to see someone else advancing on him.

'But why did they send you?' he said.

'Vivienne asked me to find you.'

His frown deepened. 'Vivienne . . . ?'

'It's your father,' I said. 'He was in London last night. He was caught in the bombing. I'm sorry.' He turned aside for a moment, jerkily, and released a quick, hissing breath, that might almost have been a sigh of relief. I stepped forward and put my hands on his arms above the elbows. 'I'm sorry, Nick,' I said again. I realised I had an erection. He nodded distractedly, and turned to me and slowly laid his forehead on my shoulder. I was still holding him by the arms. From their table the Lydon sisters looked on in unaccustomed solemnity, and Sylvia stood up and I watched her walking toward us in slow motion, shimmering through alternating diagonal slashes of sunlight and shadow, a hand raised, her lips parted to speak. Nick was trembling. I wished that the moment might never end.

*

Max's corpse had already been officially identified by that mysterious, disembodied Brevoort – who *can* it have been? – whom I had spoken to on the telephone, but Nick was determined to see his father a last time. While he sat in silence with the Lydons in the Hungaria, each of them holding one of Nick's hands and gazing at him with sympathy in which there was, on Lydia's part at least, a frank admixture of lust, I made another series of difficult and frustrating telephone calls to various centres of so-called authority, which resulted in the grudging admission that if the body of a person called Brevoort *had* been discovered in Lisle Street, which all my respondents seemed to doubt – Lisle Street had not been bombed, I was told, and what *was* that name again? – then it was likely to have been taken to Charing Cross station, which was being used this morning as a temporary morgue. So Nick and I walked up Whitehall in the hard-edged spring sunlight, past the statue of Charles I encased in its protective galvanised privy. On all sides were giant mounds of rubble over which ambulance men and Home Guard recruits were scrambling like ragpickers. In the Strand a cascading water main was incongruously suggestive of Versailles. Yet the destruction, however extensive, was curiously disappointing; the streets seemed not ruined, but rearranged, as if a vast rebuilding scheme were under way. I had, I realised, put too much hope in the air war; what the newspapers nowadays like to call the fabric of society is depressingly strong.

'Funny thing,' Nick was saying, 'a father's death. You lost yours – what was that like?'

'Awful. And yet a kind of release, too.'

We stopped where a small crowd had gathered to peer into a crater in the roadway. Down in the hole two sappers were contemplating in head-scratching dismay a huge, plump bomb, like a giant grub, lying on its side half buried in the clay.

'I thought it would be me who would cop it,' Nick said. 'I used to picture Max and poor Ma trailing along to view the bloodied remains.' He paused. 'I'm not sure that I can look at him,' he said. 'I know I was all for it, but now I've lost my nerve. Terrible, isn't it.'

'We're almost there,' I said.

He nodded, still absently watching the sappers as they got down gingerly to work.

'I wonder what it would be like,' he said, 'if that thing were to go off now.'

'Yes, the same thought occurred to me last night.'

Last night.

'Would we know we were dying,' he said, 'or would there just be a flash, and then nothing?'

In the station, an ARP warden directed us to the farthest platform, where the corpses, a great many of them, were laid out side by side in neat rows under canvas sheets. A nurse wearing a tin helmet and a sort of bandolier escorted us down the lines. She was a large, distracted woman, and reminded me of Hettie as she had been in her younger years. As we walked along she counted off numbers under her breath, and at last pounced on one of the shrouded forms and pulled back the canvas sheet. Max wore a troubled expression, as if he were in the throes of a perplexing dream. The mark on his forehead where the shrapnel had struck was surprisingly small and neat, more like a surgical incision than a wound. Nick knelt awkwardly and leaned down and kissed his father's cheek; when he stood up again, I tried not to notice him giving his lips a furtive wipe with the back of his hand.

'I need a drink,' he said. 'Do you think there are any pubs still standing?' The nurse gave him a bleak, disapproving stare.

We spent the rest of the afternoon trying to get drunk, not very successfully. The Gryphon was crowded, the atmosphere even more hysterical than usual. Querell was there, and came and sat at our table. He was predicting a general collapse of morale followed immediately by widespread anarchy and internecine fighting. 'There'll be killing in the streets,' he said, 'you wait and see.' He viewed the prospect with obvious satisfaction. Nick did not tell him about his father's death. I kept thinking of Danny, and each time I did I experienced a secret surge of elation that was all the sweeter for being, in the circumstances, so shaming.

Later, Vivienne telephoned; she had come down to London, and was at Poland Street.

'How did you know where to find us?' I said.

'Telepathy. It's in the blood. Is Nick all right?'

The telephone was hot and sticky in my hand. I was wondering if Danny were still in the house; I had an image of him appearing in the sitting room in his vest, and of Vivienne and him settling down on the sofa – that sofa – for a nice long chat.

'Nick is not all right,' I said. 'No one is all right.'

She was silent for a moment.

'What are you so happy about, Victor? Has Daddy left you something in his will?'

When Nick and I got to Poland Street it was not Danny who was with her, but Boy. They had drunk most of a bottle of champagne. Boy rose and embraced Nick, with unaccustomed awkwardness. Vivienne's eyes were red rimmed, though she smiled at me brightly. When she patted the place beside her on the sofa I recalled Danny doing the same thing the night before, and I looked away.

'Are you blushing, Victor?' she said. 'What *have* you been up to?'

Boy was in full evening dress, except for a pair of carpet slippers.

'Corns,' he said, lifting a foot. 'Killing me. But it doesn't matter, it's only the BBC, no one will notice.'

Presently Leo Rothenstein arrived, and the Lydons, accompanied by a pair of awkward young RAF pilots, and a woman called Belinda, a washed-out blonde with peculiar, violet eyes, who claimed to be a close friend of Vivienne's, though I had never encountered her before. The blackout shades were drawn, and Boy forgot about the BBC and instead fetched more champagne, and then someone put on a jazz record, and the party was under way. Later, I came upon Leo Rothenstein in the kitchen, in ponderously playful conversation with the by now drunken blonde Belinda. He gave me his most domineering smile and said:

'You must feel quite at home, Maskell – it's an Irish wake.'

And later still, when still more guests had arrived, I found myself yet again trapped with Querell, who backed me into a corner and lectured me about religion. 'Yes, yes, Christianity is the religion of the slave, of the foot soldier, of the poor and the weak – but of course, you don't consider such people to be people at all, really, do you, you and your pals the *Übermenschen*.' I half listened to him, nodding and shaking my head at what seemed appropriate moments. I was wondering again where Danny was – I had not stopped wondering that all day – and what he might be doing. I remembered the steely-soft feel of his shoulder, the hot, hard little bristles on his upper lip, and savoured again at the back of my throat the thick, fish-and-sawdust taste of his semen. 'At least I *believe* in something,' Querell was saying, pushing his face close to mine and goggling at me drunkenly. 'At least I have *faith*.'

*

Danny did not come home that night, or the following night, or the night after that. I held off for as long as I could, and then went to Boy. At first he could not grasp what I was concerned about, and said I should not worry, that Danny knew his way in the world, and could be depended on to look after himself. Then he peered at me more closely, and laughed, not without sympathy, and patted my hand. 'Poor Vic,' he said, 'you have a lot to learn; our kind can't afford that sort of jealousy.' And the following week, when I found Boy one afternoon in bed with Danny, I stood in the doorway and could think of nothing to say, could think of nothing to think. Danny, lying on his side, did not realise I was there until Boy said cheerfully, 'Wotcher,

Vic, old son,' and then he stirred, and turned his head and looked at me over his shoulder and smiled sleepily, as if I were someone he had known a long time ago, and of whom he retained only a confused and vaguely tender impression. Then something opened in me, briefly, frighteningly, as if a little window had been thrown open on to a vast, far, dark, deserted plain.

THREE

IT IS TIME for me to speak of Patrick Quilly, my quondam catamite, cook and general housekeeper. I miss him terribly, even still. When I think of him I go hot with guilt and shame, I am not quite sure why. I torment myself with the question of whether he fell or jumped, or even if – dear God! – he might have been pushed. I met him when he was working as a sales assistant in a jewellery shop in the Burlington Arcade. I had dropped in one day to buy a rather nice silver tiepin I had spotted in the window; it was intended as a gift for Nick to mark the occasion of his maiden speech in the House, but I ended up giving it to Patrick, in celebration of another, quite unmaidenly accession, when he came that night into my bed. He was tall, as tall as I am, and very handsome, in a sulky, glowering sort of way. His upper torso was remarkable, all muscle and stretched tendons and excitingly wiry body hair, but his legs were comically thin, and he was knock-kneed, a matter about which he was particularly sensitive, as I discovered when I was unwise enough to make a light-hearted allusion to it (he sulked for a whole day and half a night, but as dawn was breaking we made up, very tenderly; I could not have been more . . . accommodating). He was, like me, an Ulsterman – Protestant, of course, despite the Christian name – and had joined the army at an early age to get himself out of the Belfast slum where he was born. He went to France in 1940 with the Expeditionary Force; I often wonder if I came across his letters home, in my capacity as censor. When the Germans invaded, he was captured at Louvain and spent the rest of the war in what seems to have been a not at all disagreeable prison camp in the Black Forest.

After our first night together he moved in with me straight away – I still had the top-floor flat at the Institute then – and immediately set about reordering my domestic life. He was a tireless tidier-up, which suited me, for I am something of an obsessive myself, in that way (queers seem to come in only two varieties, the sloven, like Boy, or the monk, like me). He was quite uneducated, and of course, as was my way, I could not resist trying to introduce him to Culture. The poor boy really did work at it, much more diligently than Danny ever had, but still got nowhere, and was laughed at for his pains by my friends and colleagues. He minded this terribly, and smashed a cut-glass decanter one day in tearful rage after Nick had amused himself throughout a luncheon at the flat by imitating Patrick's Belfast accent and addressing cod questions to him on the subject of seventeenth-century painting, about which, I should point out, Nick knew somewhat less than Patrick did.

Patrick had a great love of good clothes, and frequented my tailor with enthusiasm and a blithe disregard for the state of my account. But I could not resist indulging him, and besides, he was achingly desirable in a well-cut suit. There were many places to which I could not bring him, of course, for no matter how presentable he might look, he had only to open his mouth to reveal what he was. This was a recurring cause of friction between us, though his resentment was much alleviated when I took the risk and allowed him to accompany me to the Palace on the day my knighthood was conferred. Mrs W. even had a word for him, and you can imagine the effect. (I often wonder, by the way, if Mrs W. is aware of her iconic status among the queer fraternity. Certainly her mother in her day revelled in the role of the queers' goddess, and was fond of making jokes about being the one real royal among a palace full of queens. Mrs W.'s humour, however, is less broad, though she does like to tease, in her straight-faced way. Dear me, I miss her, too.)

The advent of Patrick marked the beginning of a new phase of my life – the middle period, one might say – a time of rest and reflection and deep study which I was glad of after the hectic years of the war. The London scene had quietened dramatically anyway, especially after Boy went to America, though the tales of his doings that came back to us from across the Atlantic livened up many an otherwise dull dinner party. In the main, I was uxoriously content. That is only a technical misuse of the adverb. Patrick had all the best qualities of a wife, and was blessedly lacking in two of the worst: he was neither female, nor fertile (I ask myself, in these days of protest and the pursuit of so-called liberation, if women fully realise how deeply, viscerally, *sorrowfully*, men hate them). He took very good care of me. He was an amusing companion, an excellent cook, and a superb if unadventurous lover. He was also a resourceful pander. Utterly free of sexual jealousy, he brought me boys with the shy eagerness of a cat depositing half-chewed mice at its master's feet. He was something of a voyeur, too, and it took me some time to get over my instinctive prudery and let him watch while I cavorted in bed with these half-wild creatures.

The staff at the Institute accepted Patrick's presence in my life without remark. Of course, we were exquisitely discreet, at least during the hours when the galleries were open to the public. Patrick loved to throw parties, a few of which did become worryingly rowdy, for his friends tended to be on the rough side. The following morning, though, by the time my hangover and I had struggled up, the flat would be set completely to rights, the stragglers ejected, the cigarette stubs and the empty beer bottles cleared away, the carpets swept, the atmosphere as cool and calm as the bluish interior of Seneca's bedroom in the Poussin above my desk, which had not, after all, been stolen by one of the guests, or smashed in a romp, as I in my drunken nightmares had envisioned it would be.

Vivienne never came to the flat. I met her in Harrods one day when I was with Patrick, and after I had made the mumbled introductions we stood talking for a minute, and I was the only

309

one who was embarrassed. Nick thought Patrick a joke. I had hoped he would be jealous – Nick, I mean. Yes, pathetic, I know. Patrick on the other hand took a great shine to Nick, and had an irritating way when he came to visit of following him about, like a large, friendly and not very bright dog. It did not seem to matter how badly Nick behaved, Patrick always forgave him. Nick was advancing into middle age at a stately, seigneurial pace. He had put on flesh, but what would have been a coarsening in others was in him the assumption of a lordly mantle. He was no longer the downy, fascinatingly demonic beauty he had been in his twenties; let us be honest, he looked like a typical High Tory grandee, portly, pinstriped, with that marvellous, all-over pale-gold sheen that the very rich and powerful acquire with the years, I do not know how. That youthful pomposity, which I used to find both comic and endearing, had, like his physical self, grown steadily heavier, squashing the last traces of a sense of humour that anyway had never been one of his stronger qualities. Where once he asserted, with the enthusiasm and certainty of youth, now he pontificated, fastening on to one with the fixed, menacing stare of the bully, daring one to contradict him. He had progressed through the years, a one-man caravan, accumulating the precious goods of life, money, power, renown, a wife and children – two big bright girls, one the image of their mother, the other of her Aunt Lydia – and now wherever he appeared he carried the weight of these riches with him, like an Eastern potentate padding along in front of his retinue of veiled women and burdened slaves. Yet I still loved him, helplessly, hopelessly, ashamed of myself, laughing at myself, a prim, middle-aged scholar pining after this overfed, overconfident, pompous pillar of the Establishment. How deluded I was. Love, I have always found, is most intense when its object is unworthy of it.

At the end of one of those drunken, revelrous parties at the flat I confessed everything to Patrick about my other secret life. He laughed. This was not the response I had expected. He said he had not had such a good laugh since the day his commanding officer in France was shot in the backside by a German machine-gunner. He had known that I had been something significant in the shadowy world of the Department, but that I had also been working for Moscow he thought a grand joke. He knew what it was to live clandestinely, of course. He wanted all the details; he was greatly excited, and was particularly ardent in bed afterwards. I should not have told him all those things. I got carried away. I even named names, Boy, Alastair, Leo Rothenstein. It was foolish and boastful of me, but oh, I did enjoy myself, just letting it all spill out.

We had a row, Patrick and I, on the night that he died. This is a source of continuing, hardly bearable remorse for me. There had been squabbles before, of course, but this was the first real, stand-up, no-holds-barred fight I had permitted between us; the first, and the last. I cannot remember how it started – something trivial, I'm sure. Before we knew it we were going at it hammer-and-tongs, raving at each other, lost to ourselves in an exultant transport of fury, like a pair of demented, doomed lovers at the climax of a bad opera. I wish I had known of the real doom that awaited poor Patrick just a few hours later, for then I would not have said such dreadful, dreadful things to him, and he would not have sat up brooding into the early hours, would not have got drunk on my best brandy, would not have staggered out on to the balcony and plummeted through the whistling dark to his death four flights below in the moonlit courtyard. I was asleep when he fell. I wish I could report some bodeful dream, or say that I started awake in inexplicable dread at the moment of his death, but I cannot. I slept on, and he lay there on the stones, his poor neck broken, with no one to see him die or hear his last breath. The porter found him, when he was doing his morning rounds; the sound of the fellow's boots on the stairs woke me. *'Beg pardon, sir, I'm afraid there's been an accident . . .'*

At the time I was undergoing yet another round of

interrogations by the Department, and curiously enough, this turned out to my advantage, for Billy Mytchett and his people were as anxious as I was to keep the matter quiet. They thought that after years of questioning I was about to crack and tell all, and the last thing they wanted was the *canaille* of the press sniffing about. So someone had a word with the police and, later, with the coroner, and in the end not a mention of the matter appeared in the papers. I was so relieved; a scandal like that would have gone down very badly at the Palace, where I was still pleasurably ensconced. I stayed inside the flat for weeks, frightened of outdoors. Miss McIntosh, my secretary, brought me groceries and bottles of gin, carrying them up all those flights of stairs herself, despite her years and her arthritis, bless her virgin's kindly heart. I soon realised, however, that I would have to give up the flat. Patrick's mark was everywhere; how I wept, bent double at the kitchen table, rolling my forehead on my fist, when I picked up a tumbler one day and found his five fingerprints clearly visible on the fluted sides. I found something else, too. When eventually I worked up the courage to go out on to the balcony, I noticed that the catch on the French window was broken, in such a way that it seemed it might have been forced. I asked Skryne if the heavies had been in the flat, rummaging for evidence against me, but he swore he had sent no snoopers in at all. I believed him. Yet the doubt lingers in my mind; did Patrick come upon an intruder in the flat that night, some stealthy searcher who left no trace, unless you count a smashed body lying all aheap in the silence and the moonlight? Surely I am being fanciful? Patrick, ah, poor Patsy!

*

By the time hostilities in Europe were drawing to a noisy close I held the rank of major and had taken part in some of the most significant Allied intelligence offensives of the war (imagine here a simper of modesty, a gruff clearing of the throat). Despite my diligence, however, and my successes, I was never able to climb to the very highest reaches of the Department hierarchy. This was, I confess, a source of resentment and humiliation. Nick was at the top, and Querell, and Leo Rothenstein, and even Boy was sometimes given a hand and hauled up to take part in the Olympian deliberations on the Fifth Floor. (What a comedy they must have played out up there, the four of them!) I could not understand why I was excluded. Hints were dropped which suggested that I was seen to be a shade too raffish, that I enjoyed the deceptions and the double-bluffs too much to be taken completely seriously. I thought that rich, especially when I considered Nick's capriciousness and frequent negligence in matters of security. And if I was regarded as dangerously louche, what about Boy? No, I decided: the real reason I was consistently blackballed was that I was being punished for my sexual deviation. Nick may never have mentioned my affair with Danny Perkins, or the many other such affairs I had enjoyed *après* Danny, but he was, after all, my wife's brother, and the uncle of my children. The fact of his own scandalous liaisons – for example, the simultaneous affairs he had carried on with the Lydon sisters right up to and, some said, well after his marriage to Sylvia – did not count, apparently. I need hardly say that I refrained from voicing these complaints. One must not whine. It is the first rule of the Stoics.

Deep down I was afraid that my exclusion from the Fifth Floor might be due to something far more sinister than mere prejudice, or a poisoned word from Nick. My fear was fed by the persistence of that curious echo, that faint sonar blip, which I seemed to catch at certain significant turns in my term of service at the Department. Sometimes I would stop dead in my tracks, like a traveller halting on a country road at night, convinced he is being followed, though when he stops, the footsteps he imagines behind him stop as well. The strangest aspect of it was that I could not distinguish whether this shadowy stalker, if he existed, was friend or foe. Things came into my possession, pieces of information, documents, maps, names, which it was no real business of mine to have; these unlooked for, choice *trouvailles* made Oleg nervous, though he always allowed his greed to overcome his misgivings. There was an opposite effect, too, when this or that scrap of information that Moscow had asked for, often very low-grade stuff, would suddenly acquire a security classification that put it beyond my reach. In all of this I thought I detected a whimsically malicious note; it was as if I were being made to dance for someone's amusement, and no matter how I might struggle, the strings, impossibly delicate and fine, remained tightly attached to my ankles and my wrists.

I suspected everyone. For a time I even suspected Nick. During the war, one fog-muffled afternoon deep in winter, when I was with Oleg in Rainer's – yes, we went on meeting there almost to the end, even though it was just around the corner from the Department – I saw Nick in the street passing by the smeary window and could have sworn that he had spotted me, though he gave no sign and just pulled down his hat brim and disappeared into the fog. I went on tenterhooks for days afterwards, but nothing happened. I told myself it was all nonsense. Was it likely that Nick would go in for the kind of cat-and-mouse game that I suspected was being played with me – would he have had the subtlety, the wit, for it? No, I said, no, if Nick were to spot one of his top people, even if it *was* his brother-in-law, hugger-muggering with a Soviet controller – and Oleg was known to pretty well everyone by now – he would have pulled out his Service revolver and strode into the teashop Richard Hannay fashion, pushing chairs and waitresses aside, and marched me off to be dealt with by the Department's internal security people. The straight-as-a-die, no-nonsense man of impulse and precipitate action, that was the image of himself that Nick chose to put forward.

Boy, then? No: he might have started the thing as a practical joke, but he would have tired of it rapidly. Leo Rothenstein was a more likely suspect. That kind of elegantly contemptuous game would have appealed to a Levantine parvenu and money-aristocrat like him, but I did not believe he had the subtlety for it, either, nor the sense of mischievousness, despite his parties and his ponderous jests and his boogie-woogie piano playing. Billy Mytchett, needless to say, I did not consider at all. So that left Querell. It would have been perfectly in character for him to make a plaything of me and push me this way and that, just to amuse himself. I remember him once saying, when he was drunk, that a sense of humour is nothing but the other face of despair; I believe that was true of him, although I am not sure that *humour* is the word to apply to that malignantly playful way he had of toying with the world. Despair is not quite the word either, though I cannot think what is. I never thought that he believed in anything, really, despite all his high talk of faith and prayer and sanctifying grace.

In my calmer moments I accepted that these fears and suspicions were a delusion. No one was able to think straight in those last, frantic years of the war, and I had more to be frantic about than most. My life had become a kind of hectic play-acting in which I took all the parts. It might have been more tolerable had I been allowed to see my predicament in a tragic, or at least a serious, light, if I could have been Hamlet, driven by torn loyalties to tricks and disguises and feigned madness; but no, I was more like one of the clowns, scampering in and out of the wings and desperately doing quick-changes, putting on one mask only to whip it off immediately and replace it with another, while all the time, out beyond the footlights, the phantom audience of my worst imaginings hugged itself in ghastly glee. Boy, who revelled in the theatricality and peril of the double life, used to laugh at me ('Oh, God, here's Shiver-shanks with his scruples again!'), and sometimes I suspected that even Oleg was mocking me for my worries and my caution. But mine was more than a double life. By day I was husband and father, art historian, teacher, discreet and hard-working agent of the Department; then night fell, and Mr Hyde went out prowling, in mad excitement, with his dark desires and his country's secrets clutched to his breast. When I began to go in search of men it was all already familiar to me: the covert, speculative glance, the underhand sign, the blank exchange of passwords, the hurried, hot unburdening – all, all familiar. Even the territory was the same, the public lavatories, the grim, suburban pubs, the garbage-strewn back-alleyways, and, in summer, the city's dreamy, tenderly green, innocent parks, whose clement air I sullied with my secret whisperings. Often, at pub closing time, I would find myself sidling up to some likely looking red-knuckled soldier or twitching, Crombie-coated travelling salesman in this or that George, or Coach, or Fox & Hounds, at the very same corner of the bar where earlier in the day I had stood with Oleg and passed to him a roll of film or a sheaf of what the Department supposed were top-secret documents.

Art was the only thing in my life that was untainted. At the Institute I would sometimes slip away from my students and go down to the basement and take out something, not any of the big pieces, not my *Seneca*, still in storage there, not one of the great Cézannes, but a Tiepolo sketch, say, or Sassoferrato's *Virgin in Prayer*, and bathe my senses, swollen with guilt and dread, in the picture's serenity and orderliness, giving myself up wholly to its insistent silence. I know, and who should know better, that art is supposed to teach us to see the world in all its solidity and truth, but in those years it was the possibility of transcendence, even for the space of a quarter of an hour, that I sought after repeatedly, like a prelate returning nightly to the brothel. And yet, the magic never quite worked. There was something wrong, something too deliberate, too self-conscious, in these occasions of intense contemplation. A suspicion of fraudulence always attended the moment. I seemed to be looking not at the pictures, but at myself looking at them. And they in turn looked back at me, resentful, somehow, and stubbornly withholding that benison of tranquillity and brief escape that I so earnestly desired of them. Unsettled, inexplicably chagrined, I would at last give up and cover up the painting and put it away, in embarrassed haste, as if I had been guilty of an indecency. The dreadful thought comes to me that perhaps I do not understand art at all, that what I see in it and seek in it is not there, or, if it is, that I have put it there. Have I any authenticity at all? Or have I double dealt for so long that my true self has been forfeit? My true self. Ah.

In those years Vivienne and I did not see much of each other. With money left her by her father she had bought a small house in Mayfair, where she led what to me was a mysterious but seemingly contented life. There was a nanny for the children, and a maid for her. She had her friends, and, I imagine, her lovers; we did not speak of such things. She accepted my sexual defection without comment; I think she found it amusing. We treated each other courteously, with cool regard, and always a certain cautiousness. Our exchanges were not so much conversations as a kind of brittle raillery, like fencing matches between two fond but wary friends. As the years went on her melancholy deepened; she nursed it like a cancer. We each had our losses. She grieved a long time for her father, in her shrouded way; I had not realised how close they had been, and was obscurely shocked. Her mother died, too, after years of spectral communication with the departed Big Beaver. And poor Freddie died. He survived six months in that so-called Home and then quietly succumbed to some kind of pulmonary infection – it was never made clear what exactly it was that had killed him. 'Och, it was the heart that broke,' Andy Wilson said to me at the funeral. 'He was pining, like an old dog that you'd send away from his own place.' And he gave me a slyly venomous glance. Hettie that day was more dazed than ever. At the graveside she plucked at my sleeve agitatedly and said in a hoarse stage-whisper, 'But we've done all this *already*!' She thought it was my father's funeral we were attending. That winter she fell one morning on the icy front step of St Nicholas's and broke her hip. From the hospital she was moved directly to a nursing home, where, to everyone's surprise and no little dismay, including, I suspect, her own, she lived for another five years, confused, sometimes troublesome, lost in the far past of her childhood. When she died at last, I entrusted a local agent with the sale of the house; there are things even a heart as hard as mine cannot endure. On the afternoon of the auction I read in a biography of Blake the poet's own account of how he had walked out of his cottage on his first morning in sweet Felpham and heard the ploughman's boy say to the ploughman, *Father, the Gate is Open*, and I felt that somehow my own father was sending me a message, though what its import might be, I could not tell.

*

Boy and I went on a pub crawl the day the news came of Hitler's death. It was May Day. We started at the Gryphon and staggered on to the Reform, with an interlude at a public lavatory in Hyde Park, the big one near Speakers Corner, which was to be a favourite hunting ground of mine in later years. That first time I was too timid, despite the many gins I had already drunk, to do anything but watch the furtive comings and goings. I kept a lookout while Boy and a burly young Guardsman with red hair and extraordinarily pretty ears made noisy and, by the sound of it, not very satisfactory love in one of the stalls. While I was standing guard, an emaciated individual in a mac and a derby came in and cocked an eye in the direction of the ill-fitting door from behind which could be clearly heard, amid groans and stifled cries, the dead-fish slap of Boy's stout thighs against the red-haired young man's buttocks. I thought the fellow must be a detective, and my heart set up that curious, light, tripping measure which in the years ahead I would come to know so well in such circumstances, the source of which was a mixture of fear, wild hilarity and a wholly wanton exultation. The loiterer proved not to be a copper, however, and, after glancing once more wistfully towards the stall door and then, despondently, at me – he knew me for a beginner, I'm sure – he buttoned up his flies and ducked out into the night. (By the way, I greatly deplored, towards the end of the good old 1950s, the universal adoption of the zip-fastened fly; true, the zip greatly enhances access, especially if one is in the throes of *amor tremens*, but I used to love to see that delicate tweaking action of the hand as it undid the always slightly awkward buttons, the thumb and index finger busy as mice while what the Americans delightfully call the pinkie held itself aloof, conjuring for a delicious, absurd moment an agitated society matron reaching tremulously for her teacup.)

I woke next morning on the sofa in Poland Street, crapulous and, as always after a night out with Boy, filled with a smouldering, objectless anxiety. The telephone was harshing beside my ear. It was Billy Mytchett, with an urgent summons. He would not say what the matter was, but he sounded excited. When I came into his office he stood up and trotted around from his side of the desk and shook my hand vehemently, making little huffing noises and looking past my shoulder in a sort of agitated daze. He was by now Controller of the Department. He was still an ass.

'It's the Palace,' he said, in a fraught whisper. 'They – he – *he* wants you to come round at once.'

'Oh, is that all,' I said, picking a loose thread from my cuff; it struck me how much I should miss being in uniform. I thought of mentioning to Billy that the Queen was a relative, but thought I might have done so already, and did not wish to seem to be harping on the connection. 'It's probably about those damn drawings at Windsor that I'm still supposed to be cataloguing for him.'

Billy shook his head; excitable, hirsute and ingratiatingly eager, he always reminded me of a dog, though I could never decide which breed, exactly.

'No no,' he said, 'no – he wants you to go on some kind of mission for him.' He opened his eyes wide. 'Very delicate, he says.'

'To where?'

'Germany, old chap – bloody Bavaria. What about that, eh?'

*

A Department car, with chauffeur, was assigned to take me to the Palace, an indication in itself, in those days of severe petrol rationing, of how impressed Billy was by this royal summons. My driver brought us in by the Horse Guards gate, where a rather brutish but good-looking sentry in full fig, busby and all, sneered at my pass and motioned us on. All this seemed peculiarly familiar, and presently I realised why: I was remembering the day more than a decade before when I had been driven into the Kremlin yard on my way, so I thought, to meet the Father of the People. The anterooms of power are all alike. Not, mind you, that the Palace had much power left, though HM still retained – or believed he did, anyway – considerably more clout than his daughter Mrs W. has today. He is not highly regarded, I know, but in my opinion he was one of the shrewder of the latter-day monarchs.

'It will be the devil of a thing,' he said, 'if these Labour chaps get in, as looks increasingly likely.' We were in one of the great, glacial reception rooms which are a depressing feature of that depressing palace. He was standing at the window, hands clasped at his back, frowning out over the Palace Gardens awash with watery sunlight. In a vast fireplace a tiny coal fire was burning, and there was a vase of wilted daffodils on the mantelpiece. He looked back at me over his shoulder. 'What do you think, Maskell? – you're a sound Tory, aren't you?'

I was seated, in exquisite discomfort, on a delicate gilt Louis Quinze chair, with my legs crossed and hands resting one upon the other on my knee, looking rather prissy, I suspected, though I could not think how better to comport myself in the circumstances: tiny chair, freezing limbs, propinquity of the sovereign. HM was in his we-don't-stand-on-ceremony-here mood, which I always found hard to endure.

'I think I'm more of a Whig than a Tory, sir,' I said. His left eyebrow shot up, and I added: 'A loyal one, of course.'

He turned back to the window with a deeper frown; this was not, I told myself gloomily, an auspicious start to the audience.

'Of course, the country's lost the run of itself,' he said testily; his stammer was hardly noticeable when he was exercised like this. 'How would it not, after what we have had to endure in these last five years? Mind you, I often think it's not the war itself but its consequences that have had the most profound effects. Women in the factories, for instance. Oh, I've seen them, in their trousers, smoking cigarettes and giving cheek. I said from the start no good would come of it – and now look where we are!'

He fell into a brooding silence. I waited, breathing shallowly from the top of my lungs. He was wearing an impeccably cut three-piece suit of smooth tweed, with a regimental tie; such ease, such negligent grace, even in a bad mood – you really cannot beat royalty for poise in adversity. He was fifty, but looked older. His heart even then must have been beginning to fail.

'Mr Attlee,' I said with judicious care, 'seems a reasonable man.'

He shrugged.

'Oh, Attlee's all right; I can work with Attlee. But the ones around him . . . !' He gave himself an angry shake, then sighed, and turned and walked to the fireplace and leaned an elbow on the mantelpiece and looked resignedly at a far corner of the ceiling. 'Well, we shall have to work with all of them, shan't we. We wouldn't want to hand them an excuse to abolish the monarchy.' He lowered his eyes abruptly from the ceiling and gave me a merry stare. 'Or would we? What says the loyal Whig?'

'I hardly think, sir,' I said, 'that Clem Attlee, or for that matter anyone in his party, would attempt, or even wish, to abolish the throne.'

'Who knows, who knows? Anything is possible in the future – and they *are* the future.'

'For a time, perhaps,' I said. 'The life of a government is short; the throne endures.' Really, the thought of the moderate Left in power for any appreciable interval made me shudder inwardly. Hot, hangover breath rasped in my gullet like a flare from a furnace. 'People are realistic; they will not be fooled by promises of jam for all, especially when even the bread has not yet materialised.'

He chuckled wanly.

'Very good, that,' he said. 'Very droll.'

His gaze drifted ceilingwards again; he was in danger of becoming bored. I sat more purposefully upright.

'The Controller, sir, Commander Mytchett, mentioned something about Germany . . . ?'

'Yes, yes, quite.' He seized a second gilt chair and set it down in front of me and sat, elbows on knees and hands clasped before him, and looked at me earnestly. 'I want to ask you a favour, Victor. I want you to go to Bavaria, to Regensburg – do you know the place? – and fetch back some papers that a cousin of ours is holding for us. Willi – that's our cousin – is a kind of self-appointed family archivist. We had all got rather into the habit – a bad habit, I dare say – of giving him . . . documents, and so on, for safe keeping, and then of course the war came and there was no way of retrieving them, even if Willi would have been prepared to release them: he's a bit of a terror, is old Willi, when it comes to his precious archive.' He paused, in difficulty, it seemed, and sat motionless for a long moment with his head bowed, frowning at his hands. He had never before addressed me by my Christian name (and was never to do so again, by the way). I was pleased, of course, and flattered, I think I may even have blushed a bit, not unbecomingly, I hope, but I was shocked, too, and not a little put out. As I think I have remarked already, I am a staunch Royalist, as all good Marxists are at heart, and I did not like to hear a king . . . well, *lowering* himself in this way. Those papers, I thought, must be very delicate indeed. HM was still frowning stolidly at his linked fingers. 'I remember when you were out at Windsor,' he said, 'working on those drawings of ours – by the way, have you finished that catalogue yet?'

'No, sir. It's time-consuming work. And there was the war . . .'

'Oh lord yes, yes, I understand. I was just enquiring, you know. Just . . . enquiring.' Abruptly he stood up, almost flinging himself from the chair, which tottered briefly on its graceful little legs. He began pacing up and down before me, softly punching a fist into the palm of his hand. A king in a dither is a memorable spectacle. 'These, ah, documents,' he said. 'There are letters from my great-grandmother to her daughter Fried-erike, and some from my mother to her German cousins. Just family papers, you understand, but not the kind of thing we would wish to see falling into the hands of some American newspaper fellow, shall we say, who wouldn't be bound to silence by English law. Apparently the American army has taken over Schloss Altberg and turned it into some sort of recreation centre for their troops; I hope Willi had the sense to lock away the family jewels – and as to how he's managing his mother in the circumstances, one hardly likes to think. You'll meet her, the Countess, no doubt.' He gave the ghost of a shudder, and sucked in his breath sharply, as at the memory of something sore. 'A formidable person.'

I watched him pacing, and pondered the interesting possi-bilities of this errand I was to be sent on. I know I shouldn't have, but I could not resist pressing a little, ever so gently, on what was obviously a bruised and tender area.

'I think it would be best, sir,' I said slowly, in a tone of obsequious solicitude, 'if I were to know in some more detail which are the papers that the Palace is most anxious to retrieve. I have found, in the field' – I liked that touch – 'that the more information one has, the more likely one is to bring off successfully the task in hand.'

He heaved a heavy sigh, and stopped pacing and sat himself down unhappily on a sofa opposite the fireplace, pressing the knuckle of an index finger to his thought-tightened lips and looking off towards the windows. A fine profile, if rather weak. I wondered if he had any queer leanings – I haven't known a royal yet who did not. I was thinking especially of those summer camps for working class lads of which he was so enthusiastic a supporter. I noticed he was wearing thick woollen socks, which looked as if they might have been hand-knitted, not very skilfully; perhaps one of the princesses had made them for him – the elder, I thought, for somehow I could not picture the younger one busy with needles and pattern book. Now he sighed again, more heavily still.

'Every family has its difficulties,' he said, 'its black sheep, and whatnot. My brother . . .' Yet another sigh; yes, I had rather thought his brother would make an appearance before too long. 'My brother behaved very foolishly in the years before the war. He was terribly put out, you know, by the . . . the abdication, and all that; felt the family, and the country, had let him down. I suppose he wanted revenge, poor chap. Those meetings with Hitler – very foolish, very foolish. And it was Willi, you see, our cousin Willi, a much cleverer man than poor Edward, who was the intermediary between the Nazi leaders and my brother and his . . . his wife.'

His stammer was becoming steadily more pronounced.

'And you think,' I said gently, 'that there may be . . . documents, relating to those meetings? Records? Transcripts, even?'

He cast a glance in my direction, tentative, pleading, almost shy, his eyes drooping with misery, and nodded.

'We know there are,' he said, in a hushed, husky voice, like that of a child at bedtime frightened at the prospect of the dark. 'We are trusting you, Mr Maskell, to retrieve them; we are confident you are the man for the job; we know you will be discreet.'

I nodded in my turn, putting on a deep frown to indicate dependability and bulldoggish resolve. Oh, mum's the word, your majesty; mum's the word.

*

I was flown to Germany on an RAF cargo plane, strapped precariously to a makeshift seat amid slumped mailbags and crates of beer that chattered like teeth. Amazing devastation below, charred forests and blackened fields and roofless cities agape. At the airfield outside Nuremberg I was met by a decidedly sinister Army intelligence officer with a ragged moustache and a mad smile. He told me his name was Captain Smith, but his look said he did not expect to be believed. He greeted everything I said with bitter amusement and a sceptical twitch of the moustache, assuming, I suppose, that I too must be lying about my identity and my purpose, out of professional habit, if nothing else. Not that I was required to say more than the minimum: Smith quickly let me know how grandly, sneeringly indifferent he was to me and whatever it was I was really up to. He had a jeep, in which we drove at terrifying speed through the shattered streets of the city and out into the country. The late spring sun shone heartlessly on the untended fields. The driver was a fat corporal with little piggy ears and rounded, babyish shoulders; the stubbled back of his neck was layered in pachydermal folds. I am always attracted to drivers; there is something strangely stirring in that intent, unmoving way they sit over the wheel, so stern and somehow stately, keeping themselves to themselves, seeming to pay out the miles behind them like so many measured lengths of invisible steel cable. Smith and he treated each other with a sort of angered, high ironic contemptuousness, bickering in venomous undertones, like an unhappy husband and wife out for a Sunday drive. We travelled the ninety kilometres to Regensburg in little more than an hour.

'I'll give old Adolf that,' Smith said, 'he could build a damn fine road.'

'Yes,' I said, 'rather like the Romans,' and was taken aback when Smith turned all the way round in his seat to stare at me with an expression of mock-amazed, fiercely smiling derision.

'Oh yes,' he snarled, his voice strangulated with inexplicable wrath, 'the Romans and their roads!'

Here we are in Regensburg, an odd little town, its spindly, square towers, many of them topped with enormous storks' nests, more suggestive of North Africa than the heart of Europe, an impression intensified for me, when I first arrived, by a Moorish sickle of moon hanging askew in the velvety, pale-purple evening sky. I was billeted in a small, dingy hotel called The Turk's Head. Smith dropped me unceremoniously at the door and he and his driver roared away, the jeep giving a tremendous fart of exhaust smoke as it rounded the corner of the street on two wheels. Forlornly I carried in my bags. There were American soldiers everywhere, in the bar, in the dining room, some even sitting on the stairs, smoking and drinking and noisily playing poker. Their mood was one of dazed euphoria; they were like children who had got overtired at bedtime and were refusing to go to sleep. Children, yes: it was like the Children's Crusade, with the difference that this ragtag army of overfed striplings would not be devoured by rotten old ogrish Europe, but vice versa. But don't get me wrong, as they say themselves: I did not hate the Americans; in fact, I found them perfectly congenial, in their unheeding, heartless way. In the sixties I made a number of trips to the United States – lecture tours, consultations – and once, unlikely as it may seem, I taught for a semester at a Middle Western college, where by day I expounded to a roomful of fanatically diligent note takers on the splendours of seventeenth-century French art, and in the evenings went out to drink beer with those same students, by now relaxed and doggily amiable. I recall one particularly convivial occasion at the Rodeo Saloon which ended with me calling upon my old music hall days with Danny Perkins, and standing on a table and singing 'Burlington Bertie', with appropriate gestures, to the noisy if surprised approval of my students and half a dozen cowboy-booted old-timers who were propping up the bar. Oh yes, Miss V., I am a myriad-sided man. And it was not just the American individual that won my admiration (though I more than admired one or two of my students, especially a young, honey-hued football player with flaxen hair and extraordinary cerulean eyes who surprised me, and himself, with the gauche intensity of his ardour on the old leather couch in my locked office one steamy afternoon when a giant summer storm was stamping thunderously across the campus and the rain-light flickered excitedly between the turned-down wooden slats of the rattling window blinds) but the American system itself, so demanding, so merciless, undeluded as to the fundamental murderousness and venality of humankind and at the same time so grimly, unflaggingly optimistic. More heresy, I know, more apostasy; soon I shall have no beliefs left at all, only a cluster of fiercely held denials.

At The Turk's Head there was no dinner to be had: in Bavaria they dine at noon and are in bed by nine. I prowled the streets and at last found a *Bierschenke* that was open, and sat for a long time feeling sorry for myself, and drank enormous beakers of blond ale and ate platefuls of evil little linked sausages that looked like dried and shrivelled dog turds. The captain of the cargo plane came in, and before we could avoid it we caught each other's eye, and so, being well-bred chaps, we were compelled to spend the evening together. He turned out to have been a scholar long ago in peacetime, a specialist in medieval manuscripts. He was a large, diffident person with sad eyes, exuding an air of great weariness. In later years I ran into him again, one damp summer day at the Queen's Garden Party.

He introduced me to his wife, Lady Mary, pale, phthisic, nervous as a greyhound, with close-set eyes and a thin pale nose and a faintly demented laugh. I do not know how she and I got on to the topic of Prince George – very handsome, very queer, killed in an RAF crash in the war – but it became quickly and embarrassingly apparent to all three of us that at the time of the Prince's death Lady M. and I had both been his lover.

Now he asked in his diffident way what I was doing in Germany.

'Sorry,' I said, 'hush-hush and all that.'

He nodded, frowning, trying not to seem offended. We passed the rest of the evening discussing incunabula, a subject on which he was wearisomely well informed.

Early next morning Captain Smith arrived at the hotel in the jeep with the same fat driver and drove me out to Altberg, an unreally picturesque village clinging to the edge of a rocky eminence above the Danube and overlooked by the castle, a tall, turreted nineteenth-century horror, of no architectural interest. There was a drawbridge spanning a deep cleft in the rock, and above the gate a stone plaque bore a carved posy of Tudor roses. In the narrow, lopsided courtyard a pair of hunting dogs, enormous, starved-looking brutes, pricked up their ears and regarded us with truculent surprise. Once again Smith dropped me off with the air of a man brushing something unwholesome from his hands; as the jeep rattled away over the drawbridge I fancied I heard wafting back a cackle of derisive laughter.

The palace was in the command of Major Alice Stirling, a brisk, high-shouldered, hard-eyed woman in her thirties, remarkably good-looking, with red hair and very pale skin and a saddle of freckles on the bridge of her nose that should have softened her expression but did not. I found her disconcertingly attractive, I, who had not been stirred by a woman in years; it must have been those wide, vulnerable-looking shoulders. She shook hands energetically, yanking my arm up and down as if she were working the handle of a water pump; I felt I was being not so much greeted as cautioned. She was from Kansas; she had always wanted to visit Europe, since she was a little girl, but it had taken a war to get her here – wasn't that something? In the raftered entrance hall a series of begrimed family portraits leaned out at a sharp angle from the walls as if to allow their startled subjects a better view of these recent incomprehensible comings and goings in the family home. There were some massive pieces of dully glistening black furniture. In the middle of the floor stood a ping-pong table, looking oddly self-conscious and forsaken.

'Yes, the facilities here are not what you'd call great,' Major Stirling said, throwing up her eyes and pulling her lower jaw down sideways in an expression meant to portray despair, cheerfulness and pluck, all at the same time. 'Still, we manage to show the boys a good time.' Here a knowing twinkle in acknowledgement of the *double entendre*. 'Spirit is the thing, and we have plenty of that. Some of our guests have been shot up pretty badly, but that doesn't stop them making their contribution. And what,' without missing a beat, 'can we do for you, Major Maskell?'

'I should prefer to speak to Prince Wilhelm,' I said. 'The matter is delicate. Is he about?'

Major Stirling remained perfectly motionless, canted forward a little toward me, like one of the portraits above her, with her head pertly inclined, gazing blankly at a point in space behind my left shoulder, her fixed smile gradually going rigid and yet seeming somehow to vibrate, as I imagine a wineglass must do in the second before the soprano's high C shatters it.

'I think,' she said, sweetly, ominously, 'I can answer any questions you might have.'

I mentioned vaguely the archive, the royal papers. 'Were you not informed of my coming?'

Major Stirling shrugged.

'Someone sent a signal, yes,' she said. 'It's in my office somewhere.'

'Perhaps,' I said, 'we should find it and you can read it again. It might clarify matters.'

At this she gave a throaty laugh and tossed her head, making her russet bangs bounce.

'Clarify!' she said. 'Golly, you English do have a sense of humour. I've never seen a signal yet from your people that didn't just add to everyone's confusion.'

Nevertheless she led me to her office, a stone-floored baronial hall with a carved and varnished ceiling and yet more execrable giant pieces of mock-baroque furniture ('Don't you just love it?' with another square-mouthed, sliding-jawed grimace). The signal was found and read; the Major, frowning at it, shook her head in slow, disbelieving wonderment.

'Maybe the decoders used the wrong code books,' she said.

'I have come,' I said gently, 'specifically at the request of the King. King George the Sixth, that is. Of England.'

'Yes, that's what it says here, Major Maskell.' I wished she would stop addressing me by my rank. The alliteration was unfortunate, and seemed to me to smack of Gilbert and Sullivan. 'But I can't release a used envelope from this castle without authorisation from US Army headquarters in Frankfurt.' A toothed grin. 'You know how it is.'

'Surely,' I said in my most reasonable tones, 'if the Prince – or, indeed, his mother, who I understand is head of the family now – were to authorise removal of the documents, you could have no objection . . . ? These are private papers, after all.'

Major Stirling gave a positively mannish snort.

'Nothing private about this place any more, Major,' she said, putting on a Wild West drawl, 'no sirree.' Prince Wilhelm, she informed me, and his mother, the Countess Margarete, were confined to special quarters. 'We don't call it house arrest, you understand, but let's just say they won't be going over to

330

England to visit with their cousins at Buckingham Palace for a while. Not till our boys in the de-Nazification programme get through with them.' She nodded with humorous solemnity, and winked.

'Still, if I might speak to the Prince . . . ?'

Certainly, she said; nothing easier; she would show me the way. She stood up, smoothing her skirt at the front, so that the outlines of her suspender clips showed through. Goodness, I thought, with amused consternation, can it be that I am reverting?

*

The Prince bore a fascinating resemblance to an elderly battle-scarred crocodile. He had a thick trunk, and short, tapering legs ending in feet so small, in their delicate, pointed-toed, slipper-like shoes, that he seemed to be not standing, but balancing upright on a strong, stubby tail. His head was large and square, and curiously flat at the front and sides; his hair was shaved high up at the temples, with an oiled black saurian slick combed back fiercely from his forehead. His face was pitted and scaly, and cross-hatched with old duelling scars. He wore a monocle, which flashed urgently, like a covert distress signal, as he tottered forward to meet me, a big, beringed, liver-spotted hand held out before him, palm down, as if he expected it to be kissed. He had the distraught, desperately smiling manner of a man who has suddenly found himself at the mercy of people whom in the old days he would not have deigned to notice if they had fallen under the hoofs of his horse. He must have been alerted to my coming, for he was dressed – trussed, might be a better word – in frock coat and striped trousers, with a row of decorations pinned to his breast, among which I identi-fied the Iron Cross and the Order of the Garter. The room in which he received me was in the upper reaches of the castle, a long, low-ceilinged garret with two squat windows at the far end looking out on a fir-clad hillside. The floorboards were bare, and the few pieces of gimcrack furniture wore the contingent look of things unceremoniously shifted out of long-accustomed surroundings and dumped here.

'Welcome to Schloss Altberg, Major Maskell,' he said, in accentless English. His voice was reedy and unexpectedly high-pitched, the result, I was told later, of a wound to the throat incurred in some immemorial battle – I pictured chainmail and lance and flashing tarnhelm – and when he spoke he drew his lips back over his big yellowed teeth in a sort of snarling smile. 'I wish I could have received you properly into my home, but in these times we are all at the mercy of circumstance.'

Gravely, exploratively, he continued slowly shaking hands with me, like a doctor testing for temperature and pulse, and then circumstance in the shape of Major Stirling stepped forward and made a boxing referee's chopping motion with her hand, and at once he released me and stepped back a pace, as if to avoid a smack.

'Major Maskell has been sent here by Buckingham Palace,' the Major said, with a sceptical smirk.

'Ah yes,' said the Prince, without any emphasis at all.

Then we moved into another low room – these must formerly have been the children's quarters – to meet the Countess. She was seated in an armchair with her back to the window, large, leather-skinned, fascinatingly ugly, smelling of face powder and unwashed lace. She was straight out of Grimm – every German prince should have a mother like this. She examined me keenly, at once curious and disdainful. Major Stirling she ignored, with magnificent indifference. She asked me about life at Windsor and Balmoral now. She had been to these places many times, of course, before – she lifted a claw and made a dismissive gesture, as if throwing something away over her shoulder – before all this nonsense. The Prince had taken up a heraldic stance behind her chair, and now she twisted her great head and looked up at him with a mixture of exasperation and scorn and barked at him to order luncheon to be served. She turned partly in Major Stirling's direction but would not look at her. 'If,' she said loudly, 'we are allowed to entertain guests in our own dining room, that is?'

The Major shrugged, and winked at me again.

The meal was served in a vast, timbered hall with mullioned windows overlooking the courtyard. Liveried footmen came and went wordlessly on creaking shoon, and the pair of hunting dogs padded about under the table, snapping up dropped scraps and collapsing noisily on to their haunches now and then to scratch their fleas. We ate some kind of cold game, venison, I think, with dumplings, which looked like the testicles of a giant albino, and were so dense and sticky that after my knife had gone through them the lips of the wound would shut again with a repulsive, kissing sound. Half a dozen members of the Prince's family appeared. There was a large, stately woman, with the prominent chest and bright cheeks and glassy stare of a ship's figurehead, who must have been the Prinzessin, and her adult daughter, a washed-out version of her mother, white-faced and unreachably distant, with ash-blond plaits coiled at the sides of her head like a pair of earphones. Two sturdy, crop-headed boys, big-bottomed and virtually neckless, were evidently, if implausibly, the young Princess's sons. Every so often they would scramble down from their chairs and set to wrestling with each other like bear cubs, rolling about the floor, their shrieks flying up to the timbered ceiling and falling back again, nerve-janglingly. The Countess sat at the head of the table with me on her left hand and the Prince on the other, while Major Stirling was banished below the salt. To my left there was an unidentified, very deaf old man, who spoke to me in largely incomprehensible dialect on the subject, if I understood him correctly, of the proper method of killing and butchering wild boar. Opposite me sat a shaggy young man with a twitch, dressed in a kind of dusty clerical garb, who addressed not a word to me and who, when I tried to talk to him, stared at me wildly, his eyes rolling, as if he might be about to jump up from the table and take to his heels. It occurred to me that on other planets there might be organisms of such delicate refinement that to them human life, even at its most developed, would surely seem a state of unremitting agony and insanity and squalor.

Luncheon ended, or I should say, petered out, and my deaf neighbour excused himself with apologetic leers and mutterings and withdrew, and the bear cubs were led away by their wild-eyed keeper, their spectral mother following after, seeming not to walk out the door but fade through it, and the Countess on her stick gondoliered off to her afternoon nap, a hand clamped on the Prince's arm, and I was left with Major Stirling and the boar hounds, noisily sleeping now – the dogs, that is.

'Some set-up, eh?' the Major said, looking about with cheerful disdain.

A footman refilled our hock glasses, and she moved up the table and sat beside me, one of those big shoulders almost touching mine. She had a faint sharp piney smell. I imagined myself being overborne by her in some vague, cruel, irresistible fashion. I loosened my tie. Discovering that I was Irish, she said that Ireland was another place she had always wanted to visit. She claimed she had an Irish grandmother. I seized on this, and discoursed at some length on the charms of my native land. I really did work very hard, but to no avail; when, delicately, I brought up the subject of the royal papers again, she laid a hand on my wrist – a flash, a fizz – and gave me her iciest smile and said:

'Major Maskell, we're waiting for Frankfurt to contact us, all right? Meantime, why don't you relax and enjoy the beauties of Bavaria?' Another jauntily lewd twinkle. 'I hear you're staying at The Turk's Head? Lots of our boys billeted there. Must be a real lively spot.'

Of course, I blushed.

I found Captain Smith waiting for me on the steps above the courtyard, wrapped up in his greatcoat and smoking a cigarette; as I came up, a flaw of smoke swirled briefly about his head, as if it had come out of his ears. He was looking particularly fierce and bristly this afternoon. 'Get what you came for?' he asked, and grinned with satisfaction at my glum demeanour. The dogs were morosely prowling, and at two little windows high up in the wing opposite us the globular heads of the bear cubs appeared, gloatingly grinning down on us. Smith exhaled another ragged cloud of smoke and put two fingers into his mouth and produced a piercing whistle. Immediately the jeep came roaring through the gate and cut a semi-circular sweep across the courtyard, scattering the dogs, and drew up at the foot of the steps with a screech of smoking tyres. The driver looked at neither of us. 'Bloody tyke,' Smith muttered, and gave a bark of laughter.

We were about to depart when the little pale Princess came sidling out on to the steps with her mouse-claws clasped under her meagre bosom and, eyes modestly cast down, addressed me obliquely, in German, in a papery voice so faint that at first I could hardly catch what she was saying. Her grandmother wished to speak to me. She would show me the way.

'Wait here, Smith, will you?' I said.

We climbed, the Princess Rapunzel and I, through a maze of stone back-staircases and mildewed corridors, in silence, except for a faint crepitation made by the Princess's petticoats. At length she stopped, and I looked up, and there was the Countess, on the landing above us, leaning over the banister rail with a lace shawl wrapped about her, beckoning through the gloom with a crook'd finger and jerky, upward sweeps of her arm, like a figure in a clock tower. By the time I got up to her level, she had retreated to her room, with what must have been remarkable spryness, and was reclining now against a bank of pillows on a vast, ornate bed. She wore a faded brocade bed gown, and her shawl, and an antique little cap. She gazed at me stonily as I stood in the doorway feeling somehow villainous, and without a word pointed a finger in the direction of a large, deep cupboard in a corner. The Princess moved past me and went to the cupboard and drew open the doors and stood back, folding her pale thin hands on her breast again. Inside the cupboard was a chest, a solid wooden affair with brass hinges and an ancient padlock; the fastening was further secured with two thick leather straps lashed tight and stoutly buckled. The Princess murmured something and went out. From the bed the Countess watched me with a fierce, watery eye. I advanced toward her, my eyes fastened upon her gaze.

'*Danke schön, gnädige Gräfin*,' I said, and even made her a little bow. 'Your cousins in England will be extremely appreciative.' I thought of mentioning my relation by marriage to the Saxe-Coburg-Gothas, but her look was not encouraging. 'I shall tell His Majesty how helpful you were.'

I have never been able quite to carry off these emblematic gestures – more than once I caught out Mrs W. in that characteristic po-faced little smirk of hers, when I was in the midst of attempting some courtly flourish – and the Countess was not one to miss the hairline cracks in the enamel of even the most polished performance. Still she did not speak, but yet she made a reply, by means of a subtle transformation of her gaze, which thickened somehow, her face filling up like a wineskin with a sort of glutinous, an almost tumescent, contempt, before which I blenched, and took a faltering step backward, as if something might suddenly come squirting out of her to burn and blind me. She shrugged, making the bedsprings creak.

'My son will not forgive me,' she said, and gave a thin, throaty laugh. 'Tell that to our cousin the King.'

The Princess returned, bringing Captain Smith and the driver, whose name (it has just come back to me; one's memory is such a hoarder) was Dixon. Smith regarded the scene – frightened Princess, dowager in mob-cap, chest of family secrets – with wolfish amusement, his eyebrows and his moustache twitching. Between the three of us we lifted up the chest, which was extremely heavy and awkward to hold, and staggered with it out the door and down the stairs, Smith swearing and Dixon effortfully snorting through distended, porcine nostrils, with the Princess following murmurously behind us. We stowed our booty on the back of the jeep. Who says I am not a man of action? I half expected that Major Stirling would come flying down the steps and bring me to the ground in a football tackle, but there was no sign of her; I was disappointed; my wrist still tingled where she had touched it. As we were driving out of the courtyard, I looked up at the windows where the children had appeared earlier, and saw the Prince looking down on us impassively. What was he thinking, I wonder?

'Hope they haven't raised the bloody drawbridge,' Smith said, and gave a squawk of mad laughter, and snatched off Dixon's cap and began to beat him hilariously about the head with it.

On the outskirts of Regensburg I had Dixon pull up at the side of the road and stand guard while Smith and I jemmied open the chest. The papers were neatly sorted and stored in oilskin pouches. I looked forward to an evening's entertaining reading in my room at The Turk's Head. Smith raised a questioning eyebrow; I winked at him. And later, in a public urinal in the town square, among delicious smells, I encountered a blond young man in a tattered uniform who detained me with an evil smile, laying a thin hand on my wrist and quite banishing all memory of Major Stirling's mannish touch. He claimed he was a deserter, and that he had been on the run for months. He was appealingly emaciated. As he knelt and ministered to me I ran my trembling fingers through his hair thick with dirt and fondled his neat little ears – I always had a weakness for these strange organs, on close inspection so excitingly repulsive, with their frills and delicate pink volutes, like primitive genitalia that have fallen into disuse – and goggled in blissful stupor at a shaft of sunlight falling athwart the beautiful, glistening, grass-green slime growing on the wall behind him, above the clogged trench, and in my head everything swirled, Smith's mad eye and the Prince's scaly hand and Major Stirling's boyish shoulders, all swirled and spasmed and sank, into the hot throat of the whirlpool.

*

I have been brooding on the word *malignant*. Naturally it has a special resonance for me. I looked it up just now; really, the dictionary is full of delightful surprises. *Malignant*, according to the *OED*, derives from 'late L. *malignantem, malignare, -ari*', and its first cited definition is, 'Disposed to rebel; disaffected, malcontent'. However, I am also informed that the word was applied 'between 1641 and 1690 by the supporters of the Parliament and the Commonwealth to their adversaries'. In other words, a 'malignant' was a Cavalier, or a Royalist. This discovery provoked in me a delighted chuckle. A malcontent, and a Royalist. How accommodating the language is. Other definitions are: 'having an evil influence'; 'keenly desirous of the misfortune of another, or of others generally'; and of course, this time according to Chambers, 'tending to cause death, or to go from bad to worse, esp. cancerous'. Mr Chambers never was one to beat about the bush.

I HAVE ALWAYS derived a deep satisfaction from working in places that were made for repose. When the title of Keeper of the King's Pictures was conferred on me, directly after my triumphant homecoming from Regensburg (HM was gruffly grateful; I was modesty itself, of course), the Royal collection was still in underground storage in North Wales, and my first task was to oversee the return of the pictures and their rehanging in Buckingham Palace, at Windsor, and at Hampton Court. How I treasure now the recollection of the peace and pleasure of those days: the hushed voices in great rooms; the Vermeer light, a kind of gold gas, spreading its rich effulgence down from leaded panes; the perspiring young men, in shirt-sleeves and long aprons, solemnly trotting back and forth like sedan-chair porters, bearing between them a Holbein grandee or Velázquez queen; and I in the midst of all this muted bustle, with my clipboard and my dusty checklists, eyes uplifted and best foot forward, *The King's Man at His Duties*, consulted by all, deferred to by all, a master among men. (Oh, indulge me, Miss V., I am old and sick, it comforts me to recall the days of my glory.)

There were, of course, other, less transcendent advantages to my elevated position in the Royal household. At the time, I was embroiled in a tiresome, often ugly, though not uninvigorating power struggle at the Institute, where a lifelong overindulgence in port and a resultant fit of apoplexy had suddenly left the Director's chair vacant. I explained the matter to HM, and shyly indicated that I would not object were he to bring his influence to bear on the Trustees when they came to make their choice of a successor. This was the post I had always aimed to secure; it was, you might say, my life's ambition; indeed, even above my scholarly achievements, it is for my work as head of the Institute that I expect to be remembered, after these present unpleasantnesses have been forgotten. When I took over, the place was moribund, a dusty refuge for superannuated university lecturers and third-rate connoisseurs, and a sort of ghetto for fugitive European Jews too clever for their down-at-heel boots. I soon knocked it into shape. By the beginning of the 1950s it was recognised as one of the greatest – no, I shall say it: as *the* greatest centre of art teaching in the West. My activities as an agent were nothing compared to the wholesale infiltration of the world of art scholarship achieved by the young men and women whose sensibilities I shaped in my years at the Institute. Look at any of the significant galleries in Europe or America and you will find my people at the top, or if not at the top, then determinedly scaling the rigging, with cutlasses in their teeth.

And then, I loved the place, I mean the surroundings, the building itself, one of Vanbrugh's most inspired designs, at once airy and wonderfully grounded, imposing yet indulgent, delicate yet infused with manly vigour, an example of English architecture at its finest. By day I found soothing the atmosphere of studiousness and quiet learning, the sense one had all around of young heads bent over old books. My students had an earnestness and grace that one does not encounter in their present-day successors. The girls fell in love with me, the young men were restrainedly admiring. I suppose I must have seemed something of a legend to them, not only a champion of art but, if rumour were to be believed, a veteran of those clandestine operations that had contributed so much to our victory in the war. And then, at night the place was mine, a vast town house entirely at my disposal. I would sit in my flat on the top floor, reading, or listening to the gramophone – I have hardly mentioned my love of music, have I? – calm, reflective, sustained aloft, as it were, by the thronging silence peculiar to the spaces in which great art resides. Later, Patrick would come home from his nocturnal rambles, perhaps with a couple of ruffianly young men in tow, whom I would set loose in the galleries, among the spectral pictures, and watch them frisk and tumble in the chiaroscuro lamplight like so many Caravaggian fauns. What a risk I took – my God, when I think of it, the damage they could have wrought! But then, it was precisely in the danger of it that the pleasure lay.

I would not wish to give the impression that my time at the Institute was all high talk and low frolics. There was a great deal of bothersome and time-consuming administration to be seen to. My detractors muttered that I was incapable of delegating duties, but how is one expected to delegate to cretins? In an institution such as ours – closed, intense, hot with messianic fervour: I was moulding an international generation of art historians, after all – a single controlling sensibility was an absolute requirement. When I became Director, I immediately set about imposing my will on every corner of the Institute. There was nothing too trivial to merit my attention. I am thinking of Miss Winterbotham. Oh dear yes. Her name was the least of her misfortunes. She was a large person in her fifties, with tree-trunk legs and a mighty bust and myopic, frightened eyes, and also, incidentally, the most incongruously beautiful, slender hands. She was a minor scholar – baroque altarpieces of South Germany – and an enthusiast for madrigals; I think it was madrigals. She lived with her mother in a large house on the Finchley Road. I suspect she had never been loved. Her ineradicable unhappiness she disguised under a gratingly hearty cheerfulness. One day, in my office, while we were discussing some not very important piece of Institute business, she suddenly broke down and began to weep. I was aghast, of course. She stood before my desk, helpless in her cardigan and sensible skirt, shoulders shaking and great fat tears blurting from her squeezed-up eyes. I made her sit down and drink some whiskey, and after long and tedious cajoling I got out of her what the matter was. A bright young scholar in the same field as hers, who had lately joined us, had at once set about undermining Miss Winterbotham's position. The old academic story, but a particularly cruel version of it. I called in the younger woman, the clever daughter of French refugees. She did not deny Miss Winterbotham's charges, and smiled in my face in that feline way that French girls do, confident I would approve her ruthlessness. Her confidence was misplaced. Of course, after Mlle Rogent's abrupt departure from our midst, I had to deal with Miss Winterbotham's speechlessly rapturous gratitude, which came in the form of coy little gifts, such as homemade cakes, and bottles of noisome aftershave lotion that I passed on to Patrick, and, every Christmas, a violently hideous necktie from Pink's. Eventually her mother became incapacitated, and Miss Winterbotham had to give up her career to look after the invalid, as daughters did, in those days. I never saw her again, and after a year or two the plum cakes and the silk ties stopped coming. Why do I remember her, why do I bother to speak of her? Why do I speak of any of them, these nebulous figures milling restlessly, unappeasably, on the margins of my life? Here at my desk, in this lamplight, I feel like Odysseus in Hades, pressed upon by shades beseeching a little warmth, a little of my life's blood, so that they might live again, however briefly. What am I doing here, straying amongst these importunate wraiths? A moment ago I tasted on my palate – tasted, not imagined – the stingy-sweet flavour of those boiled blackcurrant drops that I used to suck trudging home from infant school on autumn afternoons along the Back Road at Carrickdrum a lifetime ago; where was it stored, that taste, through all those years? These things will be gone when I go. How can that be, how can so much be lost? The gods can afford to be wasteful, but not us, surely?

My mind is wandering. This must be the anteroom of death.

Those were the

Those were the years of some of my most intense work, when I conceived and began to write my definitive monograph on Nicholas Poussin. It was to take me nearly twenty years to finish. Certain pygmies skulking in the groves of academe have dared to question the book's scholarly foundations, but I shall treat them with the silent disdain they deserve. I do not know of any other work, and nor do they, which comprehensively, exhaustively and – I shall dare to say it – magisterially captures the essence of an artist and his art as this one does. One might say, I have invented Poussin. I frequently think this is the chief function of the art historian, to synthesise, to concentrate, to *fix* his subject, to pull together into a unity all the disparate strands of character and inspiration and achievement that make up this singular being, the painter at his easel. After me, Poussin is not, cannot be, what he was before me. This is my power. I am wholly conscious of it. From the start, from the time at Cambridge when I knew I could not be a mathematician, I saw in Poussin a paradigm of myself: the stoical bent, the rage for calm, the unshakeable belief in the transformative power of art. I *understood* him, as no one else understood him, and, for that matter, as I understood no one else. How I used to sneer at those critics – the Marxists especially, I am afraid – who spent their energies searching for the meaning of his work, for those occult formulas upon which he was supposed to have built his forms. The fact is, of course, there is no meaning. Significance, yes; affects; authority; mystery – magic, if you wish – but no meaning. The figures in the *Arcadia* are not pointing to some fatuous parable about mortality and the soul and salvation; they simply *are*. Their meaning is that they are there. This is the fundamental fact of artistic creation, the putting in place of something where otherwise there would be nothing. (*Why did he paint it? – Because it was not there.*) In the ever shifting, myriad worlds through which I moved, Poussin was the singular, unchanging, wholly authentic thing. Which is why I had to attempt to destroy him.—What? Why did I say that? I did not expect to say that. What can I mean by it? Leave it; it is too disturbing. The hour is late. Ghosts ring me round, gibbering. Away.

*

Perhaps the most significant, personal, result of my Royal elevation was that it enabled me to give up being a spy. I know everyone believes that I never stopped; there is a convention in the popular mind which insists that such a thing is impossible, that the secret agent is tied to his work by a blood oath from which only death will release him. This is fantasy, or wishful thinking, or both. In fact, in my case, retirement from active service was surprisingly, not to say disconcertingly, easy. The Department was one thing; with the end of the war, amateur agents such as myself were being gently but insistently encouraged to bow out. The Americans, who now hold power, were demanding that professionals be put in charge, company men like themselves, whom they could bully and coerce, not mavericks like Boy or, to a far less colourful extent, me. On the other hand, we were exactly the kind of agents – familiar, trusted, dedicated – that Moscow desired to keep in place, now that the Cold War had set in, and we were urged, and sometimes, indeed, threatened, to hold on at all costs to our connections with the Department. Oleg, however, was oddly complaisant when I told him that I wished to be released. 'I'm sick of the game,' I said, 'literally sick of it. The strain is making me ill.' He shrugged, and I pressed on, complaining that war work, and the difficulty of serving two opposing systems in their uneasy alliance against a third, had put intolerable pressure on my nerves. I suppose I did rather pile it on. I ended by warning that I was close to cracking. This was Moscow's nightmare, that one of us would lose his nerve and put the entire network at risk. Like all totalitarians, they had a very low regard for those who helped them most. In truth, my nerve was not about to crack. What I had felt most strongly at the end of the war, what we had all felt, was a sudden sense of deflation. For myself, I dated the onset of this depression to the morning following the announcement of Hitler's death, when after that night of celebratory boozing with Boy I had woken up on the sofa in Poland Street with the taste of wetted ashes in my mouth and felt as Jack the Giant Killer must have felt, when the beanstalk came crashing down and the man-eating monster lay dead at his feet. After such trials and such triumphs, what could the world in peacetime offer us?

'But this is not peace,' Oleg said, with another listless shrug. 'Now the real war is starting.'

It was a summer afternoon, and we were sitting in a cinema in Ruislip. The lights had just come up between features. I remember the sombre, shadowless glow descending from the vaulted ceiling, the hot, dead air, the prickly feel of the nap of the seat covers and a broken spring sticking in the back of my thigh – I suppose sprung cinema seats went before your time, Miss V.? – and that oddly weightless, muffled sensation that you only got in picture-houses, in those days of double bills, in the intervals between features. It was Oleg's idea that we should meet in cinemas. They offered excellent cover, it is true, but the real reason was that he was a passionate fan of the movies, especially the smooth American comedies of the day, with their sleek-haired, effeminate men and marvellous, mannish, silk-gowned women over whom he sighed like a love-sick prince-turned-frog, gazing up at them, these Claudettes and Gretas and Deannas, in a kind of entranced anguish, as they swam before him in their shimmering tanks of soot-and-silver light. He and Patrick would have got on famously.

'I rather think, Oleg,' I said, 'that one war is enough for me; I've done my bit.'

He nodded unhappily, the fat at either side of his neck froggily wobbling, and began to drone on about the nuclear threat and the need for the Soviets to get their hands on the secrets of the West's atomic weapons technology. Such talk made me feel quite antiquated; I had still not got over my amazement at the V2s.

'That's the business of your people in America,' I said.

'Yes, Virgil is being sent there.'

Virgil was Boy's code name. I laughed.

'What – Boy in America? You must be joking.'

He nodded again; it seemed to be turning into a kind of tic.

'Castor has been told to find a posting for him at the embassy.'

I laughed again. Castor was Philip MacLeish, otherwise known as the Dour Scot, who the previous year had managed to get himself appointed first secretary in Washington, from where he was reporting regularly to Moscow. I had met him a couple of times, in the war, when he was something minor at the Department, and had disliked him, finding his solemnity of manner ridiculous, and his fanatical Marxism unbearably tiresome.

'Boy will drive him mad,' I said. 'They'll both be sent home in disgrace.' Odd, how accurate the more offhand prophecies can prove to be. 'And I suppose you want me to act as their control from here, do you?' I imagined it, the endless eavesdropping, the combing through signals, the casually probing conversations with visiting Americans, the whole horrible tightrope-walking effort of keeping agents in place in foreign territory. 'Well, I'm sorry,' I said, 'I can't do it.'

The house lights were dimming, the dusty plush curtains were creakily opening. Oleg said nothing, gazing up expectantly at the preliminary crackle of scratched white light fizzing and boiling on the screen.

'I have been appointed Keeper of the King's Pictures,' I said, 'did I tell you?' He turned his eyes unwillingly from Jean Harlow's satin-sheathed backside and peered at me incredulously in the watery glow from the screen. 'No, Oleg,' I said wearily, 'not this kind of picture: paintings. You know: art. I shall be working in the Palace, at the King's right hand. Do you see? That's what you can tell your masters in Moscow: that you have a source right beside the throne, a former agent at the very seat of power. They'll be terribly impressed. You'll probably get a medal. And I shall get my freedom. What do you say?'

He said nothing, only turned back to the screen. I was a little piqued; I thought he could at least have argued with me.

'Here,' I said, and pressed into his moist warm paw the miniature camera he had issued me with years ago. 'I never learned how to use it properly, anyway.' In the flickering light from the screen – what a grating voice that Harlow woman had – he looked at the camera and then at me, babyishly solemn, but still did not speak. 'I'm sorry,' I said, but it came out sounding cross. I stood up, and patted him on the shoulder. He made a half-hearted attempt to seize my hand, but I withdrew it quickly, and turned and made my way stumblingly out of the place. The noise of traffic in the sunlit street seemed a kind of sardonic cheer. I felt at once buoyant and leaden, as if in shrugging off the burden I had borne for years I had suddenly become aware again of the long-forgotten weight of my own, all too familiar self.

At first I did not believe that Moscow would let me go, or not so easily, at least. Aside from any other consideration, my vanity was wounded. Had I been of so little worth to them, that they should drop me so unceremoniously? I waited confidently and in trepidation for the first signs of pressure being applied. I wondered how I would stand up to blackmail. Would I be prepared to risk my position in the world in order merely to be free? Perhaps I should not have made so bold a break, I told myself, perhaps I should have gone on supplying them with scraps of Department gossip, which I could have gleaned from Boy and the others and which no doubt would have kept them happy. They had the power to ruin me. I knew they would not reveal the work I had done for them – if they let one thread go, the whole network would unravel – but they could easily find a means of exposing me as a queer. Public disgrace I might have been able to bear, but I did not at all relish the prospect of a stretch in prison. Yet the days passed, and the weeks, then the months, and nothing happened. I drank a great deal; there were days when I was drunk before ten o'clock in the morning. When I went out on the prowl at night I was more frightened than ever; the sex and the spying had sustained a kind of equilibrium, each a cover for the other. Loitering in wait for Oleg, I was guilty but also innocent, since I was spying, not soliciting, while in my tense vigils on the shadowy steps of the city's public lavatories I was only another queer, not a betrayer of my country's most precious secrets. Do you see? When you live the kind of life that I was living, reason makes many questionable deals with itself.

I wondered what story Oleg had told Moscow. I was tempted to contact him again, so that I might ask him. I pictured him in the Kremlin, standing in the middle of the shiny floor in one of those vast high featureless rooms, unhappily wheezing, twisting his hat in his hands, while a shadowy Politburo listened in terrible silence from behind its long table as he made his bumbling excuses for me. All fantasy, of course. My case was probably dealt with by a third secretary at the London embassy. They did not need me – they never had, really, not in the way I believed – and so they simply cut the link. They always were practical fellows, unlike the mad fantasists who ran the Department. They even made a gesture of appreciation for my years of loyal service: six months after that meeting in the Odeon in Ruislip, Oleg contacted me to say that Moscow wished to offer me a gift of money, I think it was five thousand pounds. I refused – none of us ever made a penny out of our work for Russia – and tried not to feel slighted. I told Boy that I was out, but he did not believe me, suspecting that I was only going into deeper cover, a suspicion he thought vindicated years later when everything fell apart and I was the one who was called in to deal with the mess.

*

There was no formal procedure for resigning from the Department, either; I simply drifted away, as so many others had done in the past year. I met Billy Mytchett by chance one evening in a pub in Piccadilly and we were both embarrassed, like a pair of former schoolmates who had not seen each other since the days of pranks and scrapes. I ran across Querell, too, at the Gryphon. He claimed to have left the Department before I did. As always, I found myself immediately on the defensive before that thinly smiling, measuring, pale gaze. Boy, who was about to leave for Washington, had just returned from a tumultuous binge across North Africa – on which he had been accompanied by his mother, of all people, a still spry and famously handsome woman only slightly less given to outrageous behaviour than her son – and Querell had all the details: how Boy had got drunk at an embassy cocktail party in Rabat and pissed out of the window into a bed of bougainvillaea in full view of the ambassador's wife, that kind of thing.

'Seems he sat for a whole evening in the bar of Shepheard's Hotel in Cairo telling anyone who would listen that he's been a Russian spy for years.'

'Yes,' I said, 'it's an old joke. He likes to shock.'

'If I put him into a book no one would believe in him.'

'Oh, I don't know; he would certainly add colour.'

He glanced at me sharply and grinned; his bleak little novels had at last caught on, reflecting as they did the spiritual exhaustion of the times, and he was enjoying sudden and lavish success, which was a surprise to everyone except him.

'You think my stuff lacks colour?' he said.

I shrugged.

'I don't read much, in that line.'

We came across each other again the following week, at the farewell party for Boy that Leo Rothenstein threw in the Poland Street house. The occasion later became legendary, but what I retain most strongly is the memory of the headache that began as soon as I arrived and that did not leave me until well into the following day. Everyone was there, of course. Even Vivienne ventured down from her Mayfair retreat. She gave me her cool cheek to kiss, and for the rest of the night we avoided each other. As usual, the party started without preliminaries, all instant noise and smoke and the tingling stink of alcohol. Leo Rothenstein played jazz on the piano, and a girl danced on a table, showing her stocking-tops. On the way from the Foreign Office Boy had picked up two young thugs, who stood about nursing cigarette ends in cupped hands and watching the increasingly intoxicated goings-on with a mixture of slit-eyed contempt and rather affecting uncertainty. Later, they started a fight with each other, more for something to do than out of anger, I think, though one of them was knifed, not seriously. (Later still, so I heard, they both went home with one of my colleagues from the Institute, a harmless connoisseur and small-time collector, who woke up the next afternoon to find the thugs gone, and with them everything of value in the flat .)

Querell cornered me in the kitchen. His eyes had that odd glitter, like marine phosphorescence, that they took on when he had been drinking heavily; it was the only physical sign of inebriation I could ever detect in him.

'I hear Queen Mary sent you a present of a handbag,' he said. 'Is it true?'

'A reticule,' I said stiffly. 'Georgian; quite a good piece. It was an expression of gratitude. I had put her in the way of a bargain – a Turner, as it happens. I don't know what everyone finds so funny.'

Nick came by, morosely tipsy; Sylvia had just produced their first child, and he was still supposedly celebrating the birth. He stopped, and stood swaying, regarding me with a soiled glare, breathing noisily, his jaw working.

'I hear you've left the Department,' he said. 'Another bloody rat diving off the poor old ship and leaving the rest of us to keep her afloat.'

'Steady on, old chap,' Querell said, smirking. 'There might be spies about.'

Nick scowled at him.

'Not a decent bloody patriot among the lot of you. What will you do when the Russian tanks come rolling across the Elbe, eh? What will you do then?'

'Do give over, Nick,' I said. 'You're drunk.'

'I may be drunk, but I know what's what. There's bloody Boy hiving off to bloody America. What's the good of going to America?'

'I thought it was you who organised it,' Querell said.

Beside us, a young woman in a pink dress began to be sick into the sink.

'Organised what?' Nick said indignantly. 'What did I organise?'

Querell, laughing softly, played with his cigarette, twirling it between fingers and thumb.

'Oh, I heard you were the one who arranged for Bannister to go to Washington, that's all,' he said. He was enjoying himself. 'Did I hear wrong?'

Nick was watching with bleary interest the vomiting girl.

'What influence have I got?' he said. 'What influence has any of us got, now that the bloody Bolshies have taken over.'

Vivienne was passing by, and Querell reached out and caught her wrist deftly in his thin, bony, bloodless hand.

'Come on, Viv,' he said, 'aren't you going to talk to us?'

I watched them. No one ever called her Viv.

'Oh, I thought you must be discussing men's things,' she said, 'you all looked so earnest and conspiratorial. Victor, you do seem grim – has Querell been teasing you again? How is poor Sylvia, Nick? Childbirth can be so *draining*, I find. Goodness, what *has* that young woman been eating? Seems to be all tomato skins. It is tomato, isn't it, and not blood? Haemorrhages in one so young are not a good sign. I must go back; I was speaking to such an interesting man. A negro. He seemed very angry about something. Which reminds me, did you hear what Boy replied when that Mytchett person was urging caution on him in his new life in the New World? Mytchett said that where Americans are concerned, one mustn't on any account bring up matters of race, homosexuality or Communism, and Boy said, *What you're telling me is not to make a pass at Paul Robeson.'*

'Wonderful woman,' Querell said when she had gone. He put a hand on my arm. 'You're not divorced yet, are you?'

And Nick gave a loud, slurred laugh.

At midnight I found myself trapped in uneasy conversation with Leo Rothenstein. We were on the landing outside Boy's room, with drunken people sitting on the stairs above and below us.

'They say you're leaving the ranks,' he said. 'Bowing out gracefully, eh? Well, you're probably right. Not much left for us here, is there? Boy's had the right idea – America is the place. And of course, you have your work; I see your name about frequently. They want me to be something on the Board of Trade. Can you imagine it? Our friends will be pleased, I suppose, given their passion for tractors and suchlike. But it's hardly Bletchley Park, is it. One does miss the old days. Much more fun, and that nice warm sense of really doing something for the cause.'

He produced an impossibly slender gold cigarette case and opened it with an elegant flick of his thumb, and I saw again a sunlit garden room in Oxford long ago and the young Beaver opening another cigarette box with just that gesture, and something happened inside my chest, as if it had begun to drizzle in there. I realised I must be drunk.

'Nick is going to stand for parliament,' I said.

Leo chuckled softly.

'Yes, so I hear. Bit of a joke, don't you think? At least they've found him a safe seat, so humiliation will be avoided. I can just see him on the hustings.'

Briefly, gratifyingly, I imagined myself landing a punch in the middle of Leo's big sallow face and smashing his raptor's nose.

'He may surprise us all,' I said.

Leo gazed at me for a moment with peculiar, boggle-eyed intensity, and then laughed heartily, in his humourless way.

'Oh, he may,' he said, nodding vigorously. 'He may indeed!'

Below us, someone struck a shaky chord on the piano, and Boy began to sing an obscene version of 'The Man I Love'.

*

Everybody nowadays disparages the 1950s, saying what a dreary decade it was – and they are right, if you think of McCarthyism, and Korea, the Hungarian rebellion, all that serious, historical stuff; I suspect, however, that it is not public but private affairs that people are complaining of. Quite simply, I think they did not get enough of sex. All that fumbling with corsetry and woollen undergarments, all those grim couplings in the back seats of motor cars, the complaints and tears and resentful silences, while the wireless crooned callously of everlasting love – faugh! what dinginess, what soul-sapping desperation. The best that could be hoped for was a shabby deal marked by the exchange of a cheap ring, followed by a life of furtive relievings on one side and of ill-paid prostitution on the other. Whereas – O my friends! – to be queer was very bliss. The fifties was the last great age of queerdom. All the talk now is of freedom and pride (pride!), but these young hotheads in their pink bell-bottoms, clamouring for the right to do it in the streets if they feel like it, do not seem to appreciate, or at least seem to wish to deny, the aphrodisiac properties of secrecy and fear. At night before I went out cottaging I would have to spend an hour downing jorums of gin to steady my nerves and steel myself for the perils that lay ahead. The possibility of being beaten up, robbed, infected with disease, was as nothing compared with the prospect of arrest and public disgrace. And the higher one had climbed in society, the farther one would fall. I had recurring, sweat-inducing images of the Palace gates clanging shut against me, or of myself tumbling head over heels down the steps of the Institute and Porter the porter – yes, but it had long ago ceased to be amusing – above me in the doorway brushing his hands and turning away with a sneer. Yet what a sweet edge these terrors gave to my adventures in the night, what throat-thickening excitement they provoked.

I loved the fashions of the fifties, the wonderful three-piece suits, the rich cotton shirts and silk bow ties and chunky, handmade shoes. I loved all the appurtenances of life in those days that are so sneered at now, the cuboid white armchairs, the crystal ashtrays, the moulded-wood wireless sets with their glowing valves and mysteriously erotic mesh fronts – and the motor cars, of course, sleek, black, big-bottomed, like the negro jazzmen whom on occasion I used to be lucky enough to pick up at the stage door of the London Hippodrome. When I look back, these are the things I remember most vividly, not the great public events, not the politics – which was not politics at all, only a hysterical squaring up for more war – and not even, I am sorry to say, the doings of my children, so uncertain and needful in their fatherless teens; above all, I remember the fizz and swirl of the queer life, the white-silk-scarfed enchantment of it all, the squabbles and sorrows, the menace, the unspeakable, always abundant pleasures. This was what Boy missed so much, in his American exile ('I am like Ruth,' he wrote to me, 'amid the alien cornballs'). Nothing could make up for the fact of not being in London, not the Cadillacs or the Camels or the crew-cutted football players of the New World. Perhaps, if he had not gone to America, if he had got out, like me, or remained and gone on doing desultory work for Oleg, he might not have brought all that trouble on himself, might have ended up a sprightly old queen toddling between the Reform Club and the public lavatory beside Green Park Tube station. But Boy suffered from an incurable commitment to the cause. Pitiful, really.

I have always thought Boy went a little mad in America. He was being watched all the time – the FBI had always been suspicious of him, not seeing the point of the joke – and he was drinking too much. We were used to his enormities – the brawls, the three-day binges, the public displays of satyriasis – but now the stories grew darker, the deeds more desperate. At a party thrown for our embassy people by one of Washington's legendary hostesses – I am glad to say I have forgotten her name – he made a clumsy pass at a young man in full view of the other guests, and when the poor fellow demurred Boy knocked him down. He drove in that ridiculous car of his – a pink convertible, with a genuine Klaxon horn which he employed with enthusiasm at every intersection – at breakneck speeds all over Washington and the surrounding states, collecting speeding tickets, three or four a day, which he would tear up under the noses of the traffic policemen, claiming diplomatic immunity. Poor Boy; he did not realise how dated he had become. This kind of thing might have been amusing back in the twenties, when we were so easily amused, but now his indiscretions were merely embarrassing. Oh, of course we went on regaling each other with accounts of his latest scrapes, and we would laugh, and shake our heads, saying, *Good old Boy, he never changes!* But then a silence would fall, and someone would cough and someone else would begin loudly ordering another round, and quietly the subject would be dropped.

And then, one humid evening in late July, I came out of the Institute and found myself staring at a splotch of crushed chalk on the rain-washed, steaming pavement. In the old days this had been Oleg's signal to summon me to a rendezvous. The sight of that white stain provoked in me a medley of sensations: alarm, of course, quickening to fright; curiosity, and a kind of childish expectancy; but, most strongly, and most surprisingly, nostalgia, fed no doubt by the evening smell of summer rain on the pavement and the oceanic hushing of the plane trees above me. I walked along for a little way, with my raincoat over my arm, outwardly calm, while my thoughts were in turmoil; then, feeling not a little ridiculous, I ducked into a phone box – check the street corners, the windows opposite, that parked car – and dialled the old number, and stood in hot suspense listening to the blood beating in my temples. The voice that answered was unfamiliar, but my call had been expected. Regent's Park, at seven: the old routine. While the strange voice was relaying its instructions – how blank and timbreless they are, those drilled Russian voices – I thought I heard Oleg chuckle in the background. I hung up and left the booth, dry mouthed and a little dizzy, and hailed a taxi. The old routine.

*

Oleg seemed pudgier, but otherwise he was unchanged since I had last seen him. He was wearing his blue suit, his grey mac, his brown hat. He greeted me warmly, ducking his Christmas-pudding head and making happy burbling noises. Regent's Park was all hazy golds and pale grey-greens in the soft summer evening. There was the smell of recent rain on grass. We met by the Zoo, as always in former days, and struck off in the direction of the lake. Dreamy lovers drifted across the green-sward arm in arm. Children ran and shrieked. A lady walked a little dog. 'Like Watteau,' I said. 'A painter. French. What do you like, Oleg? I mean, what are you interested in?' Oleg only waggled his head and did that bubbly chuckle again.

'Castor wants to go,' he said. 'He says it is time to go.'

I thought of MacLeish tramping the windy grey wastes of Moscow. Well, he might feel quite at home there – he was born in Aberdeen, after all.

'And Boy?' I said.

Grown men were sailing model boats on the lake. A quite beautiful young man in a white shirt and corduroy trousers, a ghost out of my youth, was lounging in a deckchair, moodily smoking a cigarette.

'Yes, Virgil too,' Oleg said. 'They will go together.'

I sighed.

'So,' I said, 'it's come to this. I never really believed it would, you know.' I looked at the young man in the deckchair; he caught my eye and smiled, insolent and inviting, and a familiar something happened in my throat. 'Why have you come to me?' I said to Oleg.

He turned on me his blankest, most blameless bug-eyed stare.

'We have to get them to France,' he said, 'or northern Spain, maybe. Anywhere on the Continent. After that it will be easy.'

Moscow had suggested sending a submarine to pick the pair up from the shores of some Highland lough. I had a vision of Boy and the Dour Scot stumbling in the dark over wet rocks, their city shoes sodden, trying to get their flashlight to work, while out in the night the submarine captain scoured the shore for their signal, muttering Russian oaths.

'For goodness' sake, Oleg,' I said, 'surely you can come up with something less melodramatic than a submarine? Why can't they just take the ferry to Dieppe? – or one of those boats that cruise along the French coast for forty-eight hours? Businessmen use them for dirty weekends with their secretaries. They call into St Malo, places like that; no one ever bothers to check papers or count the passenger lists.'

Oleg suddenly reached out and squeezed my arm; he had never touched me before; odd sensation.

'You see, John, why I came to you?' he said fondly. 'Such a cool head.' I could not suppress a smirk; the need to be needed, you see, that was always my weakness. We walked on. The low sun shone on the molten water beside us, throwing up flakes of gold light. Oleg giggled, snuffling through his flat, piggy nose. 'And tell me, John,' he said roguishly, 'have *you* been with your secretary on these boats?' And then he remembered, and blushed, and hurried on ahead of me, waddling along like a fat old babushka.

*

Boy came back. I telephoned him at the Poland Street flat. He sounded worryingly hearty. 'Tip-top, old chap, never better, glad to be home, *bloody* Americans.' We met at the Gryphon. He was bloated and hunched, and his skin had a fishy sheen. He reeked of drink and American cigarettes. I noticed the torn skin around his fingernails and thought of Freddie. He was rigged out in tight tartan slacks, tennis shoes, a Hawaiian shirt of scarlets and vivid greens; a fawn stetson hat with a leather band sat on the bar by his elbow like a giant, malign mushroom. 'Have a drink, for Christ's sake. We'll get completely blotto, shall we? My heart aches, and a drowsy numbness, et cetera.' He laughed and coughed. 'Have you seen Nick? How is he, I missed him. Missed you all. They don't know how to have fun over there. Work work work, worry worry worry. And there I was, Boyston Alastair St John Bannister, trapped in a madhouse with nothing to do but drink myself silly and bugger black men. I had to get out; you see that, don't you? I had to get out.'

'Heavens,' I said, 'is that really your name – Boyston? I never knew.'

Betty Bowler was on her stool behind the bar, smoking cocktail cigarettes and clanking her bracelets. Betty by now had become the kind of big, blowsy disaster that buxom young beauties always turn into. In her prime she had been famously painted by Mark Gertler – cream flesh, blue eyes, burnt-sienna nipples, a pyramid of portentous apples in a pink bowl – but now, as she waddled into her late fifties, the Bloomsbury look was all lost, sunken in fat, and she had become one of Lucian Freud's potato people. I was always a little afraid of her. She had a tendency to go too far, lurching from raillery into sudden bursts of venomous abuse. It was a conceit of hers to pretend to believe there was no such thing as homosexuality.

'Thought as how you was going to bring home a war bride, Boy Bannister,' she said, doing her cockney voice. 'One of those Yank heiresses, nice big blonde with plenty of assets behind her.'

'Betty,' Boy said, 'you should be in the pantomime.'

'So should you, tub-of-guts. You could play the Dame, except you don't look man enough for the part.'

Querell turned up, wearing a crumpled white linen suit and two-tone shoes. He was in his Solitary Traveller phase. He was about to leave for Liberia, or maybe it was Ethiopia; somewhere distant, hot and uncivilised, anyway. It was said he was fleeing an unhappy love affair – *Love's Labour* had just come out – but he had probably started the rumour himself. He sat between us at the bar looking bored and world-weary and drinking triple gins. I watched a smoky pale patch of sunlight at the foot of the steps inside the door, and thought how stealthily the world goes about its business, trying not to be noticed.

'Well, Bannister,' Querell said, 'the Americans finally rumbled you, did they?'

Boy gave him a sullen, slithery look.

'What's that supposed to mean?'

'I hear Hoover kicked you out. You know he's a notorious queen. They always have a kink, don't they, the Hoovers and the Berias.'

Much later – the light at the foot of the steps had turned red-gold – Nick came in, with Leo Rothenstein, both in evening dress, sleek and faintly ridiculous, like a pair of toffs in a *Punch* cartoon. I was surprised to see them here. Since his election Nick had steered clear of the old dives, and Leo Rothenstein, whose father was on his deathbed, was about to inherit a peerage and the family's banks. 'Just like old times,' I said, and they both regarded me in silence with a peculiar, flat stare. I suppose I was drunk. Nick peevishly ordered a bottle of champagne. He was wearing a crimson cummerbund; he never did have any taste. We lifted our glasses and toasted Boy's return. Our hearts were not in it. When we had finished the first bottle, Betty Bowler brought out another, on the house.

'Absent friends!' Leo Rothenstein said, and looked at me over the rim of his glass and winked.

'Christ,' Boy mumbled, pressing a fat, sunburned arm to his eyes, 'I think I'm going to blub.'

Then Oleg telephoned. The code word was *Icarus*. Somewhat unfortunate, I agree.

ODD, the air of melancholy burlesque the whole thing had. It was all absurdly simple. Boy made an excuse, and we left the Gryphon together and I drove him to Poland Street. Above the twilit streets the sky was a tender deep dark blue, like an upside-down river. In the flat I waited, sitting by myself on the sofa, while he got his things together. The champagne was still fizzing in my sinuses, and I too felt weepy, in a distracted sort of way, and kept heaving great sobby sighs and slowly blinking and peering about me, like a drunken tortoise. Vividly I recalled tussling here with Danny Perkins, and experienced an awful pang, like a spasm of physical pain. I could hear Boy crashing around upstairs, talking to himself and groaning. Presently he came down, carrying an ancient gladstone bag.

'Wanted to bring everything,' he said mournfully. 'Left it all, in the end. How do I look?'

He was dressed in a dark-grey three-piece suit, striped shirt, cuff links, school tie with gold pin.

'You look ridiculous,' I said. 'The Comrades will be wonder-fully impressed.'

We went down the stairs, wordless and solemn, like a pair of disappointed undertakers.

'I've locked the flat,' Boy said. 'Danny Perkins has a key. I'll keep this one, if you don't mind. Souvenir, you know.'

'You're not coming back, then?' I said lightly, and he gave me a wounded look and went on, past the doctor's surgery, and out into the glimmering night. God knows why I was feeling so frolicsome.

Again I drove, the big white car eating up the miles with

callous eagerness. As we were crossing the river I wound down my window and the night howled and leaped into the car. I looked down past the bridge and saw a red ship at anchor there, and something about the scene – the glossy darkness, the bulging, restless river, that fauve-bright vessel – sent a shiver through me, and suddenly, with a tigerish thrill, I saw my life as grand and dark and doomed. Then we left the bridge and plunged among warehouses and weed-grown bomb-sites again.

Beside me, Boy was weeping, in silence, with a hand over his eyes.

Soon we were speeding over the Downs. In my memory of it, this part of the journey is all a smooth irresistible headlong dash through the startled, silvery night. I see the car swirling along, headlights sweeping over tree-trunks and moss-grown signposts, and Boy and me, two grim-faced figures tensed behind the windscreen, lit from below, jaws set and eyes fixed unblinkingly upon the onrushing road. I too have read my Buchan and my Henty.

'Wish it was day,' Boy said. 'This is probably my last sight of Blighty.'

Philip MacLeish was at his mother's place in Kent, a genuine rose-covered cottage complete with wooden gate and gravel path and bottle-glass windows all aglow. Antonia MacLeish opened the door to us and without a word showed us into the living room. She was a tall, angular woman with a great mane of black hair. She seemed always to be brooding on some smouldering private resentment. I associated her with horses, though I had never seen her mounted on one. MacLeish was sitting in an armchair, morosely drunk, staring into a cold grate. He was wearing an old pair of flannel trousers and an incongruous, canary-yellow cardigan. He glanced up unenthusiastically at Boy and me, said nothing, and went back to his contemplation of the fireplace.

'The children are asleep,' Antonia said, not looking at us. 'I won't offer you a drink.'

Boy, ignoring her, cleared his throat.

'I say, Phil,' he said, 'we need to have a talk. Get your coat, there's a good chap.'

MacLeish nodded, slowly, miserably, and stood up, his knee joints creaking. His wife turned aside and walked to the window, took a cigarette from a silver box on the table there, lit it, and stood, elbow in hand, gazing out into the impenetrable dark. I saw us all there, clear and unreal as if we were on a stage. MacLeish looked at her in baggy-eyed anguish and lifted a beseeching hand towards her.

'Tony,' he said.

She made no reply, and did not turn, and he let fall his hand.

'Time to go, old man,' Boy said. He was tapping his foot on the carpet. 'Just a chat, that's all.'

I had an urge to laugh.

MacLeish put on a camel-hair overcoat, and we went out. He had not even packed a bag. At the front door he paused, and slipped back into the hall. Boy and I looked at each other glumly, expecting sobs, shouts, hurled recriminations. In a moment he was back, however, carrying a furled umbrella. He looked at us sheepishly.

'Well, you never know,' he said.

It was midnight when we got to Folkestone. The night had turned windy, and the little ship, lit like a Christmas tree, was bobbing and rearing on the swell.

'Christ,' Boy said, 'it looks bloody small. There's bound to be someone on board who'll know us.'

'Tell them you're on a secret mission,' I said, and MacLeish glared at me.

There was the question of Boy's car. No one had thought what to do with it; obviously I could not drive it back to London. He loved the thing, and got quite agitated contemplating its possible fates. In the end he decided he would simply leave it on the quayside.

'That way, I can think of it as being here always, waiting for me.'

'Dear me, Boy,' I said, 'I never knew you were such a sentimental old thing.'

He grinned mournfully and wiped his nose with his knuckles. 'Betty Bowler was right,' he said. 'I'm not man enough.' We stood irresolute, the three of us, at the end of the gangplank, our trouser legs whipping in the warm night wind and the light from the lamps shivering at our feet. On board, a bell clanged dolefully. 'The watches of the night,' Boy said, and tried to laugh.

MacLeish, lost somewhere in the tormented deeps of himself, was staring at the narrow channel of darkly roiling waters between the ship's flank and the dock. I thought he might be contemplating throwing himself in.

'Well then,' I said briskly.

We shook hands awkwardly, the three of us. I thought of giving Boy a kiss, but could not bring myself to do it, with the Dour Scot looking on.

'Say goodbye to Vivienne for me,' Boy said. 'And the children. I shall miss seeing them grow up.'

I shrugged. 'So will I.'

He went up the gangplank, heavy-footed, lugging his bag. He turned.

'Pop over and see us sometime,' he said. 'All that caviare, that good vodka.'

'Of course. I'll sail out on the *Liberation*.'

I could see him not remembering. He was thinking of something else.

'And Victor—' he said; the wind caught the skirts of his overcoat and flapped them. 'Forgive me.'

Before I could respond – how would I have responded? – MacLeish beside me suddenly stirred himself and fixed a hand urgently on my arm.

'Listen, Maskell,' he said, in a voice that shook, 'I never liked you – still don't, really – but I appreciate this, I mean your helping me like this. I want you to know that. I appreciate it.'

He stood a moment, nodding, those crazed Presbyterian eyes fixed on mine, then he turned and lurched up the gangplank. Finding Boy blocking his way, he gave him a hard push in the back and said something sharply which I did not catch. In my last sight of them they were standing side by side at the metal rail, and all I could see were their heads and shoulders; they were looking down at me, like a pair of Politburo members viewing the May Day parade, MacLeish expressionless, and Boy slowly, wistfully waving.

*

I caught the mail train back to London, and as we clattered along – why do trains always seem so much noisier at night? – the last effects of the alcohol in my blood drained all away, and I panicked. Thank God there was no one in the compartment to see me huddled in a corner of the seat, grey-faced, stark-eyed, my hands shaking and jaw involuntarily working. It was not arrest that I feared, not exposure, not even prison; that is, I *did* fear these things, but not in any immediate, felt way. I was just frightened, frightened of everything. My mind whizzed, all out of kilter, as if some component inside it had come loose and was flapping madly, like a broken fan belt. It is a good thing I was trapped on a train, or I do not know what I might have done – gone haring back to the quayside, perhaps, and leaped on board that ship with Boy and MacLeish as it pulled out to sea and so-called freedom. The thought of London filled me with terror. I had a Blakean vision of the city, all eerily aglow and thronged with aimlessly toiling figures into whose boiling midst the swaying, shuddering train would soon eject me. A sense of desolation and irremediable woe took hold of me, and brought me back all the way to the nights of my earliest childhood, when I would lie in bed in the swooping candlelight, while Freddie crooned in his cot and Nanny Hargreaves preached to us of hellfire and the fate of sinners; and now, hurtling through the dark towards London and the suddenly real possibility of damnation, in this world if not the next, I prayed. I did, Miss V., I prayed, incoherently, wriggling in terror and shame, but pray I did. And to my surprise, I was comforted. Somehow, the great Nobodaddy in the sky reached down a marmoreal hand and laid it on my burning brow and soothed me. When the train pulled into Charing Cross at three in the morning I had got my nerves back under control. As I walked along the empty platform, past the panting, sweating engine, squaring my shoulders and clearing my throat, I scoffed at myself for my fears of the night. What had I expected, I asked myself – a posse of police waiting for me at the ticket barrier?

I found a taxi and went home. Sleep was impossible. Patrick was in Ireland, on his yearly visit to see his aged mother. I was glad; I could not have faced the prospect of trying to account for my overnight absence – he always knew when I was lying, which must make him unique in my life. How he would have enjoyed it all, though; later, when he heard what I had been up to, he laughed and laughed. Never took me really seriously, did Patrick. I drank a cup of black coffee, but it gave me palpitations, and then I downed a beaker of brandy, and that made the palpitations worse. I stood at the window in the living room and watched the summer dawn come up bloodily over the rooftops of Bloomsbury. The birds had woken, and were making a frightful racket. I had a fluttery, hollow sensation, that was not just the effect of the caffeine; it was the same feeling that I used to have when I was still with Vivienne and would come home in the small hours after a night of trawling through the public lavatories. In every wrongdoer there lurks the desire to be caught.

At nine I called the number Boy had given me for Danny Perkins and arranged to meet him in Poland Street. I slipped out of the house, feeling watched. Lemon-sharp sunlight, the smoky summer smell of London. I had not shaved. I felt like one of Querell's surreptitious villains.

Danny Perkins was working for a bookie now, in what capacity I did not care to enquire, and was all swagger and hair oil, like a real cockney. When I arrived at the house he was lounging in the doorway in the sun smoking a cigarette with studied panache. Sharp suit, loud tie, black suede shoes with crêpe soles an inch thick. The sight of him stirred up in me the old stew of emotions. He had been my first queer love, and the one who first tied me to the stake of jealousy; it was hard to know which was the more profound experience. We were flustered at first, not knowing what to do: shaking hands seemed somehow absurd, and an embrace was out of the question. In the end he contented himself with punching me softly on the upper arm, and doing that boxer's sideways ducking motion of his head and shoulders that I remembered so well.

'Hello, Vic,' he said jauntily, 'you're looking fit.'

'And so are you, Danny. Not a day older.'

'Oh, I don't know about that. I was thirty-five last week. Where does it go to, eh?'

'Still got an eye on the stage?'

'No, no; my professional days are over. I do a bit of warbling still, but it's mostly in the bath, now.'

We went into the house. The hall retained a medicinal smell, though the dodgy doctor was long gone. Where his surgery had been was a betting office now – 'One of ours,' Danny said, with a proprietorial frown – and the floor was strewn with cigarette ends and soiled racing sheets. What had been my life was disappearing under time's detritus. We climbed the stairs, Danny going ahead and I trying not to look at his narrow, neatly packed bum. In the parlour I watched his eyes slide over the sofa without a flicker of remembrance.

He had not yet mentioned Boy.

I found a half-full bottle of Scotch and we had a drink, standing in silence by the parlour window looking down into the narrow, sun-bright street. They would be in Paris by now, probably; I pictured Boy in the bar of the Gare du Nord, with an absinthe and a Gauloise, while the Dour Scot paced the pavement outside. We would all be hauled in, of course. I flinched at the prospect; I had been an interrogator, I knew what it would be like. But I was not afraid; no, I was not afraid.

I poured Danny and myself another whisky.

Boy's room bore the signs of his precipitate departure: books thrown everywhere, the grate stuffed with half-burned papers, a white shirt spreadeagled on the floor suggestive of the chalk marks at the scene of a murder. In a wardrobe I found the old brown leather suitcase with the brass corners in which he kept his love letters. Trust Boy not to bother taking them with him. He was never one for blackmail. Unlike me.

'Were you looking for something in particular, then?' Danny Perkins asked. He was standing in the bedroom doorway, nonchalantly wielding another cigarette. I shrugged. Danny gave an odd little laugh. 'He's gone, isn't he,' he said.

'Yes, Danny, he's gone.'

'Will he be back?'

'I shouldn't think so, no. He's gone rather a long way off.'

He nodded.

'We'll miss him, won't we,' he said. 'He was always a laugh.' He took a drag of his cigarette, and coughed for half a minute; he never could smoke properly. I picked up a letter and read: *My dearest Boy, you missed a real knees-up at the palace last night, with all the lads in full regalia and Dickie simply rampant . . .* 'Funny, that, when you think of it,' Danny said hoarsely, 'the good time we had, things being so bad, what with the war and all. It's like we hardly noticed. But it's all over now, isn't it?'

'What's that, Danny?'

'I say, it's all over. Mr Bannister gone, the old place empty . . .'

'Yes, I suppose you're right; it is over.'

Extraordinary, how careless people could be; half the letters seemed to be on House of Commons notepaper; there was even one with a Lambeth Palace crest.

'Well,' Danny said, 'I better be going: things to do, bets to be made good, that kind of thing.' He winked, grinning. He turned to go, then paused. 'Listen, Victor, if there's anything I can do, give me a bell. I know a lot of people, see.'

'Oh, yes? What sort of people?'

'Well, if you were ever to get yourself in trouble, like Mr Bannister has, you might be in need of shelter, say, or transport . . .'

'Thank you, Danny. I'm grateful.'

He winked again, and sketched a mock salute, and was gone.

I spent the better part of the afternoon going over the flat. Incriminating material everywhere, of course; I burnt most of it. The flames made so much heat I had to throw open the windows. Why does the smell of burning paper always remind me of childhood? I was taking a last, beady look around when I heard footsteps on the stairs. Danny coming back to offer me a hot tip, perhaps? I walked out on to the landing. A window there, that I had never noticed in all the years I had lodged in the house, gave on to a distant haze of summer greenery, a patch of park, or public gardens, with trees, and toylike figures at work, or play, or simply idle, I could not tell which; I can still see that view, perfect in all its miniature detail, a little window looking out into a lost world.

'Danny?' I called down. 'Is that you?'

It was not.

*

Everything was done with politeness and decorum; you could never fault the Department on its manners. The first one up the stairs was Moxton, from Security; I knew him slightly, a sandy-haired, weasel-faced fellow with oddly inexpressive eyes. He stopped on the return and twisted his head back to look up at me, one hand holding his hat, the other resting lightly on the banister rail. 'Hello, Maskell,' he said pleasantly. 'You're the very chap we wanted to see.' Behind him came a large, bearish young man with a baby face splotched with pimples; Security, I thought, with remarkable inconsequence, always did get the least appetising recruits. 'This is Brocklebank,' Moxton said, and his lips twitched.

So here it was at last. I was not even surprised; what I felt was a huge settling sensation, as if a tremendous weight inside me had shifted, dropping an inch with a soundless crash. Moxton and the boy Brocklebank had reached the landing. Brocklebank gave me a measuring look, narrowing his eyes in the way the thrillers told him to. A new recruit, brought out for a bit of training in the field. I smiled at him.

'Phew,' Moxton said, 'isn't it hot.' He glanced past my shoulder into the bedroom. 'Been tidying up, have you? Bannister always was a slovenly sod. Having a bonfire, too, by the smell. What do they call it? *Felo de se?*'

'*Auto-da-fé*, actually, sir,' Brocklebank said, in a surprisingly plummy accent; I would not have taken him for a public-school type.

'That's right,' Moxton said, without looking at him. 'Burning of heretics.' He strolled into the bedroom and stopped in the middle of the floor and surveyed the disarray. Security people love this kind of thing; justifies their existence, after all. Beside me Brocklebank stood breathing, a big, soft engine, smelling of sweat and expensive cologne. 'I imagine you've tied everything up here?' Moxton said, looking at me sideways from inside the room with those dead eyes, 'the loose ends, and so on?' He stood a moment longer, pondering, then roused himself and came back out on the landing. 'Look here,' he said, 'why don't you come down with us to the office. We can have a chat. You haven't been round to the old place in ages.'

'Are you arresting me?' I said, and was surprised by the cracked flute-note that sounded in my voice.

Moxton put on a look of bland startlement.

'Well now, what an idea! Takes the rozzers to do that. No, no – as I say, just a chat. The Chief wants a word.' He squeezed out a chill, flinty smile. 'They've called in Skryne, too. Bit of a flap on, as you can imagine. They'll be fretting if we delay.' He touched my arm, as if to reassure me, then nodded to Brocklebank. 'Lead on, Rodney, will you?' As we went down the stairs in the wake of Brocklebank's fat back, Moxton hummed to himself and tossed his hat lightly in his hand. 'You're a Cambridge man, aren't you?' he said. 'Like Bannister?'

'We were up together, yes.'

'I was at Birmingham.' Another wintry glitter. 'Not the same thing at all, eh?'

Brocklebank drove the car while Moxton and I sat in the back seat side by side, with our faces turned from each other, looking out of our respective windows. How calm the streets seemed, a glassy, distant anti-world, adrift with the dense soft smoke of summer. My mind churned sluggishly, in a kind of hindered, underwater panic, like a fish entangled in a net.

'You realise,' I said, 'I have no idea what's going on.'

Moxton did not turn from the window, and only chuckled. He was right, of course: you must start acting the moment they challenge you, not when you are already in the car, with the cuffs on. Or rather, you must never stop acting, not for an instant, even when you are alone, in a locked room, with the lights off and the blankets over your head.

*

Billy Mytchett had the wounded, anguished look of a fifth-former who has heard a rumour in the dorm that his mother has bolted and his father's firm gone smash. 'Christ, Maskell,' he said, 'this is a hell of a business.' I had never heard him swear before; it seemed encouraging, for some reason. We were in a safe house in a suburban avenue somewhere south of the river. Safe houses always seem to me to have something of an ecclesiastical atmosphere; a domestic setting that is not lived in must remind me of my father's study, which he never used except on Saturday nights when he was preparing the next day's sermon. There was always a chill in that room, and a faint, flat stink generated, I suppose, by years of devout labour, impassioned self-delusion, and the ever-present fear of a loss of faith. It was the same fusty smell that trickled like dust in my nostrils now as I sat on a hard chair in the middle of a brown-painted parlour, with Moxton and Brocklebank loitering silently behind me in the umber gloom, and Billy Mytchett pacing up and down in front of me on the threadbare carpet with his fists jammed in the pockets of his old tweed jacket, doing tight turns at every third pace, like an agitated sentry who suspects the assassin has already slipped past him and is even now forcing his way into the king's bedchamber. Skryne, on the other hand, was quite comfy and at his ease, sitting in an armchair at an angle to me, spruce as a visiting uncle in his neat suit and speckled tie and argyle socks, his perennial pipe going nicely. I had known him only by repute. Uneducated, but very sharp, so they said. He had been a policeman in Palestine. He did not worry me. In fact, none of it worried me; I was almost enjoying it all, as if it were a bit of foolery laid on for my entertainment and I had no real part to play in it except that of a mildly interested spectator. Then Skryne began to speak, in his pleasant, mild, pigeon-fancier's voice. They knew all about me, he said, my work during the war for the Bolsheviks (that was the term he used – so quaint, so charmingly old-world!), my meetings with Oleg, everything. 'MacLeish, Bannister and you,' he said. 'Others as well, of course; but you were the three.' Silence. He waited, chin tilted, eyebrows lifted, smiling. You will think me ridiculously fanciful, I know, but I felt exactly as I had felt that morning many years before when I had woken up in the dawn light and knew that I would marry Baby: I had the same sense of levitating, somehow, as if a seraphic version of myself were rising up out of me, gilded and afire, into the suddenly shining air. Skryne softly slapped a hand down on his knee. 'Come on, now,' he said good-humouredly, 'aren't you going to say anything?'

I stood up – I mean my real, corporeal, stark and sweating self – and walked to the window. Outside, there was a monkey-puzzle tree, looking very black and mad in the sun, and a discouraged strip of grass with a flowerless border. In the house opposite, a fat man was leaning out of a narrow upstairs window; he was so still, and filled the window frame so fully, that I wondered if he had become wedged there and was waiting for someone to come along behind him and give him a tug. Slowly I took a cigarette out of my case – whatever became of *that*, I wonder – and lit it; the gesture seemed to me impossibly theatrical. Odd, the lights one sees oneself in on such occasions. I hardly knew myself. 'Billy,' I said, without turning, 'do you remember that day at the end of the war, when you called me round to the Department and told me the Palace needed me to run an errand in Bavaria . . . ?' I threw my unsmoked cigarette into the fireplace and returned to the straight-backed chair – how disapproving a chair like that can look – and sat down, crossing my knees and resting my folded hands on them. All this had happened before; I wondered where. Billy was looking at me with a puzzled frown. I described my trip to Regensburg, how I had smuggled out the chest, and what was in it. 'Blackmail,' I said, 'has never seemed to me an ugly word. Quite the opposite, in fact.' There was the noise of a lawnmower, the old-fashioned kind that you had to push. I looked to the window. The fat man opposite had extricated himself from the upstairs window, and was shearing his lawn now, pushing the machine with a curiously antique action, bending low from the waist with arms stretched out stiff and one stout leg extended behind him. The word *felucca* came to my mind. Idle fancies, Miss V., idle fancies in the midst of crisis, it is ever thus with me. Billy Mytchett brought out his cold pipe and sucked on it, like a baby with its soother; in the pipe department, Mytchett was no match for Skryne.

'Blackmail,' he said, flatly.

I toyed with my cigarette case – what would I do without my props? – and selected another cigarette and tapped it on the lid. No one taps cigarettes like that any more; why did we do it, anyway?

'All I want,' I said, 'is for my life to go on as it is, in the same placid, unexcited way. I stay at the Institute, I keep my position at the Palace, and I still get the knighthood that HM has privately promised me. In return for this, I guarantee silence on everything I know.'

I was remarkably cool, if I say so myself. I have a way at times like that of going quite still all over, a protective instinct which is at once primitive and highly developed. I imagine my O Measceoil ancestors out on the bracken in pursuit of the great elk, hunter and hound together stopping dead at point as their poor prey lifts its magnificently burdened head and regards them out of one tragic, tear-streaked eye. There was another silence, and Skryne and Billy Mytchett looked at each other, and it seemed as if they might laugh. Billy cleared his throat.

'Look here, Victor,' he said, 'there's no need for this kind of nonsense. We're all grown-ups. That Regensburg stuff has been known about for years; no one is interested in that.' And straight away I understood. They wanted a deal, just as I did. Immunity for me was immunity for them. The flight of Boy and MacLeish was scandal enough to be going on with. I was disconcerted; more, I was dismayed. I had slapped down my trump card, and the rest of the table could hardly suppress a snigger. 'You'll have to cooperate, though,' Billy was saying with a great show of sternness. 'You'll have to talk to Skryne here and his people.' Skryne nodded, fairly glowing at the prospect of the fascinating conversations he and I would have in the coming months and years – our liaison was to last, on and off, for two and a half decades.

'But of course,' I said, making what I considered a gallant

stab at insouciance; really, their cynical practicality had shocked me. 'I shall tell Mr Skryne such things, why, they will make his eyes pop.'

Billy jabbed the stem of his pipe at me. 'And you'll have to keep your mouth shut,' he said. 'No running with stories to your pansy pals.'

'Oh, Billy,' I said.

He turned away with a disgusted grimace, as if to spit.

We broke up then, and Brocklebank was detailed to drive me home. They could not get rid of me fast enough. I tarried, dissatisfied. Everything felt so flat and anticlimactic. In the hallway I stopped beside a dusty aspidistra in a tarnished brass pot and turned to Billy.

'By the way,' I said, 'as a matter of interest: who was it betrayed me?'

Skryne and Billy looked at each other. Skryne smiled, tolerant, dismissive, as if I were a favourite nephew who had asked for one treat too much.

'Oh, now, Dr Maskell,' he said. 'that would be telling, wouldn't it.'

The evening air was heavy with the smell of cut grass. Brocklebank, stout Rodney, walking ahead of me to the garden gate, gave a yawn that made his jaw muscles crack. On the journey home he became quite talkative; no one really minds a bit of treachery, no one on the inside, I mean. I could tell there were all sorts of things he was dying to ask me. When we got to the flat I invited him up to see my Poussin; it was a device I often employed, with more success than you might expect. The majority of my invitees did not know, or care, what I was talking about, and God knows what they expected to see when I threw open the study door like a proud impresario and presented to them the spectacle of Seneca's stylised exsanguination. French-speakers probably thought I was asking them in to a chicken dinner. Rodney, however, was a bit of a snob, and pretended to know something about art. He carried his great bulk carefully, going about daintily on creaking tiptoe, as if the flat were a china shop. He proved to be something of a bull in the bedroom, too, with that big back, those unexpectedly narrow thighs. Pity about the pimples, though.

*

He left at dawn, creeping out of my bed and gathering up his clothes – dropping a shoe with a crash, of course – while I pretended tactfully to be asleep. I wondered if he would tell anyone he had been with me. Talk about a breach of security – as Boy might have said. I was missing Boy already. I lay awake watching the room whiten, beset by a profound and not quite explicable sadness. Then I got up, and changed the sheets – more than once I had caught Patrick, for all his vaunted freedom from jealousy, going over the bedclothes with the beady eye of a suspicious landlady – and went down and got out the car, in those days a big old Hillman of which I was very fond, and set off westward across the city. I did not know where I was going; I was dizzy from lack of sleep. The streets were all harsh sunlight and long, slender sharp shadows. After a while it seemed to start to rain, impossibly, out of a cloudless sky, and when I put on the wipers they did no good, and I realised that I was weeping. This was a surprise. I stopped the car and got out a handkerchief and swabbed my face, feeling ridiculous. Presently the tears stopped, and I sat for a while with my head leaning on the back of the seat, sniffling and gulping. A milkman passing by looked in at me with lively interest; I must have livened up his round for him. It was a fine morning, truly lovely. The sun. The little white puffs of cloud. The birds. I was about to drive on again when it struck me that the street was familiar, and I saw, with a small shock, that I had stopped a few doors away from Vivienne's house. Homing: the word came to me in all its ambiguity, its fatuous yearning. When had Vivienne's house, any house she had ever inhabited, been home to me?

She must have been awake – she never was much of a sleeper

– for when I rang the bell she came down at once and opened the door. Vaguely I wondered if she could be accustomed to receiving callers at this hour of the day – and was that a look of disappointment that crossed her face when she saw that it was me and not some far more interesting other? She was wearing a bright-blue gown – with a jolt I saw again Senhor Fonseca sprawled in his blood – and silk slippers, and her hair was tied up in an unbecoming knot. She had not put on her make-up, which gave her a blurred and almost apprehensive expression; if she had been expecting a visitor, it must have been an old and trusted someone, for the world was not often permitted to see Vivienne without her face.

'Victor!' she said. 'Good heavens, what a nice surprise. I thought you must be the postman.' The hall, filled with morning light, had the look of a long glass box suspended in sunlit space. Crimson roses crowding in a bowl seemed to throb in their depths, like slow hearts. Vivienne closed the door and hesitated for a moment in amused perplexity. 'Is it very late for you,' she said, 'or very early? You're not drunk, are you? It's just that you look a bit . . . odd. You do realise it's five o'clock in the morning?'

'Yes,' I said, 'I'm sorry, I don't know what I was thinking of. I was passing, and . . .'

'Yes. Well, come into the kitchen. The children are asleep.' I thought of Antonia MacLeish: should I telephone her? And say what? 'One hardly knows what to offer, at this hour of the morning,' Vivienne said, going ahead of me and opening the kitchen door. 'In the old days we would have had champagne. Speaking of which, how is Boy?'

'He's . . . away.'

'I haven't seen him in such a long time. Haven't seen anyone, really, from that world. I do seem to have lost contact. Do you think it means I shall turn into a lonely old woman, the Miss Havisham of South Audley Street? I feel positively ancient. If it weren't for the children I'm sure I shouldn't go out at all.

Would you like some tea?' She turned interrogatively from the sink with the kettle in her hand. I said nothing. She laughed softly and shook her head. 'Do tell me what the matter is, Victor. You look like a little boy who's been caught stealing apples. Are you in trouble? Have you made some awful mistake, misattributed one of the King's pictures, or something?'

I was about to say something, I hardly knew what, when suddenly I began to weep again, helplessly, in a great splurge of misery and objectless rage. I could not stop. I just stood there, in the middle of the floor, in the gaseous light of morning, choking on phlegm, my shoulders shaking, grinding my teeth and bunching my fists, with my eyes squeezed shut and the hot tears spurting down my shirt-front. There was an awful, indecent pleasure in it. It was like that glorious transgressional moment when as a child dreaming in bed I would give way and wet myself, copiously, scaldingly, unstoppably. At first Vivienne did nothing, but stood, startled and uncertain, with a hand to her lip. Then she came forward, shimmeringly, and put her arms about me and made me rest my forehead on her shoulder. Through the stuff of the dressing gown I could smell the faint staleness of the night on her skin.

'My darling,' she said, 'whatever is the matter?'

She made me sit down at the table, and fetched me a fresh handkerchief, and busied herself preparing the tea while I sat and snuffled.

'I'm sorry,' I said. 'Don't know what came over me.'

She sat down and regarded me across the table.

'Poor dear,' she said, 'you really are in a state.'

I told her about Boy and MacLeish and the dash to Folkestone. I was breathless and afraid, like the messenger kneeling at the king's feet telling him of the rout of his army, but I could not help myself, the words spilled out as the tears had done, unstoppably. Vivienne sat quite still, watching me, with almost clinical attention, and said nothing until I had finished.

'Boy has gone off with the Dour Scot?' she said then. 'But it's impossible. They can't stand each other.'

'I rather think they'll probably separate, you know, once they get to . . . where they're going.'

'To Moscow, you mean. That is where they've gone, isn't it?'

'Yes,' I said, 'I suppose so.'

She nodded, still with her eyes on mine.

'And you?' she said.

'Me?'

'Why have you not gone with them?'

'Why should I do that? I just gave them a lift down to the coast. Boy asked me. He was my friend.'

'Was?'

'Well, he's gone now. I doubt we shall ever see him again.'

She poured the tea, watching the twisting amber arc clatter into the cups. I asked if she would give me something to lace it with, but she was not listening.

'You always lied to me,' she said pensively. 'From the very start, you lied. Why should I forgive that now?'

I stared at her.

'Lied to you?' I said. 'What did I lie about?'

'About everything. Is your tea all right? Perhaps you'd like some breakfast? I'm beginning to feel quite peckish, myself. Shocks always make me hungry – do you find that? Let me fry some eggs or something.' She did not move, but sat with her fingers resting on the handle of the teapot, gazing before her and slowly nodding. 'So Boy is gone,' she said. 'I should like to have been able to say goodbye.' She blinked, and turned her gaze on me again. 'You knew he was planning to bolt, didn't you.'

'What do you mean? I didn't even know he had a reason to bolt.'

'You knew, and you didn't tell anyone. Such . . . such discretion!'

Her eyes glittered. I looked away from her.

'You're being ridiculous,' I said. 'I knew nothing.'

She went on staring at me in silence, and clenched her fist and laid it on the table before her, like a weapon. Then, suddenly, she laughed.

'Oh, Victor,' she said, and she relaxed her fist and lifted her hand and laid it tenderly along the length of my cheek, as she had so many times before had cause to do. 'Poor, poor Victor. You're right, you knew nothing, even less than you thought you did. He kept it all from you.'

The tea tasted of clay. In the silence I could clearly hear the pips for the six o'clock news from a wireless set in the house next door. I had not realised there were so many early risers in Mayfair. A jade figurine of a pot-bellied monk – one of Big Beaver's pieces – sat smirking to itself on the window sill beside me. Things, in their silence, endure so much better than people.

Chrysalis.

'He?' I said dully. 'What are you saying? What *he*?'

I could not bear her pitying smile.

'Don't you see?' she said. 'It was him. It was always him . . .'

I really must look out that pistol.

*

They kept coming back to me, year after year; whenever there was a flap on, when some new gaping hole was found in the State's so-called security, Skryne would wander into my life again, diffident, deferential, relentless as ever. During our interrogations – I say *our*, because I always think of them as something that we shared, like a series of tutorials, or a course of spiritual exercises – he would maunder on for hours in that dry, mild, schoolmasterly way that he had, asking the same question over and over, in slightly altered forms, and then all at once he would seize on a name, a word, an involuntary flicker of response in me that I had hardly been aware of, and everything would shift, and the questioning would go off in an entirely new direction. Yet it was all very relaxed and mannerly and, well, chummy. In time we even took to exchanging Christmas cards – honestly, we did. He was a match for me in patience, in concentration, in his eye for the telling detail, in his ability to take a fragment and build up a picture of the whole; but in the end I was the one with the greater endurance. In all that time – I wonder how many hours we spent together: a thousand, two thousand? – I do not think I ever gave him anything he could not have got elsewhere. I named only the dead, or those who had been so peripheral to our circle that I knew the Department would not bother with them, or not for long, anyway. Chess is too serious, too warlike, an analogy for what we were engaged in. A cat-and-mouse game, then – but who was the mouse, and who the cat?

I remember the first time Skryne came to the flat. He had been angling for a long time, not very subtly, to get in and have a look at what he called my gaff. I objected that it would be an unconscionable invasion of privacy if he were to question me in my home, but in the end I weakened and said that he might come round for a sherry at six some evening. I suppose I thought I might get an advantage by granting his harmless and in a way quite touching wish: the cocktail hour is a tricky and uncertain part of the social day for persons of his class, who think of it as teatime, and fret, I find, when they have to forgo this important repast. However, he seemed perfectly at ease. Perhaps he was a little intimidated by the empty, echoing galleries as we ascended through them, but once inside the flat he began to make himself at home right away. He was even about to light up his pipe, without asking my leave, but I stopped him, saying the fumes would be bad for the pictures, as indeed they might have been, for the black shag that he smoked gave off an acrid stink that shrivelled my nostrils and made my eyes prickle. I caught him taking a quick look round; he seemed not very impressed – indeed, I think he was disappointed. I wonder what he had been expecting? Purple silk hangings, perhaps, and a catamite posed upon a chaise longue (Patrick had not been well pleased when I asked him to absent himself for the duration of the visit, and had taken himself off to the pictures in a sulk). He became animated, though, when he spotted the little Degas drawing I had borrowed from the French Room downstairs to hang over the fireplace; I have never succeeded in liking the work of this painter, and had brought the piece up to live with it for a while in the hope that it might win me over. (It did not.)

'That's a lovely thing, isn't it,' he said, pointing the stem of his cold pipe at it. 'Degas. Beautiful.' He blinked shyly. 'I dabble a bit myself, you know.'

'Oh, yes?'

'Watercolours. It's just a hobby, though my missus will insist on getting my things framed and hanging them about the place. As a matter of fact, I did a copy of that very one, from a book. Mine's only on cardboard, though.'

'So is the original.'

'Oh.'

'And it's De*gas*, by the way; the *s* is pronounced.'

We drank our sherry in the study. He did not remark the Poussin. There were two chairs – one of them already waiting for you, Miss V., although it did not know it – yet we remained standing. I wondered what account of me he would give his missus. *The dry type, Mabel; and stuck-up, too.* It was a chrome and copper evening in October. Boy and the Dour Scot had made their first appearance in Moscow to talk to reporters, spouting a lot of solemn claptrap about peace and fraternity and world revolution; Party Congress stuff, written for them, probably, by our friends in the Kremlin. The thing was tele-vised, apparently in a snowstorm – I owned a primitive set by then; it was supposed to be for Patrick's amusement, but I was already a secret addict – and I found it a depressing and slightly nauseating spectacle. Heartbreaking, really, that all that passion, that conviction, should have shrunk to this, two raddled, middle-aged men sitting at a bare table in a windowless room in the Lubyanka, putting on a brave face and desperately smiling, trying to convince themselves and the world that they had come home at long last to the Promised Land. I dreaded to think how Boy might be faring. I remembered, that night in the thirties when I was whisked off to the Kremlin, the wife of the Commissar of Soviet Culture looking at the champagne in my glass with a curled lip and saying, 'Georgian.' A fellow from the British embassy claimed to have spotted Boy one night in a Moscow hotel, slumped at the bar with his forehead on his arm, noisily weeping. I hoped that they were whiskey tears.

'Think they're happy, your two chums?' Skryne said. 'Not much in the way of beer and skittles over there.'

'Caviare is more their taste,' I said coldly, 'and there is plenty of that.'

He was toying with things on my desk; I had an urge to slap his hand away. I do hate people to *fiddle*.

'Would you go over?' he said.

I took a sip of sherry. It was very good; I hoped Skryne could appreciate it.

'They urged me to,' I said. They had; Oleg had been anxiously solicitous. 'I asked them, if I went, could they arrange regular working visits for me to the National Gallery and the Louvre? They consulted Moscow and came back very apologetic. No sense of irony, the Russians. Just like the Americans, in that.'

'You don't like Americans, do you.'

'Oh, I'm sure they're perfectly decent people, individually. It's just that I'm not a democrat, you see; I fear mob rule.'

'What about the dictatorship of the proletariat?'

'Oh please,' I said, 'let us not descend to polemics. Some more sherry? It's not at all bad, you know.'

I poured. I like the oleaginous quality of this drink, but otherwise even the best of it has a bitter edge that reminds me of some unpleasant taste from childhood – Nanny Hargreaves's castor oil, perhaps. No, I prefer gin, with its mysterious hints of frost and forest, metal and flame. In the first days after Boy's flight I practically bathed in the stuff from first thing in the morning until the dead hours of the night. My poor liver. Probably it was then, all those years ago, that the cells essayed the first drunken steps of their dervish dance that is now consuming my insides. Skryne stood gazing glassy-eyed before him, the thimble of drink seemingly forgotten in his fingers. He often went blank like that; it was unnerving. Concentration? Deep thought? A trap for the unwary, perhaps? – one did tend to let one's vigilance slip when he went absent in this way. Late light from the window was throwing a nickel-bright sheen across the surface of the Poussin, picking out the points of the pigment and shading in the hollows. Someone at the valuers has raised a question as to its authenticity; preposterous, of course.

'Consider this picture,' I said. 'It is called *The Death of Seneca*. It was painted in the middle of the seventeenth century by Nicholas Poussin. You are something of an artist, you tell me: the civilisation that this picture represents, isn't it worth fighting for?' I noticed the faint shiver on the surface of the sherry in the glass I was holding; I had thought I was quite calm. 'The Spartan youth,' I said, 'complained to his mother that his sword was too short, and her only reply was, *Step closer*.'

Skryne gave a curious, creaky sigh. I had to acknowledge, there in the confined space of the study, that he exuded a faint but definite smell: tobacco, naturally, but something behind that as well, something drab and unsavoury; something very – well, very *Hackney*.

'Wouldn't it be better, Dr Maskell,' he said, 'if we were to sit down now, here, and get it all over and done with?'

'I told you, I am not willing to undergo interrogation in my own home.'

'Not interrogation. Just a . . . just a general clearing up, you might say. I'm a Catholic – well, my mother was a Catholic; Irish, like you. I still remember how it used to feel, when I was a lad, to come out of the confession box, that feeling of . . . lightness. Know what I mean?'

'I have told you everything I know,' I said.

He smiled, and gently shook his head, and set his glass down carefully on a corner of my desk. He had not touched the sherry.

'No,' he said. 'You've told us everything that *we* know.'

I sighed. Was there to be no end to this?

'What you are asking me to do is betray my friends,' I said. 'I won't do that.'

'You've betrayed everything else.' Still smiling, still gently avuncular.

'But what you mean by everything,' I said, 'is nothing to me. To be capable of betraying something you must first believe in it.' I too put down my glass, with a clunk of finality. 'And now, Mr Skryne, I think, really . . .'

In the hall I handed him his hat. He had a way of putting it on, fitting it carefully to his head with rotating motions, using both hands and crouching forward a little, that seemed as if he were screwing the lid on to a container of some precious, volatile stuff. At the door he paused.

'By the way, did you see that thing that Bannister said when he met the chap from the *Daily Mail* in Moscow? We haven't let him publish it yet.'

'Then how would I have seen it?'

He smiled cannily, as if I had made a sly and telling point.

'I wrote it down,' he said, 'I think I have it here.' He produced a bulging wallet and extracted from it a slip of paper carefully folded. I could see he had planned this little gesture, even down to the last-minute timing; after all, he was a fellow thespian. He put on a pair of wire-frame spectacles, threading the earpieces carefully behind his ears and adjusting the bridge, then cleared his throat preparatory to reading aloud. '*Don't think I'm starry-eyed about this place*, he says. *I miss my friends. I'm lonely sometimes. But here I'm lonely for the unimportant things. In England I was lonely for what is really important – for Socialism.* Sad, eh?' He proffered the slip. 'Here, why don't you keep it?'

'No, thank you. The *Daily Mail* is not my paper.'

He nodded, thinking, his gaze fixed on the knot of my tie.

'Are you lonely for Socialism, Dr Maskell?' he said gently.

I could hear the clank and gurgle of the lift ascending; it would be Patrick returning from the pictures, probably still in a huff. Life can be very trying, sometimes.

'I'm not lonely for anything,' I said. 'I have done my work. That's all that matters.'

'And your friends,' he said softly. 'Don't forget your friends. They matter, don't they?'

MISS VANDELEUR has just left, in rather hangdog fashion, I'm afraid. She will not be seeing me again; or, more accurately, I shall not be seeing her. Her visit was a moving occasion; last things, and so on – and *not* so on. I had bought a cake – it turned out to be somewhat stale – and put a small candle on it. I have a special licence to be silly, now. She eyed the cake suspiciously, in some bafflement. Our first anniversary, I said, handing her a glass of champagne with what I judged to be just the right shading of old-world gallantry; I would not want her to think I harbour any feelings of rancour against her. But in fact, as she pointed out when she checked back to the beginning of her by now dog-eared notebook, this was not the date on which she first came to me. I waved aside these petty details. We were sitting in the study. Although she did not seem to notice it, I was acutely conscious of the awful blank space on the wall where the Poussin should have been hanging. Miss V. was in her greatcoat, yet still seemed cold, as she always does; her mechanic must have the devil of a time warming her up – girls always blame their young men for the prevailing tempera-ture, don't ask me how I know. She also had on her leather skirt, as of old. How account for the pathos of people's clothes? I envisioned her in her room in Golders Green, in the grey light and fetid air of morning, with a mug of cold coffee on the dressing table, creakily getting into that skirt and contemplating another day of . . . of what? Perhaps there is no such room in Golders Green. Perhaps it is all an invention, her father the Admiral, her uncouth mechanic, the glum commutings on the Northern Line, my biography. I asked her how the book was coming along and she gave me a resentful stare, looking like a sullen schoolgirl who has been caught smoking behind the bicycle shed. I assured her I did not feel harshly toward her, and she put on a show of incomprehension, saying she was sure she did not know what I was talking about. We regarded each other for a moment in silence, I smiling, she with a cross frown. Oh, Miss Vandeleur, my dear Serena. If these really are her names.

'Despite appearances,' I said, indicating the champagne bottle and the ruined cake with its Pisan candle, 'I am officially in mourning.' I watched her closely for a reaction; none came, as I had expected; she already knew. 'Yes,' I said, 'you see, my wife died.'

Silence for a moment.

'I'm sorry,' she said faintly, looking at my hands.

April. Such wonderful skies today, great drifting ice-mountains of cloud, and beyond them that delicate, breakable blue, and the sunlight going on and off as if a capricious someone somewhere had control of a switch. I do not like the springtime; have I said that before? Too disturbing, too distressing, all this new life blindly astir. I feel left behind, half buried, all withered bough and gnarled root. Something is stirring in me, though. I often fancy, at night especially, that I can feel it in there, not the pain, I mean, but the thing itself, malignantly flourishing, flexing its pincers. Well, I shall soon put a stop to its growth. Mouth very dry now, all of a sudden. Strange effects. I am quite calm.

'It was dreadfully sad,' I said. 'It seems she starved herself to death. Refused to eat, just turned her face to the wall, as they used to say. Such desperateness to die! She wouldn't let them send for me; said I should be left in peace. She was always more considerate than I; braver, too. The funeral was yesterday. I am still a trifle upset, as you can see.'

Why, with death attendant upon me at every moment, tirelessly prowling the rickety defences of my life, am I still surprised when it makes a kill? I had always taken it for granted that Vivienne would outlive me. And yet when Julian telephoned, I knew, before he said it, that she was gone. We stood for a long moment, listening to each other breathing through the ether.

'It's better this way,' he said.

Why do the young always think it better that the old should be dead? The question answers itself, I suppose.

'Yes,' I said, 'better.'

She had requested to be buried by the Jewish rite. I was astonished. When we were married first she used to take the children to church services, especially when she was in Oxford, but that, I realised now, must have been merely to annoy her mother. I never knew she cared for the God of her fathers. No accounting for people, no accounting. There were more surprises at the funeral. Nick wore a yarmulke, and so did Julian, and during the prayers, the Kaddish or whatever it's called, I saw Nick's lips moving as he joined in with the cantor. Where did all this devoutness come from all of a sudden? But obviously it was not sudden.

The cemetery was on the outer fringes of north London. It took us more than an hour to get there, despite the indecent speed at which the hearse cut its way through the northbound traffic. It was a harsh, blustery grey day with squalls of rain and a gash of infernal, yellowish light lying along the horizon. In the car I sat in the back seat, feeling shrivelled and cowed. Beside me Blanche sobbed to herself, her face all blotched and swollen. Julian sat stiffly upright at the wheel, his eyes fixed on the road. The empty seat beside him was lugubriously symbolic of his mother's absence. Nick travelled alone, with his chauffeur. At one stage in the journey, when we were briefly on the motorway and our two cars drew level, I saw that he was working, papers and gold pen in hand, the Ministerial red box open beside him on the seat. He felt my eyes on him, and looked up at me unseeingly for a moment, remote, expressionless, his thoughts importantly elsewhere. Even now, when he is in his seventies, corpulent, bald, his face all fallen and his eyes rheumy and pouched, I can still see in him the beauty he once was; is it real, or do I put it there? That was what I was for, that was always my task, to keep his image in place, to kneel before him humbly with head bowed and hold the mirror up to him, and in turn to hold his image up to the world's inspection.

As we were pulling in at the gates of the cemetery, Blanche made a fumbling attempt to take my hand, but I pretended not to notice. I do not care to be touched.

For a second I did not recognise Querell. It was not that he had changed very much, but he was the last person I had expected to see here. What cheek! He was thin-haired, a little stooped, yet still possessed of a watchful, sinister elegance. Or no, not elegance, that is not the word; just sleekness, rather, at once devilish and tawdry, and an air always of malevolent anticipation, like that of an expert swimmer, say, calmly looking on as a clumsy novice ventures flounderingly out of his depth. He carries the aura of his fame with ease. I was always jealous of him. When the ceremony was finished he came and shook my hand perfunctorily. We had not seen each other for more than a quarter of a century, yet he carried off the moment as if we had been in the habit of bumping into each other every day.

'Trust the Jews,' he said, 'they always come back to their own in the end. Just like us – Catholics, I mean.' He was wearing a padded windbreaker over his suit. 'I feel the cold more, nowadays. My blood has gone thin from living so long in the south. You don't look too bad, Victor; perfidy keeps one young, eh?' I could not recall him ever before using my first name. I introduced him to Blanche and Julian. He gave them each in turn a keen, long look. 'I knew you when you were in your cradles.' Julian was curtly polite. I do admire his reserve, so rare a thing these days. 'You have your mother's eyes,' Querell said, and Julian gave that stiff little nod of his, which to me always seems to be accompanied by a phantom clicking of the heels. My poor, lost son. Querell had turned his attention on Blanche. She was all of a quiver, flustered in the presence of such a celebrity. She withdrew her hand from his as if his touch had burned her. I wonder if they know about Querell, she and Julian? It is not the kind of thing one asks one's children, even when they are grown up.

'When do you go back?' I said.

Querell gave me a stare.

'Tomorrow,' he said.

The spring wind gusted in the still-bare trees and a handful of rain spattered the wall of the marble temple behind us. Julian attempted to slide a supportive hand under my arm but I shook him off violently. For a moment I clearly saw Vivienne walking toward me, weaving her way among the headstones in her tubular black silk dress and flapper's high heels. Nick had already sped off in his car, without a word to anyone. Querell was talking about taxis.

'Oh, no no,' I said, 'let us give you a lift.' Julian opened his mouth but said nothing. Querell frowned. 'I insist,' I said. One can have fun even at a funeral.

We fairly dashed back into the city, Querell and I in the back seat now, and Blanche and Julian in front, the two of them sitting like effigies, listening intently to the silence behind them. Querell watched with narrow-eyed interest – ever the novelist – the dreary suburban streets going past, the corner groceries, the launderettes, the brand-new but already dingy shopping malls with their garish window displays and blown litter.

'England,' he said, and snickered.

At St Giles Circus we were brought to a halt by a traffic jam. It was as if we had blundered into the smouldering centre of a herd of big, shiny, shuddering animals.

'Listen, Querell,' I said, 'come for a drink.'

How like the old days it sounded! Querell gave me an ironical stare. Julian was already edging the car towards the kerb. On the pavement the wind swirled about us callously.

While Querell was doing up the complicated zipper of his coat I watched the car nose its way back into the traffic, brother and sister leaning toward each other now in animated talk. Those are the really secret lives, the lives of one's children.

'Anxious to be away,' I said. 'We have become the tedious old.'

Querell nodded.

'I was just thinking,' he said, 'my mistress is younger than your daughter.'

We turned into Soho. The day had brightened, and now a strong sun appeared, shouldering its way out of the clouds, and the sky above the narrow streets seemed immensely high and somehow vigorously in flight. The wind swooped and lunged, wringing the necks of the daffodils in the Square. On the corner of Wardour Street a crone in cocoa-coloured stockings and a shroudlike coat was shrieking abuse at the passers-by. White flecks on her lips, the grief-maddened eyes. The sun flashed suddenly, outlandishly, on a sheet of glass on the back of a lorry. Two club girls went past, in fake-fur coats and three-inch heels. Querell eyed them with sour amusement.

'London was always a parody of itself,' he said. 'Ridiculous, ugly, cold country. You should have got out when you could.'

We walked down Poland Street. After Boy's flight, Leo Rothenstein had sold the house. The upper storeys had been converted into offices. We stood on the pavement looking up at the familiar windows. Why can't the past ever leave off, why must it be forever pawing at us, like a wheedling child. We walked on, saying nothing. Miniature wind-devils danced on the pavement, lifting dust and scraps of paper in swaying spirals. I was feeling quite light-headed.

The old pub had a pinball machine now. It was noisily attended by a gang of shaven-headed young men wearing broad braces and lace-up boots. Querell and I sat in prostatic discomfort on low stools at a small table at the back and drank gin, watching the boot-boys about their raucous game, the vague old daytime topers at the bar. Ghosts glimmered in the shadows. Phantom laughter. The past, the past.

'Would you come back?' I said. 'Do you not miss it, any of it?'

He was not listening.

'You know,' he said, 'Vivienne and I had an affair.' He glanced at me quickly and away again, frowning. He turned his cigarette this way and that in his fingers. 'I'm sorry,' he said. 'It was when you were first married. She was lonely.'

'Yes,' I said. 'I know.' He stared, in gratifying startlement. I shrugged. 'Vivienne told me.'

A bus went past outside with an elephantine blare and made floor and seat and table faintly shudder, and stark pale faces on the top deck gaped in at us fleetingly in what seemed a sort of amazement. Querell with pursed lips expelled a thin quick cone of smoke towards the ceiling; there were patches of whitish stubble on his badly shaved old turkey's neck.

'When?' he said.

'What?'

'When did she tell you?'

'Does it matter?'

'Of course it matters.'

His hands, I noticed, were trembling a little; the smoke as it rose from his cigarette wavered in the same rapid rhythm. The smoke was blue before he inhaled it, and afterwards grey.

'Oh, a long time ago,' I said. 'The day after Boy defected. The day after you and the others decided to betray me to the Department.'

An argument had started at the pinball machine, and two of the young men were engaged in a mock fight, feinting and jabbing and making dangerous-looking little kicks at each other's shins, while their companions jeeringly urged them on. Querell drank his drink and exhaled a sort of whistly sigh. He took our glasses and went to the bar. I looked at him in his vulgar padded coat and suede shoes. The mystery of other people yawned before me, as if a door caught by the wind had been flung open on to dark and storm. Another bus went by, and another set of dull, astonished faces looked in at us from on high. Querell came back with the drinks, and when he was settling himself on the stool again I caught a whiff of something off him, an internal emanation, cheesy and raw; perhaps he is sick, too. I certainly hope so. He frowned into his glass, as if he had spotted something floating in it. A patch of pink, the size of a shilling, had appeared high up on each of his cheekbones; what was it – anger? excitement? Surely not shame?

'How did you know?' he said, in a thickened voice. 'I mean, about . . .'

'Vivienne, of course. Who else? She told me everything there was to know, that day. She was my wife, you see.'

He drank deep and sat bending his glass this way and that, watching the last silver bead of liquor rolling around the bottom.

'I wanted to keep you out of it, you know,' he said. 'I wanted to give them Rothenstein, or Alastair Sykes. But no, they said it would have to be you.'

I laughed.

'I've just realised,' I said, 'this is what you came back for, isn't it. To tell me about you and Vivienne, and about . . . this. What a disappointment for you, that I should know it all already.'

His lips, contracting with age, had acquired tiny, deeply etched striations all along their edges, which gave his mouth a spinsterish cast. That is how I must look, too. What would those young men have seen, if they had turned on us their menacing attention? A pair of sad old withered eunuchs, with their gin and their cigarettes, their ancient secrets, ancient pain. I signalled to the barman. He was a slender, pale youth, a Bronzino type, drawn and somewhat debauched-looking; when I paid for the drinks I brushed his cool, damp fingers with mine, and he gave me a wan glance. In the midst of death, life.

Querell was regarding me with a grim eye, feeling along his lower lip with the tip of his tongue. I tried to imagine him and Vivienne together. He blinked slowly, old saurian eyelids drooping. I smelled his mortal smell again.

'We had to give them someone,' he said.

Well, I was always able to see that, of course. There had to have been a London end to the operation, someone to receive the material MacLeish and Bannister were sending from Washington and pass it on to Oleg. It was the least the Department would have expected; the least they would have settled for.

'Yes,' I said, 'and you gave them me.'

Abruptly the dangerous young men departed, and the abandoned pinball machine seemed to take on a hurt, puzzled look, like that of a dog with no one left to throw sticks for it. Talk, smoke, the desultory clatter of glasses.

'I suppose you were in before me?' I said.

He nodded.

'I had a cell going when I was at Oxford,' he said. 'I was still an undergraduate.'

He could not keep the boastful note out of his voice.

I stood up. Suddenly I wanted to be away from him. It was not anger that was spurring me, but a kind of impatience; something else was finished with.

'I really am sorry,' I said, 'that you didn't get to see me squirm.'

Outside, on the pavement, I felt dizzy again, and thought for a moment I might fall over. Querell was waving for a taxi; could not get away quickly enough, now that his attempt at revenge had backfired on him. I put a hand on his arm: papery flesh under his coat, and a thin old bone, like a primitive weapon.

'It was you,' I said, 'wasn't it, who gave my name to that fellow who was writing the book – the one who was going to expose me?'

He stared at me.

'Why would I do that?'

A taxi pulled up. He moved toward it, trying to shake off my hand, but I clutched him all the more tightly. I was surprised at my own strength. The taxi driver turned with interest to watch us, two half-sozzled old geezers furiously grappling.

'Who, then?' I said.

As if I didn't know.

He shrugged, and smiled, showing me his old, yellowed teeth, and said nothing. I released him, and stepped back, and he stooped and got into the taxi and pulled the door shut behind him. As the taxi drove away I saw his pale long face in the rear window, looking back at me. He seemed to be laughing.

Suddenly it strikes me: are my children mine?

*

Just now a most unpleasant exchange over the telephone with an impudent young man at the valuers. Outrageous imputations. He actually used the word fake. Do you realise, I said, who I am? And I swear I heard him stifle a snigger. I told him to return the painting to me at once. I had already decided to whom I shall bequeath it; I do not think I need to change my mind.

*

He answered the telephone himself, on the first ring. Had he been waiting for me to call? Perhaps Querell tipped him off, a last piece of mischief-making before he flew south again to the sun and his child mistress. I was terribly nervous, and stammered like a fool. I asked if I might come round. There was a long pause, then he simply said yes, and hung up. I spent the next half-hour going through the flat in search of the Webley, and found it at last, with a cry of triumph, at the back of a bureau drawer, wrapped in an old shirt which, I realised with an absent-minded pang, had been one of Patrick's. Strange sensation, hefting the weapon in my hand. How antiquated it seems, like one of those domestic gadgets you see in displays of Victoriana, ponderous, weighty, of uncertain use. But no, not uncertain, certainly not uncertain. It has not been oiled since the war, but I expect it will work. Two rounds only – what can have become of the other four? – but that will be more than sufficient. I could not find the holster for it, and was in a quandary how to carry it, since it was too big for my pocket, and when I tucked it into my waistband it slithered down inside the leg of my trousers and fetched me a nasty crack on the instep. A wonder it didn't go off. That would not do; I had suffered enough ignominy without shooting myself in the foot. In the end I wrapped it up again in the shirt – broad pink stripes, plain white collar; Patsy went in for that kind of thing – and put it in my string bag. Umbrella, raincoat, latchkey. It was not until I got down to the street that I noticed I was wearing slippers. No matter.

The taxi driver was one of those tiresome monologuists: weather, traffic, Pakis, bleeding pedestrians. How unprepossessing they are, the helmsmen that are sent to ferry us through the most momentous passages of our lives. I diverted myself by imagining the consternated howls that will rise from certain stagnant backwaters of academe over a posthumous article of mine on the erotic symbolism in Poussin's *Echo and Narcissus* – I wonder, by the way, why in this picture the artist chose to portray Narcissus without nipples? – that will appear shortly in an adventurous and somewhat irreverent new American art journal. I do like to shock, even still. The sun was occluded and Holland Park had a sullen, brooding aspect, despite all those big cream mansions and toy-coloured motor cars. I got down with relief from the taxi and gave the fellow a shilling tip, or five pee, as we must say now; he looked at the coin in disgust and swore under his breath and dieseled away. I grinned; offending taxi drivers is one of life's small pleasures. Wet patches on the pavement and a smell of rain and rot. A lilac bush beside the front door was about to blossom. A furtive thrush flitted among the leaves, keeping a beady eye on me as I waited. The maid was a Filipina, a tiny, dark, infinitely sad-seeming person who said something incomprehensible and stood aside meekly as I stepped into the hall. Marble floor, Italian table, big copper bowl of daffodils, a convex mirror in a baroque gilt frame. I caught the nurse, I mean the maid, looking dubiously at my string bag, my slippers, my funereal umbrella. She spoke again, again incomprehensibly, and, pointing the way with a little brown bat's claw, led me off into the silent interior of the house. As I walked past the mirror my reflection fleetingly grew a monstrous head while the rest of me tapered off into a sort of complicated umbilical tail.

Pale rooms, dim pictures, a magnificent Turkey carpet all gules and purples and desert browns. Imelda's rubber soles discreetly squeaked. We entered an octagonal conservatory with potted plants, their unreally green, polished leaves intently leaning, and she opened a glass door on to the garden and stood back, smiling a mournful, encouraging smile. I stepped past her and out. A path of paving stones set flush in the grass led across the lawn to a great dense dark-green stand of laurel. There was a sudden swish of sunlight and something quivered in the air, quivered, and sank. I walked along the path. Wind, cloud, a swooping bird. Nick was waiting in the watery light under the laurels. Very still, hands in pockets, watching me. White shirt, black trousers, unsuitable shoes. His shirt-sleeves were rolled up.

Here it is: *The Agony in the Garden.*

'Hello, Victor.'

Now, after all, I could not think what to say. I said:

'How is Sylvia?'

He gave me a quick, hard look, as if I had made a tasteless allusion.

'She's in the country. She prefers it there, these days.'

'I see.' A fearless robin dropped from a twig on to the grass close by Nick's foot and seized a speck of something and flew up soundlessly into the tree again. Nick looked cold. Was it for me he had got himself up in this nice silk shirt, these slim-fitting slacks and slip-on shoes (with a decorative gold buckle on the instep, of course) and posed himself here against all this green? Another actor, playing his part, not very convincingly. 'I'm dying, you know,' I said.

He looked away, frowning.

'Yes, I heard. Sorry.'

Shadow, sun a second, then shadow again. Such agitated weather. Somewhere a blackbird began to cluck warningly; there must have been magpies nearby; I know about magpies.

'Who told you?' I said.

'Julian.'

'Ah. See a lot of him, do you?'

'Quite a bit.'

'You must be a father figure for him,' I said.

'Something like that.'

He was eyeing my slippers, my string bag.

'Well, I'm glad,' I said. 'A man needs a father.'

He gave me another hard look.

'Are you drunk?' he said.

'Certainly not. Just somewhat wrought. I have been hearing things.'

'Yes,' he said grimly, 'I saw Querell talking to you at the funeral. Interesting chat, was it?'

'It was.'

I crossed my ankles and leaned on the umbrella, trying to seem nonchalant; the ferrule sank into the grass and I almost lost my balance. I am at an age when one does tend to fall down. I'm afraid I rather lost control, then, and began to upbraid him, coming out with all sorts of awful things – recriminations, insults, threats – that were no sooner said than I regretted them. But I could not stop; it all came out in a scalding, shameful flood, a lifetime of bitterness and jealousy and pain, gushing out, like – forgive me – like vomit. I think I may even have unsheathed my brolly from the clay and brandished it at him threateningly. What now of my stoic resolve? Nick just stood and listened, watching me with mild attention, waiting for me to finish, as if I were a wilful child having a foot-stamping tantrum.

'You've even subverted my son!' I cried.

He lifted an eyebrow, trying not to smile.

'Subverted?'

'Yes, yes! – with your filthy Jewish nonsense. I saw you together at the funeral, praying.'

I would have gone on, but I choked on spit and had to cough and cough, beating myself on the chest. Abruptly my tremor started up, as if a vague small engine inside me had been switched on.

'Let's go into the house,' Nick said. He shivered in his shirt-sleeves. 'We're too old for this.'

Apple trees, April, a young man in a hammock; yes, it must have been April, that first time. Why did I think it was high summer? My memory is not as good as it is supposed to be. I may have misrecalled everything, got all the details wrong. What do you think, Miss V.?

In the conservatory we sat in wicker armchairs on either side of a low wicker table. The maid came and Nick asked for tea.

'Gin, for me,' I said, 'if you don't mind.' I smiled at the maid; I was quite calm again, after my little moment of catharsis in the garden. 'Bring the bottle, dear, will you?'

Nick studied the garden, his elbows on the arms of his chair and his fingertips joined before him. A tiny speck of wet laurel leaf clung to his balding brow, seeming symbolic of something or other. A gust of wind sprinted through the willows and a moment later smacked its palms against the glass beside me. A rain shower started, but faltered almost at once. All sorts of things were going through my head, bits and scraps of the past, as if a maddened projectionist in there were throwing together a jumble of old, flickering film clips. I recalled a midsummer night party that Leo Rothenstein gave in the great park at Maules fifty years ago, the masquers strolling under the murmurous trees, and frock-coated footmen gravely pacing the greensward with bottles of champagne wrapped in wetted napkins; the soft, still darkness, and stars, and skittering bats, and a vast, osseous moon. On an ornate bench beside a grassy bank a boy and girl were kissing, the girl with one glimmering breast bared. For a moment now I was there again. I was with Nick, and Nick was with me, and the future was limitless. The maid returned with a tray, and I started awake again into the awful present.

Only yesterday all this happened; hard to credit.

While Nick – old, paunched, pouchy Nick – was pouring his tea, I grasped the gin bottle by the neck and glugged out a good half-tumblerful.

'Do you remember,' I said, 'that summer when we first came down to London, and we used to walk through Soho at night, reciting Blake aloud, to the amusement of the tarts? *The tygers of wrath are wiser than the horses of instruction.* He was our hero, do you remember? Scourge of hypocrisy, the champion of freedom and truth.'

'We were usually drunk, as I recall,' he said, and laughed; Nick does not really laugh, it is only a noise that he makes which he has learned to imitate from others. Thoughtfully he stirred his tea, round and round. Those hands. *'The tygers of wrath,'* he said. 'Is that what you thought we were?'

I drank my gin. Cold fire, hot slivers of ice. The furled umbrella, which I had leaned against the arm of my chair, fell on the marble floor with a muffled clatter. My props were not behaving themselves at all today.

'Yeats insisted Blake was Irish, you know,' I said. 'Imagine that – London Blake, an Irishman! I've been thinking of that time when he and his friend Stothard sailed up the Medway on a sketching trip, and were arrested on suspicion of spying for the French. Blake got into a great state of agitation, convinced some false friend had denounced him to the authorities. Silly, of course.'

Nick sighed, making a sound like something deflating, and leaned back in his chair, the woven wicker crackling under him like a bonfire. The cup and saucer were balanced on his knee; he seemed to be studying the cup's design. The silence beat like a heart.

'I had to be shielded,' he said at last, weary and impatient. 'You know that.'

'Did you?' I said. 'Do I?'

'I was the one who was going to be in government. If we hadn't given you to them, they would have got to me sooner or later. It was a collective decision. There was nothing personal in it.'

'No,' I said, 'nothing personal.'

He looked at me stonily.

'You did all right,' he said. 'You got your job, your place at the Palace. You got your knighthood.'

'I haven't got it any more.'

'You were always too fond of honours, and having letters after your name, all that capitalist rot.' He glanced at his watch. 'I've got someone coming shortly.'

'When did you start?' I said. 'Was it Felix Hartmann, or before that?'

He shrugged.

'Oh, before. Long before. With Querell. He and I went in together. Even though he always hated me, I don't know why.'

'And are you still working for them?'

'Of course.'

He smiled, with lips shut tight and the tip of his nose depressed; age has accentuated his Jewishness, yet the one he has come most to resemble is his gentile father – that sinuous look, the pointed bald pate, those watchful, hooded eyes. The rain, having taken a deep breath, started up again with determination. I have always loved the sound of rain on glass. Tremor getting very bad now, hands all ashake and one leg going like the arm of a sewing machine.

'Was it Vivienne who told you?' he said. 'I always suspected she had. And you never let on, all these years. What a sly old body you are, Doc.'

'Why didn't *you* tell me?'

He transferred the cup and saucer carefully to the table and sat for a moment, thinking.

'Do you remember Boulogne,' he said, 'that last morning, on the ammunition ship, when you lost your nerve? I knew then I could never trust you. Besides, you weren't serious; you were just in it for amusement, and something you could pretend to believe in.' He looked at me. 'I tried to make it up to you. I helped you. I passed you all that stuff from Bletchley for you to impress Oleg with. And when you wanted to get out and devote yourself to' – a faint smirk – 'art, I was there. Why do you think they let you go? Because they had me.'

I poured another mighty gin. I was realising that I preferred it without tonic; it was brighter, more emphatic, steely-sharp. A bit late to be acquiring new tastes.

'Who else knew?' I said.

'What? Oh, everyone, really.'

'Sylvia, for instance? Did you tell Sylvia?'

'She guessed. We didn't discuss it.' He glanced at me and gave a rueful shrug, biting his lip. 'She felt sorry for you.'

'Why did you give my name to that fellow?' I said. 'Why did you have to betray me a second time? Why couldn't you have left me in peace?'

He heaved a sigh and shifted in his chair. He had the bored, impatient air of a man being forced to listen to an unwelcome declaration of love. As he was, I suppose.

'They were after me again.' He smiled; it was Vivienne's icy glitter. 'I've told you,' he said. 'I have to be protected.' He looked at his watch. 'And now, really—'

'What if *I* talk to the papers?' I said. 'What if I call them up today and tell them everything.'

He shook his head.

'You won't do that.'

'I could tell Julian. That would dull some of his filial admiration.'

'You won't do that, either.' Distantly we heard the doorbell ring. He stood up, and bent and retrieved my umbrella. 'Your socks are wet,' he said. 'Why are you wearing slippers, in this weather?'

'Bunions,' I said, and laughed, a touch hysterically, I fear; it was the gin, no doubt. He was looking at the string bag again. I shook it. 'I brought a gun,' I said.

He glanced aside, clicking his tongue in annoyance.

'Are they taking care of you?' he said. 'The Department, I mean. Pensions, that kind of thing?' I said nothing. We set off through the house. As we walked, he turned from the waist up and looked into my face. 'Listen, Victor, I—'

'Don't, Nick,' I said. 'Don't.'

He began to say something more, but changed his mind. I could feel the presence of someone else in the house. (Was it you, my dear? Come, was it you, skulking in one of those gilded antechambers?) The maid – why do I keep wanting to call her the nurse? – materialised out of the shadows in the hall and opened the front door for me. I went out quickly on to the step. The rain had stopped again, the lilac leaves were dripping. Nick put a hand on my shoulder but I squirmed away from his touch.

'By the way,' I said, 'I'm leaving you the Poussin.'

He nodded, not surprised at all; that bit of laurel was still stuck to his brow. And to think I once thought him a god. He stepped back and lifted his arm in a curious, grave salute that seemed less a farewell than a sort of sardonic blessing. I walked away rapidly down the wet street, through sunlight and fleet shadow, swinging my umbrella, the string bag dangling at my side. At every other step the bag and its burden banged against my shin; I did not mind.

*

I hope Miss Vandeleur will not be too disappointed when she comes around to do the final clearing-up – I have no doubt it will be she that he will send. Most of the sensitive things I have already destroyed; there is a very efficient incinerator in the basement. As to this – what, this memoir? this fictional memoir? – I shall leave it to her to decide how best to dispose of it. I imagine she will bring it straight to him. He always did have his girls. How could I ever have thought that it was Skryne who had put her on to me? I got so many things so drearily wrong. Now we are sitting here, Webley and myself, in silent commune. Some playwright of the nineteenth century, I cannot recall for the moment who it was, wittily observed that if a revolver appears in the first act it is bound to go off in the third. Well, *le dernier acte est sanglant* . . . So much for my Pascalian wager; a vulgar concept, anyway.

What a noble sky, this evening, pale blue to cobalt to rich purple, and the great bergs of cloud, colour of dirty ice, with soft copper edgings, progressing from west to east, distant, stately, soundless. It is the kind of sky that Poussin loved to set above his lofty dramas of death and love and loss. There are any number of clear patches; I am waiting for a bird-shaped one.

In the head or through the heart? Now, there is a dilemma.

Father, the gate is open.

ACKNOWLEDGEMENTS

Very many books have been written on the subject of the Cambridge spies; the majority of these I have not read. However, the following three have been of great help to me:

Conspiracy of Silence, by Barrie Penrose and Simon Freeman (Grafton, London, 1986)

Mask of Treachery, by John Costello (William Morrow and Company, New York, 1988)

My Five Cambridge Friends, by Yuri Modin (Headline, London, 1994)

I should also mention:

Code Breakers: The Inside Story of Bletchley Park, edited by F. H. Hinsley and Alan Stripp (Oxford University Press, Oxford, 1993)

London at War 1939–1945, by Philip Ziegler (Sinclair-Stevenson, London, 1995)

Louis MacNeice, by Jon Stallworthy (Faber & Faber, London, 1995)

Poussin, by Anthony Blunt (Pallas Athene, London (reprint), 1995)

Karl Marx, by Isaiah Berlin (Thornton Butterworth, London, 1939)